The Calling of Bara

The Calling of Bara

by
Sheila Sullivan

E.P. DUTTON & CO., INC.
New York   1976

ISBN: 0-525-07307-8
Library of Congress Catalog Card Number: 75-32658

Bara's Journey

as drawn by Tam

PART 1

Endings

AFTER THE MYSTERIOUS DEATH of General Bradwardine in 2031 all attempt at government had slowly crumbled away, because in the end it proved impossible to control the anarchy into which society had fallen. No abrupt or dramatic event had accounted for the collapse. There had been no war, no bomb; only a remorseless gearing down, from a humming urban prosperity to a life so cold and threadbare that those bewildered people who had survived the decline sometimes wondered if they still lived on the same planet. The pitiless price exacted for oil, the reluctance of men to dig coal, the hideous accidents with nuclear power – together these had choked the flow of energy which had been the arterial blood of the old industrial society. Some eighty years of bitter and protracted strikes had helped to bring poverty to millions of people, and to every country of Europe and the west; half a century of inflation had reduced money to meaningless metal and paper. By 2040 urban organization had almost totally broken down. Such water as came from the taps was rank, and had to be boiled for ten minutes before it could be drunk. Gas and electricity were so sporadic and dangerous only fools attempted to use them. The sewage system had been long since choked and useless. A rudimentary system of transport, using a mixture of gas-cars and horses (of which horses were considered the most reliable), delivered food and coal to the licensed local stores. Neighbours clustered together in small communities, often sharing coal and wood. Between each small gathering might be half a mile of fallen and abandoned buildings, where only the wind and the scuffling of rats ruffled the silence.

The summer of 2044 was warm and wet and lush. One afternoon Kate and old Charley were weeding the vegetable garden when Charley suddenly jerked his chin towards the gate.

'Who are those men who keep riding past?' he said.

Kate looked up from her weeding in alarm. She and her granddaughter Bara had met these riders three or four times on the Heath, and Kate had disliked them instantly. Bara, who was now fifteen, studied young men with passionate interest, and Kate was beginning to notice that young men studied Bara in return. The girl was not a beauty, but her face, in its mane of gold-red hair, was open and arresting, and her wide smile was freely given. She was coltish, eager in her movements, and to Kate's eye the most attractive child on earth.

The three young men rode magnificent stallions, wild-eyed, intractable creatures, one jet-black, one roan, and one piebald. The horses rather than the men had first caught Bara's eye a month ago, when they had brought her suddenly to a halt, gaping in admiration. But when she had raised her eyes to the young man on the roan her heart had faltered and her breath caught in her throat. He was superb, magnificent beyond all her dreams: eyes of piercing blue were set wide in a brown face, and his hair was a shock of quaking silver, the colour of the moon. He had stared at her coolly, up and down, smiling in approval, then glanced with irritation at Kate, and ridden away. Kate feared him immediately and told Bara what she felt. He reminded her of the fairy-tale Disney princes of her earliest youth, and she found his celluloid beauty ridiculous, but she knew that beneath it he was cruel and predatory. But after the second or third encounter, when it became obvious that the young man waited to waylay them as they gathered wood, Bara could think of nothing and no-one else. She tossed about all night and she scarcely heard when anyone spoke to her during the day. Kate told Charley that Bara must not be let out on the Heath alone, and nor should the door be opened to the young man if he came. Charley performed a nervous little hop and nodded sagely.

Then one afternoon in full summer, when Bara had gone down to Fred's store in Golders Green, and Kate was pulling runner-beans in the garden, the young man appeared in front of the house. With a yell and a toss of his silver head he urged his horse to leap the high gate, then he cantered fast up to Kate, finally reining-in so fiercely that the animal reared.

'Where's the girl?' he said, showing his white teeth.

'She's out. Will you get out of my garden?' Kate was trembling with fury at his intrusion and his flamboyant display of horsemanship.

'Where is she?'

'It's none of your business.'

'All right,' he said, fingering his whip. 'I'm used to getting what I want. If I can't have her, I'll take her.'

He turned his blue eyes full and square on Kate. Immediately she was enveloped in a chill miasma, and although she had already formed an angry reply the words fell like stones to the bottom of her mind. She stared, cold to the bone and unable to move. As he continued to gaze at her she felt her will, her compass-needle, bending from the course she had set it; her words were parried before they were spoken. Then, as he turned his eyes away, the sun was shining again and the anger flaring through her body. He bared his teeth and laughed at her, a cold, metallic laugh, then he wheeled the great horse and thundered out over the gate. Immediately Kate's anger melted into a shaking fear. How could she and old Charley ever keep this man from Bara? She knew that at sixty-two she was wonderfully strong; her thick tawny hair was only lightly streaked with sand, there were no deep lines on her face, her body was straight and willing. Nevertheless, she and Charley were no match for young men like these. Her hands shook as she continued to pull the beans for supper.

The next day Bara did not leave the house. She did nothing but sit at the window, staring onto the Heath, and Kate knew that she was ready and willing. She had had Bara in her care for ten years now, ever since the terrible day when her own son Lenny, Bara's father, had died in the cholera plague of 2034. The disease had raged all over the south of England, and a week later Bara's mother was also dead. After these ten years Kate was so used to Bara's trust that this departure into a secret, half-adult world was painful to bear. Bara was trying to escape her childhood ill-prepared and far too young; but this, Kate told herself, was what loving adults always thought. She herself had married Ralf at sixteen, so she was hardly in a position to criticize. But it was hard to watch, especially when the handsome predator who waited at the gate wanted nothing but Bara's body. Kate felt fiercely protective and full of loathing for the dashing stranger who had so dazzled Bara; but it was impossible, with only mad old Charley for a bodyguard, to protect a girl who did not want to be protected.

The young man did not appear and Bara was in despair, silent all day and crying quietly to herself at night. But she did not have to wait long; no longer than a hot, still night in August, three weeks after the stranger's visit to Kate in the garden. Kate could not sleep, for the room was stuffy and Bara was tossing restlessly inhthe next bed. There was no moon, but the stars were brilliant, with a brilliancy no-one in England had seen for two hundred years. Suddenly the velvet silence shattered in splinters. Glass was clattering, wood was rending, metal was clanging and men were shouting. After a stupefied second, Kate heaved herself out of bed, sick with terror, and fumbled in the darkness for her nailed stick. Bara cried out and pulled her blanket over her head.

When she dared to look over the edge again she saw the marvellous stranger standing by the window, his silver hair glittering in the starlight. He was beautiful, like an archangel. But he held a knife in his hand. Then Kate found the courage to swing her terrible club. The stranger leaped aside just in time, and once again his sudden gaze chilled Kate into silence. She could hear Charley screaming with pain in the next room, but while the stranger held her in his gaze she could not call out to him. Then a tall man burst into the room.

'*Her,*' said the silver stranger, pointing at Kate with his dagger. His tall friend looked at Kate for a moment, then leaped. The nails of her club caught him on the arm and he yelled with pain, but he seized Kate by the shoulders and threw her back onto the bed. He flung himself at her neck, squeezing with both hands and thrusting her head against the wall at the head of the mattress.

'No!' shouted Bara wildly, leaping up and beginning to run to Kate. 'Leave her alone!'

But the stranger caught her by the arm, and in one movement bent it behind her back and pressed her against his body.

'Lie down, sweetheart,' he said softly. But Bara could hear Kate choking. She screamed and kicked, frantic to reach Kate.

'A wildcat, I see', said the stranger, pinning her arms and pressing his mouth so hard to hers she could not breathe. Then he raised his head and said to his friend, 'Let the old woman alone. Have her if you like.'

His companion straightened up. 'No thanks,' he said. 'An old hag like that?'

He strode out of the room, leaving Kate moaning on her back. The stranger had relaxed his grip and Bara took her chance to wriggle free and rush towards Kate's side. But before she could cross the room he grabbed her by the waist and swung her violently back on her own bed. Her head struck the iron bedhead, half stunning her, but she saw the knife at her breast and felt his body fall heavily on top of her. Kate's breath came in rasps, forcing a passage through her swollen throat, and her throbbing head was filled with cries she could not separate from her pain. Something terrible was happening – here? – there? She could not locate the focus of her panic, she could only battle with the pain that threatened to overwhelm her.

Bara was sobbing when the stranger lifted himself off her. She was torn and bleeding and she wanted only to die.

'Come on, sweetheart,' he said briskly. 'You're too beautiful to leave here.'

He pulled her up and lifted her limp body in his arms. His tall companion blocked the doorway, and behind him stood the dark, bearded man who had been tormenting Charley in the next room.

'My turn for the girl,' said the bearded man.

'Think again, Turk,' said the stranger, preparing to carry Bara outside.

'No.' Turk barred the way. 'You've had the girl. Who do we get? The old woman over there?'

'Out of my way. The girl's mine.'

Kate moaned from her bed and the sound of her voice stirred Bara from her stupor. She struck out with her nails, tearing at the stranger's face, and in his surprise he dropped her. She tried again to rush to Kate, but Turk seized her in his arms and pressed her to him. Then the stranger's fist came crashing into his face and he staggered back, losing his hold on Bara.

'You find your own woman,' said the stranger. 'I told you, she's mine.'

Kate saw him trying to hold Bara's face still between his hands, so that he could compel her with his eyes, but the girl bit and struggled, resisting with every muscle. His cold, glittering laughter rang around her, mocking her helplessness, until he had dragged and pushed and finally heaved her into the garden and almost up to his horse. Then he stopped abruptly and let her drop. He stared into the darkness and his face was white. For there, naked on the gravel, stood Charley, his eyes wild, his withered hands raised and spread. He murmured strange words as he moved in a slow circle, widdershins, keeping his eyes fixed on the rising moon. The three men stood aghast.

'It's an incantation,' whispered Turk. 'It's to raise the devils of hell.'

'Come on,' said the stranger hoarsely. Sweating with fear the three men leaped onto their horses and galloped off into the night.

The next day Kate's neck was so swollen she could not swallow. Even disposing of her saliva was a conscious, painful effort. For several days she lay on her bed, occasionally sipping the warm milk Charley brought, and slowly the pain subsided. She began to sit up and feed on slops, but she was so haunted by the events of the night, and so wretched for Bara, that she could not sleep. For three days Bara could scarcely walk, but Kate believed the real injury was not to her body. Far worse was the fact that she had been savaged by a man so beautiful she would have given herself to him freely and with joy. As she lay on her bed day after day, with her throat burning and her head aching, Kate was tormented with the thought that Bara might never be able to forgive the race of men what one of them had done to her that night. How bitterly Bara's first love contrasted with her own. Weakly, she allowed her thoughts to wander back to Ralf. The Revolution of 2003, of which Ralf had been a leader and of which he held such hopes, had turned sour with a year. Instead of flowering into a new People's Government, it had become twisted into yet another military dictatorship, and Ralf had had to flee for his life. From far down where he prowled in the shadows of her memory, he swept up suddenly before her; solid, corporeal, knocking the breath from her lungs. Even after more than forty years her feelings about her lost husband were still so distressing she tried not to dwell on them. That she hated him, there was no doubt; she hated his cold indifference to the fate of his family, she hated him for the slow withdrawal of his love in the years before the Revolution. She hated his idiotic passion for that stupid, useless Revolution, which had first taken him from her, and she hated him for the coolness with which he had left her for ever. She cultivated these feelings of anger because they kept her desolation at bay; but she could never forget the tempest of love that had struck her when she was sixteen, in the first week she had met Ralf, and she knew she would never forget their first year together, when all doubts and irritations had been consumed in the blaze of her love. Because, for all her bitterness, she had never forgotten that time, she had decided to manage without a husband, and to bring up their son Lenny without a father. Even at the height of her passion for other, later, men, she had never thought of any of them as a husband, for no man she had ever met could survive as husband or father in the compelling shadow of Ralf.

For days old Charley was abject, bitterly ashamed of his failure to help the women. However much they tried to comfort him, he would accept no excuses. He tried to redeem himself in his own eyes by fashioning a brutal club, with a knife protruding from the end and a head studded with nails. He assured Bara that the men would not return, but Kate felt certain they would be back. The conquest had been too easy. Bara moved silently about the house and garden, and Charley accompanied her every day to and from her job in Joddy's stables. He held his new club in one hand and he clutched Bara's arm with the other. He felt foolish, and frightened, but he thought he was regaining a little of Bara's trust, and that gave him courage. He sensed that Kate was quite unable to shake off the depression that had settled on her like a winter cloud. She spoke very little, and she found few words of comfort for Bara. Violence and brutality had broken into her life many times, but the shock had never numbed her as this had done. The outrage on Bara seemed to her so terrible that she had no feelings adequate to meet it.

And so it was Charley who moved briskly around, muttering of this and that, and getting things done with some pretence at normality. He contrived what he could, with the aid of some neighbours, to strengthen their pathetic defences. The huge neo-Georgian house, once the pride of Ralf's father, stood in a large garden overlooking the old Hampstead Heath Extension. When Ralf was a boy, in the eighties and nineties of the last century, the tower-blocks built to house the armies of the homeless had encroached year by year, until they smothered in concrete the green fields and paddocks of the Extension. The blocks were now in ruins, and Ralf's old house was habitable in only one corner of the ground floor. Kate and Bara slept in the old study, Charley slept next door in the junk room; the sitting-room, though very damp, was usable because of the wood fires they burnt there half the year; and the kitchen was the only other weatherproof corner. Half the windows were boarded up, damp spread in ever-widening circles up the walls, the outside door swung on rusty hinges. Charley nailed more slats over the broken windows, then he turned to the old palisade he had built fifty years before for Ralf's father. He paid Tam, the young carpenter who lived nearby, to find suitable wood, and between them they replaced the weakest of the stakes and pales. But they worked without conviction. There was no wire to be found anywhere. Once not long ago there had been miles of the stuff, from the ripped-out electrical circuits of houses and factories, but already it was almost gone, used up in the binding of fences and windows and shacks and furniture. Any that remained had been sequestered by the ruthless and powerful dealers who traded in the remains of the old urban society, and whose demands in money or barter were far beyond anything Kate could afford. So, in spite of the strenuous efforts of Charley and Tam, the palisade remained a feeble defence. However, Bara seemed pleased with it and that was important. As she walked round its circumference, running her finger along the slats, she seemed to recover a little of her old spirit. She even half-smiled at Tam, who reddened, then immediately bent again to glower over his work. He was stubby and swarthy and plain, but there was something about him she trusted, and she knew very well that he looked at her often. She was sure he was gentle and kind, and she suspected he was beginning to love her. What a fool she had been, what a bloody, bloody fool, to have worshipped that silver stranger.

Kate was astonished at Charley's activity. She guessed something of what drove him, for she knew he had an acute sense of shame, and she knew how much he prized Bara's love, but she had never seen him so positive in all his long life. This new adversity, which had crushed her own spirit almost to breaking, had made a new being of Charley. And yet, for all his new vigour, he was clearly quite incapable of defending the house. His spindly body had never been much more than a bundle of twigs, and now that he was over seventy the sap in his bones was fast running dry. He was brittle, and although he could move slowly all day through the garden, he could no longer rise to a sudden violent effort. As Kate lay listlessly on her bed, hearing him patter about the house, she remembered Ralf's father describing to her long ago how Charley first came to him. By the nineties of the last century the mental hospitals had been so overwhelmed that every householder had been required to take one patient a day for domestic work. Charley's chief concern had been to escape the vultures who were out to eat his liver. He lived high up in a tower block, where he was sure the vultures could get him, so part of his therapy was to meet harmless garden birds at ground level. After a week he had announced that he wanted to come and live in the garage and be the gardener. He hated his tower block, and his dad called him a barmy nit. So, fifty-four years ago, in 1990, he had come. He had been as thin and angular then as he was now, his body had scarcely changed. Everything about him was still pointed, from his spikey hair and his spikey nose and his spikey chin, down to his spikey knees and his spikey toes. His eyes had remained the palest blue that Kate had ever seen. All his life he had retained his habit of performing little leaps and capers, then peering sharply round to make sure he was unobserved. He was lovely, Kate thought; mad, devoted, a gardener for whom everything burgeoned green and succulent. But he was no good as a guard.

Then one morning the dark and surly Tam provided the answer to the problem of defence. He and a girl called Suz arrived at the house and demanded to see Kate. Tam came straight to the point.

'You need company,' he said.

'Well, I'm certainly worried about looking after ourselves,' said Kate warily.

'I'll look after you. We'll move in if you like, me and Suz.' Tam struck his thumbs in his belt and looked darkly at her.

'I can help too,' said Suz, who was brown and sharp, like a sparrow.

'I'll have to think about it,' said Kate, confused by the directness of his approach.

'I don't see why,' said Tam gruffly. 'We're sick to death of our shacks. It's damn difficult trying to build old cars into a house. We're bloody cold and we can't seem to stop the rain coming in. You let us live here and I'll look after you, and Suz'll help in the house.'

'You give me a roof and a bed and some food, and I'll work,' said Suz.

'How much?' asked Kate suspiciously.

'What do you mean?' said Tam. 'It's a swop. A decent house for some work and protection.'

'I'll have to talk to Bara. But it sounds a good idea.' Kate smiled. 'Are you and Suz together now?'

'Yea,' said Tam briefly. 'She tags along with me.' Suz smiled sideways up at him. 'She won't make any trouble with Bara,' he added.

When Kate told her the plan Bara smiled for the first time in many days.

'I'd love it,' she said happily. 'I'd feel really safe again.'

So two days later Tam and Suz moved into the sitting-room. The young man flushed with pleasure when Bara smiled at him, but instead of feeling the expected quiver of excitement in his admiration she was astonished to find herself filled with fear. Her stomach knotted, her heart raced, and she left the room quickly. She was immensely relieved that Tam had a girl with him. A load of marquetry and ormolu, looted from Kenwood, accompanied the move. Four dining-room chairs with curving arms and backs like lyres, were stacked in pairs and dragged up the stony path; a large oval table, beaded and inlaid, was manhandled into the sitting-room; an ormolu sideboard with curly golden legs was wedged into a corner of the kitchen; a marquetry corner-cupboard was shoved into the corner by Kate's bed. The furniture was stained and chipped and mildewed, but it was usable, and Bara considered it added a great air to the tumbledown house. The gilt chairs – though considerably less comfortable – were certainly more refined than the old car seats which lined one wall of the sitting-room. Kate watched in silence as the magnificent, mouldy pieces were heaved and kicked into position. She remembered being taken to Kenwood as a child, in the eighties of the last century, when the house had been a warm and sumptuous museum of an age even more luxurious than the one into which she had been born. She had been expected to admire a vast collection of silver shoe-buckles and boring pictures, and she had cried because she had wanted to play outside with the dog. A few of those pictures now hung around her, in her own house, for when Bara was a child she and her friends had spent many days of many years playing in the ruins of Kenwood; and once, exploring a gardener's shed, overgrown and almost buried in ivy, they had stumbled upon a great stack of pictures. Bara had liked and brought home with her a glowing little picture of Venice; a girl with ringlets playing a guitar; a tempestuous painting of fishermen struggling with boats; a huge picture of a country inn, with the signature of 'G. Morland' on the inn sign. Kate smiled to herself, then shook her head abruptly to dispel the cloud of memories, and laughed aloud at the banging and yelling and singing that accompanied Tam's move. After the silent death of the last month since the visit of the strangers, the place was alive again. Two days after Tam and Suz moved in, two friends of theirs, Christo and Jank, appeared, and three days later settled into the garage. Tam assured Kate of their good behaviour and Kate felt weak with relief. For the first time in many years their defences were properly manned.

And then the strangers came again. Late on a frosty afternoon in September, with the sun a ball of fire through the black trees, Bara heard the thudding of distant horses. She cried out, stiff with fear. Kate rushed from the kitchen, seizing a long knife as she went, and grabbed her club from its position by her bed. She swore to herself that if anything happened to Bara this time it would be only after she herself was killed. A determined old woman could do some damage with these ghastly weapons. Tam leaped up from where he was mending a chair and tore with his dark eyes blazing to find Charley's club. He stationed himself by the door, swinging the savage implement in his right hand and clutching his knife in the other. In the corridor behind him, Charley fluttered in agitation, wielding an iron bar.

The men drew up their horses at the gate, then the stranger shook his silver hair, the colour of the moon, and smiled his marvellous smile.

'Get her,' they heard him say. Turk, the bearded man, urged his piebald against the gate. They heard the straining of the wood and Turk swearing at his horse. The gate held for a moment, but the weight of the great beast was too much for it. Suddenly the wood splintered and horse and rider were through. The mocking laughter

of the stranger floated through the frosty air. Turk dismounted, drew
his sword and strode up the path, grinning through his beard. Tam
opened the door and stood with his club raised and his knife up. His
knees shook, his eyes began to darken, and for one terrible moment
he thought he was going to faint.

'Hey boy,' said Turk, still grinning. 'A new man about the place?
Enjoying the women, boy?'

'Get out,' said Tam.

'Oh, come on,' said Turk. 'Stand back and you won't get hurt. You
don't want to get hurt, do you, boy?'

Tam swung his club in a wide arc, but Turk leaped swiftly back.

'All right,' he said, no longer smiling. 'If that's the way you want
it.'

He held his sword in front of his body and advanced slowly on
Tam. Tam knocked the sword sideways and tried to hold it down
with his knife while he lunged with the blade at the end of his club.
But Turk slewed his sword sideways and dodged the lunge. As Tam
recovered his balance, Turk slashed at his legs, but the long blade of
Tam's knife intervened and for a moment Turk's body was open to
the club. Tam swung it furiously and crashed it into Turk's left
shoulder. The man screamed in pain. The nails bit so deep he was
impaled, but he still had his sword arm free and before Tam could
wrench his weapon away Turk had swung at him with the edge of
the sword. Kate forced herself to watch, but in the narrow confines of
the doorway she could not reach Turk with her weapons. She
glanced at the other men to see if they might be coming to Turk's
aid, but they still sat on their horses, silent and smiling. Tam was cut
in the ribs, and he staggered sideways, blood welling through his
jerkin. His club was still entangled in Turk's tunic, but as Turk lifted
his sword for the kill Tam threw himself forward and plunged his
long knife through Turk's body. Turk gasped and fell forward. Kate
pulled Tam inside, Charley slammed and bolted the door. Through a
slit in the boards they saw the two mounted strangers staring at each
other. Kate's hands began to shake in terror, for surely they would now
attack together. But they did not. The silver stranger raised his sword
and gazed upward at the point, glittering red in the sunset.

'Malcontent!' he cried. 'The omens are against us.' Then they
wheeled their horses and spurred away.

Tam lay on the floor, groaning and clutching his side, his face very
white. Kate and Charley ran for some water and clean cloths, calling
to Bara that the men had gone. Bara came out of her room and
screamed when she saw Tam doubled up on the ground. She knelt

sobbing by his side, trying frantically to stop the bleeding with her bare hands.

'It's all right,' called Kate from the kitchen. 'It's not a bad wound.' She bathed and bandaged it and in a few minutes Tam grimaced and pulled himself slowly up. Kate took his hands and kissed his stubbly cheek, quite unable to express her thanks, and Bara sobbed on his shoulder, her words welling up from depths of gratitude. But Tam hated the performance. He mumbled something about only doing his job and he escaped as soon as he could. His leather jerkin had saved him from a lethal cut, and in a few days the wound healed over, leaving him with very little pain. Kate prayed, and indeed half believed, that these terrible beautiful men would never come again. The next day Tam and Charley hauled Turk's body onto the old Heath and flung it in a bog, where it sank without a trace.

Until these last few months, the years of Bara's childhood had been among the happiest of Kate's life. Although she had been enraptured by her son Lenny, both as a baby and a boy, that had been a time of unceasing anxiety and her memories were clouded with strain. After the final collapse of the big banks in 2030 money had been scarce, and she had lived in constant fear that thieves might discover the floorboard under which she kept her savings. None of them had yet found it, and at last Kate felt that she had a satisfactory pile of money behind her. Money was still used for the exchange of goods, alongside the increasing practice of barter, but the state of the coinage was chaotic. The decimal coins of the last century still circulated, some of them worn almost smooth, but mixed with them were stray half-crowns and pennies and sixpences from pre-decimal days, and alongside these again were the millions of coins looted from museums and collections. Sovereigns, Roman pennies, Georgian crowns, Spanish guineas, Tudor groats all mingled pell-mell with the modern coins, and there was no standard value to any of them. The only rough and ready rule was that gold was best, silver next, and the assortment of brown metals, which included most of the Roman coins, were least valuable of all.

By 2044 the number of coins in circulation had no longer to be divided among so many people, because by the mid-thirties of the century there were not nearly so many people about. Their disappearance was a source of constant surprise to the remaining dwellers in the towns. Kate remembered London seething with people; anonymous, moving people, standing and circling, swerving and running, or simply forging urgently ahead. The biological success of her species had appalled her in her youth. But now the people were no longer there. The long grey streets stood empty. The gradual collapse of town life, gathering speed in the twenties, had sent anarchic bands of hungry men pouring out into the country. All through those rough years there had been a steady march away from London and all the great cities, because when there was no food left in the towns townsmen remembered that food grew in the country. So to the country they had flocked, millions of urban sparrows. The farms in countries surrounding the cities had all been attacked and occupied long since. They had been carved up into smallholdings, often heavily fortified, and there the unskilful townsmen grubbed a kind of living from the soil. Bands of homeless beggars roamed the lanes as they had once roamed the towns, fighting and murdering for food. Fishermen had fortified their villages and sunk the boats of any townsmen who attempted to fish for a living. Suspicion and hostility lurked everywhere, for even in the wide acres of the shires there was not room for so many people. Then, slowly, the numbers had begun to dwindle. The very old and the very young starved or died of exposure. Others in their thousands died of illnesses once reasonably under control: flu, blood-poisoning, gangrene, bronchitis and pneumonia, typhoid and dysentry. By the thirties there were far fewer people about.

Kate noticed that as ammunition had gradually run out, so violence had subsided. The horror of guns, she thought, was that they were such fun. Everyone enjoyed them, and many people had begun to kill just for the sport. Fortunately the more primitive weapons did not share this attraction; knives and clubs did not seem to be used with quite the same abandon, and violent death was no longer the everyday occurrence it had been in the first quarter of the century.

By the thirties many people were peacefully cultivating their own fortified patches of fruit and vegetables, and many had settled into some essential trade. Carpenters, cobblers, chandlers, candlemakers, coopers, wainwrights and other craftsmen were not hard to find. Others made themselves a livelihood from services, earning their keep by carting water from the wells, or carrying passengers or goods in carts, or helping with smallholdings or repairs to houses.

There had been no mechanical means of transport for many years now, and the horse had come into its own again. On all the main tracks was a constant clopping and snorting of horses; great brown roans and little Shetlands, Shires and Punches and mountain ponies, mules and donkeys shoulder to shoulder with high-stepping Arabs and hunters. Anything that could be found to breed had been put to work, and horse dealers had become among the wealthiest men in the land. Horse traders, car dealers, horse traders again. Whatever their merchandise, Kate thought, they had always been shifty and rich. Often she had carried Bara as a baby to the nearby London road, where the child would gaze entranced at the great beasts swaying past with their loads. Bara always remembered the scene; the warmth of Kate's arms, the cries of the drivers, the beautiful, frightening march of horses on the London road.

The wreckage of industrial England was now overwhelming in its mass and extent. All over London, all over the Midlands and the North, the factories and the pits stood silent, their vaults and galleries echoing, their benches looted of everything that could help a man to live. Rust, the lethal enemy of metal, was eating steadily through the machinery of a civilization. Broken aircraft rusted in the hangers, trains rusted to their tracks in the sidings, the ripped-out hulks of rusty cars cluttered every road in the land. The rubbish accumulated in the break-up of the technical age dominated every town, and every landscape that was not utterly remote. Miles of pylons and concrete lamp-standards, marching across town and country, mouldered and fell apart in wind and frost. Huge mounds of indestructable plastic, packings and boxes and cartons and stinking household rubbish littered the borders of every town. The wind moaned through collapsing complexes of bridges and flyovers and junctions the length and breadth of the land. In the corner of Kate's garden stood a large irregular mound, smothered in ivy and honeysuckle and clematis, which concealed not earth or stones, but an abandoned electric cooker, two TV sets, a washing-machine, a boiler, and six electric fires. The freezer and the refrigerator she had kept in the kitchen because they made useful cupboards. Indeed, much of the debris was of some practical use. When her frying-pans wore out Kate found she could substitute the hub-caps of abandoned cars; when the electricity had finally failed, back in the early thirties, she had stuck a long candle in the socket of the standard-lamp; old radiators had proved useful for palings and workbenches and repairs to crumbling masonry; Charley eagerly sought out broken glass and perspex for repairs to windows and garden cloches.

Everybody who had reached middle or old age found the food monotonous, but few went hungry. There was usually bread to be had at the stores, or people made it themselves. There was meat, albeit unidentified; there was bacon; occasionally as an expensive treat there were butter and cheese and cream. Kate would like to have kept a cow and a goat and a few chickens, but she knew that without powerful defences, and strong men to guard them, the animals would be stolen in under a week. All she could hope was to protect the fruit and vegetables. Charley's skill provided them with potatoes and leeks and onions and sprouts and cabbage and spinach and runners and peas. His trees gave apples and pears and plums, his canes gave raspberries, and in every odd corner of the garden sprouted great trunks of rhubarb. Kate did not greatly regret the elaborate foods of her youth, but there were many men and women of her age who ached for the hot, rich meals they had once taken for granted. In the last years of the previous century the meats and desserts and exotic vegetables so relished by the well-to-do were rapidly vanishing, and many were now merely words in stories and children's games. Aubergines? Bananas? Peppers? Oranges and lemons? What were they? Nowadays the potato was king of vegetables and the apple queen of fruits. Between them they made the basis of almost every winter meal, and by the time March came round every year Kate was sick of the sight of sprouting potatoes and crinkled apples. However, taken all in all, she found the life they lived in 2044 was reasonably ordered and comfortable. She was always a little colder than she would have liked, and the abrupt fall in temperature between the two rooms in which they kept fires – the kitchen and the sitting-room – and the other rooms and corridors never ceased to chill and startle her. Central heating, a distant memory of her childhood, had been very agreeable indeed. And baths. A hot, steaming bath from a tap. More than anything she missed that. Compared with the luxury of urban life in the last century this was a beggar's life to a king's, but it was no longer utterly brutal as in the first years of collapse.

Oats and fodder were an important part of the trade at Fred's store in Golders Green. The store was no longer licensed by a central authority, for there was none, but Fred held doggedly on, sending out into the country every week armed scouts whose job was to return with cartloads of whatever fuel or food or goods they could find. He even arranged a relay which brought salt and opencast coal from the Midlands. Rumour whispered that half his stock was loot, but Kate thought it was probably rather less than half. Although Fred did not care for girls, who struck him as shameless and pert, he was a kindly old man who had known both Ralf and Ralf's father before him, and he offered Bara a job in his store. She was loth to leave Joddy's stables, where one of her daily duties was to groom the shuddering silken flanks of Dark, the great black Shire, who stood nearly eighteen hands, and to comb out the white mops of hair which fell over his hooves. But Fred could pay her twice as much as Joddy could offer, so she arranged that she would work in the store by day and at the stables on three evenings a week. Fred wanted her to assist the boy who had recently come as accountant, for although this new youth had a way with numbers his reading and writing were not of the best. It was becoming increasingly difficult in the mid-forties to find people who could read and write well, and Kate realized with relief that these talents would stand both her and Bara in good stead.

The chief priority, she thought, as she urged herself into activity again after the attack, was more money to spend on defence. The garden paling was not strong enough, the front door should be renewed, the broken windows must be more stoutly boarded. Thanks to Fred, Bara would bring home money or goods (as she chose) from her new job in the store. Kate herself must work half every day with Charley among the fruit and vegetables, to make sure they had food to eat and plenty over to sell or barter. Although she was now sixty-two she did not expect to find the work a hardship to her muscles, and it would not be dull. She had recently begun to take an excited interest in the crossing and improving of the vegetables, and she felt that some of her seed stocks were already a distinct improvement on their originals. The other half of the day she must do something to earn money. She might try to start a little school. Or she might take in sewing and mending. Or she could be a washerwoman – or even a scrivener.

The boys had arranged that one of them would be always in the house, while the other two went off to work. Christo and Jank continued to build and repair shacks, but Tam had moved on to become a skilled wainwright, building carts for Joddy at his stables. Bara soon began to notice that although his day's work was done by the time she arrived for her evening job at the stables, Tam would often work late when she was there, or perhaps pretend to be urgently engaged on a task over which she knew there was no hurry at all. She sometimes wondered idly how he explained himself to Suz when he got home. She allowed herself to feel a faint, flattered amusement, but she could not face the thought that he might love her. Suz was brisk and cheerful in the house, except when she had had a row with Tam, when she would become morose and refuse to speak at all. Kate knew very well that Tam's eyes were more for Bara than for Suz, but she said nothing. When Suz was happy she talked far too much, and Kate was often glad to escape to the potting-shed. She became more and more absorbed in the breeding of peas, and as she worked to create new combinations of size and flavour and colour she sent her homage back across two centuries to Mendel in his monastery garden. When the new Dark Ages ended, and civilization rose again, would Mendel be still remembered, or would all be to do again?

Christo and Jank cooked for themselves in the garage, but Tam and Suz ate in the house, sitting with Kate and Bara on the lyre-backed chairs round the oval inlaid table from Kenwood. Sometimes Kate astonished the young people by suddenly laughing aloud at the grotesque incongruity. Plaster fell off the ceiling every month, damp stained the walls in rising columns, the carpet was reduced to shreds of cord, and half the windows were boarded up. Yet here they sat with these pieces of furniture, the choicest the eighteenth century could fashion, hand-picked by experts a hundred years ago to grace a palace. Tam ate everything with his great sheath-knife. Kate had trained Bara to eat with knife, fork and spoon, and now Suz was rapidly acquiring the art. When she and Bara giggled at Tam's barbaric methods he growled and looked as if he might whack them. Yet he liked to be teased too. Kate found him an intriguing, complicated character, if somewhat rough, and she was delighted to help him in his passion for reading. Clearly his job as a wainwright occupied only a corner of his active and searching mind.

Six weeks after he had arrived, when he had already read at devouring speed almost every book they had on their shelves, Kate suddenly remembered an odd fact she had forgotten for well over forty years. Surely Ralf had told her that during those awful three years before the Revolution, when the cult of the book-burners had raged like plague all over the country, he and his father had hidden about a thousand books under some floor? The more she thought the more certain she became that this was no fantasy. Ralf's father had been a publisher, and therefore a special target for the book-burners – the Children of Eden, as they had called themselves. So he was a very likely person to have hidden books away. But where? The creakiest and most uneven boards in the house were in her own bedroom, which had once been the study. So one summer evening when Tam came home from Joddy's, she told him what she had remembered, and watched his dark eyes light up with excitement. He rushed for some tools and was prising up the boards before she had finished her story. In a few minutes they knew the books were there. Rows of flat cardboard boxes, meticulously stacked, lay side by side in the dark cavity below the floor. The cardboard was streaked white and green with mould, and so sodden that a finger went straight through it. But the books within had survived. Many of the leather bindings were mildewed, and a few volumes were soaked to pulp, but the vast majority were merely stained and damp. In a fury of excitement, like a man discovering treasure, Tam tore up more and more floorboards, revealing more and more boxes of books. When the late dusk gathered to darkness they lit candles and worked on. By the time they gave up three hours later Kate was exhausted, and the sitting-room was stacked high with a thousand books.

Tam did not go to bed that night. By the light of guttering candles he cleaned up a leather-bound first edition of Gibbon, he pored over *The Wealth of Nations,* he turned the pages of Mill and Russell like a man discovering a new country; he worked through an illustrated Mandeville, he browsed in *The Anatomy of Melancholy,* he devoured Bacon's *Essays* and Hume's *History* till his eyes ached. He was trembling with joy at what he had unearthed, he was shrinking in despair at the shortness of one lifetime in which to read it. When Kate woke him for work in the morning he was slumped over the table with his dark head on a volume of Voltaire.

Kate eventually decided that in order to earn the money she required she would first try her hand as a scribe. She had word put about that she was prepared to write notes, documents, agreements, bills, love letters or anything else, and that she was prepared to teach pupils how to write. She nailed up notices in her best hand in Fred's store and on her own gate, then waited for results. People were slow to come, for although so many under thirty could neither read nor write they were still unwilling to acknowledge the fact in public. Then Joddy sent her a ledger, which registered his sales of horses and ponies and carts. It was written so wildly that at first she could hardly decipher a line. 'Like an inky spider running all over the page,' Bara said. Kate did her best to copy it, writing large and legibly, and Joddy was delighted. He propped the book open in a box in front of his stables, as an advertisement for his establishment, but its real effect was an advertisement for Kate's calligraphy. Work flowed in from carpenters, market gardeners, wheelwrights, blacksmiths, water-carriers; even from illiterate lovers. Sometimes by the end of a morning's work Kate's hand ached painfully, and she was glad to lay aside her pen for an afternoon's work in the garden.

Soon it was late October, to Kate's eye the most ravishing season of the year. The sun shone softly through a long St Martin's summer. The wide acres of the Heath, and the derelict suburban gardens, now spread over fallen brick and masonry, burned in red and yellow and tan. In the early morning the sequined webs of spiders stretched geometrically between the brambles, and above them squirrels flitted in chestnut and beech and oak. To his delight Charley had tamed yet another robin, the thirtieth, he reckoned, in the fifty-four years he had worked this patch of garden. The robin would now eat from his hand, and ride round the garden perched on his battered felt hat. Bara was happy in her jobs, Kate's copying was profitable and enjoyable, the young lodgers were behaving well, and all was running easily, when Bara began to be sick in the mornings.

For four days Kate heard and watched her, but she said nothing. That Bara could have conceived a baby in that one act of rape was too cruel to believe. On the fifth morning Bara was so white Kate persuaded her to stay at home from work.

'You know what it could mean,' she said warily. 'I mean, on top of your missing and all—'

'Oh yes, I know. The bloody beautiful bastard.' Bara stared angrily out of the window, her pale face yet more pallid.

'What do you want to do about it?' asked Kate, making a pretence of dusting the table.

'Get rid of it. If that's what it is. I'm only fifteen. I'm not interested in babies. Specially his.'

'There's no sure way, you know. Nowadays there's only the old wives' remedies.'

'Let's try them. I'll try them all.'

'Some of them might make you pretty ill. And they might not work either.'

'I don't care. I'll try them all. What are they?'

'I don't know. We'll have to find someone. Mother Huff I suppose. She knows all these ghastly things.'

'That old bag. They say she stinks.'

'I expect she does. Never mind, she'll know what you should take.'

'What did they do in your day?'

'Surgical abortion. It's the only certain way.'

'Why can't I have that?'

'Because there aren't any proper surgeons any more, and I'm not having some old woman stick her filthy instruments in you. We'll do it with witches' potions.'

'Ugh.'

'There's no nice way of getting rid of a baby. They're made to stick.'

Mother Huff looked so like a witch in a fairy-tale that Kate and Bara had to suppress their smiles. She did not wear a tall hat, and there was no sign of a broomstick, but she was old and bent, with a long arched nose and wispy grey hair. She enveloped herself in a ragged red shawl, and her smile was bent and toothless. She lived in the one weatherproof corner of a ruined mansion in Bishop's Avenue. As Bara and Kate stepped through the broken lintel they were struck by a smell so foetid they could hardly force themselves to move on.

'Come in, come in, my dears,' cried Mother Huff, hobbling round the dark room and swiping wildly at the cats which occupied every chair. 'You've come to the right place, you know. Mother Huff knows a thing or two to help a young girl in trouble. Is it a love potion, my dear?' She thrust her sharp face at Bara, and tried to stroke her cheek with a bony finger. Bara started back in disgust.

'No,' said Kate, 'not a love potion. She wants to be rid of a baby.'

'Ah, naughty, naughty,' cried Mother Huff, grinning archly. 'Another little girl in trouble, eh?'

'Can you do anything for her?' said Kate sharply.

'Oh yes, oh yes. You've come to the right place for that. Mother Huff knows a thing or two to help a girl in trouble. How long?' she asked abruptly.

'About six weeks,' said Kate. The smell of the place was overpowering.

'Six weeks, six weeks. H'm.'

The old witch hobbled over to a dark corner where long shelves lined the wall. On every shelf were rows and rows of bottles, of every colour, shape and size, rescued from dumps and looted from hospitals and larders. Mother Huff ran her knotted finger along one of the shelves.

'We'll try this first,' she said, lifting down a squat bottle containing a brown liquid. She spat on the glass and wiped the grime with a corner of her shawl.

'What is it?' asked Bara faintly.

'Ah, that's my secret, dearie. That's Mother Huff's secret. But it works, it often works at two months.'

'Can you give me any idea of what's in it?' asked Kate. Mother Huff turned sharply, her eyes contracted into little black beads of venom.

'No!' she hissed. 'It's my secret, see? Mine. No-one's having it off me. No-one. You takes it or leaves it, see?' Bara stood flat against the wall, reeling with nausea. Kate turned to her uneasily.

'Well, we'd better have it I suppose,' she said.

'Ah, but what do I ask for it?' croaked Mother Huff, once more ingratiating. 'What does a poor old woman get for her trouble?'

'What do you want?' said Kate. 'We can pay in goods or money.'

'Golden money's what I like, dearie. That's what I take for my potions.' Kate had a precious sovereign with her, and she passed it over. Mother Huff's eyes glinted, and her fingers wrapped tightly round it.

'How much at a time? And how often does she take it?' asked Kate.

'Two spoonfuls three times a day. It may make the girl feel rather poorly. But if we will be naughty we must pay for it, mustn't we?' She grinned her toothless grin and tried again to touch Bara's cheek. Kate took hold of Bara's arm and pulled her through the maze of cats out of the room. In the fresh air again Bara revived.

'What a place,' breathed Kate.

'What a hag,' replied Bara. They took deep breaths of the soft autumn air as they walked home along the brambled pathways that intersected the ruins of Ingram Avenue. Kate held the bottle tight. My God, she thought to herself, so this is what the ancient and noble art of medicine has come to.

The potion did nothing but harm. Bara's morning nausea now continued all day. She suffered raging headaches, pain crept into all her joints. And there was no sign of abortion. Kate steeled herself for another visit to Mother Huff and returned with a different liquid. Bara recovered her health and was unaffected by the new green medicine, but apparently the baby was unaffected also. Bara rode the stable horses furiously, she leaped from high places, landing as flat-footedly as she dared; she lifted enormous weights, and she drank the medicine in double doses. She had moments of wild desperation when she would shout and punch the furniture, and she had periods of desolation when she could only lie on her bed and sob.

One day Kate returned from Mother Huff with a third potion, and before she could retrieve it Bara drank the contents of the bottle in one wild gulp. In a few moments she was violently sick. That night her temperature rose and she was shaken by an acute dysentery. Kate sat up with her all night, fighting to suppress the swarming visions of Bara's death. But in the morning Bara was a little better, and in a week she was well again. Through it all the baby showed no signs of shifting. There were now no more potions to try, and Kate feared what Bara might do in one of her desperate moods. Ever since the failure of the first medicine Kate had wanted Bara to have the baby. She tried occasionally, when Bara seemed in a receptive mood, to describe how adorable babies could be, but Bara would not listen.

Then one afternoon she heard Bara laughing in the garden. She heard her begin to sing. Kate moved in astonishment to the door, and stared out at Bara where she stood digging potatoes. She walked over to Bara's side and watched, waiting for the girl to speak.

'Grans,' said Bara, smiling up sideways through her hair, 'I'm going to have him. If he's as tough as this I'm going to have him. It would be such an awful waste to lose such a terribly tough character.' She straightened up, and they both half-laughed, half-cried in each other's arms.

'Of course you're right,' said Kate. 'It would be the most terrible waste.'

Bara returned to her job in Fred's store, and to her evenings at the stables. Her pregnancy was happy and easy, she never lost confidence and she had no regrets about her decision. Kate thanked heaven for the miracle by which this hated foetus had become a wanted human creature. One evening, in the May of 2045, Kate and Suz delivered the baby. The first they saw of it was a fuzz of flaxen hair, tinged with silver. Then it emerged, flailing, a solid nine-pound boy. Although he was very plain, with a large nose, this fact was not apparent to Bara. She was enraptured.

'I'll call him Con,' she said.

'Whatever for?' said Suz.

'I don't know. Because I like it.'

Con was the third baby Kate had had in the house – first there had been her son Lenny, then Bara, and now there was another boy. She found she never grew tired of them, even when they were as demanding as Con. He was a noisy devil, every bit the tough character Bara had predicted, a baby who was instantly enraged if he were not picked up and fed the moment he awoke. His fists would whirl and his round legs would pump, while his face turned slowly purple and red. As soon as he was picked up all was calm again. He held his fair head steady very early, and he stared about him with eyes of astonished blue. The women of the house doted on him, but Tam found him of no interest at all.

'He's ugly,' he said, 'and he's smelly, and he's noisy. Maybe I'll like him later,' he added, to placate the fuming Bara.

When Con began to smile, at seven weeks, Bara's enslavement was complete. Fred allowed her to bring him to the store, where she could feed him when he was hungry and then leave him out to sleep in the overgrown yard at the back. When his fury at being left alone rose to a pitch Bara could ignore no longer, she would bring him into the store, where he could watch her and the other company. Fred was sour about this arrangement at first, but when he saw how liberally

Con bestowed his toothless smiles, and how well they were received by the shoppers in the store, he began to regard the baby as a free advertisement. When Con was three months old, and gulping solid foods with relish, Fred propped a placard against his basket, which read 'This baby is fed with foods from this store'. Bara felt that Fred was hardly in need of such promotion, for the nearest rival store was two miles away, but she supposed his early training in management had left him with a firm belief in the power of advertising.

Bara's cheeks had filled out during her pregnancy, and her pallor had been slowly overlaid with a healthy pink. Her figure was returning to its bony, coltish outline, but that too, Kate thought, would probably remain a little rounder. She would never be beautiful, but she was handsome and striking, and an intolerable distraction to the unfortunate young book-keeper she was supposed to help. Kate felt there would be plenty of trouble with men. She noticed that Jank eyed Bara appreciatively, but for the moment he and Christo were both involved with other girls, and so far Suz had contrived to keep Tam for herself.

No-one ever spoke of Con's father, but one day Kate suddenly felt she might begin to talk to Bara about Ralf. As a child Bara had been reluctant to hear anything about either her grandfather or her father, and Kate suspected that she bitterly resented their departure, interpreting it in her infant mind as a betrayal. She still shied away from any mention of Lenny, but suddenly she was interested in hearing about her grandfather. Kate had caught her eye several times recently, when Ralf's name had been mentioned, and she sensed a new probing curiosity in Bara's glance. Then, one winter evening, when Con was in bed, Kate and Bara sat in the kitchen with Tam and Suz and Charley over a bottle of elderberry wine. Outside the wind blew and the rain clattered down, plopping in steady drips through the roof of the uninhabited part of the house. Slowly Bara turned her green gaze on Kate.

'Tell us about Ralf,' she said. Kate stopped her mug of wine half way to her lips. The image of Ralf as a young man in that very room surged up before her. Charley fidgeted on his chair and suddenly his pale eyes were awash with tears.

'Where is he?' he said to Kate, his voice cracking. 'Why isn't he here? Why did he go away from us?'

'You remember, Charley,' said Kate, putting her hand over his bony fingers. 'You remember why he had to go. The police were after him. They might have killed him.'

'No, I don't remember. Why didn't he come back to us?'

'I suppose he couldn't. He thought he'd be killed.'

'He was a very clever man, wasn't he?' said Bara. 'I mean, really extra clever?'

'Yes, he was,' said Kate, gazing into her wine. 'He was an extraordinary person. He knew so much it made you reel. Latin poetry from end to end, molecular biology, the physics of particles, Greek drama – I don't know what all. The maths he worked at was so advanced no-one else could see it wasn't just gibberish. And he played the fiddle – oh, marvellously. And he helped to organize a national, bloodless Revolution. He was clever beyond all explanation. Learning seemed to fall out of the air into his head. It wasn't – it wasn't quite natural somehow.'

'Funny to think of him being your husband,' said Bara, gazing intently at her grandmother.

'Yes, funny.' Kate controlled her voice with difficulty and drank her wine at a gulp.

'What did he look like?' said Suz.

Tam shifted in his chair. 'What's it matter?' he said gruffly. 'You always want to know what people look like.'

'Why not?' said Kate hastily. 'It has a bearing. Well, he was very tall, and very dark, with square-cut black hair and a line of beard round his jaw, and a lovely smile. His hair flopped about when he was angry. His hands were very big.'

'Sounds nice,' said Suz. 'Tall, dark, and handsome.'

'Oh for Chrissake,' muttered Tam. 'You think he escaped to Ireland, don't you?' he continued, turning to Kate.

'That's what he said he meant to do. Lenny was always sure he'd got to Ireland. I suppose that's why Lenny loved the Irish legends so much.' Bara turned her face away and would not look at Kate.

'But why Ireland?' Tam insisted. 'Why did he go to Ireland?'

'I can't really remember. I suppose it was far enough away, but still possible to get to.'

'But the Irish wars. What about the Irish wars?' Tam leaned forward, scowling with concentration. 'The wars were terrible. I've just been reading about them. Two million people killed. The North fighting King William's War, the South fighting the Holy Crusade. It was absolute carnage. Why choose *there*?'

'Oh, I can't remember,' said Kate wearily. 'I think the wars were over by then. He didn't go till 2003.'

'It must have been awful for you when he went.' Once again Kate felt Bara's thoughtful gaze upon her, and she understood that this evening for the first time Bara had recognized her as a separate person, with a being of her own. This was the first adult apprehension that some close and beloved relative was not merely an extension of oneself; the breaking of one of the great links with childhood.

'Why shouldn't he go to Ireland anyway?' said Suz. 'Who wouldn't? It's a magic place, all green and gold, and everyone's happy.'

'I know everyone says that,' said Bara. 'I wonder if it's true.'

'Of course it's true. The sun shines all the time and everything grows in a week, and if you want gold you only have to dig for it.' Suz gazed wistfully out into the dark night. 'People bathe in cream there,' she said, 'and there are trees that grow up to the sky, and strawberries in every field. Everyone knows that.'

Tam glanced at her scornfully, but Kate stared in amazement. She remembered that fifty years ago there had been strange stories about Ireland, for even Ralf had been influenced by them, but she had no conception that those old tales had branched and flowered into such a legend. So Ireland was now the Happy Land, Eden and El Dorado; the golden image which drew the fantasies of all who were poor and discontent.

'I'd like to go there,' said Bara.

'You couldn't', said Suz. 'It's the other side of the world.'

'No it's not. I'll show you.' And Bara rushed to the sitting-room for Ralf's battered old atlas, to try to show Suz how Ireland lay in relation to London. But Suz could make nothing of it at all. Tam took the atlas from Bara and frowned over it a long time, but he would not ask her for any explanation. When the girls were out of the way next morning he asked Kate to explain it to him.

Five years passed in clear, unsullied weather of sun and rain and snow. By the year 2050 the blanket of dust and gas and ice, which had swathed the planet in ever increasing fog for two hundred years, had almost dispersed, and once again the sun's rays burst at dawn in a fierce and primitive glory. No violent events occurred to disturb the humdrum placidity of Kate's household. Occasional news and rumours floated in from the tinkers and gypsies who roamed the world outside. There was a new kingdom of Cornwall, where any man who spoke English instead of Cornish was hung from the nearest tree; there was constant warfare on the borders of Sussex and Kent; there was a growing Doomsday cult centred on St Albans; there had been a series of sacrificial murders in Winchester; a young and beautiful chieftain with silver hair was terrorising Colchester and its countryside. The world of Kate's childhood, once drawn almost into the dimensions of a single city by the power of TV and radio, was now fragmented into a cosmos as vast as that of the stars. No-one knew what was happening beyond the shores of Britain. No-one knew, and no-one very much cared. Kate's own horizons, once as wide as the world, were now drawn through Hampstead, Highgate, Golders Green.

Con grew sturdily, his positive character showing no sign of softening. As soon as he could heave himself up on his legs, at eleven months, he was staggering everywhere and into everything. His flaxen hair grew thick and tufted, and whenever light shone on it there was a gleam of silver. His wide blue eyes seemed perpetually surprised at what they saw. When Bara could no longer bring him to the store he was left with Kate and Suz during the day, and Kate found him much the most difficult of the babies she had had in her charge. Her own son Lenny had been gentle and ready to please from the moment he was born, and Bara had been a cheerful infant, easily diverted from mischief or danger. Con was very different. If he set his mind on breaking up a burning candle, or stepping fully clothed into a bucket of water, or climbing up the tail of a horse, he became outraged at any attempt to divert him from his chosen course. His absorbed little face would crumple suddenly into a grotesque mask of rage, and he would hit out wildly at anyone who was interfering with his object.

'You'd never have dislodged him,' Kate said to Bara, after a particularly exhausting day in Con's company. 'Not in a hundred years. Not with all the Mother Huffs in the world.'

Bara laughed. 'He's a horror,' she said adoringly.

Kate was now sixty-eight, but she looked ten years younger. Her thick sandy hair was streaked with white, and a few deep lines had scored themselves on her forehead and round her eyes, but her back was still very straight and she was brimming with energy. She had one dread only, which she kept to herself. The youth drugs she had taken in her teens were almost always effective, but there were known to be certain people, undetectable in youth, who between the years of about sixty and seventy would begin to age with terrifying speed. Kate looked anxiously in her bit of mirror every day, to see if she might be of this company, but so far the signs were good. She felt that at all costs she must keep her health and strength, at least until Bara settled down with some man or into some permanent occupation; besides, she enjoyed her youthful looks, and dreaded decrepitude.

Although she still loved working at the stables, Bara was becoming more and more bored with her job at Fred's store. She had worked there for five years now, and the days were becoming increasingly tedious. The book-keeper no longer needed her assistance, and he had been both disappointed and relieved when her presence had been removed from his side. She now helped to serve the customers, a job far more responsible than in past days, for each buyer would offer some coin or object that the assistant had to measure against the value of the sale. Bara might be offered pre-decimal coins or Greek coins, or coins from any place or time; oddments of clothing or household equipment, knives, ladles, brushes, buckets, pans; or garden tools, seeds, vegetable roots; or ornaments, brooches, buckles, rings, many looted from museums and once of inestimable value. One day to her delight she was offered a stuffed parrot. Often she had to consult Fred on the barter, and he would grope about in his long experience trying to remember what he could expect to receive for the proferred object. The system was chaotic, and gave rise to endless anxiety in both buyer and seller, but without any central authority no enduring standards of value could be established.

There seemed no better job for Bara to do, and the money was good, so in spite of her boredom she held reluctantly on. She would come home in the late afternoon to see Con and put him to bed, then on three evenings a week she would walk across the ruined tower blocks on the Heath Extension to Joddy's stables, where she would feed and groom Dark, the black Shire, and make him comfortable for the night. She was always tired and often cross when she came home, and Kate began to sense a new unease, a restless conviction that something different had to happen soon. Bara was a sharper, less trusting character than she had been once, and given to bouts of despair she could not account for. She fiercely rejected any attempts by men and boys to see more of her, and she struck Jank with a stick when he said he was tired of his girl, and how about it? Even now, five years after the rape, she never spoke of Con's savage and beautiful father. Kate did not dare to refer to any incident from that terrible time, for although she suspected Bara's wounds were unhealed she did not see how she could attempt their cure. One day, if fortune was kind, some loving and gentle man would be the physician Bara required.

Tam had grown up into a very serious young man, desperately anxious to improve and educate himself. He would take nothing at all from Bara, who could at least read and write and understand an atlas, but he would devour as much instruction from Kate as she had time to give him. He was a silent companion, and Kate could not make out if all this learning was for the love of it or no. She suspected he had political ambitions (if you could call them that in so disorganized a time), for he was deeply angry about the conditions under which many people lived, and he must have realized by his twentieth year that both men and women seemed prepared to follow his suggestions and do what he asked of them.

At much the same time as she began to notice Bara's restlessness, Kate became sharply aware that Tam had had more than enough of the company of Suz, and that the tenacious Suz was not prepared to lose him quietly. Sometimes, aggrieved and whining, she would follow him from room to room, until his looks became so thunderous she was frightened into brief silence; sometimes she would prance before him with her sharp, bird-like movements, chattering brightly about nothing. He tried ignoring her, but she would not be ignored; he tried shouting angrily, but she revived in a moment like a cork in water; he tried the effect of studied politeness, but his irony was lost on her. Kate would watch him bristling like an angry dog, frustrated by his inability to be rid of her. He knew that Suz had as much right in the house as he had himself, and that there was nowhere for her to sleep but in the sitting-room with him. He might have been able to bear it, Kate supposed, had Suz shown the faintest sympathy for his passion for books. But she saw them as a rival to herself, and more than once she had ripped up some volume he was reading and flung it into the fire. Kate knew that the excitement which had flared in him when they had first discovered the hidden boxes still burned as fiercely as on that summer night five years ago. He was now familiar with the contents of all the two thousand books in the house but he knew as intimately as he knew the shape of his body the volumes on philosophy and politics and government. Kate also realized that the attraction he had felt for Bara ever since he was a boy mending the fence had long ago deepened into a love which neither Bara's indifference nor Suz's clamour could begin to touch. No doubt he believed he was successful in concealing his passion from all watchers, but Kate knew with absolute conviction where his heart lay. The undertows tugged in all directions, the atmosphere was increasingly brittle; one violent word might soon be enough to shatter the calm that Kate worked vigilantly to preserve. She was nagged by this new tension in her young household, and depressed by her inability to soothe it. Expectancy hovered uneasily, and Kate was too old to welcome expectation.

One late autumn evening, when the colours of the leaves were muted in the darkening light, Kate wrapped herself in a blanket and went to sit outside on a log in the garden to talk to Charley as he worked. The old man was ageing rapidly. He had never known his exact age, but he reckoned he must be about seventy-six, and Kate could not understand how his thin, creaking body still survived what he demanded of it. He was like a ghost, she thought, a being who occupied no solid space. He could not possibly last much longer, and however hard the rest of them worked when he died, his bosky, luxuriant garden would never be the same again. A terrible ending was to come, and it could not be long. Charley was something no-one could have expected from life. Even now he never stopped working. He still flitted all day round his fruit and vegetables, winter and summer alike, and under his loving care the garden burgeoned so richly that Kate was able to sell quantities of stuff they could not possibly eat themselves. Kate looked up at Charley's Pippin, now a large tree which still grew vigorously, thrusting out branches and buds and fruit every year. She smiled as she remembered the morning fifty years ago when the young Charley had burst at a spindly run full tilt into the kitchen. Usually he stalked stealthily into rooms, but not that day. He had been holding in his hand a little red, rough-skinned apple.

'Look,' he had said, trembling with excitement, 'look, it's Charley's Pippin. I'm calling it Charley's Pippin. I made it. It's mine.'

In the end she and Ralf and Ralf's father had discovered that four years previously Charley had grafted some kind of pippin onto some kind of russet, and at last the little tree had borne some fruit. Charley cut the apple into three, everyone shook his hand, and Ralf poured water over the core, saying 'I christen this apple Charley's Pippin.' That day Charley had performed a great many of his secret little skips and hops. For half a century the generations of local children had teased him about his tree. 'We're going to cut it down, Charley!' they'd shout. 'We're coming with a big chopper tonight!' He still derived his chief entertainment from his feud with these children, whom he regarded with thrilling hatred. If one of them set so much as a toe in the garden he would skip up and down in fury, hurling potatoes and pebbles and insults until he was satisfied his territory was again secure. Whatever else went on in his crazy head, he knew this territory was home, where he was useful and beloved.

Kate leaned forward, easing her weight on the hard log and cupping her chin in her hands. It was the belonging that mattered, she thought. The vanished comforts of a vanished civilization were of little importance as long as there was food for survival and some shelter from the cold; and as long as the thin, naked human soul had the love of its own kind. She herself was a fortunate being; she had Bara's love, and Con's love, and Charley's love. She had had Lenny's love and she had had Ralf's – but had she? Had she ever really possessed Ralf's love? A worm of doubt had been gnawing through her mind for half a lifetime. For one marvellous year no shadow had crossed the blaze of noon in which they lived. Yet, looking back down the long valley of time, she knew that even then he had given her only his body and the outer edge of his attention. He had held himself behind his frontiers, and they had never broken before her. During the three years before the Revolution, when he had been away more often than at home, he had retreated further and further from her and from his family, into a black cloud of political passion and commitment where she could not find him at all. And when he had finally left, early on New Year's Day in 2003, in an attempt to escape Bradwardine's police, he had scarcely seemed to realize what either his capture or his escape would mean to his father or to her. The conviction that she had never found her way through to him intensified the bitterness she had fostered ever since he left. She had never tried to forgive him because she knew she could not; and anger was a more acceptable companion than pain. She shook her head sharply and thrust Ralf's face down into the secret places of her mind. The night was suddenly very dark, Charley had disappeared, the wind was rising. She must get to bed.

Wrapping her blanket tightly about her she heaved herself up from the log, and set off down the path. Perhaps it was the worst thing of all, she thought, this hellish bucket in the outside shed. Charley had been sick so often emptying it into a hole in the ground that for years she had done the job herself, until Tam had relieved her of it. The wind whipped round her legs, straight through her tattered trousers. She stumbled in the dark and a bony hand caught her arm. She started in terror, but of course it was only Charley. Kate thanked him, and they made their way together along the path to the shed, supporting each other against the wind. Kate was frozen to the bone as she cursed the form that life on this planet had taken. These tiresome excretory processes might have been avoided altogether if cellular evolution had taken only a slightly different course. But to Charley she said, 'Thank you Charley. Get to bed and sleep well.'

'Say good-night to Bara and Con,' he said, as he said every night.

Next morning the leaves swirled in a bitter wind. When Charley did not come in for his breakfast Kate looked for him outside, then went to his room. She found him lying stiffly on his mattress, his knotted fingers clutching at his blanket like the claws of a bird. His eyes were open but there was no doubt he was dead. Kate stood gazing down at the frail body, no more than a bundle of sticks, and she knew that for the first time in may years her courage was going to fail her utterly. She stood helpless, watching the breaking wave swelling towards her. For over fifty years Charley had tended this garden, and she could not believe it could exist without his fluttering presence among the fruit trees, in the old shed, between the rows of peas and beans and cabbages. The wave tore towards her, the breaker curled over her head. She fell heavily onto the mattress beside Charley's body and she began to cry. She wept as she had never wept before, losing all control of her sobs. The great retches of sound wracked her muscles and invaded her bones. She wept for the crazy devotion of old Charley, she wept for Lenny, she wept for Ralf, she wept for decay and desolation and the tragedies of everyday that men are scarcely strong enough to bear. She wept for her youth, and for the death of the world she had known, and she wept for the loneliness which wrapped her like a mist of dawn.

They buried Charley in the overgrown graveyard of the old parish church in Hampstead. The church had fallen in ruins long ago, and the graveyard in autumn was a jumble of broken masonry and coloured leaves. No-one bothered any longer about burial in consecrated ground, and Kate herself had no religious feelings about death, but she passionately wished that old Charley should lie in that wild and hallowed place, where every spring and summer snowdrops and bluebells and dog roses rioted over the broken ground.

Joddy washed down his best cart, groomed the black Shire until he shone, then drove slowly with Charley's body over the hill to Hampstead. The cart ran softly on four old car-tyres, which absorbed much of the jolting from the broken road. Bara and Kate rode with Joddy on the cart, Fred walked on one side of the horse, Tam and Christo on the other. A crowd of neighbours and acquaintances followed, for Charley's innocence had made him many friends. Kate had asked Tam and Christo to dig the grave the night before, and they were to lower Charley's coffin into the ground. Kate held Bara's hand tightly, and stared unseeing at the swaying haunches of the horse. Endings, more endings. She knew the growing point in her had now finally shrivelled. A finger of ice lay over it, and under that touch nothing could grow again. The young were restless, the old wished only to die. She was lost in a daze of memories, a nightmare in which Ralf and Lenny and Charley advanced, retreated, spun and fell, in spirals of darkness and light. She was drained of all feeling, possessed by the past, so drawn into memory that they had to shake her gently when they reached the churchyard.

A mile across the wildest region of the Heath, on the slopes which led down to the lake, was a long tangled bank of brambles in which were hidden four foxes' earths. Kate and Bara sometimes sat nearby, downwind and very still, in the hour before dusk on a spring evening. Birds twittered in the high trees, and an occasional squirrel bounded through the undergrowth, but otherwise the hour was hushed. They would grow stiff and chilled as they waited, enduring the crawl of insects over their arms and legs, but several times they had been rewarded by the sight of fox cubs emerging warily from their holes. Once, with their twitching noses held high in the air, the cubs had taken the human scent and had scrambled back over each other into their earth. But more usually they stayed out unsuspecting on the open bank, tumbling and scuffling and nipping, and chasing their own tails in tight circles. Bara had taken Con there for the first time when he was two, carrying him in a shawl on her back, and they had had the fright of meeting an old dog fox face to face on a dark path. Bara had gasped but Con yelled with delight, and immediately the fox had fled. Con could not return to the fox holes often enough, though usually his loud excitement made certain that no cubs ever appeared.

On a pale afternoon in the first week of the January of 2051, Kate decided she would take Con to the holes. A misty sun shone on a thin layer of snow and the sky was very blue. Con at the age of five would be able to trot most of the way himself, and Kate felt easily strong enough to carry him on her back the rest of the journey. Her copying was finished, there was nothing urgent to do in the garden, and it was Suz's turn to cook the supper. She called to Tam, who was on guard duty, to tell him they were going out, and he looked up from his books to shout an acknowledgement. Her spirits soared as she stepped hand in hand with Con into the pale sunlight and over the crunching snow. A shower of gold dust filled air. She brimmed with wellbeing, and never gave her exhilaration another thought. The birches shone silver and black, the leaves which made a perpetual carpet on this part of the Heath were each rimmed with frost. Kate could find no words to measure up to what she saw. Con bounded and lurched from side to side of the path, foraging in the leaves and shouting his discoveries to Kate. She smiled at him and began to tug him along behind her, moving confidently through the dense maze of birch and elm that covered the hummocky ground. Only one defined track led across this half-mile of woods and bramble, but they scorned to use it, for this was ground Kate had known all her life. Across the open glade, through the forest of birches and down into the dell they went, then up again into the frosty sunlight on the steep slope towards the road. Con had no notion of conserving his energy and already he was whimpering and tired. Kate felt full of strength as she bundled him into her old shawl and tied him to her back.

'You're a horrible weight,' she said. 'All beef and butter.'

Con laughed and clung to her shoulders, urging her on as if she were a horse. Up on the crest the old concrete road from Hampstead to Highgate survived in broken blocks only as a carters' track. As she crossed it Kate felt a sudden chill and glanced up at the sky. A soft grey mist obscured the sun and more cloud was drifting across the blue from the east. Well, she thought, we shall get wet. But she crossed the track and tramped on down the long frosty slope, and eventually into the shade of the beeches. Suddenly it was very cold, and much darker. She unwrapped Con from the shawl and made him walk a quarter of a mile along the path through the trees until they reached the high bank above the fox holes. As they began to slide down the slope Con fell and rolled over, laughing wildly, and the noise of his laughter resounded eerily in the still air. Dusk was thickening every moment and Kate felt the first naggings of anxiety. Con was now far below her down the slope, staggering and rolling on the silver grass, still yelling with delight.

'Come back, Con!' called Kate. 'We must go.'

He stood still in amazement, far down at the bottom of the bank, and looked up at her.

'But I haven't seen the foxes,' he shouted.

'It's going to rain or snow or something.'

'I want to see the foxies. Look, I can smell them!' and he ran off along the bottom of the slope past one fox hole and towards the next.

'Con, come back!' Kate shouted.

'No. I want to see the foxies.'

'You won't see them. You're making too much noise. Come back here.'

'I can smell them. Look!' He thrust his head and shoulders down a hole. He was very excited and Kate knew she would have to go all the way down to fetch him. She picked her way cautiously on the slippery bank, zig-zagging down the steeper parts. When she reached the bottom she was surprised to find her thighs were aching. Con had emerged from the hole and stood alert, staring at her with mischief on his face.

'Come on, Con,' said Kate sharply, angered not so much by him as by an anxiety she could not focus. As she stretched to take his hand he leaped away, grinning and gurgling. He moved fast for a five-year-old, and it was a minute before Kate caught him.

'Come on,' she said. 'I'm angry with you.' She tugged at his hand, but he was unabashed.

'I'm tired,' he said. 'Carry me.'

'No, I won't. It's too steep.'

He began to whimper as she dragged him up the long slope. She found it weary work, pulling herself upwards and dragging Con as well. Her legs began to ache again and when she reached the top of the bank her knees were trembling. As she stood recovering her breath the first flakes of snow began to fall, slow and heavy, thickening all the time.

'Quickly, Con,' said Kate, 'come on now.'

He had flopped down on the ground and she tried to pull him up.

'No,' he said, and he began to cry, quietly and miserably, as he always did when he was deadbeat.

'Christ,' said Kate aloud. She had a mile to go, she had Con to carry, and she was now shivering in every muscle. She looked about her, but she could see nothing through the snow, which was falling in a thick white cloud. No-one was coming along the tracks, and no-one lived in these benighted stretches of wild land. She struggled to lift Con, who was now a dead weight of misery, and covered in snow. She tied him into the shawl and somehow heaved him onto her back. Everything had seemed so easy only an hour before, when the sun had shone and she had felt such strength in her limbs. She set off through the beeches and up the long slope towards the carters' track. The snow was already half-an-inch deep and falling so quickly in the gloom Kate could not see four yards ahead. She had had new boots from the cobbler recently, so her feet were still dry, but her coat was threadbare and her worn gloves were already soaked through. Although he was protected by her body, Con was moaning with cold, and instead of helping her by clinging to her shoulders he sank down into the shawl. She knew that if she kept up this slope she would eventually reach the Highgate road, but when she emerged from the trees she had no idea where she had struck it. She leaned sideways against an elm, resisting the temptation to sit down in the snow. Her shoulders ached painfully from the weight of Con, her thighs and her knees turned to water when she stopped. She shivered violently, and knew for certain she was ill. Her temperature must be rising fast – it was the first hint of that rise that had accounted for her exhilaration an hour and a half ago. But somewhere across that track was home, and she felt sure she would soon recognize landmarks in a country she had known so long. She pushed herself upright, adjusted the weight of Con as best she could, and crossed the track to the treacherous downward slope on the other side. Once she slipped over, and if Con had not screamed the temptation to remain lying in the snow would have been irresistible. She staggered up, pulling at a branch and dislodging a shower of snow onto their heads. They seemed to be in an open meadow, and if that was so they were too far up the hill. She turned into the trees, stumbling on the tussocks hidden by the snow. Although the air was darker under the branches, the snow was less dense, for it was caught in the interlocking boughs. Kate stood still and looked about her. There should be a bog on the left, and a hillock with two oaks, and a dense patch of bramble and gorse. She could see none of them. The branches of the bushes were already weighed half to the ground, making familiar tracks unfamiliar and impassable. The snow had evened out all the smaller dips and mounds. She found herself in a strange country, anonymous and white, a totally unknown landscape.

Which way should she go? A general downward direction was what she wanted, so she set off down a slope, moving too fast for her strength. Her legs would scarcely obey her. Her knees wanted to fold up, their muscles seemed to have left them. Knives stabbed her shoulders from the weight of Con. She concentrated the last dregs of her energy in forcing her body to work. She moved each leg doggedly forward, slower and slower, with her head down and her eyes blinking to dispel the purple lights that flashed across them. There was pain and whiteness, whiteness and pain. Then, dizzily, trying to focus, she saw her own footprints and she knew she had been round in a circle. The last thread of determination snapped, and she sank in merciful blackness onto the snow. Con cried out and was still.

For two hours in the thickly falling blizzard Bara and Tam and Christo searched desperately for Kate and Con. Neighbours turned out to help them, but no-one knew which way to look. No-one had any idea where Kate had gone, and it was an hour after they had begun searching that in the darkness of the snow and the night Tam found footprints among the beech trees above the fox holes. Only under the densest trees had footprints survived, so it was impossible by the feeble light of lanterns to track Kate's direction home across the open ground. Her route had been so devious that another hour had passed before Christo came upon traces of prints fifty yards from where Kate lay. The searchers were frozen and exhausted, but at last they felt they must be near.

When Kate recovered consciousness she was almost smothered in snow and she could not move a muscle. Somewhere out of the frozen waste which was her body she heard a cry. Some sense of space and time resolved itself. The cry came again. Was it within her or without her? From Ralf? From Lenny? Again the calling. She knew that voice, sometime, somewhere, far away. And another, higher cry.

'Grans!' it called. 'Grans, Grans!'

'Kate!' cried a deeper voice. 'Kate, Kate, Kate!' More voices, coming nearer. She tried to call, she tried to move, but her body was absent; so numb it did not exist. She was only a mind, a disembodied pattern of lights, which flickered for a moment, and then went out. When Tam raised her from the snow ten minutes later, Kate was dead.

PART 2

Journeyings

THERE WAS LITTLE physically wrong with Con that a hot fire and a long sleep could not put right. He had been shielded from the fiercest of the cold by the warmth of Kate's body, and although he had fallen into a dangerous sleep he had been found before he had been damaged. But he was now terrified of finding himself underneath anything. Kate had rolled sideways when she fell, half-smothering him, and now even the sight of Bara looming above him as he lay in bed provoked screams of terror. For many weeks he would wake gasping in the night, beating away an attacker with his arms, and Bara would have to raise him and bring him to her own bed. She often brought him in there anyway, even when he was not crying, because she found comfort in the stirring of his plump, warm body in the bed beside her.

A dead weight of misery lay night and day on Bara's spirits. She had never dared contemplate Kate's death, she had never let her thoughts even approach the subject, and now here she was with the mainstay of her world gone and only Con for company. She was constantly in tears, at home and at the store; and yet, for all her tears, she could not really believe that Kate was gone. Surely she would appear in the sitting-room door laughing at Con; she would round the corner of the road as she trudged up the hill; she would come wandering into the kitchen puzzling over a handful of her beloved peas. The force of habit was so powerful that even the certainty of Kate's death could not dispel the expectation of seeing her. Bara felt utterly alone, and too restless to settle to any occupation for more than a minute. She had never realized how much she had talked to Kate, how often they had discussed Con, how much they had wandered idly over the events of the day.

Everyone became bored with her miserable face. Fred, Tam, Suz, the boys, the neighbours – they had all been sympathetic and kind in their several ways, but after a month or so they expected Bara to be a little less tearful and depressed.

'People die all the time,' said Suz, who bore the brunt of Bara's misery. 'You just have to get used to it.'

'It's not the same for everyone.'

'Maybe not, but it is for a lot of people.'

'Who've you lost then?' said Bara angrily.

'My mum and dad, for a start.'

'You never knew them.'

'Maybe. But I lost them, didn't I?'

'It's utterly bloody different,' retorted Bara.

'Why?' said Suz, her voice rising. 'Yours was only a gran, wasn't she? Mine was my mum and dad.'

'Oh, shut up, you cats,' said Tam angrily. 'I'm trying to read.'

'Shut up yourself,' said Suz. 'Why don't you stop reading for once? I'm only telling Bara it's time she stopped moping around and blowing her snotty nose.'

'Well, she happened to like her Gran.'

'We all did,' said Suz, unmollified. 'She was a nice old bag.'

Bara turned sharply away to the window, tears welling again in her eyes. That Suz should equate the casual liking of her own mean little heart with Bara's love; that she should call Kate a nice old bag – Bara was too choked with outrage to find words to reply.

'Damn you all to hell,' she whispered, beginning to sob quietly.

'It's all right, it's all right,' said Tam, gently laying his hand on her shoulder.

'O-oh,' said Suz furiously. 'It's like that, is it? All right, if you two want to be left alone –' And she rushed away, banging the door behind her.

'Come back!' shouted Tam. 'Oh bloody hell,' he said, thrusting his hands in his pockets and turning away from Bara. 'Now you're both crying.'

Bara tried to rub the tears out of her eyes. 'I'm sorry,' she said, not quite knowing for what.

'She's clumsy, is Suz,' said Tam. 'But she's right too. It's time you did something about yourself. She wasn't an old bag, she was damn special, but you can't go on mourning over her for ever.'

'I feel so lonely, Tam.' She was not thinking of Tam at all, but in the long pause which followed she felt him staring at her back, and she realized miserably that her words could be taken as an invitation. He came close to her.

'I can help you,' he said quietly, putting his arm round her and his face close to hers. 'Any time. You only have to say the word.'

Bara knew she did not want him, yet in the chaos of her feelings the first thing she said was, 'How about Suz?'

'She was only because I couldn't have you. All the time. Right from the beginning. Just because I couldn't have you.' He leaned forward but she drew away sharply.

'I don't want to,' she said, suddenly hating his square dark head and his thick neck and his great hairy hands.

'What's the matter?' said Tam angrily. 'Still dreaming of Con's glorious father?' Before he could dodge it, Bara's hand had stung him hard across the face.

They all began to avoid each other as much as they could. Bara took food for herself and Con to their bedroom, Tam and Suz ate at different times and did not seem to be on speaking terms. A couple of nights later Suz moved herself out to the garage with Christo and Jank. Everything that Kate had kept steady and sweet was disintegrating in bitterness. Bara sat one evening on the edge of her bed in her cold room, trying to rock Con to sleep. It was all impossible, she thought. Their small society was already in pieces. If she had the energy and the courage she might be able to salvage it somehow, but she could not face the task. And anyway this house was haunted for her by the ghosts of the past. The images of childhood clutched and held her. In this place she could never go forward. Tears rolled down her cheeks onto Con's flaxen head as she thought of the happiness of her childhood in this house, as far back as she could remember, with her adored, enfolding Grans. She had not the courage to stay and exorcise the ghosts. She and Con would go away. She laid her cheek on the thick hair of his sleeping head and she wept without restraint.

There was never any doubt in Bara's mind where she and Con would go. The image of Ireland had begun to haunt her long before she had questioned Kate and Suz. What Suz had said only confirmed her longing to see that magical place. There she would find love and kindness, and a clear sun forever shining on burgeoning flowers and fields and trees.

When she told Tam that she and Con were going to Ireland, he was incredulous. He scowled and cocked his head as if he had not understood. When she persisted, he exploded.

'Don't be so bloody idiotic,' he shouted, waving his arms. 'How could you listen to those stupid baby stories? I thought you were supposed to be educated.'

'They're not stupid. They couldn't have got such a grip if there hadn't been something in them.'

'Rubbish. Look at all those stories of heaven and the Garden of

Eden and all that stuff. There's no truth in them is there?'

'This is different.'

'It isn't different at all. People have always wanted to believe in some beautiful happy land, whatever its name might be.'

'But Ireland's a real place.'

'It's a real place all right, but not in your stories it isn't. It's just a substitute heaven. It's as real as h.:re, but it's all dolled up in people's minds to look like the Islands of the Blest. God's Christ, can't you see that?' His dark face was red with anger, and he thumped the kitchen table as he spoke.

'No, I can't see it. And bloody well stop shouting at me.' She swung away from him and her long hair swept across his face.

'Bitch,' he said, grabbing her from behind and pressing her hard against him. 'You're not to go. You're damn well not to go.' He kissed the hair on the back of her neck but she kicked back at him and struck his shin.

'Damn and blast all men,' she shouted as she pulled herself free, swamped with a bewildering fear. 'Damn damn damn.' She rushed from the room, more than ever certain that somehow she and Con must get to Ireland. Ireland would be her beacon, her light on the dark sea, and until she found it their journey would be her only thought.

The next day Christo and Jank came up to her when she was playing with Con in the garden.

'They say you're crazy about Ireland. You think you only have to dig for gold and you'll find it,' said Jank. 'You're mad you know. That's how mad people think.' Christo flushed and pulled him away, but Bara stood absolutely still, frozen by his cruelty and frightened for the first time that perhaps he could be right. She wanted to talk, she wanted someone to run to, and there was only Tam. She wanted arms around her and she wanted comfort. But she could not go to him; she knew he loved her, and so, perversely, she could not go to him. Con cannoned into her and grabbed her legs.

'Throw this stick,' he said, smiling up at her. 'I'm a puppy, I'll fetch it.' To his astonishment she seized him in her arms and kissed and hugged him, and took no notice at all of his loud demands to be put down.

Bara would not listen to reason. As soon as her decision to go became known, everyone tried to persuade her to stay, at least until the next summer when Con would be six. Old Fred was horrified at her madness, and he paid a private visit to Tam one winter afternoon to ask him if he thought Bara was all right in the head.

'I mean,' he said, 'well, it's barmy. Ireland, for God's sake. Is she – I mean, is she –?' His wizened face screwed up in concentration.

'I know,' said Tam, 'I know what you mean. But it's not like that. She's all there, she's sane. It's just that she's got this one crazy idea. When it comes to that she won't listen to any reason at all.'

'How does she think she's going to get there, for God's sake?' said Fred.

'She just thinks you go. On foot, with a baby of five.'

'Christ,' said Fred, twisting his bony hands. 'How mad can you get? Hasn't she noticed what the world's like? A girl like that, just wandering about on her own. I knew her dad and I knew her grandad and I knew her great-grandad too. I feel sort of responsible.'

'Have you talked to her?'

'Talked. I've talked till my throat went dry. I might as well be talking to a brick wall. By the way,' he said, his eyes lighting up as he leaned forward on his elbow, 'do you know they're making real good bricks again? In Bedfordshire?'

'Good,' said Tam, excited. 'That's good. Now they'll have to find an old man who knows how to put them together.'

'I'll put a notice up,' said Fred eagerly. 'We'll dig up someone. But that's not what I came to talk about,' he continued wearily. 'She'll need provisions. I'll give her those.'

'Not too many though. She'd only be robbed.'

'Suppose so. She ought to have a horse and cart too.'

'She wouldn't keep it for ten miles. Someone'd have it off her.'

'Well, a horse then. Can't you go with her, for God's sake?'

'No,' said Tam, getting up abruptly.

'Why not? You like her, don't you?'

Tam turned quickly, his face drawn in pain.

'Damn you Fred, she doesn't want me. Don't you understand? Do I have to spell it all out? She doesn't want me. She wants to get away from everyone and everything she's ever known. She just wants to be alone with Con.'

Fred looked down at his hands. 'Sorry,' he said. Tam shrugged and flung himself into his chair again. 'I hear a lot of rumours in my shop,' Fred continued. 'I think half of them are bums' tales. But they do say the boy's father is White Michael.' Tam looked startled.

'White Michael? That savage?'

'Yep. And White Michael doesn't leave his by-blows lying around.'

'What's he do?'

'Takes them to his court – so-called. Where he lords it around in

Colchester. They say there's something magic about him.'

'Magic? What do you mean – magic?'

'Some power or other. He only has to look at people and they do what he wants. Anything. Murder, robbery, rape—'

'Oh balls!' said Tam.

'Balls yourself,' said Fred, jerking his grizzled chin in anger. 'I've heard plenty. There's something funny about that man. And he'll be after his boy soon. They say he comes for them when they're five or six.'

'What about their mothers?'

'Oh, he leaves them to rot. Unless he still fancies them, then they come too. But they don't see their kids again.'

'Christ. Does she know?'

'I don't think so. I haven't told her. But I don't think there's any mistaking that boy's hair. He's White Michael's all right.'

'We'd better not tell her. But it changes things about her going away. We could never stop his lot if they came.'

'No, we couldn't,' said Fred, rising stiffly. 'Well, we'll let her go then. But we'll see she has a horse and some things.'

'We'll try,' said Tam doubtfully.

Bara was insistent that she would leave before February was out. Images of Ireland obsessed her and she would not wait a moment longer than necessary before she began her journey. Fred ceased to shake his white head every time he saw her, and instead busied himself drawing up lists of what she must carry with her. Tam no longer nagged or tried to hinder her preparations. She was grateful, but also a little hurt at their apparent readiness to see her go, for there had been something comforting about their resistance and abuse. She laughed at Fred's long lists, and took no notice of Tam's insistence that she should have a horse. How could they possibly afford a horse? She would take a basket, and leave her back free for carrying Con. Fred and Tam found their exasperation swelling to the point of explosion.

'Can-you-not-see,' said Fred loudly and slowly, 'that you can't set off for a five-hundred-mile journey to Ireland with *one small basket*?'

'We'll be all right,' said Bara shrugging. 'We'll be all right.'

'You're a bloody fool,' said Tam shortly. 'You need a handcart at least. I'll make you one.'

'I *don't want it*,' Bara shouted.

'Oh God Almighty.'

Then, a week before she was due to start, there was a knock on the door in the early morning. Tam stumbled out of bed, grabbing his knife from the floor, and went to see who had knocked. There in the cold light of dawn stood Joddy, with Dark, the great black Shire, stamping and shaking his huge head beside him.

'He's for Bara,' said Joddy shortly. 'She'll need a horse.'

Tam stared at him.

'But we – the cost – we haven't –'

'He don't cost nothing. He's free for her. She's took good care of him ten years now. He likes her. She can have him.'

'Joddy,' said Tam, smiling and taking his hand. 'God, what a present.' Joddy smiled and shifted his feet. Tam turned and rushed into Bara's room.

'Bara. Get up. Come and see. Come and look at this.'

'For God's sake,' she said sleepily. 'What's happened?'

'Come on.'

She rolled reluctantly out of bed and wrapped a blanket round her shoulders. Tam bundled her along the passage and flung open the door on Dark, who stood quietly, tethered to a tree.

'It's Dark,' said Bara, stroking the horse's neck. 'Why's he here?'

'He's yours. Joddy's given him to you. He's a present. Joddy, Joddy, where are you?' he called. But Joddy had slipped away.

When Fred heard about the horse he brought up two huge panniers, packed with food and clothing, to sling over Dark's back. Tam fitted a nailed shaft and a long knife into the pannier by Bara's right hand, then spent two days training her to use them effectively. She took little interest, for all she wanted was to be off.

'What the hell's the matter with you?' said Tam, exasperated. 'Do you think you're under divine protection or something? You'll be carrying valuable stuff. People want clothes and food and horses. Not to mention girls. You've got to be able to defend yourself.'

'All right,' said Bara wearily. 'Let's do the thrusting thing again.'

At last, early in February, they were off. Bara sat astride Dark, with the panniers in front of her knees, and Con sat behind her. Tam had made a harness which would strap him either to Bara's back or to her front, so that he could even sleep in the saddle if he wished. Con trembled with excitement as he clutched Bara's waist, too enthralled with his adventure to take any notice of the few people who stood around. Bara had insisted they keep the time of her departure secret, and so on the sparkling winter morning when they left, only Tam and Fred and Christo stood around to wish them goodbye. Just as she was about to mount Tam seized Bara in his arms and kissed her fiercely.

'I don't care if you like it or not,' he whispered as he let her go.

Then Christo kissed her on the cheek, and Fred pecked gingerly at her forehead.

'I wish you'd let someone come with you,' said Christo.

'We'll be fine,' said Bara. Her spirits soared. She felt the energy of joy in every muscle. She smiled and laughed and waved, her long gold hair swinging to the rhythm of Dark's swaying walk. When they turned the corner onto the downward hill that would lead them north and west, she did not bother to look back.

All day the pale sun shone. Dark paced or trotted through the derelict suburbs and the abandoned factory land of north London. They moved in and out of the wintery gloom of trees which had grown up to meet across the broken roads. For miles about them stretched the empty desolation of an urban, industrial world. Broken factory chimneys pointed jaggedly to the sky, fallen girders rusted in heaps on broken concrete floors and roads, complexes of mutilated railway-tracks crossed and re-crossed the blighted land. Many sections of rail had been lifted to do duty as beams or anvils or fences, and very few wooden sleepers remained anywhere, for their uses were manifold. There were few people about, except in the villages which had congregated in the ruins near water. Most of the people who saw Bara simply stared, but a few waved, and some look covetously at Dark. Bara unpacked their rough bread and hard-boiled eggs somewhere on the road to Beaconsfield. Con was so excited that she had to let him exhaust himself running six times round a group of elms. Then they laughed for sheer joy, and hugged each other, and mounted again.

After the afternoon's ride they slept rolled in their blankets in straw in a barn, and for the next two days rode in the sun, through Beaconsfield and the deserted factoryland of High Wycombe, towards the beech woods on the crest of the Chilterns. When they finally emerged from the woods, in the sparkling light of noon, Bara drew her breath sharply. The chalk scarp fell steeply away below them, to where the plain of Oxford spread in tans and browns to the far horizon.

'Look, Con,' said Bara, filled with delight at a sense of height and distance she had never known before.

'What?' said Con, peering round her shoulder. 'I don't see anything.'

The novelty of the ride was already wearing off for Con. He had very soon begun to complain of an aching bottom, and even now when Bara put him on the ground his trembling knees would hardly support him. He sat down abruptly on the chalky bank by the road and began to cry.

'Oh come on, Con,' said Bara. 'It's not as bad as that.'

'It is,' he said, tears rolling down his cheeks. 'My legs don't work.'

'They're only stiff. They'll get used to it. All the greatest riders are stiff when they begin.'

'Will I be a great rider?' he asked, snuffling and rubbing his eyes.

'Oh yes, you'll be a mighty rider. The best of all.'

They ate a hunk of cold meat and a little bread, then Con fell almost instantly asleep and Bara lay back on the bank, gazing over the plain.

She raised herself lazily and found an apple in her pannier for Dark. A silver winter silence lay on the beech woods and Bara sank down on the grass again, unwilling to move on.

Suddenly there was a rustle in the bushes above her. She jumped up, turning as she leaped, and there, parting the undergrowth with his hands, stood a bearded man. He wore a wide-brimmed hat and a long grey cloak. For an instant they stared at each other, then Bara turned and ran for the weapons in her pannier. She remembered in panic that she should never have dismounted without them. She pulled out the club and looked up the bank at the rough-looking stranger. He was staring at Con, but as Bara advanced, trying tremulously to remember what Tam had taught her, the man vanished into the scrub. The sun still shone, Con still slept, but the hour of peace had become an hour of menace. She bundled the half-sleeping boy into the saddle and mounted Dark. The horse was unwilling to move but she kicked him into a steady pace, and they descended the winding track down the scarp. She wanted to move faster and whenever the road flattened a little she urged Dark into a lumbering trot. But he was heavily loaded and they could never hope to escape any serious pursuit. For the first time Bara felt a sense of foreboding. Perhaps they had been right all along, Fred and Tam and the rest of them, perhaps she was an utter fool. Or perhaps she was mad.

When they were nearly at the bottom of the hill she kicked Dark into an unwilling canter. Con whimpered as he was flung about on the saddle. Dark could not possibly keep up a canter for long, but it was worth tiring him in order to get as far as possible from the man who had stared at them. The road on the plain became very broken, and Bara had to slow Dark into a trot and then a walk. As soon as he began walking she heard a faint sound far behind. She drew up and listened. Without any doubt it was the clopping of hooves. Then it became a drumming. Whoever it was was coming fast. She urged Dark into a trot again, then turned him sharply to the right along a rutted path leading to a copse. She drove him into a canter again, regardless of the danger to his legs, for at any cost they must reach the shelter of the trees. Con began to scream. The drumming of Dark's hooves drowned any noise from the road, and Bara dared not stop to listen. The riders behind might be perfectly innocent – simply people in a hurry – but again they might not. Dark was in a lather when they reached the copse and Con was howling with fright and pain.

'Shh, Con,' said Bara, twisting round and holding a hand over his mouth. 'Hush. We'll stop here.' She could hear them now, thudding on the road, riders trotting fast and cantering where they could. Con caught her fear and they both sat silent and still. When she judged the riders must have passed the turning, Bara sighed with relief and lifted Con down.

Although it was still afternoon she bedded him down in his blanket, and for once he was happy to lie quietly. Then she gave Dark some oats from the pannier, wiped him down and threw a blanket over his back. He snorted and stamped and allowed her to nuzzle his head. Then she took out her weapons, wrapped herself up in her blanket, and fell into an uneasy sleep.

She woke suddenly. The night was now pitch dark, although she supposed it must be only early evening, and through the bare branches shone a sharp sliver of moon. She looked round, wondering what had woken her. Twigs crackled on the far side of Dark, then a lantern shone out. Bara lay rigid with fear.

'What the devil—' said a puzzled voice. A man emerged from behind Dark and cast the light of his lantern over Bara and Con. Shadows from the candle flickered on his face, making him old and devilish. Bara gripped her knife and pointed it towards him as she tried to scramble out of her blanket.

'Don't shoot,' he said, suddenly exploding into a toothless cackle. Con woke and Bara put her free arm over him.

'I won't hurt you,' said the man, hunched like a gnome over his lantern. 'But what the bloody hell are you doing here? Where's your man?'

'We're travelling. We haven't a man,' said Bara, scrambling to her feet and still pointing her knife.

'Ah,' said the little man. 'Travelling. Are you a travelling circus?' And he cackled again.

'We're on our way to Oxford.'

'And sleeping rough? I know who you are.'

'You what?' Bara was bewildered.

'Some gentleman was asking for you.'

Bara felt her stomach contract.

'Some gentleman – ?'

'Aye. Couple of hours ago. Man with a beard and his mate. Long grey cloaks and big horses. Outlanders, they call themselves.'

'How do you know they wanted me?'

'Not you exactly. It's the boy they wanted.'

'Con? They wanted Con?'

'I don't know his name, do I? Small boy with white hair they wanted. And a young woman on a horse. It's you lot all right.'

'Christ.' Bara felt the breath knocked out of her. She had thought they might want Dark, or her provisions, or even herself, but Con –.

'It's the boy they want, they said.'

'Did you tell them anything?'

'Hadn't seen you then, had I? So that's what I told them. They gave me money though.'

'What for?' But she felt she knew.

'To look out for you, of course.' He grinned again, his face thrown into fiendish shadows by the lantern. Bara stared at him, her eyes wide.

'Will you tell—?' she faltered.

'Naw. Why should I? I got the money, haven't I?'

'You might get more for telling. If I thought you'd tell I'd kill you.' And Bara moved forwards, holding her knife as Tam had shown her. For Con she knew she would torture or mutilate or murder. There was nothing she would not do to protect him. She was a vixen now, a tigress, and fear could sap her strength no longer.

'Put that bloody thing down,' said the man, twisting his face angrily. 'I told you I wouldn't talk. I leave people alone, see? As long as they don't do me any harm. You'd best get safe to Oxford in the dark.'

'Thanks,' said Bara, lowering her knife and feeling foolish. 'We'll try. Will we be safe there?'

'Oh, Oxford's a queer place these days, it's a very queer place. There's lots of people, very queer people. But they don't do much harm, so let 'em be I say. You'll get easy lost among that lot.'

Bara began to pack up quickly by the light of the lantern. Con was wide awake and no longer frightened.

'I like that,' he said shyly, pointing to the lantern.

'Aye, it's a good lantern. Want to hold it?'

'Oh yes.' The old man grinned his toothless grin and showed Con the shutter.

'Have you any children?' said Bara, smiling at him.

'Lost count,' he said, cackling again. 'Fifteen or twenty I reckon. I'll come part of the way with you,' he said. 'God's Christ,' he exploded angrily, 'that bloody sheep. Where's she bloody gone?' He peered into the darkness as if expecting his sheep to loom up before him. 'I was looking for her when I found you lot. Left her in that thing,' he continued, waving his arm towards a kind of shack constructed of battered cars.

'Been stolen, perhaps,' said Bara, strapping Con into his harness and mounting herself.

'Like as not. Bastard sheep-stealers.' He spat.

'Perhaps the Outlanders had her for supper,' said Bara, surprised at her sudden cheerfulness. He grunted, unamused, and set off in front of them, holding his lantern high. His legs were bandy but he walked fast, and he never hesitated among the criss-cross of paths. Whenever he thought he heard bleating he would stop, standing in his yellow pool of light with his head on one side. As the moon rose higher it shed a brighter glimmer on the rough grass and the small squares of ploughed land. Then in a gap between some trees Bara suddenly saw a red glow in the sky far ahead. The man stopped and pointed to it.

'That's Oxford,' he said. 'Reckon they've got a big fire this evening.'

'You mean the town's on fire?'

'No, just bonfires. They often have them. You'll see.'

'Are you going back now?'

'Aye. Bastard sheep's lost all right. Silly cow.'

'Thanks,' said Bara. 'Thanks for showing us the way, and for not telling, and everything.' She pulled a silver coin from the purse in her pannier.

'Here,' she said. He came over and held up his wrinkled palm. Then he spat on the coin and rubbed it.

'But it's silver,' he said.

'I know. Take it.'

'I bloody will,' he said, clutching his fingers over it. 'I may have lost a bastard sheep but I've done all right today.'

He smiled his toothless smile at her and as Dark moved off she saw him bend his wizened face over the coin again.

Dark picked his way carefully along the rutted tracks and round the potholes, so that Bara had only to guide him in the direction of the glow. Con soon fell asleep again, his arms around Bara's waist, but she herself kept alert, straining her ears for the sound of horses. Once she heard them drumming far away on the road and she pulled Dark into a wood. But the sound passed away, and they moved on hour after hour towards Oxford.

In the cold misty dawn they stopped on a high hill beside the most massive mountain of abandoned cars that Bara had ever seen. The summit of it was lost far above her head somewhere in the early mist. She turned to look down on Oxford. Two huge fires still raged, illuminating the tumbled buildings around them, but the rest of the town was ghostly grey in the early light. There seemed to be towers and spires, perhaps half a dozen, such as Bara had seen only in old pictures, for there had been no towers or spires left standing in London for many years. It was not easy to find a way down into the town without using the road. Bara blew on her frozen hands, allowing Dark to pick his own way down a steep track through a wood. Near the bottom she saw a river ahead. They rode towards it, down the long sloping fields, as the light turned slowly from grey to white. A girl came trudging along the river bank, slopping milk from buckets on her yoke.

'Morning,' said Bara. The girl stopped and looked at them in astonishment. Her cheeks were fat and pink.

'Who are you?' she said.

'Strangers. We're travelling. Where are we?'

'Marston this is. Where you going?'

'We want to get into Oxford.'

'Ferry's just down there. My dad'll take you over.'

'Thanks. Could I buy some of that milk?'

'Aye. How much?'

'This bottle full.' Bara pulled a large empty bottle from her pannier.

'Bottle? You got a bottle? Haven't seen a bottle in years.'

'They're very rare.'

'Here.' The girl dunked the bottle in the milk and drew it up full. Bara wondered what she should offer for it.

'That'll be a few coppers. Four maybe. Or what else have you?'

'Apples?'

'Oh aye, apples. Four apples.'

'Two. They're big ones.'

'Let's see them. All right, three. The ferry's down there.'

The wide flat-bottomed ferry carried them easily across to the other bank.

'What's the river?' Bara asked.

'Cherell.' The boatman was so sleepy and morose she asked him no more.

Almost at once they were in the town, or the ruins of the town. As the cold light increased they rode slowly through the empty suburbs. The rutted roads crossed each other frequently, intersecting the acres of fallen red brick and rampant bramble. Obviously this had once been a populous and a prosperous place, but now there were only a few people living in scattered groups. As Bara turned into the old Woodstock road she saw once again the light of the fire in the distance. She was riding down a wide street, lined with grey stone buildings, then suddenly through a small wooden gate in a long stone wall she saw flames. A fire would be a comfort. She squeezed Dark through the gateway and rode across a cobbled courtyard, under an arch, and out into a huge walled field. There in the middle was the end of the bonfire, still flickering with low flames and glowing a furious red. Surrounding it, and spread across the acre of field away to the distant walls there were people asleep. Bara had never seen such a concourse of sleeping people. They lay singly, they lay in pairs, they lay in groups, covered with bright blankets or carpets or sacking or clothes. They were a wild looking lot, Bara thought, the men with tangled hair and uncut beards, the women with their hair wrapped round their necks for warmth and rough scarves tied over their foreheads. A small urchin suddenly scrambled out of a sack at Dark's feet and piddled against a bush. He was dressed in a rough leather jerkin and breeches and his hair fell over his eyes.

'Hullo,' said Bara. He turned his head and stared at her.

'Hullo,' he replied, making for his sack.

'Where's this?' said Bara.

'What yer mean?'

'Well, what's its name? This field, and this building?'

'Oh. Sinjons. We had a party. I wanna go to sleep.'

Bara noticed that many of the people she had thought asleep were lying with their eyes open, and many others were twitching and muttering and sometimes crying out. She became uneasy, then frightened. Perhaps they were all mad and it was a madhouse she had come into. She turned Dark to go, but the archway was blocked by a woman who was just coming through. She was much like the others, dressed in long skirt and tunic, with wild hair and a red scarf round her forehead. She stood with her hands on her hips surveying the scene. She was very brown and probably not much over twenty-five.

'They had a right do,' she said, looking up at Bara. 'you join in?'

'No, I'm a stranger.'

'Ah.' The woman turned her head away, uninterested. 'There'll be no work done today, I can see that,' she said.

'Was it a party?'

'Sort of. A celebration.'

'Are they drunk?' asked Bara.

'Drunk?' The woman looked up at her in astonishment. 'Where do you come from? You never heard of the Oxford Rout?'

'No.'

'God's sakes. I thought everyone had heard of us. We live on drugs.'

Tara was bewildered. 'On drugs?' she said.

'Well, we eat a bit too sometimes. But they take your appetite away.'

'But if you don't eat you die.'

'Oh a lot of us die,' she said casually, wrapping her shawl around her and leaning her head against the wall. 'Overdoses, starvation, accidents. All the usual things too – dysentery and that.'

'I didn't know there were any drugs nowadays.'

'Where the hell do you come from? We grow our own stuff here, we don't have any shortage. Opium poppies, mushrooms, hemp, pomea – lots of stuff.'

'But do they all grow in this climate?'

'Some do, some don't. Haven't you seen the glass-houses Hinksey way?'

'Glass-houses? Whole glass-houses?'

'Glass, perspex, plastic – we collect all of it round these parts. Travel miles for it. Have to steal it sometimes. Got to. Couldn't grow our stuff without it.'

'Can I see them? The glass-houses?'

'No-one's allowed up there, 'cept the Doctors.'

'The Doctors?'

'Aye. The Doctors. The bosses. They do the sacrifices and that.' Bara stared, absolutely bewildered. The woman was gazing idly across the field of bodies.

'Sacrifices?' said Bara at last.

'What? Aye, the goats. The sacrifices.' The woman looked up sharply, her eyes very black. 'You're nosey, aren't you?' she said. 'Too many questions. I'd be off if I was you.'

Bara continued to stare blankly at her, then she looked out again over the field. It was now full light of a cold morning and bodies were beginning to move out of their coloured coverings. There was a muttering and groaning, and one or two huddled shapes shuffled over to warm their hands at the dying fire. A man in a long rusty coat relieved himself against a tree and cackled as he made patterns with his water on the trunk. The woman had not taken her eyes off Bara's face and Bara could feel her antagonism rising.

'Go away,' said the woman suddenly, spitting out the words.

'All right.' Bara urged Dark through the arch and Con woke with a jerk.

'I'm cold,' he said, beginning to whimper. 'And I'm hungry.'

'Watch out,' the woman called over her shoulder. 'Funny things happen to strangers sometimes.'

Bara was too concerned with Con to take much notice. They picked their way back across the courtyard, avoiding the loosest cobbles and the worst of the tipped flagstones, and through the wooden gate into the street. There were more people about now, as ragged and colourful as those in the field, but they all seemed to be moving aimlessly, taking no interest in Bara or the huge horse.

She turned left into the grey street, looking for somewhere to dismount and give Con some breakfast. There was a broken carved column ahead, like an old market cross or a memorial, with steps around the base, and she turned Dark towards it. When they were within a few yards she dismounted and tied the horse to some railings.

Con's legs were so stiff and cold that when Bara lifted him down once again they would not bear him. He sat down hard on the ground and began to cry. He looked so absurd with his plump legs stuck out straight in front of him and his face so pathetically crumpled that Bara laughed. She knelt beside him and hugged him. Then, in an instant, without any warning, she found she was crying. She stood up quickly, realizing she was dog-tired and hungry. She picked Con up and sat him down on the convenient step of the memorial. The stone seemed damp but she did not feel like bothering about that. Turning a few steps back to Dark, she pulled down the pannier and found some bread and milk and hunks of cold meat. Suddenly Con cried out, and she heard an edge of terror to his voice.

'Mam!' he shouted again.

He was shrinking back, gripping the edge of the step and pressing his head hard against the stone column behind him. He faced a circle of people, rapidly increasing in number, all of them staring at him and muttering angrily. Bara pushed through the gathering crowd and picked him up. His hands and the back of his clothes were covered in blood.

'Who's hurt you?' she said, bewildered.

'No-one,' he said, 'it's on that.' And he pointed to the steps of the memorial.

'Christ,' she murmured, hustling him back to Dark and not daring to look into the faces of the angry crowd. They were shouting at her now, pointing at the memorial and up the street. They were all dressed in the same kind of tattered gaudy clothes as the sleepers in the field, no-one's hair was cut and the men were wildly bearded. Bara flung Con onto Dark's back, untied the reins and clambered up. The crowd was still muttering and gesticulating, but no-one seemed to be moving into an attack. Bara noticed exactly where the handles of her club and her knife emerged from her panniers, but as there was still no threatening advance from anyone she moved Dark on towards the road ahead. As she left the murmurings grew louder and she heard the words 'desecration' and 'sacrifice' and 'death'. She knew now what last night's orgy had been celebrating. The Doctors had been officiating at the sacrificial stone.

They rode aimlessly for an hour or so around the grey decaying town, meeting everywhere groups of the abstracted, gaudy inhabitants. Turning up a narrow street, they came upon a vast pile of stone rubble, long since blackened and scorched by fire. An old townsman, creeping past on a stick, told them it had once been a great library, with a dome up in the sky, but the Children of Eden had burned it nearly half a century ago.

'I heard from my Grans how they got the British Museum library too,' said Bara. But the old man stared at her blankly and hobbled on.

They turned back into the main street, then they moved on down a hill where a cracked bell was tolling in a tower, and there below them was a river again. Now that they were away from the memorial no-one took any notice of them and they rode unmolested into a great water meadow. Pale sunlight was beginning to filter through the mist. Bara laid out their precious piece of sheeting and Con galloped down to the river to wash the blood off his hands. She heard him shouting and throwing stones at some ducks, then he came stumbling back over the tufted grass, loudly demanding his breakfast. His white hair shone, flopping up and down as he jumped. Bara turned Dark loose to graze on the poor winter grass, then she and Con sat down and ate. When she was finished Bara lay back against a hummock of grass and gazed up into the cold blue of the sky.

Suddenly a shadow fell across her face. A very tall man was standing looking down at her. Her breath caught in fear, as she realized that once again she had no weapon, and Con was gone. She kicked fiercely up at the man's groin.

'Hey!' he shouted, leaping back, 'What the hell's wrong with you?'

He stood eyeing her, a lanky blue-eyed man with cropped hair and no beard. Bara heard Con tormenting the ducks by the river, and her fear faded.

'Sorry,' she said, scrambling up and feeling abashed. It seemed that already the most ordinary incident was fraught with terror, and they were only at Oxford. She smiled and apologized again.

'I didn't quite know what was happening.'

'You're not from here,' he said, looking her over.

'Nor are you,' she answered. His clothes were sombre and neatly patched.

'What are you doing then?' he asked.

'Oh, just travelling. What about you?'

'Corn chandler. Thought you might like something for the horse. That's why I came along.'

'Thanks, I would.' He walked off to his cart on the road and Bara fumbed through her pannier for some money. She smiled with pleasure at meeting an ordinary human being in this place. He came back with a sack of bran and she handed out some of the old decimal coinage.

'Nice,' he said, turning it over appreciatively. Bara scooped out some bran for Dark and dropped it into his nose bag, then turning up the meadow she called his name. Slowly, with his head bent, he came plodding towards her.

'You two know each other,' said the man, running his eyes admiringly over Dark.

'For ages. Since I was a little girl.'

'You're not so old now. Have some cider.' He sat himself down on the sheeting and Bara sat beside him. He had a stone bottle in his pocket and he offered her a swig.

'Thanks,' she said. 'It's good.'

'What do you think of the Oxford Rout?' he asked between gulps. She wished he would stop staring at her hair.

'Well,' she said cautiously, 'they're very strange.'

'Strange? They're bloody crazy. They had a party last night. Know what that means?'

'Yes, I think I do.'

'Nasty business. The kids smear themselves with the goat's blood.'

'Ugh. Why do they do it?'

'Oh, make the drugs grow or something. Ignorant savages.'

'Who are the Doctors?'

'They're the bosses. There's half-a-dozen of them I think. They've scarves round their heads and long knives in their belts. They're not bad at doctoring either, when they're not too high. They've got the herbal stuff worked out.' He turned and looked at her straight, wriggling nearer.

'Let's talk about you and me shall we? I'm Wat. Who're you?'

'Bara. Tell me more about the doctors.' She pretended to do up her shoe and edged away from him.

'That's all I know.' He put out his arm and stroked her hair. 'Lovely stuff,' he said, shifting nearer again. 'Red and gold in one.'

Bara shook her head impatiently and tried to get up, but he put his hand on her shoulder and pressed her down.

'Lie down,' he said gruffly, rolling over her. Bara let fly with both hands and beat him round the head. At the same time she raised her knee sharply into his groin. He shouted in pain and slapped the side of her head hard. Suddenly Con was there, screaming with rage and terror, throwing stones from less than a yard away.

'Get away! Go away! Stop it! Get off!' he yelled.

Wat leaped up, blood streaming from his face where a stone had caught him, and he dived for Con. Bara thrust out her leg, tripping him heavily. She rushed for her club, pushing Con behind Dark's legs, then she stood by the horse, holding the weapon ready. But instead of attacking Wat arose slowly and stood looking at her. He held a rag to his bleeding cheek. Suddenly he smiled, a wide smile of pure amusement.

'Well, well,' he said. 'A little red vixen and her cub. You're too much for me, mates. I only hunt when I've got weapons.'

He waved with his free hand and strode off towards his cart on the road. Immediately Bara liked him and wished he would not go. But Con was pale and trembling, frowning angrily at Wat's retreating back.

'I hate him,' he shouted. 'I hate him, I hate him.' Bara knelt, putting her arms round him, and pressed his head into her shoulder. She must decide what to do next. No doubt the Outlanders were still looking for them and the crowd in Oxford might be a good place to be lost for a day or two. She looked down at Con's shining flaxen head and decided it must be covered. What with his hair, and her own hair, and the gigantic size of Dark, they made too easy a target for their enemies.

There was a long red brick building behind them, more than half ruined but probably habitable in some corner. The winter sun threw faint shadows along its jagged pinnacles and gables and bow-windows. After she had packed up and lifted Con onto Dark, they moved slowly up the meadow making for a fallen arch where the building divided. They picked their way through the rubble and found themselves again in a large court, like the one at Sinjons. A few gaudy people wandered about on the grass, apparently doing nothing. A young man was walking towards them, his dark hair curling on his shoulders, his beard black against a tattered red tunic.

'Hullo,' said Bara, hoping to ask him where they could stay. But he walked on, gazing straight in front of him. She would have to find someone less transported. She tied Dark's reins to a lump of masonry, but no sooner had she started her knot than Con began to whimper.

'No,' he said, 'my way.' He was in a frenzy of irritation. 'Let me down.'

Sighing heavily Bara lifted him down and he retied the reins in a knot unknown to Bara. She set off across the court towards a tall man with a yellow scarf knotted round his head. He turned as she approached and she saw a long knife in his belt. He must be a Doctor. She stopped and began to back away. Again she had come away from Dark without her club.

'Hi!' called the man, stroking his beard. 'What's wrong? Who are you?'

'A traveller. I'm just going.' She turned to flee.

'Don't run away,' he called. He sounded friendly and she looked back at him. 'I won't hurt you. This thing's just for show you know.' He touched his knife. 'Mostly, that is,' he added. 'What do you want?'

'I'm looking for somewhere for us to stay tonight.'

'Well, this is as good a place as any. Some of it's quite weatherproof.'

'Can we just go anywhere?'

'Why not? Look, try over there.' Bara called to Con and he came trotting over, leading Dark. The man started when he saw Con.

'That your boy?'

'Yes, he's mine.'

'You're lucky you've still got him. I heard what you did.'

'I'm sorry. I didn't know. I didn't know it was a special sort of – of – memorial.'

'Well, it is, and you'd better remember. And it's not a memorial, it's the Holy Stone. Keep away from it.' Then his voice changed again to its former friendliness.

'This is a good part,' he said, stopping by an archway.

Bara could just make out a few letters carved on the stone lintel. *Me--ow -uild--gs.*

'Help yourself to a room,' the Doctor said, 'And get the horse in if you can. Someone might take a fancy to him.'

'Thank you,' said Bara, 'it's very nice of you.'

But the Doctor had turned away and wandered off, his mind already on some other matter. The rooms were small and bitingly cold, but they seemed dry and some even had old pieces of carpet and sticks of furniture scattered round. One room contained a rusty iron bedstead and at the sight of it Bara felt limp with weariness. It was only four days since they had left home, yet already it seemed a month, and she was tired to the bone. Images of Ireland shimmered in her mind, a thousand miles in distance and a century in time. All that would have to wait.

She awoke sometime in the early night. She found that Dark had both wetted and messed on the floor in the passage, but in this weird place she felt sure no-one would mind. Con was still asleep, rolled in his blankets at the foot of the bed. Bara looked out of the empty window-frame. The stars pricked out sharply from the blackness of the sky, but there was no moon and the meadow was visible only as a denser darkness. The night was bitterly cold. The window on the other side of the room looked over the great court and somewhere over to the left was a glow of firelight and a subdued murmur of many people. Suddenly Bara smelled cooking, and she realized they had had no hot food since they left home. She picked up the protesting Con and slinging him into the shawl on her back she stepped carefully over the cobbled court in the direction of the glow.

She climbed some stone stairs and found herself in a huge hall, whose raftered roof was lost in shadows. All down one side were crude stoves and ovens, flickering red, but the main light was from torches thrust in sconces on the wall. Down the centre of the hall were long narrow tables, at which a few groups of people were eating and drinking. Everyone was long-haired and brightly dressed – the familiar people of the town – and the cooks who moved around the stoves looked no different. A fair young woman passed by, trying to stuff long wisps of hair behind her ears. Then she stopped and turned.

'Who're you?' she said.

'Bara. Just travelling. Where am I?'

'Com'n'l kitchen. Want some food?'

'Yes we do. I can pay.'

'Pay?' said the girl scornfully. 'You don't have to pay. Can you cook?'

'Yes, a bit.'

'Good, I want to go. Take my place.' She pushed a long wooden ladle into Bara's hand and was gone. For three hours Bara ladled soup and stoked fires and cut up vegetables. The heat was intense and sweat poured from the brows of all the cooks, none of whom showed any surprise at Bara's presence. From time to time she drank some thick soup and ate hunks of the bread which lay about on the tables. Now and then she fed Con, but after every mouthful he fell asleep again, slumped along a bench. Eventually one of the cooks came and stood by her as she stirred a pot of stew. He had long fair hair which fell into his beard, and his chest was bare.

'You can go,' he said. 'Take what you want with you.'

'Thanks,' said Bara. None of these people seemed very conversational, so she said no more.

'And listen.' He spoke quietly without looking at her. 'Cover that boy's head.' He pulled a red woollen cap out of his belt and thrust it at her. 'They're after him you know.' .

Bara dropped her ladle which splashed into the stew.

'The men in grey cloaks?' she whispered.

'Aye, the Outlanders. They were here earlier. White Michael's men.'

'White Michael?' Bara was bewildered.

'He's the boy's father isn't he? No-one else has hair like that.' Bara stared at him, her throat so tight she could not speak.

'Christ,' she breathed at last. 'So that's who he was.'

'They know you're here somewhere. I should go fast, while it's still dark. Get on the Burford road, west.'

'I will. Thanks. Did the Doctor tell them?' she asked over her shoulder as she roused Con.

'No, he wouldn't do that. We don't like those bastards. We live and let live here.'

Bara took as much as she could carry of chicken and bread and carrots and in an hour they were on the road west. There was a gleam of moonlight now, just sufficient to pick out the line of the huge, cracked motorway. Con sat in front of Bara, wide awake, and still glowing from the heat of the hall. He kept up a cheerful barrage of comment and question, but Bara's attention was not on him. She was straining to hear the clop of hooves on the road, and every few moments her eyes would stray to the handles of her weapons, just discernible in the faint light. Her cheeks tingled in the icy cold, her toes and fingers were almost numb. For three hours they travelled along the wide valley of the Windrush, making for Burford and hoping to leave the Outlanders behind in Oxford. Bara urged Dark into a cumbersome trot, but he would go no faster than his own chosen pace among the uneven blocks of the road. When she slapped his flank or kicked with her heels he twitched his skin but made no change in this rhythm. Con had begun to sing, working his way through the repertoire of nursery rhymes that Kate had taught to Bara, and she to him. He waved his arms, swaying dangerously as he sang, trying to provoke Bara into taking more notice of him. He was pleased with his red woollen cap and took it off several times to admire it, complaining that he could not see its lovely colour in the dark. She pulled tight on the reins.

'Shhh,' she said. 'Listen.'

'Horses,' said Con, cocking his head.

Faint and elusive, somewhere in the distance, horses were moving rapidly. Suddenly Bara found herself obstructed by the vast steel network of a pylon which had fallen across the road. Solid walls of stone prevented her turning right or left into the fields. Urgently she pressed the reluctant Dark straight through the pylon, over and under, this way and that, until at last they emerged onto the clear road again. They had lost valuable time, but at least the stone wall on the right had now given way to a hedge of thorn. Somewhere they must find a way through the thorns and into the fields. She forced Dark over a pile of rubble that had once been a wall, but he would not move fast where he could not see, and meanwhile the hooves were thudding near. She reined in behind a clump of bushes in the field, praying Dark would not whinny or snort, then she bent over Con and whispered that there were kidnappers coming and he must be very quiet. His eyes grew round with fear and he shrank back against Bara's body. The hooves slowed down. Bara laid her hand on her club and her breath came in spasms. There was cold sweat in her palm. The horses had slowed to walking pace, and a dark shadow paused at the gap in the wall. Bara felt a warm liquid in her mouth and realized she had bitten into her lower lip. Fiercely she gripped the handles of the knife and the club. Then suddenly the shadow passed, the horses were trotting, and the clopping of their hooves receded into the distance. Bara's body sagged in relief as she put both her arms round Con.

'Have they gone?' asked the boy.

'Yes, but be quiet.' Perhaps they had only been farmers, or some of the Oxford Rout. But she did not feel very convinced.

She knew from the lines of abandoned cars which heralded the outskirts of every town, that they were almost at the junction with the Burford road, so the riders must have continued due west. Bara turned north, off the huge carriageway, through the village and over the black waters of the Windrush. The Cotswolds lay before them, cold and lonely in the night.

For two weeks of sun and wind they hid in a remote farm above Bourton, overlooking in all directions the bare, brown uplands. When Bara had knocked and asked if they might bed down in the barn the farmer and his wife had been astounded and delighted to seem them.

They gave Bara and Con real beds in a dry room, and a pile of warm blankets to wrap up in. But the smell of the blankets was so pungent Bara supposed they must have been used to wrap up lambs and ailing sheep. The stench was altogether too much for Con, so surreptitiously she fetched their own blankets from the pannier. Dark had a watertight stable, and the company of his own kind, for the farmer had two stringy ponies whose duty was to pull the cart to Moreton market once a month. The panniers were already rubbing sore patches on Dark's shoulders and Bara was glad to be able to give him a few days' rest from them. On the first evening when she had combed him down and given him his nose-bag he had bent his great head down, nuzzling her shoulder, and she knew that the affection which had bound them for so long had been deepened further by their companionship of the road.

The farmer told Bara to call him Trigg and to call his wife the Missus. Bara barely understood their thick rural accents, but she realized she was welcome and she responded as sensibly as she could to their torrent of friendly words. The farmer was fifty or so, she guessed, with short grizzled hair and beard, both chopped roughly with a knife. Huge eyebrows bristled above small, dark eyes and his face was deeply rutted. His wife was angular and grey, but she had a wide smile that suddenly revealed the sweetness of her youth. They were both openly delighted to see anyone friendly, for their lives were as isolated as if they lived on an island. And indeed they did live on a kind of island, Bara thought, as she looked out over the brown valleys spread below her. What pleased her hosts most of all, she found, was having someone to talk to. She need make no effort to respond, she was required simply to listen. She would sit out with them in the cold sun in the farmyard, drinking her warm goat's milk, and letting the soft tide of their voices lap over her hour after hour. Occasionally she woke up to what was being said, and bent her mind to interpreting the words. The farm was built on an old Roman road, the farmer told her, old even beyond the Old Times. His grandfather had been to school and knew about the Romans. He pointed to the distant shoulder of a hill and said it was Edbury Camp, where the Romans had had their castle. His wife was a sadder person than he, for she had never recovered from the departure of their three sons, who had left the farm to look for something better and had never come back. It was a hard, lonely life, she said, and the flock grew smaller every year.

Con would rush about the fields, chasing Jem the sheepdog, tormenting the goats, terrifying the hens, and attempting to stroke the few spindly sheep that wandered in from the fields. He spent many happy hours climbing in and out of a rusty, half-dismembered combine-harvester which Trigg had hired over twenty years ago in the glorious summer of 2022 to help him with a record crop of barley. But the owner of the machine had gone bankrupt and cut his throat, and the harvester had never been collected. Trigg had ceased to try to grow barley on his windy fields, so the great machine, lined up alongside the useless tractor, had quietly died in an open shed.

Bara worked most of the day round the house and farm. She was amused to find that the Missus, like Kate, made use of hub-caps for frying and eating. The Missus described in close and tedious detail the uses she had found for other pieces of debris, and Bara was happy to let the soft burr hum round her. Neither of her hosts showed any curiosity at all, and they never asked why she should be travelling alone with Con. One mild morning, two weeks after their arrival, Bara sat out on the drystone wall and gazed contentedly over the wide hills and skies. This felt like some kind of a home. They would stay a little longer, she thought, as the Triggs urged, safe from the Outlanders and all the dangers of the road. She could earn her keep here, and Ireland could wait. For the first time she wondered why they were going there at all.

On the first night of March the wind dropped and the temperature rose. The air was warm and muggy, and at midnight the rain came. Bara scarcely slept, for the hours of darkness were coloured by fantastic dreams which would not disperse when she awoke. She dreamed of a fabulous country, painted in green and gold, and she knew it was Ireland. All night she was haunted by a stream of images; fields of emerald enamelled with flowers, grey towers against an azure sky, a tall white ship shimmering in silver and blue. The visions tugged remorselessly, their brilliance hurt her eyes. As she tossed and raged in her efforts to get some sleep, the name of Ireland tolled like a bell in her head. The wet dawn came as a relief. She arose, stiff and tired, and woke Con. He sat up and rubbed his eyes.

'We must go to Ireland,' he said loudly. Bara looked at him in astonishment.

'Why do you think that?' she asked.

We just must, that's all.'

The Triggs thought Bara was mad. Indeed it was the first time, she supposed, that they had noticed her as a person at all, instead of just something receptive to talk to.

'You can't go in this,' said Trigg, staring at her and waving his arm at the pouring rain.

'We'll be all right,' said Bara, packing up.

'Stay wi' us,' said the Missus coaxingly. 'Leastways till the rain leaves off.'

'But we have to go to Ireland,' said Con, looking up at her with wide blue eyes.

'Oh, that little lad's hair,' she said, stroking it. 'Tis like a magic fleece.'

The Triggs were subdued as they said good-bye, and Bara knew their gaze was that of people who doubt another's sanity. She thanked them effusively for their kindness but they only nodded.

'Where be ye making for?' asked Trigg, never taking his eyes off her.

'West.'

'Make for Cheltham. There's good inns there.'

They waved sadly as Bara and Con rode out of the farmyard in the rain. As she turned the corner of the barn Bara heard the Missus speak to her husband.

'Reckon he's a changeling, that lad,' she said.

They moved off slowly down the track, Dark's hooves squelching as he picked each in turn from the mud. Bara had wrapped the two precious pieces of sheeting round their shoulders but the soft rain was penetrating and in an hour their legs and arms were soaked.

Dark plodded steadily, his head down, as Bara guided him along tracks and over the slopes of the hills. There were trees in the valleys, where they took shelter when the rain was heaviest, but most of the time they pressed doggedly on through the mist and drizzle. In the middle of the morning Bara gave Con an apple and asked him if he was all right.

'We must get to Ireland,' was all he would say.

In the village of Guiting Power they bought some warm milk and
ate some of the cooked chicken the Missus had given them. Dark was
bedraggled but undeterred as they made their slow way along the
western track. The mops of hair around each hoof dripped with
black mud. The path climbed and fell, over the crests and down into
the valleys with no regard for contour. Sometimes they crossed a
stretch of broken dual carriageway, occasionally they caught a
glimpse of a pylon or a water-tower. But to Bara these artefacts of a
once populous age only served, as ever, to intensify the loneliness of
the land. The rain continued into the afternoon, soft but steady, and
the wide landscape was shrouded in grey mist. It was a miserable
ride, eight hours in the saddle with nothing to do but endure. Bara
tried to sing songs with Con, but he would not join in. Darkness fell
early, intensifying the gloom of the day, and they began to look for
somewhere to stay the night. Cheltham should not be far away, but
Bara could see no sign of a town and there was no-one to ask. Then,
glancing left into a wood, she caught a glimpse of a large white
house. They turned up the overgrown track and stood looking
critically at the huge pile of ruined masonry.

'There may be somewhere dry inside,' said Bara without
conviction. 'But we must be careful it doesn't fall on top of us.'

Con tied Dark to a broken pillar in front of the main door, and
cautiously they crept in. The huge hall was dark and cold.

'I don't like it,' said Con, drawing back.

'Come on, it'll have to do.' Bara dragged him along, and after
some minutes' exploring she found a small, round room which
seemed watertight. There was even a fireplace, and a pair of
ripped-out car-seats shoved against the wall.

'Look,' she said, 'this is lovely.' Simulating a jollity she did not feel,
she said, 'We can have a fire and make toast and sing songs. It'll be
fun.'

Con continued to look frightened, but he helped fetch food and
bedding from the panniers while Bara found a room dry enough to
feed and stable Dark. As she told Con to look around for firewood she
felt a small spark of childish excitement began to glow. She
remembered the days at Kenwood, where she and her friends had
their headquarters as children, when they would tear down old
mantelshelves and bookcases to pile on the fire in the great library.
Disentangling it from the remains of the electrical wiring, Con
peeled some dry wallpaper off a wall and added it to a heap of
broken chairs he had found in the kitchens. His spirits rose with
Bara's, and as soon as they had the fire started they pulled off their

soaking clothes and draped them on the car-seats round the flames. The once polished floorboards were covered in a powdering of plaster and everything they put down became white. Con rolled himself over and over in the dusty powder, screeching with pleasure. 'Look, I'm a snowman!' he shouted, waving his arms. They piled more wood on the fire and watched the shadows of the flames flickering on the curved walls of the room. There were white painted panels with flecks of gold on the beadings. Bara propped herself against the wall and laid her head back. It was wonderful to be warm and dry. Then they made their toast, and baked potatoes in the glowing cinders, and scorched pieces of chicken in the flames. After an hour or two, gorged and happy, they bedded down on the floor.

Con woke first, to the distant clopping of hooves on the road. 'Mam!' he cried, shaking Bara. 'Wake up!'

The rain had stopped and in the soft darkness the sound was sharp.

'Quick,' she said, scrambling up.

Her teeth were chattering with cold or fear, she did not know which, and when she quickly hugged Con she felt his heart thudding. They bundled up their bedding in the light of the embers and stumbled down the corridor to Dark. Bara saddled him with fumbling fingers and shoved everything pell-mell into the panniers. The riders were still on the road, moving beside the long wall towards the entrance to the park. If they were the Outlanders they would see the fire. Bara manoeuvred Dark into the hall and tugged him unwillingly over the fallen columns towards a door at the back of the house. The night was dark, but down a long slope ahead of them they could see the dull glint of water. They mounted and set off silently over the grass.

Suddenly there was a shout from the house. 'There they are!' a voice yelled.

Bara realized they must be silhouetted against the paler light of the lake. She kicked and smacked at Dark, trying to urge him into a canter. Suddenly to her astonishment he flew forward, breaking into an earth-shaking gallop. She heard Con laughing behind her, then his hand was in front of her face, showing the sharp flint which he had dug into Dark's flank. The horse thundered over the turf, the night rushed by, Bara and Con clung for life itself to the saddle and each other. Suddenly they were over water, on a bridge across the lake. Dark never slackened his pace, though the panniers struck his shoulders and the wooden bridge was rutted beneath him. Then blackness yawned ahead, and the gleam of water stretched below.

The bridge was broken. Dark could not stop, for he was galloping like the horse of a hero, but for a moment his stride faltered, he gathered himself, and he leaped into the blackness. Con screamed, scrabbling at Bara's back. But the water did not rise to meet them. Dark thudded heavily onto wood and the remains of the bridge held. Behind them they heard shouting and skidding, as horses were savagely reined at the edge of the broken bridge. Dark crashed away into the trees and the shouting grew faint behind them. Bara squeezed Con's arms which were clasped round her waist. She was laughing, flooded with relief, so overwhelmed with gratitude to Dark that she could not speak.

They had a good start now. The pursuers had not dared to jump and now they would have to ride all round the great sheet of water. Bara slowed Dark down to a walk, for his flanks and shoulders were lathered with sweat. When they struck the road she turned him left down a mud track where his hooves would not be heard. It was still dark but a faint tinge of light was creeping up the sky. Slowly the grey paled to white, but they found they still could not see ahead, for they were enveloped in mist, so thick in places they could not make out the hedge by which they rode. Bara rummaged in the panniers, packed so hurriedly that nothing was in its place, and eventually found some bread and carrots and milk. They ate and drank in the saddle while Dark plodded on. There were no sounds of pursuit and they felt safe for the moment, wrapped in the fog.

All morning they moved on, over the shoulder of a high hill and down into the valley. Everywhere was mist and silence. They kept off the roads, making use of tracks when they could and otherwise riding over grass and scrub. They passed a ragged old man drawing water from a well and they turned due west up a steep hill, as he directed them. The path wound through a pine wood, utterly silent and stilll, where the only sound was the cracking of twigs beneath Dark's feet. They climbed steeply up, oppressed by the silence and the brooding air of the wood.

'I don't like it,' said Con, hugging Bara's waist. 'There are things here.'

'There's nothing here at all,' said Bara, trying to sound confident. 'That's why it's not nice. It's just empty.'

'No birds,' said Con.

'No birds, no rabbits, no foxes, no nothing,'

'Remember the fox holes?' said Con, brightening.

But Bara did not reply. She refused to think about the last occasion on which Con had been to the fox holes.

At last they emerged into the open, but the mist on the hillside was very thick and Bara was thankful for it. They must be high and exposed where they were, a target for any searchers, but no-one would see them today. There was a strange lump ahead of them, which turned out to be a long grassy mound, about ten feet high and forty feet long. One end was scooped out into a kind of bay and some huge stones had fallen across each other at the apex of the inward curve. It seemed a good place to rest. When they had stripped off Dark's harness and panniers, they gave him a nosebag and rubbed him down. Bara threw a blanket over him and stroked him long and fondly. With his long gallop and his mighty leap he had saved them from capture, and perhaps from death.

'You're my hero,' she said to him as she stroked his ear.

'He doesn't know he is,' said Con.

They spread their sheeting within the arms of the bay, and Bara decided it would be safe in this mist to light a fire. Although the day was not too cold the air was clammy, and everything they touched felt damp. So it was pleasant to sit hidden in the fog, beside a small crackling fire, with the encircling arms of the mound to give privacy and a frontier. They decided they would stay there for the night.

When dusk approached they tied Dark to one of the great stones and bedded themselves down close to the bank. Bara stoked up the fire to a full blaze, and they left a pile of dry wood from the pine forest to feed the flames in the night.

Bara woke to hear Dark stamping restlessly. Then she heard voices. She scrambled up, seizing her club and her knife, and stood trembling in front of the sleeping body of Con. Almost at once a man and a horse loomed out of the darkness. The man stopped, just visible in the firelight, his grey cloak about his shoulders and his wide grey hat low over his eyes.

'Well,' he said. 'So there you are then. A bloody pretty dance you've led us too.'

Another figure emerged into the firelight.

'I'm afraid that's right,' said the second man in a high voice. 'But no more dancing now, my sweet. Well, well. On Bela's Knap too. How somehow – *suitable.*'

Con woke and cried out, cowering back against the bank. The second man swept off his wide grey hat and bowed.

'Most highly favoured lady,' he said in his thin voice. 'My name is Cantor and my rough friend here is Grett. May we have the honour of conveying the young lord to his father at Colchester?'

Bara did not move or speak. She held her weapons rigid, as Tam had taught her, but her knees were shaking.

'Come on, girl. We don't give a damn about you,' said Grett. 'We can't even be bothered to hurt you. Just hand over the boy.'

Still Bara did not speak. She stood absolutely still, watching them both and poised on the balls of her feet ready to spring.

'All right,' said Grett wearily. 'If that's how you want it.'

'I greatly regret it,' said his shrill companion.

Without hurry they both removed their grey cloaks and hats and threw them on the ground. Never taking their eyes off Bara they slowly drew their long swords, moved to the right and left of her, and closed in. She parried their first thrusts with her weapons, but she knew they were only playing with her. They were even smiling. Soon they would kill her, but before they did so she would have to kill Con. She would not leave him, even in death.

Cantor slashed, and as Bara parried the blow his sword became entangled in the massed nail-heads of her club. As Grett glanced over at him Bara took her chance to stab at him with her long knife. He yelled as the blade pierced his arm, but meanwhile Cantor had wrenched his sword away and lifted it above his head to bring it down on Bara. Suddenly a stone flew past Bara's face and struck Cantor full in the eye. He swung round, dropping the point of his sword, and Con flung another stone at his companion. But as the stone flew wide of him, Grett swept savagely with his sword, knocking Bara's knife to the ground. Cantor recovered, lunged with his blade, and tangled again with the club. Bara was now impeded on her left and defenceless on her right. Grett moved in on her and struck her with his fist to the ground.

When she recovered consciousness she was bound hand and foot, propped up against an arm of the bank. Con was tethered by his wrists with his back to the great stones. His sobs faltered briefly when he saw Bara move her head and try to smile at him.

'I thought you was dead,' he said, snuffling and trying to rub his eyes with his tethered hands.

'No. We're both all right,' Bara said. But her head was pounding and there was terrible pain round her jaw.

The two men were sitting with their backs to the fire, eating and drinking.

'They're eating our things,' said Con. 'They've been all through our panniers. I could kill them.' Grett looked round. 'Little lion cub, eh? Easy now, boy. You don't want your ma hit again, do you?' Cantor turned his head.

'Most gracious lady,' he said, 'I greatly regret my companion's boorish ferocity. I hope you will forgive him?'

Bara closed her eyes.

'We have told you our names,' Cantor continued, 'but have we told you that we are the Outlanders, the servants of the White Prince Michael? As I believe I mentioned, we have come to take his son home to his father's castle at Colchester.'

'Let me have him over here,' said Bara, failing to hold her voice steady as she held out her bound arms to Con.

The pain of her injuries had faded completely in the realization that it might be only minutes before she was parted from him. She had failed miserably, and now they were helpless.

'Please let him come,' she whispered.

'No,' said Grett, his mouth full of bread.

'Oh come Grett,' said Cantor. 'She won't have him for long now. Untie the boy and let him kiss his mother. It'll be a pretty sight.'

Con stumbled into Bara's lap. Their tears, their hair, their arms mingled with each other as they clung together.

'A pretty sight indeed. Very affecting,' said Cantor, standing up and stretching. 'She's a nice girl, eh Grett? Grett likes you, my dear, I have noticed him eyeing your contours. It is fortunate for you, I think, that our master does not permit us to lie with his women.'

'I'm not his·woman!' shouted Bara, raising her head.

'I beg your pardon. He does not permit us to lie even with his *discarded* women. And now it is almost dawn. A fitting time, I think, for our little ceremony. Stoke the fire, Grett, and heat the knife.'

With her arms around Con and her face buried in his hair, Bara saw nothing of what was being done. She could not speak to comfort him, she could only weep. If they clung tight enough together perhaps even the combined strength of Cantor and Grett could not tear them apart. But rough hands were already tugging at them. Grett put his boot on Bara's breast and both men dragged at Con. He screamed and kicked and bit, but they held his arms and heaved together. Bara clung wildly to his legs, crying and screaming, but Grett brought his boot down heavily on her arm and she rolled over on the ground.

'Bela's Knap is a charming place for the ceremony,' said Cantor, smiling thinly and looking about him. 'Its fitness pleases me. It is of course an ancient burial mound. A centre of ritual and ceremony to our ancestors.'

'What are you going to do?' whispered Bara, seeing for the first time the long knife heating in the fire.

'Nothing very terrible, my dear. The Prince requires that his sons shall be branded, that's all. A very sensible precaution, don't you think? Other than this, the boy will not be hurt. The Prince appreciates it if his sons are delivered to him whole.'

A cold light spread slowly over the hill. The embers of the fire glowed in the encircling arms of the barrow and the line of the pine forest was just visible in the dawn. Dark had moved slowly up the slope, into the arms of the bay, and now stood silently near the fire.

Grett hauled Con to his feet and stood foursquare in front of him, pressing him against the tall stones.

'Stop struggling, you little bastard!' he shouted, slapping Con's face. Con gave up and lay exhausted against the rock, moaning with terror. Carefully Cantor took the long, red-hot knife from the fire. Bara screamed and rolled over, pressing her face into the ground and tasting the sour earth in her mouth. Then she forced herself to look up again, for Con might turn towards her and need her to be there. As Cantor advanced holding the knife in front of him, Grett took Con's head in his hands, forcing it steady, and at the same time he shoved his knee into Con's stomach to hold him still. Cantor rested his arm on Grett's shoulder, with the hot knife pointing at Con's head. Bara trembled, holding her breath, and forcing herself to look towards the child. Cantor slowly advanced his arm. There was a wild scream from Con, a scream so eerie it surely could not have come from a human throat. As the smell of burned flesh filled the air, Bara flung her head forward between her bound legs, fighting the faintness which surged through her eyes and limbs. Con screamed again, a long scream without pause for breath. Bewildered and terrified, Dark shuddered violently, threw back his head and let fly with one of his back legs. As Cantor bent to put the knife on the ground, Dark's flying hoof struck him square on the side of the head. He crumbled without a sound, the whole side of his skull stove in.

Grett spun round, letting Con fall to the ground, and stood aghast over the body of Cantor. Bara scarcely noticed him, or the body. Her remaining consciousness had room only for Con, who lay motionless where he had fallen. She could see the savage weal on his forehead, drawn from his hairline two inches down his brow. The wound was dark red but his face was whiter than his hair. She bit her lip and tried to scrabble herself along the ground with her heels. Grett seemed to be in a daze.

'Cantor,' he repeated stupidly, still gazing at the heaped body. 'He's dead.'

Bara paused a moment in her efforts to reach Con. She closed her eyes, struggling to find some elusive wisp of sense and reason. Bound up like this she could do nothing for Con. He must certainly be alive.

A burn that size could never kill him, therefore she must be free to help him.

'Grett,' she said unsteadily. 'Listen, Grett. The boy may be dying. Look at him.'

'Let him die. Cantor's dead. I don't know what to do.'

'Listen. If the boy dies White Michael will blame you, won't he? He'll say it was your fault. And you won't escape him. No-one ever escapes White Michael. He'll have you murdered.'

Grett looked slowly round at her, comprehension dawning in his face.

'Look,' she went on, 'you can't do anything for Cantor. His head's smashed in. But we can save the boy, and White Michael will be pleased with you. If you untie me I'll be able to help you.'

Grett looked round at Con and tried to prop up the limp body. 'He's dead too,' he said. 'The knife went too deep.'

A sickness rose in Bara's throat, but she went on.

'No, he's not dead. I'm sure he's not. But he will be dead if we don't do something. Untie me and I'll help. I know what to do.'

Grett looked at her, then shrugged and began to untie the ropes that bound her.

'If you try to run away I'll kill you,' he said, glaring into her face. But he moved clumsily, still in a state of shock, and Bara knew her wits were returning faster than his. She half-staggered, half-ran to Con. She knelt by him and gathered him in her arms, whispering his name. He was warm, he was breathing, and when she slipped her hand under his tunic she could feel his heart. She held him only for a moment. As Grett dragged Cantor's body away from the fire she went over to her panniers, determined to find something clean for Con's wound. She found a small square of old cotton, worn thin but apparently clean, and very gently she laid it over Con's brow. If the wound had not become dirty when he fell there was now a good chance of keeping it free of infection. She wet another cloth with some water and held it to Con's temples. Then she propped herself against the bank, with Con in her arms, and waited for him to open his eyes.

Grett wandered aimlessly about, pulling at crusts of bread and staring at Cantor's body. Once Bara saw him prepare to kick savagely at Dark, but he thought better of it and turned away, cursing. It was light now, still grey and cold, but the mist had thinned, and from where she sat in the encircling arms of the mound Bara could see along the bleak hillside to other hills and valleys beyond. It was a high and lonely place, unfriendly to men.

'There's nothing to dig a hole with,' said Grett, 'I don't know what to do with his body.'

'Dump it in the pine wood,' said Bara.

'No. I've got to bury him right. He might come back if I don't.'

Bara stared at him. So he was afraid of ghosts.

'Well, put it in there then. That's a proper burial place.' And she nodded towards the great tumbled stones at the entrance to the barrow.

'In there?'

'Yes. People used to be buried there. Cantor said so. And he seemed to like the place too.' Bara was savage in her irony.

'Yea. Might do. I'll see.' He set himself to pulling apart the fallen stones.

Con stirred and began to groan. Soon his lids fluttered and his great blue eyes looked full at Bara.

'It hurts, Mam,' he said, screwing up his face. He tried to put his hand up to his forehead, but Bara held it down. She smiled and hugged him close. 'It'll hurt for a bit I'm afraid. It's a nasty burn. But it'll get better.'

He groaned, twisting his head, and began to whimper.

'It's horrid. It's so sore. What happened?'

'Never mind.' She gave him a drink and he moaned every time Grett crashed one stone onto another.

After half-an-hour's work the man had forced a gap large enough to squeeze through. 'It's a sort of hole in here,' he shouted from inside, his voice muffled. 'But it's mostly fallen in.'

'Is there room for Cantor?' called Bara.

'Reckon so. Just enough.'

For the next hour Grett worked at his task. At the end of that time Cantor was laid out flat within the dark tomb, his arms folded across his chest and his entire body covered in a pall of pine needles.

'Reckon that should satisfy him,' said Grett, surveying his work from outside.

'I'm sure he'll like that,' said Bara, choking down her anger.

'I'll put some food in for him, then I'll block it up.'

Bara was furious to see their precious scraps of food purloined for a corpse; but she said nothing. For another half hour Grett heaved at the boulders, and eventually fitted them together into a solid barrier.

'Time to go,' he said. He seemed to have recovered his wits, and with them the habit of command. 'We were going to take the boy and the horse and leave you here, but I reckon now you'll have to come a bit of the way and look after him. I'm not a baby's bloody nurse.' He glanced at Con, then looked quickly back again, obviously worried by what he saw. 'Hope he's all right,' he said uncertainly.

'If he's not then me or White Michael will kill you,' said Bara savagely.

'Bloody silly chit,' he replied, hauling her roughly up by the arm. 'Get packing those things.'

She laid Con gently by the fire and began to pack the panniers, while Grett went up the hill to fetch his horses. When Dark was loaded he tied a thick rope to his own pommel and knotted it to Dark's bridle. 'That'll stop any funny stuff,' he said. He strapped Bara's weapons across his saddle-bag and tied Cantor's horse on a long rein on his right. Bara made Con as comfortable as she could, propped up in front of her where he could lean back on her body. He was still dazed, and moaning with pain. Even his hair seemed lifeless.

'You'd better take care of him right,' said Grett. 'It's a long haul to Colchester. I got to get him back alive.'

At last they set off. The bare hills lay all around them, brown and winter green. Here and there were patches of budding trees, and away to the south was a thin column of smoke from a lonely farm. A pall of cloud hung low over the sky, and a damp chill struck at the riders' faces as soon as they left the circle of the fire.

Grett rode slightly ahead, leading the way eastwards down a track which skirted the pine forest. Bara could think only of Con. She held her arms round him and laid her cheek against his hair, crooning his name and trying to bring him some comfort. His hand would stray continually up towards his burn and gently she would press it down again. But at the back of her mind she knew she must start to think. It should be possible, it must be possible, to escape from this stupid Grett.

They rode all morning, stopping only to replenish their water at a well. There was little left to eat, so with Bara's money Grett bought some bread from a woman in a village. Con would not eat, but from time to time he sipped a little water. Grett kept glancing back at him, worried by the thought of his own future should Con be dead when they reached Colchester. They pressed on eastwards, climbing or descending the bleak hills, past the village of Stow and down gentle slopes into the valley of the Evenlode. It was mid-afternoon now, still grey and cold, and Grett was irritable with hunger. He had finished the bread, without offering any to Bara, and he had eaten her last apples.

'Must find a hen,' he muttered. 'We'll camp when it's dark and cook it.'

They rode alongside the river for several miles. Grett was looking for signs of villages and farms, distracted by his hunger from the task of guarding his prisoners. Now would be the time to do something – but what? Bara had nothing with which to cut the leading rope, and Grett had taken her weapons. Perhaps there would be a better chance when they camped for the night.

Then she saw, straight ahead of her, about a hundred yards away, a line of six or eight magnificent trees. They were great bare beeches, no doubt the remains of some avenue, and their trunks were only some three yards apart. The path led towards them, then diverged and ran parallel. Bara felt stealthily in Con's pocket and found what she wanted. There was rough grass between them and the trees, now some seventy yards away, and a scattering of gorse and bramble. Grett was beginning to pull the horses to the right, along the curve of the path, when Bara with all her strength struck Con's flint deep into Dark's flank. She kicked and yelled, but at the blow of the flint, which had pierced his skin, Dark had already leaped. Like a torrent released, he rushed forward, his ears back and his nostrils flaring. Grett's horse was jerked sideways and dragged into a stumbling gallop. Grett tugged furiously at the rope, yelling and swearing at Dark to stop. Together they thundered over the field towards the trees. Grett was straining at Dark's rope on his left, and at the same time trying to pull at his right on Cantor's horse. Bara dug the flint in again, closing her mind to Con's screams of agony. Dark lowered his head and thundered over briars and brambles for a gap in the trees.

Suddenly Grett realized his danger. Dark was ahead, there were only twenty yards to go to the trees, and unless he could untie himself from Dark he and his horse would crash into one of those huge tree-trunks and be killed. He wasted precious moments fumbling with the knot at his pommel before he remembered his knife. He whipped it from his belt and slashed at the thick rope. He did not cut it clean and he had to slash again. Dark burst between the trees, the panniers crashed against the trunks, Dark stumbled and Bara clung frantically to Con. But Dark recovered and they were through. Behind them Grett and his horse lay smashed on the ground.

Although Grett had cut the rope, his horse had had no time to pull up or change direction. Man and horse had crashed with the full force of their gallop against the huge tree. Bara could not bear to look at what was left of them. Con was screaming with pain and terror as she lifted him down and tried to reassure him. When his screams had subsided she laid him in a blanket by the bole of a tree, and walked over to Grett's horse to retrieve her weapons. Her legs shook violently, but she forced herself to unstrap the saddle-bags from both Grett's and Cantor's horses, for she knew they contained good blankets and probably much else besides. Then she cut Cantor's horse loose and let him go. There were no pine needles here, and few dead leaves, so she dragged up some brambles and covered the dead bodies as best she could. Then, without warning, she was very sick.

After a cold and sleepless night Bara decided they had better return to the main west road. She judged it must be somewhere to the south of them, and she hoped they might strike it further along by travelling southwest. Con's pain seemed less and the spark of life in him was reviving. Before they set out she saw him smile up at Dark and pat his leg.

After the first few miles it was a rough ride, for none of the tracks seemed to go in their direction and Bara was growing weary of trackless fields and hillsides where she had to pick out paths for Dark. As they forded the Dikler in the afternoon a pale sun struck through the mist, and towards evening they rode into Windrush. At the crossroads an old man was sitting perched on the familiar overgrown mountain of discarded domestic machinery, which together with the hulks of cars marked the approach to every town or village. In the summer, brambles and bindweed smothered these mountains in green, but in winter the sightless screens of televisions and the empty maws of washing machines gaped through the stems and thorns.

'The big road's a mile off,' said the old man. 'Charlt'n Kings they call it. Never been that far meself,' he added. 'You come far?'

'Quite far,' said Bara. 'We've come from London.'

'Where's that?' he asked, putting his head on one side. Bara replied briefly and they made for the road. Somewhere on the main track there would be a place to sleep. The thin sun still shone in the west and Bara felt wildly elated. Con was alive, the Outlanders were dead, and once more they were on their way. She sang to Con as they rode, but the dusk closed suddenly as they turned west on the main track and her elation drained away with the daylight. Con was complaining of the pain, he was limp with weariness, and they might yet have some way to go. It was stupid not to have stayed in Windrush.

After a few minutes there was a clopping and a rumbling on the track behind them. Bara subdued her spurt of fear, for of course the Outlanders were dead, and pulled Dark onto the verge to let the cart go by. As it drew level there was a shout from the driver.

'Hi! You there! Is this all the far you've got?' It was Wat, the young man who had sold her corn in the Oxford meadow, and next to him on the driver's bench was a young woman wrapped in a green shawl.

'Hullo,' said Bara, laughing with pleasure to see a familiar face.

'I met this lot in Oxford,' said Wat, turning to the girl. Then, looking back to Bara, 'This is my wife, Bel.'

The girl smiled and Bara smiled back, thinking Bel was very pretty. Wat peered forward, straining to see in the gathering dusk.

'Is the boy hurt?' he said, staring at Con's bandage.

'Yes. They branded him.' Bara's voice choked as she spoke.

'Who?' said Wat sharply.

'The Outlanders. White Michael's men.'

Wat unfolded his long body and put his hand across onto Dark's neck. He leaned over from his cart and lifted up the edge of the white cloth on Con's wound.

'Christ Almighty,' he breathed. 'The bloody bastards.' His wife had risen also. 'Look,' said Wat, 'you must let Bel see this. She knows about these things.'

Bel clambered over him and looked under the cloth.

'It's stuck,' she said. 'It needs dressing. But it looks clean. God, what a thing to do.' Con lay against Bara, his eyes half shut, as they talked over his head. 'The kid's exhausted,' Bel continued. 'And she is too,' she added, looking hard at Bara. 'Let's have them in the cart.'

'Let's,' said Wat, jumping onto the road. 'Both of you.' There were bed-rolls and parcels and sacks filling the back of the cart, but in a few moments they had Con bedded down with blankets and an old pillow, with a space for Bara next to him. Bara stood in a daze as they bustled about, too stunned by her good fortune to speak. It was utter sweet relief simply to lean against the cart while arrangements and decisions were made for her. Then she was told to get in and lie by Con. Dark was given apples and tethered to the back rail, the lamp was lit, and they set off through the dusk, rattling west.

Bara slept the sleep of the exhausted. Somewhere along the road they must have stopped for the night, but she knew nothing until she woke with a start in the pale sunlight of the next day. The cart had pulled up and a babble of cheerful voices filled the air. Bara blinked and rolled over, trying to make sense of the confusion of light and noise that swam in on her sleep. Someone pushed her gently.

'Mam. Wake up Mam.'

She looked up and there was Con, perched on the edge of the cart, smiling down at her. He had a fresh bandage round his head and there was colour in his cheeks again. His eyes were very blue.

'Con. It's you.'

Bara smiled and heaved herself up to a sitting position. He dropped into her lap and she laid her cheek against his warm hair.

'We're there Mam. This is Wat's house.'

Bara raised her head and looked round her. They were in a paddock, drawn up beside a jumble of sheds and outhouses, and on their right was a wide slow river, banked by green water meadows. All over the paddock lay tools and timber and boats and bits of boats. Then, when she looked behind her, she saw a house so fantastical she wondered if she were still asleep. It was all angles, pitches, dormers, gables, chimneys, porches, turrets; some parts were painted white, some green, some blue, some red. It was something flung together by a giant playing with children's bricks. Wat emerged from beneath a complicated wooden porch. He loped over and leaned on the cart, smiling at Bara.

'We're here,' he said.

'But where?'

'At my folks' place. Where I was a kid. Bel and me come here to see them every year. That's why we was coming this way.'

'Oh.' Bara looked so bewildered Wat laughed at her.

'You look a proper mess,' he said. 'You hair's all ropes and knots and your face's all over smudges. Come in and wash.'

Bara seemed quite unable to collect herself. 'Are we – I mean—?'

'You're stopping here. As long as you want. I've fixed it.'

To her utter astonishment Bara began to cry. Tears rolled down her cheeks, washing clean runnels in the dirt. Then she clutched Con and began to laugh. He looked up at her in consternation.

'Don't!' he shouted. 'Stop it Mam!'

Bara rubbed the tears from her eyes.

'Sorry,' she said. 'I don't know what's wrong with me.'

'You've been through enough,' said Wat, looking at her gravely. 'Come inside and meet me Ma and Da. He's a boatbuilder,' he said, waving towards the litter on the grass.

Bara climbed down from the cart and stood for a moment gazing at the crazy house. Wat smiled.

'I suppose it is a bit funny,' he said. 'I don't notice it any more.'

'It's marvellous,' said Bara. 'It's like a picture in a book of fairy tales.'

'Trouble is my Da just loves building things. If he's not building boats he's building another bit to the house. Whenever he's in a bad temper he just goes and throws out another turret somewhere, and all's well again.'

Bara laughed, and taking Con's hand, she went into the house. It was gloomy in the stone-flagged room, except for the fire roaring in the kitchen range. Around a large scrubbed table were seated three people: an old man, whose face was almost entirely concealed in a grey mane of hair and beard; a round old woman, whose eyes were overwhelmed by two great apple cheeks; and Bel, who rose as Bara and Con came in. The old ones remained seated, staring intently at the newcomers.

'This is Bara,' said Wat to his parents, 'and this is her boy, Con.'

Bara smiled at them both but they continued to stare stolidly back.

'Have some tea,' said Bel.

'Tea?' said Bara, astonished.

'Grimony tea,' said Bel. 'Ma makes it.'

The old woman nodded, as if to acknowledge the reference to herself, but still she did not smile. Bara and Con were handed steaming mugs of pale liquid, and given places on a new deal bench.

'Just made that, Da?' asked Wat, examining the bench.

The old man nodded, without removing his gaze from Bara. She felt herself beginning to flush under their relentless scrutiny.

'The burn's much better,' said Bel. 'There's scar tissue coming. But it'll leave an awful mark.'

'Branding always does,' said Wat. 'It's not meant to go away.'

'When did you bandage him?' asked Bara, realizing how long she must have slept.

'Last night, and again this morning. We stopped in an inn at Cheltham. We didn't want to disturb you so we left you in the cart. Con was so sleepy he didn't really know what I was doing.'

Bara gazed at her gratefully.

'I don't know what would have happened if we hadn't met you,' she said. 'Con would probably have died of gangrene.'

'Well, don't think about it,' said Wat, draining his scalding tea at a gulp. 'You'll be all right now.' Then he leaned forward on his elbow, looking intently at Bara. 'What exactly are you doing anyway?' he said. 'You and the boy travelling on your own like this?'

'Well,' said Bara slowly, 'I know it sounds stupid, but we're really travelling to Ireland.'

There was an astonished pause, then a hiss and wheeze broke out across the table. Bara realized the old lady was laughing.

'*Ireland*?' she creaked. 'Ireland's the other side of the world, child. You'll never get to *Ireland*.'

'Yes we will,' said Con, glaring at her and swinging his legs.

'Listen to the little lad,' growled the old man, and possibly smiling beneath his growth of beard.

'Not yet, anyway,' said Bel, rising, and clearing away the mugs.

'It's a funny idea,' said Wat. 'Tewksbry's west enough for me.'

'Is that where we are?' asked Tara.

'Aye.' For the first time the old man spoke to her, and she felt accepted. 'Quite near enough the Marches here,' he said, his voice muffled in his beard. 'Those Welshies are a terrible lot.'

His wife shook her head gravely and clucked her tongue.

'Don't want to go there,' she wheezed. 'That's the Wild Lands. Witches and monsters and men with heads growing out of their chests and hair all over.' Her eyes grew round with awe.

'I like witches and monsters,' said Con, taking an interest.

'Not those, you wouldn't,' growled the old man, laying his gnarled hand on Con's head. 'There's Droods too, to cut your heart out and eat it raw.'

'Ooo, go on,' said Con, enchanted. The old man turned away.

'He don't understand,' he said wearily. 'It's still all stories to him.'

'Time enough,' said his wife, her cheeks rising in a smile which almost extinguished her eyes.

'Come and see round,' said Bel, taking Con's hand. 'Come and see the boats.'

March merged into April. The yellow rays of coltsfoot faded, primroses opened in the woods and hedgerows, damp leaves uncurled from the buds of the may. For many days together the pale sun shone, then for a week or more it would be obscured by low clouds. In all the weeks she stayed with Wat, Bara never moved away from the house and boatyard. Sometimes Wat took Con into Tewksbry in the cart, but Bara never wanted to join them. Her courage had seeped away, the image of Ireland had faded into the recesses of her mind, no more urgency of purpose drove her on. The outside world was wholly inimical, and she could never rest easy until Wat had brought Con safely home from their outings. Here, and only here, in this house and yard, was there safety.

Old Wat worked all day and every day on his boats. Bara discovered he was accounted the best boat-builder from Severn to Wye, and he could not keep pace with the orders he received. His boats varied from flat-bottomed craft for fishing the upper reaches of the rivers to substantial coastal vessels with cabins. Three boys from Tewksbry were employed in the yard all the year, and during his annual visit Wat worked long hours beside his father. Bel told Bara that they came early every spring, not only to see the old people, but to help old Wat catch up with his orders.

'Why did young Wat ever leave?' asked Bara one day.

'Oh, he couldn't work with the old devil the whole time,' said Bel.

Bara could understand that, for old Wat was an exacting taskmaster, who roared and bellowed at his assistants for the slightest misdemeanour or slackness. With his eyes flashing and his wild grey mane trembling, he presented a vision so terrifying that many of his assistants fled and never returned. It was after these outbursts that he would throw up some new addition to his already contorted house. All evening he would bang away by lantern-light, while his wife in the kitchen clucked and wagged her head until her cheeks wobbled. Next morning there would be a new lean-to, or a new porch, or a new turret, and old Wat's temper would be sweet again.

Con loved the yard. In one corner was a rusty pile of old brass and iron ten feet high, from which pieces would be selected for the boats. Against one end of the house was a forge, a glowing den of mystery and excitement. The anvil was a piece of the old London-Gloucester railway-line. Sometimes he was allowed to work the bellows and his joy was unbounded. A smell of tar and caulking and glue lurked in every corner, but it was strongest in the main workshop by the water's edge, where huge pots of sticky dark substances stood in rows on the benches. It was here that Con was most often to be found, thrusting his fingers into pots and fooling with the shining, razor-sharp tools which hung along the walls. He had completely recovered from his branding. The weal was hideous, over a inch long from his hairline down his forehead, but he felt no more pain and most of the time his hair fell over the scar and hid it. Bel was sure it would never go, though it might fade a little, but as it showed only when Con thrust his hair back, or hung upside-down in a tree, Bara worried about it no longer.

Old Wat's wife lived entirely between the kitchen and the bedroom. During the day she was for ever heating cauldrons of water and boiling kettles for grimony tea. Pink as an apple in autumn, she seemed to Bara to be permanently enveloped in steam, and her breath was never free from the hisses and wheezes which seemed like escaping steam themselves. After her first implacable scrutiny she had accepted Bara without question, and she never ceased to smile and wheeze when Bara helped her in the kitchen. Nothing and nobody could persuade her to venture outside. 'It's bad for me complexion,' she would say, wrinkling up her face and creaking with laughter. She was always feeding Con juicy titbits of new-baked bread or meat or biscuit, and he soon discovered that he had only to smile and open his mouth for some delicious scrap to be dropped into it. 'Oh the little lad,' she would say, stroking his head, 'is he hungry then?'

Bara had liked Bel from their first meeting on the road. Bel's dark face with its large black eyes and frame of curly black hair appealed strongly to the fair-skinned Bara. The two of them would sit for hours in the kitchen, if the weather was bad, or outside on an upturned boat if it was fine. Bel's father had been a corn-merchant in Oxfordshire and he had given his business to Wat before he died. She and Wat had met one day at Cheltham market four years ago, and they had been together ever since. Only when she looked at Con and spoke of children did Bel's face seem tight and drawn.

'Just nothing happens,' she said miserably, as they sat one day with their tea by the range. 'I can't start one. I don't know if it's him or me.'

'I'm sorry,' said Bara, confused by the wild tumult of her feelings.

'Fifty or a hundred years ago they could have fixed us,' Bel continued. 'The story in my family is that my great-granddam was a nurse, a very grand nurse in a big hospital, like they had then. A lot of what she knew has come down the family and that's why I know about it all.'

'I think you know more useful things than they did. You know how to make medicines from plants, and anyone can find those when they need them. My Gran told me everything had to come from laboratories once. No-one bothered to know how to make a poultice of burdocks then.'

'Or grimony tea,' said Bel.

They laughed and made faces at the bitter brew.

'I'm the nurse back home,' Bel went on. 'Everyone comes to me from miles around. I'm often out all night delivering babies. I used to love that but I hate it now.' She poked savagely at the range. 'It's not fair.'

'No,' said Bara, 'it's bloody well not. Just once I'm raped and I get Con, and you try for years and get nothing.'

'Oh well,' said Bel, rising and collecting up some dishes. 'I suppose there's hope for another twenty years or so.'

A few nights later Bara woke with a start to find Wat kneeling by her bed. She jerked away from him, swamped with fear, but he only smiled and gently stroked her hair.

'Don't be afraid,' he whispered, laying his cheek on her pillow. 'You know how easy I'm frightened. You frightened me before, remember?'

'Go away,' said Bara huskily, pulling her blanket around her.

'Why? Don't you like me?' He rubbed his face against her hair.

'No I don't. Go away.'

'Oh come on. Most women like me. I thought you might think different this time.'

'Well I don't.' Bara's heart was thudding and her throat was tight.

'Just try. Try me and see.'

He put his arm around her shoulder and tried to pull her onto the pillow again. Anger blazed in her and she caught him a stinging slap across the face.

'Oh hell,' he said, jumping up. 'Not again. Am I going to get a stone in my eye too?' He stood over her, grinning and rubbing his cheek.

'If you try again you will,' said Bara, ashamed of her violence.

She tried to smile but her mouth trembled. He paused for a moment at the door and looked back.

'It was worth a try,' he said. 'Sleep well.'

But Bara did not sleep. She tossed and turned, filled with a prickling unease, and longing for some sound to break the black silence. To Wat, she thought angrily, the incident had been little more than a joke; but to her it had brought a turmoil of feelings irreducible to any kind of order. Somewhere deep in the confusion she knew she felt desire for Wat, but surrounding it, above, below, interfused on every level, were revulsion and fear. Damn him and damn him, and now she could not sleep.

The next day, to Bara's utter confusion, Bel asked her if Wat had been to her room in the night. Before Bara had recovered herself, Bel nodded and smiled.

'I thought so,' she said. 'Did you make love?'

'No.'

'Why not?'

'I – well – I didn't want to.'

'Most women do. Women like him.'

'Don't you mind?'

'No, not if it's just sometimes. I'm not perfect that way myself.'

She looked straight into Bara's eyes and smiled a woman's smile of complicity. But Bara could not respond and turned away.

'I don't mind it sometimes,' Bel went on, 'but if anyone tried to take him away from me I'd kill her.' Her gentle face set hard and Bara believed her.

'I won't try,' she said.

Bel laughed. 'You haven't tried much yet anyway. I think you're afraid of him. I think you're afraid of men.'

'Perhaps.' Bara shrugged, not wanting to discuss it. She moved to the door but Bel's voice pursued her.

'It's not like being raped, you know. I expect that's bloody awful, but it's quite different with a nice man.'

'I suppose so.'

Bara escaped into the cold grey morning, and began busily to hang up wet clothes.

Wat made no reference to his visit, but from time to time he winked at her heavily, and she understood she was supposed to be amused. Then in the bright early days of April she found to her amazement that she was constantly thinking of Tam. He had scarcely come into her head since they had left home, but now his presence in her mind seemed so solid it was almost physical. She often stopped to ponder what she saw there. Everything about Tam was square, his body, his face, his hands, and his stance too. He was trustworthy and steady, and his mind was as sturdy as his body. She found herself thinking about him most of the day, and he even began to invade her sleep at night. Had Wat unwittingly done this for her? Had his visit to her bedside somehow dragged up the memory of Tam, where it had lain drowned so long in the deeps of her mind? She felt driven, almost against her will, to talk about him to Bel; to speak about his long love for her, which had persisted through her own indifference and through his affairs with other girls. She began to think she had never really seen him before. Perhaps he had been too near her for too long, perhaps only time and distance could bring him into focus. She woke trembling from a dream of him one night, and she wept to think how many miles and dangers he was away.

April was sharp and bright, bringing lambs to the watermeadows and fishermen to the banks of the river. The tracery of winter branches was blurred in a mist of opening leaves, and the orchard across the river was dotted with tight pink buds. Even old Meg came as far as her kitchen door, to sniff the clean spring air.

'Come out!' shouted Con, pulling at her skirt. 'Come outside!'

'Oh no,' she wheezed, resisting him. 'It's a deal too cold out there for these old bones.' She laughed, wobbling like a jelly, and rolled back into the cavern of fire and steam which was her home.

Try as she might, Bara could not shake herself free of this new obsession with Tam. As she washed the clothes, as she scrubbed potatoes, as she worked in the garden or carried water or mended blankets or exercised Dark – all the while she was absorbed by memories of Tam. One morning in the middle of April, as she sat on the river bank shredding a dandelion, Wat and Bel came over and one sat each side of her.

'Why have you gone so dreamy?' asked Wat gently.

'Is it Tam? said Bel.

Bara finished dissecting the flower, then she nodded.

'Well, what's the problem?' said Wat. 'Go back to him. You're crazy to think you can get to Ireland anyway.'

'Do you think perhaps he wouldn't want you any more? Is that it?' asked Bel.

'No.'

'He would want you?'

'I think so. He always has.'

'Then go back to him,' said Wat emphatically. 'Whenever you want.'

Bara leaped up in one movement and smiled down at them both.

'All right,' she said happily. 'I will.'

The depression which had weighed on her dispersed like mist in the sun. She shook out her hair and felt as if she shone all over. Her happiness was so infectious that Wat abandoned his work, and they took Con out in a boat for an afternoon on the river. Wat rowed slowly in the sun, through a river country scoured clean and bright by winter. They fished, they splashed, they sang, they idled on the banks, they saw a kingfisher flash between the willows. Sometimes Wat shipped the oars and let the lazy river bear them aimlessly along. There was nothing in the world for Bara but love and friendship, larks and sunlight and water. She lay back, brim-full of content.

That evening, as she laid Con's head on the pillow, she told him they were going home to Tam. He stared at her aghast and sat bolt upright.

'It's all right, Con,' she said, startled. 'You know, home. Where we came from.'

But his small face was rigid with worry.

'We can't,' he said. 'We're going to Ireland.'

'It's too far and too dangerous. I've changed my mind. It would be nice to go home, wouldn't it?'

'No!' Con shouted, clenching his fists. 'We can't go home, we're going to Ireland.'

The corners of his mouth turned down and tears gathered in his eyes. Then his face crumpled and he began to sob.

'But Con—' Bara was bewildered. 'It doesn't really matter so much, does it? We've come a long way and seen a lot of things and now it would be nice to go home.'

'No it wouldn't! We can't.' He hit his head with his fists and his body heaved with sobs. 'I just know we can't.'

'You know we can't?' said Bara. 'How do you mean, you know we can't?'

'We just can't. I know we can't.'

'But how do you know?'

'I just know.' And he dropped his head in his hands, his small body jerking with the force of his weeping.

'All right, all right.' Bara held him tight and tried to kiss away his tears. 'I didn't know you felt like that. It's all right, don't worry,' She crooned to him for half-an-hour before he was composed again, and ready for sleep.

'So we won't go back,' he murmured sleepily, turning on his pillow.

'It's all right. Go to sleep.'

Bara was deeply shaken by his outburst, and by the strangeness of his words, but she tried to shrug it off and told herself he would be all right in the morning. They had a cheerful evening in the kitchen, drinking old Meg's brew of cider, and when Bara went to bed herself she had dismissed Con's misery from her mind.

Sometime during the night she awoke, prickling with sweat. A welter of dreams still dragged at her, confusing her sense of place and time. She felt a presence in the dark room, pressing from every corner, but there was no sound. With trembling hands she struck her flint and lit the rush by her bed. Angular shadows flickered, casting the beams of the roof into unfamiliar shapes. The room was certainly empty; nevertheless something alien was there. Bara shrank back, clutching her blankets. Then suddenly out of the blackness there sailed in perfect formation a fleet of small white ships, and she knew they were sailing on the tide to Ireland. The vision faded into the familiar green meadows, enamelled with flowers, through which stepped slowly a line of men in blue robes, each bearing a golden crown. Bara closed her eyes and shook her head, trying to escape the insistence of these waking dreams, then her muscles relaxed and she sank quietly back into her pillow. She realized now that she was not frightened. Whatever was in her room, its presence was benign and wished her well. But the pressure did not lift. She was inhabiting another mind, whose power was dominant. Her head began to ache and she knew that this had happened before. In the Cotswold farm. A voice spoke, booming, though it was noiseless.

'Come,' it said, 'Come, come, come.'

'But I don't want to,' cried Bara, raising herself on her elbow and holding a hand to her throbbing head. 'I want to go home. I want to see Tam.'

But her mind's glimpse of Tam was immediately swamped by a

deluge of images, green and gold and blue; golden trees in a green meadow, white flowers by a blue lake, green islands in a blue sea. *Ireland Ireland Ireland* drummed in her head. Her eyes ached, her body was running with sweat, the pressure in the room began to crush her. She fell back exhausted on her pillow.

'All right,' she whispered, turning her head from side to side. 'All right, all right, I'll come.'

Immediately she was free. There was no-one and nothing. She lay for a moment, aware of a sweet, deep sleep closing up on her, and then she knew no more.

Their departure three days later was just as their previous departures had been. When they had left London, when they had left the Cotswold farm, the same suspicion of her sanity had spoken from the silence of her friends. Bara was almost becoming used to it, but she found it very painful that Wat and Bel should think less well of her. Bel concealed her misgivings in a flood of medical lore and advice, but Wat made no attempt to cover his scorn.

'It's so bloody stupid,' he kept saying, and Bara caught him looking oddly at her many times. He thought she was touched, and his suspicions hurt. Old Meg simply shrugged when she heard the news, as if to say that the vagaries of human nature were quite beyond her. But she retreated to the depths of her kitchen and for two days increased the intensity of fire and steam to such a pitch the others could scarcely bear the heat. At the end of that time she had made provisions enough to last Bara and Con a month. From her oven came bread and buns and chicken and pork and biscuits; from her pans came soup and stew and potatoes and carrots; from her pantry came butter and eggs and milk. Bara did not see how Dark could carry it all, or how she and Con would ever eat it before it was bad. But somehow it was all packed in, together with more blankets, herbal medicines, tapers, flints, warm clothes, and a few precious scraps of ancient plastic sheeting from the barn. Old Wat had repaired and decorated Dark's harness, and young Wat had made Con a pair of stirrups of his own. He had also hafted a razor-sharp knife into a pole, so that Bara had a spear to add to her knife and her club.

When the day of their departure came, near the end of April, Bara could only weep. Dark was brought in from the meadow, where he had wandered contentedly for the last two months, and the bursting panniers were strapped across his back. Even then Bel begged them to give it up and stay. But Bara shook her head angrily through her tears. She cried in the arms of each one of them in turn, utterly unable to express the depths of her gratitude. She said she had met no-one like them anywhere, and since her Gran had died she had forgotten such good and kind people existed. Old Meg's cheeks were wet with tears as she folded Bara and Con into her skirts. 'It's those tribes in Wales I'm afeared of,' she said.

But through it all Con was merry as a cricket. 'It's nice here,' he said politely, bouncing in his saddle. 'But, you see, we have to go to Ireland.'

At last Bara was mounted and ready. Con's high spirits were having their effect and everyone managed to smile and wave and put on a show of cheerfulness. Old Wat looked gravely up at them, seated on Dark's back, then he looked from Bara's golden hair to Con's silver. ''Tis like the sun and moon,' he said.

Wat was to walk with them to put them on the track for Ross, where they would pick up the main road west through Wales. They turned out of the yard and along the river bank. In a few moments trees would hide the house. Bara turned in the saddle for a last look at the colourful jumble of gables and towers and balconies and chimneys.

'It's a lovely house,' she said.

'Aye,' said Wat, 'it's where I was raised.'

When they reached the road he pulled Bara's head down and kissed her long and hard.

'Good luck,' he said, smiling, and relaxing his long body again. 'I'm sorry we didn't make it.' Bara laughed, and made as if to slap his face, then she turned off onto the rough road for Wales.

Instead of the black depression she had expected, Bara's spirits rose high. Con was swinging his new stirrups, singing with his head thrown back, at the top of his shrill voice. The tug of Tam and home had vanished as if they had never been, and the joy of travelling west was in her once more. The wide valley of the Severn had quickened into full spring, and the lushness of its fields and trees filled her with content. They ate a princely meal under the opening buds of an orchard, they rested later in luscious grass by a stream, and after a gentle climb out of the valley they came down in the evening to the small grey town of Ross.

They crossed the Wye on the old stone bridge, much repaired with tree-trunks, and they turned down the narrow valley for Monmouth. Sometimes the wooded banks of the Wye rose steeply above them, sometimes they looked over a cliff's edge at the river meandering below. The weather turned grey in the evening, with sudden bursts of rain, and once Con asked crossly why they couldn't go back to the kitchen at Tewksbry. This time it was Bara who shook her head and said they must go on.

They had met very few people after leaving Ross, and some of those from whom they had asked the way spoke only some strange lilting tongue, which Bara took to be Welsh. Occasionally a woodcutter crossed the road, and sometimes belches of smoke from the fires of charcoal burners rose above the trees. Once Con saw a boat far below them on the river, loaded with wood.

'It's one of old Wat's boats,' he said confidently. 'Everyone had his boats round here.'

Suddenly round a bend they came upon a dilapidated gate, closed across the road. A large dark man shuffled out of an old railway carriage by the roadside. His arms hung loosely forward as he walked, and his face was almost smothered in roughly cut stubble.

'Toll-gate,' he said gruffly.

'Why?' asked Bara, who had never encountered such a thing.

'Because I say,' said the man, loping over and clutching Dark's bridle. Bara laid her hand on the shaft of her hidden knife.

'This is a public road,' she said.

'Come on,' he said, baring his teeth. 'Don't argue.'

Bara eyed the gate but she could not ask Dark to jump it with such a weight on him.

'What's the toll?' she said.

'Good money.' He leered up at her. 'Or you, if you like. One or the other.' Bara brought out a few old pennies and showed them. 'Not enough,' he said. 'More.' She found a small silver coin and added it to the pennies. 'All right.' He took the money but he did not let go Dark's bridle.

'Let me pass.'

'No. You as well. In my carriage.' And he grinned up at her, pulling Dark towards the shed. Bara drew out her knife and held it over his arm.

'Let go,' she said. With unexpected agility he spun round and lunged at her hand with his fist. He knocked the weapon upwards but Bara still held it. She swung her arm down and felt the blade bite into his shoulder. As he yelled with pain she urged Dark forward straight at the gate. For a moment it resisted, then it fell in splinters before his weight and he responded to Bara's kicks by lumbering into a trot. There was no sound of pursuit, so after a mile Bara slowed him down. Con was very silent and she was not sure if he had been badly frightened or not. In their weeks on the road he had learned to be quiet in moments of trouble, and to keep his fear to himself. She knew he could be relied upon to throw a stone if he had one, but otherwise he retreated and watched.

'I didn't like him,' was all he would say about the toll-man.

Monmouth was deserted. They met no-one, they saw no-one up the side-streets or through the windows of the broken houses. Except for the clopping of Dark along the rutted road there was no movement and no sound. No birds twittered; not even a cat stirred. Broken lamp-standards and road-signs lay across the street. Broken windows hung like sightless eyes in the stone walls of the houses. The silence was thunderous, a positive and menacing enemy. Bara shivered, for she knew that good shelter was deserted only when there had been some fearful calamity. Perhaps this was a plague town, where every living thing had either fled or died. She urged Dark on, determined not to linger in Monmouth.

They camped for the night in a deserted cottage on the hill outside the town. The hills were closing in on them now, and there were high mountains ahead, cut clearly against the pink evening sky. Bara felt well satisfied with their progress. As she sat by the little fire they had made in their cottage, struggling to comb out the knots in her hair, she glowed with confidence in her ability to get safe to Ireland. She had beaten the toll-man, she had worked out and accomplished the death of Grett. It was true her performance against the two Outlanders together might not have pleased Tam, for she felt she had been clumsy with her weapons, but with luck they would not be attacked by two armed men again. Anyway, she would practise.

After they had eaten she jumped up and picked a scrap of sharp slate from the floor. Then on the bare stone wall of the cottage she scratched the rough outline of a man. 'You watch,' she said to Con. 'You watch me do my soldier-training.' He leaped up and stood in front of the broken window, his hands on his hips, making a sturdy square against the light. He was too small to lift the weapons for more than a moment, but he had decided views on how they ought to be used. Half-laughing, half-serious, Bara leaped and dodged and feinted and swung at the outlined figure, trying to co-ordinate the sweep of the long knife with the thrust of the shafted spear. Con was not satisfied.

'Your legs are wrong,' he said. 'You'll fall over. That one ought to be *here* when that one's *there*.' Then he added, 'Your tummy's all open. Those things are all on the sides.' He pointed to the dagger. 'Tam said hold it up, with you behind it.'

Sweat streamed down Bara's face as she sprang from corner to corner of the dim room. The dust on the flagstones was thrown into

swirls by her feet, and still Con urged her on. Sometimes she told him
he was talking rubbish, but he would reply stubbornly that he knew
it should be his way, and she would know he was right. A familiar
feeling of unease crept through her, and she looked at him sideways
as she put her weapons away. But he only smiled up at her and said
he was hungry again. His mop of silver hair was almost over his eyes
now, completely covering his scar, and it flopped up and down when
he ran. Everything about him was still plump and babyish, yet he
looked much older than when they had left home three months ago.

The next day they moved lazily along the soft green valley of the
Usk. Inside the huge keep of Raglan Castle they ate a lunch of pork
and pickles and bread, and after it Con rolled wildly down the side of
the dry green moat. The weather was dull, and sometimes a light
drizzle fell, but the air was warm and Bara felt lethargic. The image
of Tam returned and hovered in the back of her mind. Sometimes
she spoke silently to him, and watched his slow smile. The thought
that she would never see him again seemed curiously without sting.
She had him there in her mind's eye, and that for the moment
seemed good enough.

In the early evening they jogged into Abergavenny. The town was
seething with people. Since they had left Oxford they had not seen a
quarter so many people; but this crowd was very different from the
Oxford Rout. These were small dour men, most of them dark, and all
of them dressed in sober leather breeches and sheepskins. The streets
were not only full of men, they were full of sheep. Bara asked a bony
woman leaning against a wall if this was market day, but she was
met by an uncomprehending stare. The woman's small black eyes
looked hostile and she only shrugged, drawing her leather cloak
tighter over her shoulders. Bara then tried a fair young man, who
stood outside an inn with a mug in one hand and a long shepherd's
crook in the other.

'Aye, it's the Threeday Fair,' he said. 'Every year it's the sheep fair
at the beginning of May. More of a shindy than anything,' he added,
raising his mug and winking.

'I'm glad to meet someone who speaks English,' said Bara.

'Aye. Heathen black-eyed savages. You have to know a bit of their
lingo or it's no good trying to trade here. But it's a goddam lingo to
get your tongue round.'

'Is this an inn?' asked Bara, peering into the dark crowded room
behind her.

'Aye. The Woolpack.'

'Do you think they'd put us up?'

'Prob'ly full. You could try.' He waved his arm towards the door, then settled down seriously to the contents of his mug.

They were shown by a serving-girl into a small raftered room in the attic. The beams were cobwebbed, but the floor seemed clean and the thick straw palliasses looked comfortable enough. There were odd piles of sacking here and there, which puzzled Bara, but when she asked about them the girl merely shrugged and made off with the candle. Bara shouted after her from the gloom of the doorway, but the girl was already almost back to the bar, and preferred not to hear.

They unloaded the panniers in the street and Bara gave a boy a penny to help her get them upstairs. When she had seen to Dark's stabling she thought they might as well settle down for the night. They lit a candle and stuck it in a piece of metal tubing, torn from an old gas pipe. Although it was barely dusk outside, the skylight had been boarded over, and the small opening overlooking the street was hung with thick sacking. They lolled on the palliasse, eating and drinking from the rich store in the panniers and listening to the uproar from the bar and the street. A crowd was singing in the bar, weighing heavily into some song whose rowdy chorus repeated every three or four lines. Outside in the street two men were playing fiddles and two were beating drums and pans while the crowds danced and sang confusedly. Bara could not imagine they would ever get to sleep, but Con fell into a deep slumber almost as soon as she had tucked him up in a corner of the straw.

The mirth and the noise and the music continued unabated. Bara lay back on the palliasse with an arm over Con and gave herself up for a long time to thoughts of Tam. Suddenly the door burst open and a small dark man, indistinguishable from a hundred others in the crowd, tumbled headlong into the room. Bara sat up, clutching her blanket round her and seizing her knife. But instead of attacking her the little man bowed solemnly from the waist.

'It is a good night we are having, I am thinking,' he said. 'But I have had enough now.'

'This is my room,' said Bara.

'Oh, but it is mine too,' said the man, trying to arrange a pile of sacks. 'I have been told.'

'But I've paid for it.'

'Oh, and me too. It is good to be an innkeeper at the Threeday Fair.'

He modestly turned his back to Bara while he removed his

sheepskin jacket and shirt. Then he cocked his dark cropped head and said in his lilting voice. 'As you are a lady I will not remove my breeches. My name is Dai. Good-night.'

He curled himself up in the bundle of sacking and began breathing heavily. Soon he was snoring, with an exact repitition of pitch and volume that soon drove Bara to a frenzy of irritation. She knew she would never sleep now. Finally she threw her shoe at him. He grunted, turned his head, and resumed his snoring. Bara lay back, deciding to keep the candle burning and resigning herself to a sleepless night, but as she gazed at the flickering shadows in the rafters her eyelids slowly closed and she fell into an uneasy doze.

The door crashed open and once again Bara scrambled up, grabbing her knife. A man stood propping himself up on the doorpost. Wisps of white hair escaped from under a shapeless hat and his red face was contorted into an enormous grin. Bara held her knife pointing straight for him, but he had not even seen her. Some incomprehensible song came bubbling from his mouth as he lurched into the room. Suddenly he saw Bara and tried to pull himself straight, but already he had tripped over the prone figure of Dai. The little Welshman leaped up, his fists clenched and his black eyes glittering.

'What the bloody – oh it's you,' he said, kicking the drunkard with his toe. 'Drunken bastard. He is a friend of mine,' he explained politely to Bara. The friend still lay on the floor but he had managed to prop himself up on an elbow.

'He is called Rhys the Drunk,' said Dai. 'I am sorry, but he will not do you any harm.'

'I am indeed delighted to meet you, madam,' said Rhys thickly, attempting to remove his hat and rolling over on his face as he did so.

'You stay there, you boozer,' said the Welshman. 'Sleep it off now, or I'll pour a bucket over you.'

'I want to piss,' said Rhys into the floor.

'Get on with it then, and let us get some sleep, for God's sake man!'

'Not in front of ladies I won't. My ma always said—' He rolled over onto his back.

'What was it she said then? I forget. Oh, she said don't piss in front of the ladies, Rhys. Rhys, she said, don't piss—'

'Oh for Chrissake we heard you the first time then,' screamed Dai. 'Do it out of the window then.'

'Can't get up. Very sorry but I can't—' He rolled over again and immediately fell asleep.

'Let him wet himself,' said Dai, scrabbling with his sacks like a dog making a bed. 'I am very sorry ma'am,' he went on, 'but indeed it is always like this at the Threeday Fair.'

Bara lay back again on her straw, smiling broadly at the ceiling, and she began to tell Tam in her head what had happened. Strange fantasies on the borders of sleep crept into her narration, and again she slept.

This time she leaped as if she had been attacked and in the same instant Con gasped and shrank back in terror. Yet another small dark man had burst into the candlelit room, and no sooner was he inside than he tripped over Dai and fell heavily forward onto the drunken Rhys. Rhys groaned loudly and rolled over, but Dai leaped once again to his feet.

'What the bloody hell this time?' he yelled, shaking his fists at the newcomer.

'I am sorry, I am sorry, indeed I am sorry,' stammered the new arrival, 'but I must get away. He will find me and he is a big man.'

His teeth were chattering with fright as he seized a spare pile of sacking and began feverishly to knot the pieces together.

'What the bloody hell—' repeated Dai, circling the newcomer with his fists still raised. 'It is the middle of the night now and what is it you think you are doing?'

'I must get away from him. He's downstairs, he's looking in all the rooms. I can't go down that way, he'll see me.'

'Who will then? Is the devil who's after you?'

'Very like the devil. A huge big fellow he is.'

'What's he want you for, be Jesus?'

'Oh – well – he thinks I stole his sheep.'

'And did you?'

'Indeed I did not. I only got it mixed up for one of my own.'

He jumped up and pulled aside the sacking on the window to peer down to the street below. 'That'll do, I think,' he muttered. He picked up his pile of knotted sacks and with shaking hands tied one end round a rafter.

'It won't reach the ground, but it will do, God help me.'

He began to thread the sacks out of the window but before he was half done there was a terrible roar from the stairs. The floor shuddered as an enormous red-headed man thundered into the room.

'He must be here,' the man yelled. 'I know he's – ah!' And he caught sight of his quarry's head disappearing over the window ledge down the sack rope to the street.

'I've got you now, sheep-stealer!' he bellowed, taking three gigantic strides to the window. 'Welshman! Taffy!' He placed his

great hands on the sacking and heaved himself over the window-
ledge. There came a terrible rending and a bellow of fear. Uproar
rose from the street below and into the room burst two more small,
dark men. They rushed to the window and leaned out.

'There's a bit of sack left,' said one, leaping over the window ledge.

'Not for me,' said the other, tripping and kicking his way back to
the door.

Dai was twisting angrily this way and that, demanding to know
what was going on.

'Who are they?' whispered Con. 'Are they goblins?'

Both men vanished but the row from the street was unabated.

'I wonder if he's hurt?' said Bara.

'I hope they all are,' said Dai venomously. 'Indeed I hope they are
all dead. And if anyone else comes in this night I'll kill him I will.'

He searched around the corners of the room until he found a loose
board, which he managed to jam against the door.

'Bastards,' he muttered. 'It's worse than any Threeday Fair I ever
knew.'

Rhys groaned and hiccuped. 'Go to sleep, you sodden pig,' yelled
Dai, kicking him in the behind. Then, remembering Bara and his
manners, he turned and bowed and said, 'I am very sorry. You will
not be thinking much of Abergavenny.'

Bara smiled and replied politely that it was a very nice town. Con
was both bewildered and delighted with what he had seen, but he
allowed himself to be settled down without protest. At last the
hubbub in the street subsided, and they all slept.

The road from Abergavenny to Brecon wound along the wide valley
of the Usk, shadowed by the foothills of the Black Moutains on the
one side and the outlying ranges of the Brecon Beacons on the other.
On a dark day it was a sinister track, overhung with trees and in
places falling away to the river below. The clouds were grey and low
and an oppressive silence hung over the valley, broken only by the
clopping of Dark's hooves and the occasional screech of a jay. Con
was subdued and Bara's attempts to make him sing met with no
success. She tried to cheer him by describing the antics of the
previous night, but he remained preoccupied and unamused.

Dark picked his way down to the river, where they ate some meat
and drank a little of Meg's cider. The rushing water swirled and
chattered in the shallows, where Con sat with his legs dangling,
moodily throwing stones.

'Come on,' said Bara, oppressed by his gloom. 'We must get on.'

'I don't like it here,' said Con. He looked round apprehensively as he settled himself on Dark's back.

Two or three miles further they met the trouble he feared.

From time to time they thought they heard a rustling in the thick trees above the road, but they could see nothing. Bara had her weapons half-drawn from the panniers and her hands sweated on the reins. Then round a bend the attack came. Two men rushed down from the trees, two more scrambled up from the scrub on the river bank and three appeared abreast on small ponies across their path. Before she could use them Bara's weapons were knocked from her hands with wooden staves, and Dark's bridle was seized on both sides. Con kicked one of the men in the face before he was dragged from the saddle and tied up. Bara wrenched an arm free and grabbed her spear, the only remaining weapon. She aimed it at the men who were tying up Con, but she dared not throw it for he was rolling and flailing on the ground and she was as likely to hit him as his captors. In a few more seconds it had been knocked from her hand and all her weapons were gone. As she watched Con trussed up and laid over the saddle of one of the ponies she beat her fists helplessly on Dark's neck.

'Don't take him away!' she shouted. 'Don't take him away from me.'

As she began to sob into Dark's mane one of the men came quickly over to her. They all appeared identical, short and dark and dressed in filthy sheepskins.

'Please don't take him away!' Bara whispered, trying to subdue her panic. 'I'll give you anything, anything.'

The man looked at her and spoke haltingly, as if in a foreign tongue.

'We do not take him from you,' he said.'We do not hurt him. You see, nobody has hit him.' She realised this was true. Although Con was tied and laid over the saddle, he had been bound gently and no-one had struck him.

'We do not hurt you either,' the man continued carefully. 'But you must come with us. If you try to get away, then you may be hurt.'

He turned and mounted his pony. Like the other two animals, it was black and shaggy, only half the height of Dark.

'Please let the boy sit up,' said Bara, hearing Con moan. 'He can ride and I promise he won't run away.'

The leader looked doubtful, then he said, 'All right.'

He spoke in Welsh to his companions and Con's feet were untied. He was set astride the leader's pony, on the front of the saddle between the man's arms. Two of the party still held Dark's bridle, two riders rode in front, and the rest followed. After a few hundred yards they came to a rough stone pack-bridge, whose slippery surface appeared only just above the level of the river. The little ponies stepped across it without fear, but Dark stopped, his ears back, disliking the rushing water and the broken stones.

'Don't beat him,' said Bara. 'He'll go in his own time. Just coax him.'

The leader looked back at her and there was the flicker of a smile on his bearded face.

'You do not need to teach us about horses,' he said. 'And yours is a noble beast.' Bara saw that his men were gentle with Dark, speaking softly to him and easing him quietly onto the first stone.

'He is a good animal,' said the leader, watching. Then he whinnied softly and Dark pricked his ears as he stepped carefully to the next stone. Bara patted the horse's neck and whispered to him.

'You are good to him,' said the leader approvingly. 'You love him.'

Bara smiled and nodded, coaxing Dark on until he was over. One of the men at the bridle grinned up at Bara and said something in Welsh.

'He says the horse believes what you tell him,' translated the leader. 'He has – he has –'

'Trust?' said Bara.

'Yes. Trust. Come.'

They formed a single file up the narrow path onto the foot hills of the Beacons. The bare hillside lifted steeply out of the valley, but the leader took an easier path round the shoulder of the range. The ground was rocky, the grass thin, the great mountains rose blackly above them. The leader turned in his saddle to Bara, who rode just behind.

'The Beacons,' he said, pointing to the peaks. 'Where we live.'

They climbed for three hours, sometimes picking their way up stony paths, sometimes descending to cross a stream, sometimes riding across plateaux of heather. Slowly, the details of the peaks became clear, and Bara saw that they were heading for a cleft between the highest points. As they approached she began to notice more and more sheep. Some were browsing on their own in small groups, some were in larger flocks, some were in the charge of a shepherd, who waved to them and urged his dog along the mountainside to greet them. 'They are ours,' said the leader. 'Our men. Our dogs. Our sheep.'

The day grew darker and the uplands were cold; the peaks ahead loomed high and forbidding. Con had fallen asleep in the saddle leaning against the leader, and the man let him be. Bara's first relief at the gentle treatment they had received was giving way to fear. What could these men want with her and Con? They had not touched her, they had not robbed her, they had not even looked in the panniers. Yet they must have had spies after her, they must have ridden many miles over rough country in order to cut her off. Was it her they wanted, or Con? The wind bit through her and she shivered, but whether with cold or fear she did not know.

At last they had ridden through the rocky cleft. They emerged at the upper lip of a broad grassy basin, almost ringed by mountains, but with openings at either end. The valley was about a mile wide in both directions, and dotted white with sheep. At the lowest point was a village of round huts, closely packed and tightly stockaded. Smoke drifted from the pointed roofs, and even at this distance a faint smell of cooking made the men sniff the air and set off down the rough slope at a reckless trot.

As they descended the half-mile of grass, Bara saw a crowd begin to gather at the gate of the stockade. More and more people arrived and soon they had spilt out of the gate onto the slopes of the valley. As they came within shouting distance the leader raised his staff and called out in Welsh. There was a faint answering cry and the crowd began to move slowly towards them up the slope. As they approached, the leader roused Con and stood him up on the saddle for all to see. It seemed to Bara that a sigh of satisfaction floated across the valley, but no-one spoke. When they came to the nearest groups the crowd parted for them, and as they rode in silence up the path that was cleared all eyes were on Con. So it was him they wanted. Bara clenched her teeth and vowed that this time she would not fail him.

At the gate of the stockade stood an old man. He too was in sheepskins, but he wore a band of iron round his head and a white beard flowed over his chest. The leader of Bara's group raised his staff in greeting and the two men exchanged words in Welsh. Then the old man took Bara's bridle and led them through the gate. He smiled up at her.

'Welcome to the Shepherds' Kingdom,' he said.

They were led through a maze of huts to a central clearing, where the old man stopped. Standing high on a plinth in the centre of the open ground was the huge stone head of a monster. The teeth and the eye-sockets were worn but well-defined, and there were rough excrescences along the top of the skull. Bara felt she had seen something like it in an old book of her great-grandfather's at home, but she could not remember the picture clearly. She turned round and saw to her astonishment that both the old man and her captor were kneeling before the stone monster with their foreheads bent to the ground. As the old man raised his head he saw her amazement.

'It is our Dragon,' he said, as he rose stiffly from his knees. 'It is the Dragon of our Kingdon. You must learn to venerate it.'

Bara said nothing, half angry and half amused at the idea that she should abase herself before a stone. She and Con were led off and shown to a large hut on the edge of the open circle. There were raised stone beds round the walls, covered in sheepskins and heather, and there were three large wooden chests arranged round the central fire. The fire smouldered on a flat stone, its smoke wafting about the hut until it finally escaped through the hole at the apex of the roof.

'Be comfortable,' said the old man. 'This is one of our best houses, for you are important people.'

Bara's heart thudded.

'Why?' she asked hoarsely.

But the old man only spread his hands and smiled. He shouted something in Welsh, bringing a man and a woman hastily into the room. The man was like all the other men, except that he was even smaller, but the woman was remarkable for the length and luxuriance of her black hair. It fell in shining swathes over her shoulders and down her body almost to her thighs, and she moved as though she were conscious of it. They both bowed to Bara, who held Con by the hand.

'They are your servants,' said the old man.

'And my guards?' said Bara angrily.

'If you like. I did not say so. But we have trailed you all the way from the plague town and we would not like to lose you now.'

So they had been followed all the way from Monmouth.

'Why do you want us?' Bara asked again, holding Con's hand more tightly. But as before the old man only spread his hands and smiled.

'You are our guests,' was all he would say.

The little man was introduced as Fen and the woman as Fanwy. Both of them smiled and set to making Bara and Con comfortable.

They brought hot water in wooden tubs, and they brought clean woollen shirts and sheepskins. Neither could speak any English, but as she combed out Bara's tangled golden hair Fanwy made her admiration plain. Fen made devilish faces at Con as he washed him all over, and Con made ferocious faces back at him. Suddenly Fen exclaimed and jumped backwards. He began talking excitedly to Fanwy, and Bara realized that he had found the scar under the hair on Con's forehead. He held the hair back gently and he and Fanwy exchanged rapid words. Suddenly Fanwy rushed out of the hut and Fen smiled broadly at Bara. She and Con were bewildered, but in a moment Fanwy came running in again, followed by the old man. They parted Con's hair again and showed the scar. It was red and crinkled and hideous, but the old man touched it without distaste and spoke to Fen. Then he backed two steps away from Con, and bowed low. Fen and Fanwy did the same, while Bara and Con stared at them in astonishment.

'He is perfect,' said the old man, smiling at Bara.

'But it's only a horrid old scar,' said Con.

The old man smiled and stroked Con's white hair forward over his brow again. Without saying any more he left.

Fanwy followed him and returned in a few minutes with wooden platters piled high with mutton and potatoes. Suddenly Bara and Con realized they were famished. After they had eaten, they were full and warm and satisfied enough to push anxiety from their minds. They lay down wearily on their sheepskin beds and before darkness fell both were asleep.

They discovered the next day that they were allowed to wander as they pleased within the confines of the village. The inhabitants were a quick, bustling people who moved sharply and turned fast and seemed always in a hurry. They were very friendly, forever smiling at Bara and stroking Con's hair, but there was something about their smiles that made Bara uneasy. They were complacent, proprietary smiles, and they held some secret she could not fathom.

If ever she and Con wanted to walk on the hillside Fen would be ready to go with them. He was a sprightly, bright-eyed little man, constantly pulling faces at Con, and always ready to turn somersaults or walk on his hands for Con's amusement. Often they would go to the stables to visit Dark, where he towered above the little black ponies, or they would walk out to find him on the mountainside, where he browsed on the rough grass. Sometimes when they were out on the hill Bara would think they were alone, but if she looked around carefully she could always find Fen observing them from some distant rock or bush. Fanwy spent her working time between the kitchens and the hut, but most of the day and half the night – so it seemed to Bara – she simply sat combing her magnificent hair. And as she combed she smiled the small, satisfied smile of a woman who is pleased with herself.

Bara and Con explored the village thoroughly. Outside the main stockade, but still heavily guarded, were two great barns, one used for grain and one for hides and wool. There was a tanning shed, where the stench was overpowering, and there was a tailors' room, where hides and skins and wool were made into clothes. Behind Bara's hut, against the stockade, was the long kitchen, where mutton was continually roasted and boiled. There was no other meat, and there were no other clothes than those made of wool and sheepskin. Bara slowly realized that the entire life of the place was based on the sheep. Wool, leather, meat, and seasonal milk came from the flocks. Nothing but grain and vegetables were brought up from Brecon, where they were exchanged for the products of the sheep. She also noticed a total absence of the usual useful debris from the old world. There were no car seats, no wire or cable, no freezers or fridges, no corrugated iron, no asbestos, no plastic sheeting or cartons or buckets or bowls; indeed, no plastic of any kind. Of course the heavier objects would be very difficult to drag into these high, remote moutains. But the smaller, lighter things? Could it be that these people would have nothing to do with the old world? That they regarded its products as corrupting? There seemed to be nothing in the entire village that was not made of wood, stone, leather, hempen rope, or wool. The flocks dotted the hillside and moutains as far as one could see, the remote sound of bleating mingled all day with the barks of dogs and the whinny of ponies. During the early days of May the sun shone and the moutains were clear and wide. If she had not been nagged by constant anxiety Bara felt she could have been happy in this place.

On the 14th of May, Con would be six. Bara knew that May had come but she had no idea of the date, and could find no trace of calendar reckoning in the village. So she picked a sunny day at random and told Con he was six. She went to the tailor's workshop where she begged some strips of leather, with which she plaited him a broad belt, and she lit six tapers in the hut that evening. Fen was good-humoured, but bewildered, so Bara assumed that birthdays were not acknowledged by these people.

They had noticed several times on their walks that there was some kind of alignment across the valley, between two blocks of stone which stood in clefts in the moutains, facing each other and rather to the south of the village. There was a large round hole in each stone, and Bara found that if she positioned herself carefully on a fine morning she could see the sun gleaming through the eastern stone, and in the evening through the western. This must be an alignment on the sun, which appeared to pass through the point in the village where the dragon's head stood. On Midsummer Day, Bara supposed, the rising sun would perfectly fill the eastern hole. One morning she took a stick and drew in the dust a plan of the world, marking the equator and the position of Britain. Then she looked questioningly at Fen, hoping that he would explain the alignment. But he looked puzzled, then he smiled and shrugged, and added a few curly lines to improve her pattern.

'No,' said Con, frowning. 'Like this.' He stretched out his arms with opposite hands pointing to the two distant stones.

'Yes,' said Bara. 'East-west.'

'No,' said Con, still frowning. 'Like this.'

He took the stick and drew a line roughly south-east and north-west, from the point where Bara's equator bisected the eastern edge of the globe, to the position of Britain.

'It's not east,' he said. 'It faces east and – and – '

'South.'

'Yes. East and south.' Bara stared at him.

'How do you know?' she said. As usual he only shrugged.

'I just know,' he said.

As he turned away Bara saw the old man approach. He was staring angrily at her diagram in the dust. He stood for a moment looking down at it then he rubbed it out fiercely with his bare foot.

'That is not for you,' he said. 'Such knowledge is forbidden to all but the Elders.' Bara turned her back, exasperated. 'He's absolutely barmy,' she said to Con.

The old man glanced at Bara, looked away, then suddenly turned his head back to her again. He was staring at a row of yellow buttons down the front of her shirt. He took a step forward and held one of them in his gnarled hands while he examined it, then he pursed his lips in anger and his face flushed.

'You cannot have those here,' he said, tightly controlling his voice. 'Those are impure things.'

Bara started back angrily, but he still held her shirt with one hand and kept his eyes fixed on the buttons. The other hand he extended towards Fen, who immediately passed him a knife. Before she could move again Fen grasped her from behind, and with four strokes of the knife the old man slashed off the four yellow buttons. Bara's anger subsided in bewilderment. Then suddenly she understood. The buttons were plastic, from the old time, and therefore contaminated, unthinkable. The old man held the buttons out to Fen.

'From the High Pass,' he said. 'Throw them from the High Pass tonight. And remember the prayer.'

Every morning and evening there was a ceremony in the central circle, around the stone dragon's head. Often Bara struggled to remember exactly where she had seen the picture of such a head, and what its name could be. She had certainly seen it somewhere, in one of those mouldering books at home. Then one morning, with no effort at all, the old picture and its caption swam lazily into focus in her mind. This was the head of a fossil dinosaur, and its name was Iguanadon.

The ceremonies were always conducted by the old man, dressed in a white woollen robe and carrying his staff. He would begin with an obeisance to the Dragon, and the crowd would follow him. Then he would turn to the eastern stone in the morning, or the western stone at dusk, and each time he would sing in a thin wailing voice, waiting for the crowd to join in responses. Bara could not accustom herself to the absurdity of the fossil dinosaur, but there was something weird in the singing which chilled her, and she stopped attending.

By the time they had been about four weeks with the Shepherds, and her anxieties had sunk almost to the back of her mind, Bara began to sense a growing urgency and excitement among the people of the village. At the same time Fen became very subdued, as if he had something on his mind. Often Bara caught him looking at her reflectively, but he would always turn his head away without smiling. Then one day in early June he brought Bara a stick with eighteen notches scored into the side. As he stared gravely at her he scored out a notch at a time with his finger. When he had scored out the last notch he put his hand up to cover his face. Then he looked to see if she understood him. But Bara could make nothing of his demonstration and she shook her head. He tried speaking, very softly and slowly, but she could not understand. She listened closely, aware from his strained face that he had something important to tell her. There were eighteen – eighteen something. Days? Sheep? People? She could not tell, nor could she understand why he crossed the notches off. Then he heard Fanwy coming and he turned sharply away, thrusting the stick under his sheepskin.

Some two weeks after Fen had shown Bara the stick there was a ceremony which lasted all night. The day had been full of inexplicable bustle. The people were so busy they forgot to smile at Bara or to stroke Con's hair, and for the first time they both felt ignored. Bara was sharply reminded that they were captives, who did not belong. Fen continued to watch and attend to them, but even he was abstracted. Fanwy had vanished to the kitchens, where she could be seen moving sulkily among the pots and stoves. Clearly she preferred the role of lady's maid to that of kitchen hand, for when she attended to Bara she had plenty of time to comb her hair.

On the evening of the ceremony a ring of fires was lit round the dragon's head. Bara and Con were preparing to go out and watch when the old man appeared in the doorway. He was wearing a red woollen robe, and his iron coronet had been replaced with gold. He had discarded his plain wooden staff and in its stead he carried a magnificently carved and jewelled bishop's crook.

'I would not have you think you were forgotten', he said solemnly. 'Tonight we hold our fire ceremony for the healing of the sick. We know that fire is cleansing and will drive sickness away. It is exactly one week from the summer solstice.' He looked at Bara hard, but she could not interpret his expression. He dropped his eyes to Con and smiled. 'You may both observe the ritual if you wish,' he said. Con stepped forward and put a finger on the carved crook.

'It is from the old religion,' said the priest. 'It is very old and very holy.'

Con smiled up at him and nodded. The priest felt for Con's scar with his finger and murmured some words in Welsh. Then he was gone.

Night had fallen and the drums were beating insistently when Bara and Con reached the edge of the circle. The drum-skins were stretched over wooden frames and the drummers were tuning them carefully by holding them up to the fire which encircled the Dragon. Opposite the drummers seven people were propped up in a row, two old men, three women, and two children. The girls who attended them made sure their sheepskins were wrapped warmly round them, and that they had water when they wanted it. The priest had abased himself before the Dragon, where he lay absolutely still, while the whole population of the village arranged themselves into a jostling circle. Suddenly the drums struck up in concert and the crowd was instantly hushed. As there was no moon the people could see each other only in the light of the flickering fire. Slowly the priest rose and spread his arms to the Dragon. In a shrill voice he began to intone. The drums beat softly and the crowd murmured responses. Then the priest began to move slowly, first from one foot to the other, and then in a shuffling circle. The drums beat louder, in a more intricate rhythm, and the priest stamped slowly round the circle of fire, passing his hands through the flames. The drums altered their rhythm again and as the priest raised his crook high in the air the crowd began to sing. To Bara's ear it was a strange, tuneless sound, thin-throated and far away, but she saw that many of the singers had their eyes closed in rapture. At a wave from the priest the seven sick people were brought forward to the edge of the fire-circle, each carried on a rough bier, face towards the flames. Bara thought they all looked frightened and ill, and ought to have been in bed.

Suddenly the drums burst into thunderous sound. Con jumped with fright, then smiled shamefacedly up at Bara and turned to watch again. The priest stood on the far side of the circle, with his head thrown back and his eyes closed. His arms were spread above the sick, and he stood absolutely still while the drums crashed behind him. The singing had stopped, and there was no sound or movement in the crowd. Only the drummers moved and only the drums sounded. Bara felt Con's grip tighten on her hand. Still there was nothing but the beat of the drums. Something would have to break. A man leaped out of the crowd, his teeth bared in a contorted face. His eyes were dilated, his breath came in gasps. He crouched for a moment in the circle, then he jumped into the air and began to throw himself into rigid postures. Still the crowd was silent and still the priest did not move. The boom of the drums and the stamping of the dancer filled the darkness. Another man flung himself out of the crowd. He too had wild eyes and he did not seem to see the first dancer, who was now leaping and stamping to the increasing rhythm of the drums. The newcomer flung himself round the circle like an acrobat, shrieking after every somersault and tumble. Soon there were two more, and then another. The space outside the fire-circle was filled with frenzied dancers while the drums beat louder and faster and the priest stood rigid with his arms raised. The fires were now smouldering a luminous red, and their light was steadier. For a long time the dancers stamped and writhed and twisted. Their bodies were streaming with sweat but they whirled inexhaustibly. The insistent beat of the drums became almost unbearable to Bara, and Con had his hands over his ears.

'Shall we go?' she whispered.

'No,' he hissed.' 'I want to see.'

Then one of the dancers fell, his body exhausted. In a matter of minutes all five were lying prone. Then at last the priest moved, taking a step to one side, and as he did so the thudding of the drums dropped to a muffled roll. Still with his arms held high he stepped into the glowing embers. Bara stifled a cry of horror and Con stuffed his fist in his mouth. Slowly and deliberately the priest stepped through the fire. His head was still thrown back and his arms outstretched. No sound came from him or from the crowd. When he had walked the circle of fire around, he slowly lowered his head and then his arms. His face winced with pain as his rigid shoulders moved again, but at once he composed himself and murmured some words. Very softly the crowd responded. Then from the sinking fire he picked a firebrand, red-hot with a few small flames flickering at the end. He approached the oldest of the sick men and held the torch above the old man's forehead. As he brought it down to touch the skin a wild scream split the silence. Con saw Cantor's iron approach his forehead on Bela's Knap.

'No!' he screamed, 'No, no, no!'

The crowd turned on him in fury. Bara had never before seen anger so twist men's faces. The priest paused and raised his head. He spoke a few angry words in Welsh, then rough hands seized Bara and Con and dragged them away. Women and children spat in their faces as they were buffeted to their hut. There they were thrown onto their sheepskins and left with Fen as their guard. Con was sobbing violently as he lay in Bara's arms. She would not dare to think what they might do to him now. As soon as the angry crowd left, Fen darted from his position at the door and knelt beside them. His small face was desperate as he tried to think what he might do to help them. Then he turned away to stoke up the fire, and in a few moments he had ewe's milk heated up. Bara smiled gratefully and tried to persuade Con to sip. He quietened a little, and between his sobs he drank some of the warm milk. Bara knew he was reliving his branding and she held him tight for over an hour until he slept.

In the morning the priest came to the hut. He was in his white robe again, with the iron band for a crown and a plain staff in his hand. But this time there was no bow and no smile.

'Because of the boy's cry,' he said, 'the sick will not heal. The purifying power of fire was obstructed in its work.'

Bara had been frightened, but now anger rushed through her like a storm and she leaped for him.

'It's rubbish,' she shouted. 'It's all a load of stupid childish mumbo-jumbo.'

The old man glared, suppressing his anger and moving no muscle.

'I am not accustomed to being shouted at,' he said quietly. 'Nor do I listen to blasphemy.'

Bara did not heed him.

'It's so stupid,' she cried. 'How can you call it Con's fault? He was right to scream, he knows you only *burn* people with fire, you don't *heal* them.'

The old man bit his lip and unclenched his hands slowly. Bara realized for the first time how angry he was.

'You are a child,' he said. 'An ill-educated stranger.' His voice was rigidly controlled. 'If it were not for these things I would have you bound and whipped before the people. As to the boy, because he is what he is, and because the time is short, I have ordered that he be forgiven.'

Bara stepped back, her heart racing with sudden fear.

'What do you mean? Because of what he is? *What* time is short?'

But the priest had bowed and left.

Three days of brilliant weather followed, but they had no effect in raising Bara's courage. She was frightened, and she hardly slept. The people of the village smiled as before, but always she sensed some double meaning in their looks. In spite of what he had done, Con was still fondled and admired, which only increased Bara's unease. She would not have expected such interest in a child who had ruined a holy ceremony and prevented the sick from growing well. But Con glowed with the attention he received and he was full of smiles for anyone who heeded him.

'I like all these black little people,' he told Bara, 'and they like me.'

As he could not talk to them he would smile and laugh and shake his hair and show how high he could jump or how fast he could run. Bara noticed that his blue eyes and his silver-white hair were very attractive to these dark, brown-eyed people. Sometimes one of the women would lift Con's fringe and look at the scar, muttering low words to her companions. When Fanwy found time from brushing her own dark tresses she would smilingly insist on brushing Con's, working away at his tangled fleece until he fidgeted so violently she had to let him go.

The village seemed very busy again. There was an air of expectancy and purpose in the way people went about their business, just as before the Fire Healing. Day after golden day of June the sun shone in a cloudless blue, and the mountain air was bright as silver. The wide green valley, the high peaks, the bleating of the scattered flocks – these should have made a scene of perfect peace, but Bara was now so agitated she could enjoy none of it. She was short-tempered with Con, she suddenly loathed mutton, her sleep was full of turbulent dreams, her longing for the comfort of Tam's arms was almost more than she could bear. Fen would sometimes watch her smiling at vacancy as she thought of Tam's square, and warm body and the perpetual expression of faint puzzlement on his face. She felt alone and helpless. *Because of what he is. Because the time is short.* What had the old man meant? He was an eerie being, with his civilized behaviour and his barbaric beliefs. He was a savage, whose cultivated manners were simply a wrapping for barbarism.

One evening Bara sat on the wooden chest, clutching its sides with her fingers and staring into the small fire in the hut. Something was about to happen. As she sat she bit her lip and hurt her knuckles with her grip on the chest. She watched herself, as fear slowly seeped through her limbs, melting the strength of her muscles and paralysing her thought.

But nothing happened. Then Fen came bursting through the skins across the door, letting in a flood of sunshine. He glanced at Bara, then began to make up the fire. In another moment Con came plunging in, cracking a whip and imitating the cries of carters. He galloped round the hut, he cracked his whip at Bara, he leaped over Fen's crouching body, and he rushed out again. Fen laughed, but he stopped abruptly when he saw the tears on Bara's cheeks. He came and squatted in front of her, gazing up with a frown on his small face. She only bowed her head and shook it in despair. As her shoulders slumped Fen leaped up to support her. He spoke softly in Welsh and she tried to smile at him, but the effort of responding was too much for her. She turned away and rubbed her eyes. Fen moved rapidly over to his bed by the door. He fumbled under the skins for a moment, then he glanced quickly outside and returned to Bara. Once again he held the notched stick in front of her. She stared at it, noticing that he had cut lines through all the notches but two. Perhaps that meant two days? Fen was whispering urgently, but Bara could understand nothing. He covered his face with his hands in despair, then stood up with his arms folded, staring into the fire. Suddenly he seemed to have decided something, for he turned slowly to Bara and held up two fingers. Two fingers, two notches. Then he raised her gently and stood moving his body before her. Suddenly she realized he was representing the act of sex, and she leaped back angrily. But he sprang forward and covered her mouth with his hard hand. At the same time he shook his head vigorously and held up his two fingers again. Bara sank down on the bench, understanding at last. In two days' time she was to be raped.

But he had not finished. He was holding his hand about two feet off the ground; then he began to gallop round the room, cracking an imaginary whip. So now he was talking of Con. He stopped in front of her and looked at her steadily. Then slowly he drew his hand across his throat. Blackness rushed at Bara from all the corners of the room and she fell heavily across the chest. When she came round, she was aware of a stabbing pain in her shoulder. She was lying on her bed and Fanwy was bending over her, smiling her soft smile. Something cool was laid on her cheek. Fen began to demonstrate how Bara must have tripped and fallen on the edge of the fire, but his manner was frenzied, and half-conscious as she was, Bara could see he was utterly overwrought.

In the afternoon the priest came. He bowed to Bara, who lay stiff with fear on her bed and made no move to greet him.

'I am sorry about your accident,' he said, 'but Fanwy's medicine will heal the pain very soon. In two days it is our great festival, the Summer Solstice. This is when we ensure prosperity and fertility for our flocks in the coming years. It is time to prepare yourself and your son for the honour that will be done you at our ritual.'

Bara clutched her sheepskin and opened her mouth to shout at him, but she caught sight of Fen's face, contracted with terror, and she remembered his life was in her hands. He would almost certainly be killed if his betrayal became known. So she stifled her cry and said nothing.

'You are not pleased?' asked the priest, surprised.

'I'm sorry. My cheek and my shoulder hurt a lot.' Bara forced out the words then turned her back on him. No doubt it was he who would rape her, and he who would cut Con's throat.

She say very still, trying by the stillness of her body to calm the confusion of fears that swarmed through her. An escape must be planned, and quickly. Whatever the dangers, anything was better than the fate that awaited them in the Shepherd's Kingdom. First she must find Dark, to see that he was near the stockade and not too far up the mountain. Once they had reached and mounted him he would easily outstrip these little mountain ponies.

When Fen brought them food in their hut at midday Con showed an intense interest in Bara's burn. Fanwy had dressed it with grease, which made it look red and raw. Three times she had to show it to Con before he was satisfied. Then he said, 'She shouldn't have put that stuff on.'

Bara stared at him. 'What do you mean? How do you know?'

'Oh, I just know.'

He lost interest, and ran out into the sun bleating like a lamb.

In the afternoon Bara walked casually round the village, trying to appear unconcerned. She strolled to the gate and pointed out into the valley, smiling at the guard. He glanced behind her and seeing Fen was nearby he let her go. Up the grassy slopes she found Dark, who came plodding slowly with his head down at the sound of her whistle. She laid her cheek against his neck, rubbing his nose and pulling his ears. He lowered his head and nuzzled her shoulder. Then she took his rope and led him down the mountainside, passing Fen on the way. She had half-expected him to stop her but he stood aside and nodded vigorously, as if he approved of her action. She led Dark into some scrub near the stockade and as she pretended to sit for a rest on the grass she tethered his rope to a low thorn. She sat for a while, praying the rope would pass unnoticed and that Dark would not tug on it and complain. Then as she rose she started violently, for Fen loomed up on the far side of the thorn. He must have seen what she was doing and she waited wretchedly for him to untie the rope. But he did nothing. After looking at her gravely for a moment, he turned suddenly and walked away. Bara's spirits soared as she ran leaping after him over the grass. She knew now that he would not hinder their escape, and she wanted to hug him and have him turn somersaults for her. But as she drew near he whipped round, his face twisted with anger, motioning her fiercely away and hissing some words in Welsh. She stopped dead, realizing how stupid she had been. If he was to help them he must not be implicated in any friendship with her. He was endangering himself enough already.

Bara composed herself again and began to stroll casually round the stockade. It was a long sunny walk, through lush grass and patches of scrub, but her attention was solely on the fencing. She had no eyes for the purple peaks around her, or the white speckle of the sheep on the hillside, or the cloudless summer sky. All that mattered now was to find a weak point in the stockade, and to identify its relationship to the buildings within. She marked one or two possible places where the stakes seemed further apart or the palings loose, then, when she had completed her round, she smiled at the guard and entered again by the main gate. He looked keenly after her, but she hoped more in admiration than in suspicion. That very night they must get away. If they could force the stockade and find Dark the escape should not be too difficult. Fanwy often left the hut in the evening, and Bara was now certain that Fen would give them some opportunity to slip away. They would have only the clothes they wore, but at least by the evening of the summer solstice they would still be alive. She shied away from the possibility that they might be caught. They must get away, and they would.

She stopped dead as she turned the corner to their hut. For standing in a line in front of the door were four guards, armed with staves and daggers. Between two of them stood Con, his eyes wide with fear. Bara flew to him and the guards did not prevent her from kneeling beside him.

'They keep pointing to the priest's house,' he said miserably. 'I have to go there.'

'All right. I'll come with you.'

Bara was shaking with fear, but she steadied her voice for Con's sake. What had gone wrong? Fen had said there were two days yet.

Then two of the men placed their hands gently on her shoulders. The two who held Con began to move, urging him in front of them, but when Bara tried to step after him she was held firmly back.

'But I must go with him,' she cried.

For reply one of the men pointed in the opposite direction and spoke in Welsh. Con screamed as he was pushed forward.

'Mam! Mam! Where are they taking me? Come with me Mam!'

Bara struggled to reach him but she was firmly held.

'Con, it's all right, it's all right,' she called, her own voice breaking.

'But I want you, I want you!'

His cries died away as he disappeared among the huts, and Bara found herself edged firmly in the opposite direction. She clenched her teeth and fought to hold down her panic. There were two days yet, two days; she must hang on to that.

She was brought up sharply in front of a hut she had never seen before. It lay behind a long wattle screen and was more elaborate than any other building in the village. There was a gabled wooden porch, carved and painted, and a thatch cut in an intricate pattern along the roofcrest. Carved wooden models of the dragon's head faced each other along the length of the thatch. In the doorway stood an old woman, wrinkled like a tortoise. Her back was bent, and a wizened arm clutching a staff protruded from her long blue cloak. She leered at Bara and stood aside for her to enter. The interior was very dark, without the customary fire, and there was an unpleasant musty smell. Carved pillars supported the roof, white sheepskins lay on the beds, but the room was dominated by an enormous wooden chest, carved in an intricate tracery of flowers and fruit and corn. It was brilliantly coloured in green and gold, quite as magnificent in its way as the bishop's crook used in the Fire Ceremony. As Bara stood gazing round she heard the door sharply locked from the outside. She spun round, and found herself face to face with the crone, who grinned toothlessly at her alarmed face.

'It's all right,' she said in lilting English. 'I am not as frightening as I look.'

Bara sat down heavily on a bench by the wall.

'I see I'm a prisoner,' she said.

'You are my honoured guest,' replied the old woman. 'My name is Skene.'

'Honoured guests aren't usually locked into their rooms,' said Bara angrily.

'The great moment of your life is at hand, my dear. We would not wish to lose you.'

Bara's mouth went dry.

'How soon?' she whispered.

'The summer solstice. The day after tomorrow.'

Bara dropped her head in her hands.

'Here, drink this,' said the crone, holding out a steaming silver bowl.

'What is it?'

'Just milk. Hot milk with a posset.'

'To poison me?' said Bara, pressing back against the wall. 'Or to drug me?'

'Tut-tut, my dear. Neither. You are far too valuable to be poisoned or drugged. It will make you feel calmer, that's all.'

'Where's Con?'

'He's quite safe, I promise you. He's with our Priest King and he will be well looked after.'

'Is he valuable too, then?'

'Oh yes, you both are.'

'Why?'

'Ah. Drink this.'

Bara covered her face with her hands.

'I want to see him,' she said.

'You will see him again. I promise you. Drink, it will help.'

Despairingly Bara took the bowl in her hands and drank. Now what would happen to them? Her plan was in ruins. She was locked in this hut, Con was under guard on the other side of the village, Fen was no longer in charge to overlook their escape. She dropped the bowl on the ground and walked unsteadily over to one of the beds, where she flung herself down and gave herself up to despair. Her body was aching with sobs and the sheepskin was wet with tears before she cried herself to sleep.

When she awoke she could not tell if it was day or night. There were no windows in the hut, the door was still shut, and two smoky lamps burned on each side of the great chest. A plate of cold mutton and potato stood by her bed, but the sight sickened her. Her stomach felt like a ball of stone. She knew she must have been heavily drugged, or she could never have slept. The old woman was rocking to and fro on a bench in a corner, hugging herself with her arms. She grinned as Bara raised herself onto an elbow.

'How do you feel, my dear?' she croaked. 'You have had a long sleep. Behind that partition you will find a good clean earth-closet.'

'I don't want it. What time is it?'

'Early evening.'

'Which day?' Bara sat up abruptly, clutching the sides of the bed.

'Which day? Two nights before the great day.' The crone gazed abstractedly at one of the smoking lamps. 'I had my great day too,' she said. 'The Priest King and I did our duty for our people and we honoured the Dragon. He was good to us. The flocks multiplied, the pasture grew green far into the autumn, the winter was gentle, the lambs were many in the spring. The people showed their gratitude.'

'How?' said Bara, drawn against her will into the old woman's memories.

'How? They made me Guardian of the Treasures. They gave me this lovely house and they made me Guardian. Many, many years I've lived here, guarding the Holy Chest, and every year I look after the – the beautiful girls who are brought to me at the summer solstice.'

The old woman heaved herself up and hobbled across the room. She bent to run her bony hand along Bara's golden hair. Her intention was kind, but Bara shrank away, detesting her touch.

'You are very beautiful,' said Skene. 'You and your son are the most beautiful we have ever had. And he is branded as the son of a king. Together you will make a wonderful year for us, and your honour will be great among the people.'

She crept back to her seat, but Bara did not see her, for she had buried her face in her bed again. She wrenched tufts of wool from the sheepskin and bit the leather underneath. She needed some violent action, she wanted to fling the old bitch to the ground, to kick with her feet at the bolted door, to hurl the lamps onto the sheepskins and set the place ablaze. But this was exactly what she must not do, for it could only result in a more rigorous guard. So she turned and twisted on the bed, trying to devise some plan of escape which had even a remote possibility of success. The hut was impregnable. If it were physically broken down the noise would be so great the whole village would be roused. There was no window, no chimney, no access except the bolted door to the world outside. And the door opened only when the guard brought food. And he was a man, and armed. And she had no weapon. And Con was guarded on the other side of the village. It was hopeless. She sat up and rubbed her eyes.

'Have I got to stay in this room for another two nights and a day?' she said.

'It is a privilege.'

'But there's no light. There's no sun. I want to go out. I want to see my son.'

'You will see him.'

'When?'

'On the great day. Tonight you will sleep well again and on midsummer eve tomorrow we will make you beautiful for the High King.'

Bara gripped one of the carved pillars, tightening her throat against the nausea which swept through her. But she said nothing, for her only chance was to dissemble and retain the friendship of this old witch. Antagonizing her would mean stricter control – and there was something else. For all her rational upbringing there lurked in Bara a fear of this wizened crone. The was no telling what her ugly powers might be, and it was safer to have her friendship than her enmity. So she looked round the hut and said:

'Well, what am I going to do all night and all day?'

'To do? Well now. Do you play chess?'

'*Chess*?' Bara was so astonished she could only gape.

'Yes, chess. Ah well, never mind, no-one plays chess now.' Skene shrugged resignedly.

'But I can,' said Bara. 'At least I could once, a bit.'

Skene's eyes lit up and her face split into an empty grin.

'That is wonderful.'

She heaved herself up, and for the first time it occurred to Bara that this crinkled bag of bones was a real person, with skills and hates and loves and even a real past of her own. Skene shuffled over to one of the plain chests and lifted the lid.

'There,' she said, leering with pleasure.

On the bottom of the empty chest stood a large wooden chess set, polished to a shine by the rubbing of countless fingers. The board was made of two roughly jointed rectangles, the black squares stained, the white left in natural wood. It stood all ready set up for a game, and the old woman had only to lift it without disturbing the arrangement. Her face was still lit with pleasure as she carried it carefully over to her bed, and motioned Bara to sit on the far side. Bara had almost forgotten her danger in her astonishment. She sat down as she was bid and bent her mind to remembering what Kate had once taught her.

'I always play black,' said Skene, 'that is, if you don't mind. At least, I always used to,' she added. 'I haven't played for years and years.'

There in the dim smoky hut they sat, hour after hour, planning and plotting and manoeuvering, enmeshed in the weird patterns of the game. After an hour or so, during which Skene had collected half of Bara's pieces, Bara began to remember what could be done; the moves shed their rust and shone in her mind. Occasionally the old woman glanced at her in surprise.

'You can play,' she said once. And after a long time she added, 'I've lost count of the years since I had such a game. We played often in my youth.'

'Was that here?' asked Bara, as they drank the milk the guard had brought in.

'No, not here.'

'Where then?'

'I belong here.'

'But not always?'

'You ask too many questions. This is my home and my people. They have honoured me.'

'I know all that,' said Bara in irritation. 'But where did you live before you came here?'

'You are too persistent.'

But Bara had started a train of thoughts leading back over half a century, and she knew that in the old this is not easily deflected. So she waited, and after a few minutes Skene spoke again.

'If you really wish to know,' she said, 'I was born in the Marches, in Shropshire – oh, so long ago. My father grew fruit in the summer and root-crops in the winter. Early on summer mornings we would take our stuff in the cart to Ludlow market – oh dear, an old woman's memories are very long.'

She rubbed a watery eye and shook her head.

'But how did you come here?' asked Bara.

'I was taken from the fields where I was working. I was a fine looking girl with long fair hair. They like them fair you know, these little black people.' Suddenly she pushed the chess away and rose stiffly.

'But it was a great honour,' she said fiercely. 'A great honour.'

'Yes,' said Bara softly, watching her.

'I gave these people a prosperous year, one of the best they ever knew, and they have held me in the highest respect.' She straightened her bent shoulders. 'I am Guardian of the Treasures,' she said.

The long games of chess had exhausted them both, so after a hot meal of lamb and carrots Bara was glad to lie back on her bed. The brief respite was over and again she felt cold with foreboding. Somehow in the night she must get out. If only she could find a loose stave of wood she might be able to kill the guard when he brought them food. Or perhaps she could seize his knife. Plans of escape churned in her head, some fantastical, none of any use. The bed was hard and the sheepskin hot. She was intensely irritated by the whistling breath of Skene, she could not keep her mind from the horrors of the summer solstice, she could not think of any workable plan, she regressed further and further into hopeless dreams of Tam, his square body, his dark smile. Her head ached as the long evening wore slowly into night.

Finally she roused herself and shook up her bed. Perhaps she would play a game of chess with herself, for Skene still slept the deep childish sleep of the old. Or perhaps – she stared at the ornate chest, whose carved leaves and flowers and tendrils twined in green and gold over the sides and lid. Why shouldn't she pass her time in looking over the treasures? Presumably the chest was full of ceremonial crowns and robes and chalices and suchlike – perhaps the bishop's crook was kept in there. If it was not locked she would open it. She moved softly across the hut and pulled gently at the lid. Inch by inch it began to open. A musty, foetid smell seeped out into the air, then the hinge creaked sharply. Bara jumped and dropped the lid with a crash as a wild shriek from the old woman pierced the silence. She was bundling herself off her bed, her wrinkled face contorted with fury and her mouth chattering wild words.

'All right, all right,' said Bara, her momentary fear turning to anger. 'I was only going to look.'

'Those are holy things,' hissed the old woman, shuffling over to Bara and thrusting her face up at her. 'Those are not for profane people to gape at. And they may not be examined except in my presence. I am their Guardian and only I can show them to you.'

'I'm sorry,' said Bara wearily, turning away. 'I didn't mean any harm.' Skene was a little mollified and spoke more gently.

'I suppose you didn't know any better,' she muttered, 'but don't do it again.'

'Will you show them to me then?' asked Bara.

'Perhaps later tonight,' said Skene. 'If you are good.'

Bara shrugged, unable to raise the expected smile, and pointed to the chess set.

'Shall we play?' she said. The crone's face split into a delighted grin and she settled herself by the board.

'Three to me so far,' she said, 'and one to you. You begin.'

They played till Bara's eyes were sore and her limbs stiff with the effort of sitting still so long. The back of her neck was rigid, and one of her feet had gone painfully to sleep, but she had taken two games to Skene's one.

As the guard laid out a late supper of milk and bread Bara sat back and debated her chances of escape through the unbolted door, but obviously there was no hope. The guard was armed with a dagger and he hardly ever took his eyes from Bara as he set the food out on one of the chests. Even if she managed to seize his dagger and get past him, there was a shadow just beyond the doorway which was almost certainly that of another guard. She asked Skene to let her have some news of Con and the old woman translated the guard's reply.

'He is well,' she said.

'I want to see him. Please.' Tears pricked her eyes. 'He must be so miserable.'

'You will see him on the day,' was all that Skene would say.

Bara sank down on her bed again with her head in her hands. It looked like the end of the journey. A long, unlucky journey it had been, but surely worth more than death on a midsummer morning. For death it must be for both of them. If Con was to have his throat slit, then somehow, whatever she might have to do, she would die with him. And she would die before she had been raped by that repulsive old man. She pulled the sheepskin round her shoulder, in a vain attempt to quell the cold which crept outwards from her bones.

'Now,' said Skene suddenly, making Bara start. 'Now I shall show you our treasures.'

'No, thank you,' said Bara, rolling over.

'Yes, you must see them. Come over here.'

Bara had no strength in her muscles, but somehow she heaved herself up and moved wearily over to the chest. She leaned against a pillar and watched without interest. Skene had put on a blue woollen robe and jewelled belt, presumably in honour of the treasures. She bent low over the chest, chanting some kind of incantation in a high voice. The lamps had been freshly trimmed by the guard, and their smoky light wavered across the hut, casting deep shadows and pools of yellow brightness. Skene came to the end of her chant and there was a long hush. Then slowly she raised the lid, releasing again the foetid smell. Everything in the chest seemed to be wrapped in blue wool, so that Bara had to wait while Skene slowly unwrapped the first object. It appeared to be heavy. Finally Skene removed the last wrapping of fine wool and held out a grey, polished stone. Bara looked at it in astonishment.

'Is that all it is?' she said. 'Just a stone?' But Skene did not hear her. 'This is the wind-stone,' she said softly. 'With it I can raise a wind against our enemies, so they will be blown down from the high passes and smashed on the rocks below.'

Then she unwrapped an object that rattled in her hand, and Bara stared in surprise again at a rusty old lock, of a kind they had on their doors in London. Skene touched the key with her thin forefinger.

'This must always be unlocked when any of our women is in childbirth,' she said, 'and also every spring when the ewes are lambing. Otherwise they cannot give birth and the infants die.'

Bara stared at her, contemptuous but also frightened. Then Skene bent to lift another roll and when she had carefully unwrapped the blue cloth she held the object out to Bara, smiling crazily. It was a withered human hand, severed at the wrist, and twisted in arthritic shapes.

'It is the Hand of Glory,' whispered Skene in ecstasy, 'the hand of a hanged man. The warriors hold it before them when they go on a raid, so they can never be repulsed.'

Bara held tightly to the pillar and closed her eyes, struggling to contain the sickness which clutched at her stomach. But the old woman took no notice and busied herself unwrapping the next bundle. When she had finished she held out between her fingers a long length of wizened cord, with a lump of dried gristle at one end.

'It is the birth-cord and placenta,' she murmured, 'from an unborn baby.' Bara clenched her teeth and shut her eyes again. 'If it is ever knotted the flocks will die, and the Shepherds' Kingdom will be at an end.'

She thrust the grisly object forward but as Bara caught a whiff of its smell her eyes swam and she sank, retching, to the ground. Hastily Skene pushed a sheepskin under her head and laid another over her body. As soon as Bara opened her eyes the crone began to bustle round her.

'You aren't well,' she muttered in agitation. 'But you must get well at once. You must be well and beautiful for the ceremony.'

Bara's mouth was parched and her head ached.

'I want some water,' she said.

'Water, water. Yes.' Skene fetched a mug and filled it from a leather jug. 'Are you all right? Are you sure you're all right? I'm responsible for you, I'm the person they'll blame if you're not well.'

She shuffled aimlessly around, muttering to herself, picking things up and putting them down for no reason. Bara did not heed her. She gulped her drink then hauled herself onto her feet.

'I'm all right,' she said curtly. 'But I'm going to bed.'

Her lids were heavy, her limbs were lead, her brain was bursting out of the iron band of her skull. She lay down with relief, taking no notice of the old witch who still hovered round her.

'You will be well after a good sleep. Yes, sleep is the best thing,' said Skene. 'And tomorrow we will bath you and dress you for the evening ceremony.'

Bara turned her head.

'The evening—?'

'The ritual begins on midsummer eve, my dear. Though the main ceremony is the next day, on the solstice.'

On the solstice, on the solstice, on the solstice. The words thrummed in Bara's head as she turned and twisted, trying to find some ease for her aching body. The hut seemed hot and stuffy, yet if she kicked off her sheepskin she was chilled. What did it matter anyway, she thought, if she had only a day and a half to live. She began to wonder how she would kill herself. It was going to be a pain past all understanding to watch Con die, yet she must do it. She must seize a knife from someone and plunge it into Con's heart, feeling in a split second, as Tam taught her, for the space between the ribs. As Tam had taught her; Tam so far away. Tears stung her eyes, then came welling unrestrained as in her hopelessness she lost control of her thoughts and sank in a welter of waking dreams. Tam, Tam, Tam. She would never see him again and he would never know she loved him. For a moment his brown face loomed before her, his arms enclosed her – but then he was gone, whirling on a wind far away.

She drank her posset when it came, but could take no food. Her stomach was hollowed out, her bowels began to run, several times she had to shut herself in the stench of the closet. Skene still hovered in agitation, asking again and again how she was feeling. Bara answered briefly at first, then not at all. She knew the old woman's concern was for her own welfare and not that of her charge. Again she tried to sleep, but she could not subdue the turmoil in her mind. She lay half-waking, struggling in a sea of fantasies, in which the images of Con and Tam and Kate advanced and spun and faded in a hellish dance. Several times she started up, warding off some menace which faded as she tried to grasp it, then fell again into a fitful sleep. Once when she woke, gasping for breath, she saw that Skene had retired to her bed and only one eerie lamp remained lit. A wave of sickness swept her as the smell of the cord and placenta returned. She fell back on her bed, and at once the withered hand began to crawl out of the chest into the turmoil of her mind. It crawled up Con's neck, Cantor's knife glowed red hot above his head, Tam lay dead on his face in the plague-ridden streets of Monmouth . . .

She cried out in horror as panic flooded through her. She could no longer control these voices and these visions, she could not banish them, she could not drown them, she could not capture them at all. She was invaded and swamped, yet she was not asleep, she was certain she was not asleep. She screamed again, for she knew now she must be going mad. She pressed her hands with all her strength to the sides of her head, trying to hold in the sanity that was escaping in storm-clouds from her brain. Her body was rigid, every muscle taut as she struggled to hold against the tempest which threatened to blow her into the void. The next moment hallucination had escaped from the confines of her skull, and she knew for certain she was mad. For there, foursquare in the doorway, stood Tam.

His finger was to his lips as he moved rapidly forward, glancing at the sleeping body of Skene as he came. He knelt by Bara's bed and raised her gently, scarcely recognizing the girl he saw. Terrified eyes stared from a white face, tears and sweat mingled on the drawn cheeks. Bara stood up in a dream, pulling her sheepskin round her, uncertain if she was asleep or awake, sane or mad, but Tam's arm supported her and she walked slowly forward towards the door. Then she stopped abruptly.

'Con?' she whispered.

'I've got him,' said Tam.

He looked at her with deep concern, for it seemed as though she were sleep-walking, but he had no time to find out. He helped her through the outer threshold, then very softly pulled the door shut and slipped the bar down. Bara felt disembodied, as if she were half-drunk. She had the sheepskin round her shoulders but she had left her shoes behind and the dew on the grass was cold. The night was very dark, with no moon. She stepped where Tam guided her, along the inner wall of the stockade, treading softly and feeling the touch of his hand on her back as her only point of reality. Everything else was a dream. Tam stopped and gently pulled at a slat in the stockade. It moved sideways, creaking slightly, and at once his hand clamped down on his long knife. He paused and looked round for a moment, but nothing stirred in the blackness so he pulled at the slat again. The space he made was very small, no more than the diameter of a man's skull, and he put his own head through to test it. Where the head could pass the rest of the body could be squeezed through sideways. He stepped back to help Bara through, then he eased himself after her. They were outside. Some sense of reality began to return to Bara and she smiled in amazement at Tam. He bent quickly and kissed her, then he took her hand and began to move swiftly up the dark hillside. The ground was stony and sharp to Bara's bare feet, but she scarcely noticed. It was dawning on her mind, as the sun dawns on the night, that this was Tam, and he was rescuing them from death.

A lamb bleated softly to the left, and Tam immediately changed direction to climb towards the sound. The bleat came again, nearer, then suddenly Fen was before them, with the great shape of Dark forming in the blackness behind him. Next to him, clutching his hand, was Con.

'Hush!' whispered Tam urgently, but Bara had flown to the boy, and he to her. They stood in each other's arms while Bara moaned with relief and Con rubbed his cheek on hers.

'We mustn't make a noise,' he whispered, 'we're escaping, you see.'

Bara would not let him go until she felt Tam's hand pull at her shoulder. Then she turned to Fen and took both his hands and kissed them. He withdrew them quickly, embarrassed, and patted Con's head. Then he smiled.

'Good-bye,' he said awkwardly, carefully shaping the only word he had ever spoken in English. Tam took his hand, Fen raised his arm in salute, then melted into the night.

'Up,' said Tam, helping Bara onto Dark's bare back. There was only a sack for saddle, with rough stirrups of rope and a long cord for reins. 'We couldn't get the saddle,' whispered Tam. 'I'll take Con up with me.' Bara looked round, for she had thought they were all going to ride on Dark, but as Tam whistled softly another horse emerged from the night, fully saddled and bridled, with a long pack lying over his flanks. Tam slung Con up onto the pommel, then mounted himself. He leaned over and whispered.

'We must move quietly for a few hundred yards, unless we hear them coming. If we do hear them, then we must go like the bloody wind till we drop.' He turned his horse's head. 'I only know one way out of this damn place, so we'll have to stick to that.'

Bara dug her knees into the sacking and turned Dark to follow Tam. It would be hard work riding bareback, for Dark was very broad and she was unused to riding after so many weeks out of the saddle. She kept her eyes on Tam's back ahead of her, for although she still felt only half-awake, and altogether too buoyant to be real, she was able to bend her mind sufficiently to the task of following Tam. Somewhere deep within her, biding its time, was an explosion of joy.

They moved quietly along the mountainside, descending obliquely to the bottom of the bowl and making for the southern pass. Now that her eyes had adapted to the darkness Bara could discern the shape of the horses and the faint divide between mountain and sky. They could see the glow of a few lamps in the village behind them, but nothing stirred. Except for an occasional bleating, darkness and silence filled the valley.

They rode on for a quarter of an hour, hearing only the light knocking of horseshoes on the stony ground. Then suddenly behind them a shriek hurtled through the night. Tam turned in his saddle, clutching his knife.

'Was it an owl?' he said.

'No. It was the old woman. She's found I've gone.'

'Christ, we must move.'

'Will they catch us?' cried Con.

'No.'

Bara came up alongside and they urged their horses forward, into a trot, into a canter, into a gallop. Dark did not care to move fast where he could not see, so Bara had to thump with her bare heels and slap his haunch with her open hand. They flew through the darkness, scattering sheep and stones in their wake, but even above the clamour of their riding they could hear yells and horns from the village, and when they glanced back in the saddle they saw the place was ablaze with torches.

'They'll never catch us,' shouted Bara. 'Not on those little ponies.'

'They've got stamina and they know the country. They could run us into the ground or they could cut us off. Come on, come on.'

Dark had settled into an easy gallop, though his ears were back and he did not like it, and Tam's horse was having trouble in keeping up with him. Tam kicked and thumped and shouted, and together they thundered on through the dark towards the pass.

Then the pursuit was on. They heard the whinnying of ponies and when they looked back they could see the flames of torches moving fast. They rushed on over the rocky ground, then between the looming cliffs of the pass, where Bara was forced back by the narrowness of the passage, then out onto the slopes of the Taff below. They were descending steeply now, and although the horses slowed their pace they slithered often and had to be tightly reined. The track was just discernible in the darkness and they stuck to it along all its zig-zags as the safest route. It eventually led them to a bridge of stepping-stones, exactly such a one as Dark had disliked when they first rode to the Shepherds' Kingdom. Again he baulked, and Bara lost valuable moments coaxing him over while Tam fretted and swore on the other bank. Suddenly he pointed. High above them were the torches of their pursuers, streaming through the pass.

'Those ponies will come down that slope like goats,' said Tam. 'Come on.' The track led north-south along the river and they kept to it, turning south. The horses crashed into a gallop, relieved to be moving on level ground, and the torches of the pursuit receded again. They rounded a rocky shoulder of the hill, and before them the track divided. One arm continued south along the river, the narrower branched to the west. Tam reined in and bit his lip.

'We'll risk this one,' he said, turning his horse into the smaller western path. 'I hope to God it doesn't just stop in the mountain.'

Bara did not care which they took. In her relief at having decisions made for her she said nothing and simply followed. Again they urged their horses on, cantering in single file along the narrow path, which bit deep among rocks and heather. Bara knew they were taking mad risks with their horses, for any rock protruding in the darkness, or any hole washed out by rain, could cause a broken leg. But there was nothing else to be done, so they tore wildly on.

After half an hour or so the path skirted a wood and Tam pulled up. The horses were lathered and foaming, and unable to go much further without a rest. As Bara dismounted her knees almost gave way beneath her. She staggered against Dark, clutching at his mane, then she noticed Tam was sitting still in the saddle, listening. There was no sound above the panting and snorting of the horses. Tam relaxed his body and swung himself down.

'Let's rest in the wood,' he said. 'We must do something about the horses.' Con slipped down and ran to Bara, who hugged him and took his hand. 'Did you like that ride?' she asked, smiling.

'Yes, but I want to sit down.'

Tam frowned but he said nothing, and they led their horses up into the birch wood to tether them.

'I haven't much stuff,' said Tam, looking worried. He pulled down his saddle bag and delved inside. 'We'll have to mop the horses down with this,' he said, producing a dirty rag, 'and I've only got two small blankets.'

While they attended to the horses Con propped himself against a birch and closed his eyes. Rummaging in Tam's bag Bara found a lump of bread and she tore a piece off for Con, then lumps for Tam and herself. She and Tam stood smiling at each other in the darkness, while they tore at the dry bread with their teeth. He bent forward and kissed her lightly on the nose, then he turned and began to pack his bag again. Suddenly Bara lifted her head and stood motionless.

'Listen,' she whispered. Muffled, distant, but unmistakable, was the thudding of hooves.

'God Almighty,' said Tam softly. They crouched by Con under the birch and Tam drew his knife. Bara's heart was racing as she grabbed Tam's arm.

'Listen,' she whispered urgently. 'Listen, Tam. For God's sake don't let them get us. Do you understand? Kill us first, with your knife. Kill us before they get us. Both of us, Con and me. Kill us—' Her voice was rising in hysteria as he put his hand gently on her mouth.

'All right,' he murmured. 'I'll do that. I promise. And myself too.'

The hooves were nearer now, on the approaching path and coming towards them. There was nothing they could do but pray their pursuers would not notice the broken brambles where their horses had forced their way into the wood. They came on, louder and faster, less than fifty yards away. Bara held and held her breath, scarcely noticing the pain in her chest, and Tam's knuckles were white on his knife. The horsemen were almost at the wood, still galloping full tilt – and they had not drawn up. They clattered past, and on. Bara's head fell on Tam's shoulder, and he let it lie for a moment before he raised her up.

'Come on,' he said, 'we must get out of here.' Con clutched Bara's hand and would not speak. They packed the horses' blankets, then Tam heaved the silent Con up into his saddle.

'You can sleep up here,' Tam said to him, 'we shan't be going fast. We must get away from that path,' he said to Bara. 'We'll have to pick our way over the mountain.'

They emerged from the wood on the far side and began to move slowly up the slope, but it was too dark to see more than ten yards ahead and the ground was rough. Heather and rocks covered the hillside, the ground was treacherous and uneven. The horses held their heads low, trying to pick their way in the darkness, but often they stumbled. Rounding an outcrop of rock Bara suddenly heard the hooves again, but they were far below now and apparently still travelling south-west along the track.

'We'll just go west,' said Tam, 'and hope to God we don't hit that track again.'

They rode laboriously on, screwing up their eyes in their effort to detect rocks and hollows ahead. Con slept fitfully, waking with a start every time the horse stumbled or slid.

'What's his name?' asked Bara, nodding at Tam's horse.

Tam smiled. 'Moon,' he said.

'Why Moon?'

'To go with Dark of course. Dark and Moon.'

Bara looked away, not understanding why the tears rose in her eyes.

Often they drew up abreast and stood motionless, listening for the sound of hooves, but now they could hear nothing except the soft rustle of the wind in the heather. After an hour or so they rounded the shoulder of the mountain, and as they began to descend they heard the clatter of a stream below them. Just after they had crossed it Con exclaimed.

'Look!' he said. 'It's getting light.'

'Shhhhh,' said Tam. 'Don't talk so loud.'

Bara realized she could now discern the swaying haunches of

Moon up the slope ahead of her. Soon the edge of the mountain thickened against the western sky, and when they stopped to look back the hills behind were sharply etched against the grey eastern light. Then came streaks of yellow, a flush of rose, and a pale dawn spread over the sky in a rising tide. In a few minutes, in a cleft of the mountains to the south-east, the fiery sun sailed slowly up the sky, holding the promise of a glorious midsummer's eve. Bara turned to Tam and they looked at each other a long time, not smiling. Then Tam lowered his eyes.

'Still alive,' he said cheerfully. 'We'd better find somewhere to hide up for the day.'

'Why not further up the stream?'

As far as they could judge the track had curved away south and there were no paths up the little valley. They turned northward, alongside the water. The banks of the valley grew steeper and rockier, tiny falls and rapids splashed the horses as the stream clattered down its steep bed. Suddenly the western bank curved away and there before them was a small black lake. Con leaped in the saddle, but Tam's hand was over his mouth before he could shout.

'You mustn't make a noise,' said Tam angrily. 'You've got to remember we're in danger of our lives. We're escaping from enemies.'

'I forgot,' said Con. 'Sorry. Can I get down?'

The little valley was a secret place, almost encircled by the heathery slopes. They decided to camp between two great boulders on the western shore of the lake. Part of the shore was rocky, part was peat, and in front of their camp was a little beach of dark sand. Tam sat on a rock with his elbows on his knees.

'What the hell are we going to eat?' he said. 'I've hardly got anything left.'

Bara tipped out his bag and found only half a hard loaf, some carrots, and a small piece of sacking full of oats.

'I could wolf the lot of it now, oats and all,' said Tam.

They divided the oats among the horses, gave them a carrot apiece, then turned them loose on the hillside to find what green they could.

'I suppose there might be fish in the lake,' said Bara, as they sat chewing the dry bread.

'I should think there must be,' said Tam. 'But how do we get them?'

Con looked puzzled, then suddenly his face lit up and he jumped to his feet. 'I know!' he cried, and he raced off to the rocks fifty yards up the shore. They watched him fall on his stomach on an overhanging ledge, then slide his hand very softly into the water. He lay motionless for several minutes.

'What's he doing?' said Bara.

'He must be tickling for trout I think. I read about it somewhere but I don't really know what you do. How does he know?'

'Oh I don't know,' said Bara. 'He knows everything. It scares me sometimes.'

She told him of how Con knew about knots, and making fires, and building boats, and how to hold weapons, and the alignment of the sun. At the end of her recital Tam shook his head.

'There's something strange going on,' he said. 'Very, very strange.' He stood up. 'I'm so ravenous I could eat the bloody horses. I'll see if I can catch something over there. Where the stream runs out of the lake.'

He went off with some rags from his bag and Bara watched him sorting out long stems of heather. Perhaps he was trying to make a dam. She looked down at her bare feet, bruised and chafed by the constriction of the stirrup ropes. She rubbed them idly, realizing the skin would soon break, then she lay back on her sheepskin with her hands under her head, and looked up at the morning sky. Already it was a clear blue, with only a few wisps of white cloud strewn here and there, and already the sun had climbed high enough to come slanting onto the western shore where she lay. She closed her eyes and smiled to herself. She was warm, she was safe, contentment filled her to the brim. The terrors of the night had vanished like wraiths.

She awoke to see Con standing above her, carefully directing the drips from a fish's tail onto her face.

'Con! You've got one!' He laughed and jumped, swinging the fish in circles in the air.

'I knew I would,' he said, 'You just have to wait.'

'How did you know what to do?'

'Oh I just knew. Let's make a fire, Mam.'

Bara scrambled up and they began to gather dead heather. Up the slope were a few thorn trees, which supplied twigs and some dead branches. When the wood was assembled, and the fire laid by Con, they ran along the shore towards Tam. Long before they reached him they could hear him cursing. He had made a kind of dam with two long sticks and the rags stretched loosely between them, but he was finding that whenever a fish swam into the ballooning cloth it leaped away again before he could grab it.

'It's hopeless this way,' he said angrily as they came up to him. 'Look, you go over there, and when a fish comes we'll tip the whole thing up sideways.'

Bara crouched on the other side of the narrow channel with her hand on the stick. There was a strong current pulling towards the opening and plenty of fish were caught in it.

'Now!' yelled Tam as two fish were swept together into the cloth. They whipped the contraption sideways, like a loose stretcher. One fish leaped back to the lake, Tam's leg slipped into the water, Bara grazed her knuckles on the rock – but there in the makeshift net was one small fish, landed and secure.

'Thank God,' said Tam, slapping its head on the rock. 'One mouthful anyway.'

'That's not much good,' said Con. 'I'll go and do it my way.'

He skipped off along the lakeside, his hair flopping in the sun. Tam and Bara worked for another hour and they caught three more fish, two small and one large. They carried them back to their camp and found Con's offering of another large trout. Apparently he had lost interest after his second catch and had wandered off among the rocks along the shore. They lit the fire with Tam's tinder and broiled the fish on flat stones. The heather burnt fast so they had to work hard in the growing heat of the morning to keep the fire red. When at last the fish were cooked Bara called Con back, and they all ate ravenously, burning fingers and tongues in their greedy haste.

Bara made a heather bed for Con in the shade of a boulder and he fell asleep almost at once. Then she turned back to Tam, and stopped abruptly as she saw his face. They stood trembling for a moment in the gaze of each other's eyes. Bara knew that Tam's entrails were being tied in knots, because the same was happening to her. Like two magnets their bodies moved together until there was no light to be seen between them. The familiar bellyful of fear, which had sickened Bara for five years whenever she was in the presence of a man, was no longer there. She did not tauten or retreat. And Tam knew, as his heart turned over and her lips moved on his, that everything was going to be all right. Without speaking they sank in each other's arms onto the grass.

When eventually they awoke the sun was declining in the sky. Con still slept on, so they lay on their backs in the last of the sun, looking across the dark lake to the purple slopes on the other side. Sometimes a bird twittered in the rocks, only intensifying the quiet with his small, lonely sounds. Both Tam and Bara were reluctant to intrude on the sunlit silence. At last Tam spoke.

'There's so much to tell you and so much to hear about I don't know where to begin,' he said. 'You haven't got very far on your journey anyway. Nearly six months getting to Wales is just a joke.'

Bara smiled, gazing down a long perspective at the dangers and terrors of the journey.

'It wasn't much of a joke,' she said. 'I'll tell you why it took so long.' And she told him, lying close with his arm under her head. She told him about Oxford and the Oxford Rout, the pursuit of the Outlanders, and Cotswold farm, the branding at Bela's Knap, the death of Grett, the weeks with Wat and Bel. She told him of plague-ridden Monmouth, and the crazy night at Abergavenny, and the beauties and horrors of the Shepherds' Kingdom. Only when she began to describe the midsummer rituals did her voice falter, for the dangers of the present suddenly rushed at her. Tam held her tight.

'But why did you go on?' he asked. 'Why didn't you come back to London?'

'Oh it's so difficult,' she said. 'I don't know the answer. Right from the beginning I just had to go on. I still have to. Even when you and Fred thought I was mad it wasn't any different. Twice I've meant to go back, once at the Cotswold farm and once at Old Wat's. But each time something – or someone – some kind of presence – told me I had to go on. All the time I resisted it was horrible. Then when I gave up resisting the presence just went away. And my dreams wereall bright pictures of Ireland, like a child's book. Con's full of it too, even more than me. He gets absolutely hysterical when I say we must go back.'

Tam was propped up on his elbow, with a frown on his face.

'It was just the same with me,' he said slowly, lying back again. 'Only I haven't had the Ireland pictures. What I've been compelled to do is find you and Con. If I hadn't come I honestly think this – this presence thing – would have driven me mad. I couldn't sleep and I couldn't think straight – it was on at me all the time. I got to the stage where I began talking aloud and everyone thought I was going crazy. I kept shouting I knew you didn't want me, I knew you'd just send me back—' Bara gripped his hand so tight it hurt '—and anyway, I said to the thing, how the hell was I to find you between London and Ireland? A girl and a small boy in all those hundreds of miles? But in the end I couldn't sleep at all and after three nights I said all right, I'll go. Damn you to hell, whatever you are, but I'll go. And the thing just melted away, like that. I slept for eighteen hours and the next day I left.'

'It's eerie,' said Bara. 'What's happening to us?'

'I don't know. What's it all about? Why Ireland? Why us?'

'Maybe it's really to do with Con,' said Bara thoughtfully. 'He's so peculiar, knowing all these things nobody's told him.' Tam looked at her sharply. 'Of course,' he said, after a pause. 'Of course that's it. It's Con. You're to take him and I'm to help you – it fits. But who wants him? And why?'

'Everyone seems to want him,' said Bara. 'His revolting father wants him, and that barbaric High Priest wants him, and someone in Ireland wants him.'

'Do you think it's evil, this thing that's going on at us?'

'No,' said Bara slowly. 'It's persistent all right, but I don't think it's evil. In fact when it gets its way there's a feeling of peace - and kindness.'

'I found that too. I think it's benign. It wishes us well. But we've bloody well got to do what it wants.'

'How did you ever find us?' asked Bara after a silence.

'I picked up the trail in Monmouth.'

'The plague town?'

'Yes. There are some kids living there whose parents died. They watched you ride through the town.'

'But it was absolutely silent. It was deserted. Empty.'

'They were there. Then I picked you up again at the Woolpack at Abergavenny - the barmaid remembered your hair. Then some woodcutters had seen you with the shepherds, and they told me where the Shepherds' Kingdom was.'

'How did you speak to them?'

'Signs. It was a long business.'

'And how did you find us when you got to the shepherds?'

'That little dark man.'

'Fen?'

'I suppose so. I hid up in the mountain during the day, and I saw Dark and I thought it was odd he was tethered. When it was night I brought Moon down the mountain and tied him up beside Dark. Then I turned to go down to the village and I got the fright of my life. This little man just loomed up at my feet. I nearly had my knife in him - he sort of catapulted himself away in a backward somersault. It was incredible.'

'That was Fen all right,' said Bara, laughing.

'Then I realized he was making signs. He pointed to the village, then to Dark's back, then away down the valley. When I nodded he nodded too, and he got very excited. He took my hand and led me round to the gate of the stockade. We waited till the guard turned his back then I crept up on him and stabbed him with my knife. He just sank without a sound. It seemed so easy. I've never killed anyone in cold blood before. Then this little man - Fen - he led me round the back of the huts to a stone building. The guard was asleep across the door and Fen looked at me and tipped his head back as if he was drinking. I think he'd drugged the guard with a drink, and I think he had a plan of escape for you all on his own. Anyway, he stepped over

the man and he slipped up the bars of the door, then he opened the
lock with a key. The lock looked very greasy and well-prepared.
Then he just brought Con out and locked and barred the door. We
crept round the palings again and he showed me your hut and then
he took Con off to the horses. You know the rest.'

'Fen,' said Bara, gazing at the lake. 'Why did he do it for us?'

'Well, I'd have botched it up completely without him. I didn't know
where you were, I didn't even know if you were together or separated.'

'God, I hope he's all right. I hope they didn't find out.'

'I don't think they will. He's too sharp. He dropped the key by
Con's hut and he showed me how he was going to give himself a bang
on the head and lie by the guard. So I hope they'll be deceived.'

'I hope to God they will.'

Con's head appeared over his boulder.

'How long have I been asleep, Mam?'

'Hours and hours. We all have.'

'I'm hungry.'

'Oh hell,' said Tam, scrambling to his feet. 'We should have been
catching fish. We could have kippered them in the sun. Let's do an
evening's fishing before we get off again.'

'Fish rise in the evening,' said Con. 'For the insects. It's the best time.'

Bara and Tam glanced at each other and shrugged.

'Well, I never told him,' said Bara. 'I didn't even know.'

For three hours in the deepening dusk they struggled to catch fish,
but for all their experiments they could find no better methods than
those they had used before. The six fish they eventually landed had
taken a heavy toll in anger and frustration. All three of them were
tired and hungry when they began to assemble another fire. Night
had almost fallen and because Tam was worried about the light of
the flames they surrounded the fire with rocks and stones and tried to
keep it low, but they knew the glowing point of light must be visible
from any crest around the valley. So with the fish only half cooked
they stamped on the fire and crammed the burning flesh into their
mouths. Tam had two fish, Bara and Con had one each, and the
other two they wrapped in wet rags to take with them. Tam gave
Bara his shoes but they fell off her, so she had to bind her sore feet in
strips torn from her woollen shift. Darkness had gathered by the time
they harnessed the horses and set off again down the valley. The
night was warm, so Bara used her sheepskin for a saddle and rode
comfortably, enjoying the sway of Dark's great body beneath her.

'I expect the shepherds are missing us,' she said cheerfully,
convinced the pursuit was over.

'Didn't you say the party started this morning?'

'Yes. midsummer's eve. My part began then. What the old hag called the greatest honour of my life.'

'Rape.'

'Yes, by a disgusting old man. In public.'

'Barbarians.'

'But they were so civilized in some ways. Kind and gentle and orderly and hard-working. Then there was this awful savagery too.'

'What were they going to do to us, Mam?' asked Con, from where he rode between Tam's arms.

'Oh, nasty things, Con. Let's not think about it.'

'Fen wasn't nasty.'

'No, Fen was good.'

Again they were having to pick their path, as they turned obliquely west, away from the stream and over heathery ground. The night was very dark, for although a thousand stars lay strewn above them only the faintest glimmer reached the earth. A soft west wind blew in their faces as they moved watchfully on.

For two weeks of summer weather they rode through the western hills and valleys of Wales. Once they had crossed the Mynydd Du and come down into the broad valley of the Tywi, they left the mountains behind them and rode through gentler country of pasture and woods. After the summer solstice had come and gone they rode openly along the public tracks in full daylight. There was no sign of pursuit, so they assumed they had evaded it while it was on, and now that the solstice was over they were no longer required. With Tam's pocketful of money they had bought some rough moccasins for Bara, and every day they bought bread and milk and eggs from farms. Once when they did a morning's haymaking for an old widow they were rewarded with a chicken. They contrived to rig up a rod and line, and with some rope the widow gave them Bara made a net which served for catching both fish and rabbits. Wherever they rode, across moors, along valleys, by the shores of rivers, they searched for nests, and there were few days on which they did not boil the eggs of grouse or pheasants or ducks in Tam's old saucepan. In the evenings they lit their fire to cook fish, eggs and potatoes, or a rabbit if they had one. And every night when Con was asleep Bara lay in Tam's arms by the dying light of the fire, watching for the terror that had once consumed her and finding nothing but warmth and rapture. Sometimes they whispered far into the night of their childhood, or their journey, or the course of their love, but often no words were said at all.

One fine morning, in a wooded valley in Pembrokeshire, they were riding the horses across a splashing river when Con saw a salmon leap upstream. In the course of the next hour they caught more salmon than they could eat or keep. They caught them in the net, they caught them in their bare hands, they pounced on those that fell slapping on the rocks. The fish came on unendingly in a silver stream, so many that the fishers threw the small ones back in the tumbling river and watched them leap obstinately on. For the three humans, always on the edge of hunger, this was a riot of gluttony. All morning they cooked their salmon, splitting them open with Tam's knife and smoking them on a fire or grilling them on the rocks in the sun. They stuffed themselves with fish until they felt ill and could eat no more, they laughed and shouted and leaped about on the rocks, intoxicated with freedom and plentitude and sun. And once again, as always when she was happy, there crept into Bara's mind a nagging doubt about their journey. It seemed insane to leave these valleys and mountains, where they could live so cheerfully with a few sheep and a cow. It seemed lunatic to press on through further dangers and across an unknown sea to an unknown land where unknown dangers awaited them. How were they to know if the voice that was compelling them required them for good or ill? Full of rebellious thoughts she sat against a rock by the river and closed her eyes. How long she slept she did not know, for she was woken by an explosion that rocked her very bones. She screamed and held her head, expecting the sky to fall and the earth to crack, but when she opened her eyes the world was as it had been – green, silver, serene. The explosion was within her. It came again, striking with such power she felt herself disintegrating, nerve ripped from muscle, muscle from bone. She held on grimly, taut as wire, until slowly the naked force resolved itself into a form she could understand. She was scarcely aware of Con's terror or Tam's urgent words, for before the thunder shaped itself again she knew what form it would take.

'All right,' she shouted wildly, raising her face to the sky. 'All right, all right. I'll come.'

At once the fury died away, her body relaxed, and she was sitting at peace by the stream. She wiped the sweat from her forehead.

'Mam, Mam!' shouted Con in desperation. 'What is it? Talk to me.'

Tam was speaking too, his face white with anxiety. Bara reached up and touched his cheek, then she pulled Con onto her knee.

'It's all right.' She smiled at them both. 'I'm all right.'

'What happened?' said Tam. 'Was it the thing?'

'Yes. It nearly blasted me to bits.'

'Were you thinking we wouldn't go on?'

'That's right. Just that. Don't ever let the thought even begin to cross your mind. Next time we'll all be blown sky-high.' Tam grinned in his relief.

'We haven't much choice it seems,' he said. 'Take this.' And he crammed a huge lump of sun-grilled salmon into her mouth.

Four days later, at the beginning of July, they reached the coast of Pembrokeshire. None of them had ever seen the sea. They stood like children on the huge sands of St Bride's Bay, gazing at the glittering expanse which swept away to meet the sky on a long horizon. Small waves broke in white crests. Shallow pools shone in the warm sand, deeper water filled the hollows of the rocks. At first Con held tightly to Bara, then he looked down and curled his toes in the wet sand, then he stepped aside into a little pool. Suddenly he was off, yelling with excitement, down to the water's edge, and into the curling waves. Tam smiled at Bara, then hand in hand they raced after him. Bara's hair flew about her face as they rushed along the shallows, splashing and jumping and shouting. In a few moments Con had soaked himself trying to jump the waves, and Bara's chafed feet were stinging with the salt. Tam roared after Con, flailing his arms.

'I'm a sea-monster. I'm coming to eat you!' he bellowed.

Con screamed in delighted terror and fell over himself in the surf. He came up spluttering and laughing, his white hair plastered over his eyes. They spent the whole morning on the beach, alternately paddling and drying off in the sun. Then at noon they made a fire of driftwood on the edge of the sand and baked potatoes for lunch.

'Now we've got to find a boat,' said Tam, chewing some bread beside the fire. 'How much money have you left?'

'I've got a sovereign and some decimal and some old silver. It should be enough.'

'What about when we get to Ireland?'

'Oh that'll have to look after itself,' said Tam, wiping his mouth with the back of his hand. 'Perhaps they don't use money. Perhaps they barter with snakeskins or something.'

'There aren't any snakes in Ireland,' said Con, cramming a whole potato in his mouth.

'Who told you that?' asked Tam.

'No-one. I just know.'

'That's what he always says,' said Bara.

Tam gazed into the fire.

'Sometimes I just know things too,' he said. 'Things I'm sure I've never read and no-one's ever told me. When I was reading books at home – like Bentham and Russell and Rousseau and things – I found I knew it all. I knew their ideas, I knew what was coming over the page.'

'You told Grans something about that.'

'Yes. But I'm surer of it now. It's as if the ideas were just hovering round me, like tame birds. I only have to reach out for them and they come. I know so much – it staggers me – about political theory and methods of government and the ordering of societies. I'm not boasting. I just do. It's so easy. I wish to God I could put my ideas about it into practice somewhere. That's what I do in my mind – try to make it all work. To create a just and happy society. There couldn't be a better ideal to put your mind and your energy and your life towards.'

'No, I suppose not. Do you know about other subjects too?'

'No. I'm not like Con. I don't know about all these facts and skills and things, like he does.'

'You give me the horrors,' said Bara getting up and stretching. 'Both of you. I never know anything at all.'

'You have other qualities,' said Tam, squinting up at her and running his hand up her leg.

For three days they rode round the coast, meeting a few fishermen and asking as best they could with sign and gesticulation if anyone could take them to Ireland. They discovered the Welsh for Ireland, but still their words and gestures met with blank incredulity, and when they looked at the tiny inshore fishing boats they could understand the amazement of the men.

'Old Wat would make us a boat,' grumbled Con. 'His would be good enough.'

Finally somewhere beyond St David's they met a grizzled old man who did not gape at them as if they were mad. He pointed north along the coast and repeated, 'Fishgar, Fishgar, Fishgar'.

'Marvellous!' shouted Tam, digging his heels into Moon. 'He means Fishguard. I remember it in the atlas. Fishguard-Rosslare it said, and it was the shortest way across.'

'How many miles?' shouted Bara, galloping after him.

'About fifty I think.'

'Fifty miles!' she screamed. 'Across that?' And she waved her arm wildly towards the ocean.

'Don't be stupid,' shouted Tam, 'people used to sail right round the world.'

Bara laughed and swung her streaming hair out of her eyes. They cantered along the green cliff-top, gazing down at the gleaming wastes of the sea below. It was too beautiful to leave room for worry.

In the evening they reached Fishgar Bay. As they approached the town they passed for the first time in many weeks the familiar mounds of rubbish from the old world; rusted cars, broken machinery, tins and plastic of every description. They could see that there had once been a town in the south-western corner of the bay, but it was now overwhelmed with heather and bramble and thorn. Only a cluster of inhabited houses remained, hugging the line of the harbour. Although the end of the mole had fallen into the sea, the rest was solid enough to protect the huddle of little boats that sheltered behind it. But Tam and Bara had no eyes for the smacks and coracles. For there, alongside the end of the mole, was the largest boat they had ever seen. The paint was flaked, the anchor and chains were brown with rust, the deck glistened with the slime of fish; nevertheless it was a sturdy and seaworthy boat.

Two days later they were aboard. The lanky captain had taken a day to sober up, after celebrating his last catch with a night's drinking of potato spirits, but when eventually he became coherent Tam and Bara found to their delight he was an Englishman. He was a fair-skinned man, with long mousy hair lying in tangles on his shoulders, and hollow cheeks criss-crossed with myriad tiny red veins. He was very lean, as well as very tall, and his face had the battered, ageless look of seafaring men. He introduced himself as Cap'n Stark. Looking down on them from his great height, and swivelling his bleary eyes from one to the other, he told them how he had come down from the north. He had been shipwrecked on the Welsh coast ten years back and he'd lived with the bloody Welshies ever since. There was more fish down this way, he said, and anyway he'd been sick and tired of his family in Livpool. He'd found a cabin in Fishgar, and a Welsh woman he'd knocked some English into, and he was all right. He wiped his mouth with the back of his hand constantly, as if he had just taken a swig from a bottle. And between wipes he spat ferociously. Con watched in amazement, from where they all sat in a row on the harbour wall, as the great jets of spittle shot further and further out into the sea.

'Aye, I could go to Ireland,' he said nonchalantly. 'She's a trim little lugger, that one. I could get there if you made it worth my while. I've often seen the coast but I never landed 'cos of the savages. This lot's bad enough,' he said, wiping his mouth and jerking his head back towards the village, 'but they say the Irish are worse. Real heathen savages, painted all over.'

Bara glanced in alarm at Tam, but he seemed unperturbed.

'How much do you want to take us over?' he asked

'Eh, well now.' A jet of spittle flew into the sea. 'Depends how much brass you got now, dunit?' Tam pulled half a dozen pieces of silver from his pouch and Stark's attention riveted on his hand.

'Christ,' he said, wiping his mouth hard. 'That's a fair showing. Got any gold?'

Tam hesitated. 'Isn't this good enough?' he said.

'Gold's better.'

'Well, it won't be both,' said Tam firmly. 'Silver or gold, but not both.'

'Let's see the gold then.' The small bloodshot eyes stared as Tam produced his sovereign.

'Whew.' The captain whistled through his teeth. 'I ha'n't seen any of them since I were a right lad.' He picked up the sovereign and bit it, then he placed it gently in a pocket of his tunic.

'I'll have t'gold,' he said.

'And you'll take us to Ireland? And the horses?'

'Aye, when the wind and tide's right. I'll do like I said.'

So it came about that two days later, in the creeping light of dawn, Tam and Bara were stabling the horses in the black stench of the ship's hold. Both animals were angry and frightened, their hooves slipping on the slimey floor and their nostrils flaring against the dank smell. Bara had taken nearly an hour to get Dark up the gangplank, even though Moon had gone ahead of him, and he was still restless and protesting.

The captain's tiny cabin, where Bara and Tam and Con were to sleep, was only slightly less repellent than the hold. The stench of rotting fish was everywhere, even in the coarse blankets of their bunks. The long spell of summer weather had intensified the stink and the captain had done little to wash it away. Only Con was filled with rapture as he rushed all over the boat, tugging at the rigging, climbing on the ropes, swinging on the boom, and tearing up and down the small companionway.

Tam and Bara watched in horror as Stark staggered on board, clutching a bottle and wiping hectically at his mouth. His surly Welsh crew took no notice of him, but Tam saw with relief that even in his stupor the captain seemed to know what he was doing. In half an hour the ship was under way, moving slowly out of the harbour into the Irish Sea. Even early in the morning the sun was hot, and there was so little wind they were an hour clearing the coast. Con sat joyfully squeezed up in the bows, staring ahead, his hair a mop of quaking silver in the breeze. Tam, who was already feeling sick, stood gloomily against the rail with his eyes shut, in no mood for any company, so Bara left him and curled herself up on a coil of rope in the stern, out of the way of the crew. As she sat gazing into a vacancy of blue the incredible thought began to flower that they were now, almost, at last, in Ireland. Somewhere in the mist of the horizon was the country whose image had obsessed her for so long. Was it a green and golden kingdom, was it a land of milk and cream, a world of everlasting sun, as Suz had told her? Was it the heraldic tapestry of her dreams, gules and argent and vert, painted in primary colours on an azure sea? Or was it a land of cold bogs and painted savages, as the captain believed?

The ship rode easily on a light swell, but even that was too much for Tam. He tried to interest himself in the crew's activities, he watched carefully the paying-out of the great net from the stern, but slowly his face turned white, then green, and he began to retch. He hung miserably over the rail, trying to appreciate Bara's comforting words but wishing only that she would go away.

'Is he ill?' said Con, gazing aghast.

'He's sea-sick,' said Bara. 'Lots of people are.'

'Why? I want something to eat. I'm hungry. I want six eggs.'

'Oh, shut up,' growled Tam, as his stomach heaved again. Bara hated to see his swarthy face drained of all colour and she did not respond to Stark's guffaw as he strode past and noticed Tam's plight.

'Eh, that's no sailor,' he grinned, spitting far out over the rail. 'I'll take on the little lad though,' he added, ruffling Con's hair. 'He's a bright one.'

Bara felt herself a little mollified and raised a faint smile, but the captain had passed on and did not notice. She climbed down to the hold to see if the horses were any calmer, but she found them still restless and unwilling to eat even the carrots she offered them. So she returned to her coil of rope in the stern and turned to face the breeze. Even out here on the open sea the heat was oppressive, and the wind so light that the ship made very little headway. Bara looked round for some shade but there was none to be found except in the cabin, and that was too stinking to bear. The thin woollen shift in which she had escaped from the Shepherds' Kingdom was unbearably hot and prickly on her skin. Whenever she pulled it away from her body it fell stickily back. Angrily she envied Tam and the crew their bare backs and legs. Then, propped against the rail, she closed her eyes and fell asleep.

Almost at once, it seemed, shouting broke in on her dreams. One of the crew stood high on the ratlines, pointing ahead and to port, calling out words in Welsh. Stark came striding by, almost tripping on Bara's legs.

'It's a ship,' he said, looking sharply down at her. 'Big ship on the port bow.'

The crew rushed to the port rail and stared at the western horizon. While Bara had slept, the burning blue had paled and a milky haze was spreading over sea and sky. In a moment she saw in the mist the white sails of a tall ship, growing perceptibly as they watched.

'I've never seen her before,' muttered Stark. 'She's tacking our way.'

One of the crew spoke rapidly in Welsh, but Stark only spat. Then other men began to mutter among themselves, and one of them spoke again to Stark.

'They want to go back,' said the captain, turning to Bara. Tam seized his arm. His face was still white but his voice was strong and angry.

'You said you'd take us. You took my gold.'

'Aye.' The captain scowled.

He wiped his mouth and spoke to the crew in Welsh. They listened, on the edge of mutiny, but when he had finished they shrugged and dispersed and went about their jobs. But clearly they were worried, for all of them cast anxious glances over their shoulders at the approaching ship.

'I told them we hadn't a hope in hell of getting away,' said Stark to Tam. 'Not in this tub. Yon's a huge ship. Christ, look at those sails. Like a bloody brig she is. If it's pirates reckon we'd just better say our prayers.'

'Pirates!' Con's eyes widened in excitement.

Tam put his arm wearily around Bara's shoulders.

'It looks as if we aren't there yet,' he said.

Bara made him sit down against the rail, for he looked half-dead and his legs were trembling. He closed his eyes but he did not let go her hand.

'I hope it's not the end,' he muttered.

'Don't,' said Bara, crouching beside him and kissing his cheek. 'You're just sea-sick and depressed. Look what we've come through. This won't be any worse.'

He opened his eyes slowly and gazed at her.

'Don't you know what pirates *do*?' he said.

'It's all stories. We don't know anything real about pirates. We only know a lot of old wives' tales.'

'Perhaps.' He stretched against the rail and pulled out his long knife. 'Perhaps not. Rape, then robbery, then massacre. That's the usual order.'

'So the story goes.'

Bara forced a contemptuous tone into her voice but his words filled her with horror. She sank down and laid her head against his shoulder. Would they never find any peace? For six months now, danger and fear had been their constant companions, walking beside them like wraiths that no sunlight could ever dispel. Tam slipped his arm round her waist.

'Do you want me to promise the same thing again?' he said. 'The same as when the Shepherds' nearly caught us in the wood?'

'Yes. First Con – but don't let him see. From the back. First Con, then me.'

'Then me,' said Tam rubbing his thumb across the edge of his knife.

Stark loped past them, white-faced and violently wiping his mouth.

'Christ Jeeze,' he said, looking down on them. 'They'll be on us in quarter of an hour. Good thing you've a knife – we'll need all we got.'

'Are you sure they're pirates?' said Bara.

'Bound to be. Yon's no fishing boat.'

He strode off, shouting orders at his crew and inspecting their fish-knives as he went. He directed the men how to stand in line along the rails and up on the lines, on whichever side the pirates chose to grapple them. If any man muttered or grumbled Stark bent from his great height and spat in his face. If the man persisted he received a clout from the flat of his captain's hand.

Bara pulled herself up on the rail and looked towards the pirate ship. It was approaching fast, looming out of the shining mist with all sails set, and she could see people moving on deck. The milky haze had thickened across the sky and the edge of the sun was fuzzed and soft. Bara's shift, so recently soaked in sweat, now lay chill on her back. She screwed up her eyes, trying to make out more clearly the figures on the deck. How could pirates have such a lovely ship? The white sails breasted the mist on two tall masts, a high carved prow rose and fell, cutting long bow waves. Stark came striding up the deck, roaring in Welsh at his crew and roughly disposing them along the port rail. Then he grabbed Con by the shoulder and thrust him at Bara.

'Get below, you lot,' he said.

'But I've got a knife,' said Tam, heaving himself to his feet.

'Aye, and you may be wanting it too. Get down to the cabin and look after those two.'

Tam passed his arm across his forehead and Bara took his elbow. With Con leading they climbed down the companionway to the foul-smelling cabin. Tam began to retch again, so he stood by the door, leaning on the post. The mist was thickening, and the sun was merely a source of diffuse, pale light. Tam felt the chill on his bare chest and he shivered. He fingered the shaft of his knife, knotty in his hand, while he and Bara both strained to hear the first shout. Con fidgeted, and grumbled, wanting to see the pirates.

Both ships had furled much sail and slowly changed course, so that they were roughly alongside about two hundred yards apart. Stark and his men stood silently by the rail, their fish-knives ready in their hands. The ships veered and slewed, as the breeze and the swell dictated, but slowly the gap between them closed.

'Ahoy!' came the cry from the other ship, where men also lined the rail.

Tam looked over the top of the companion-way and saw a man on the big ship leap onto the rail, holding onto the lines with one hand. He had cropped sandy hair and his blue tunic was caught in with a wide leather belt.

'Ahoy!' he shouted. 'Can you hear me?'

'What do you want?' yelled Stark, while the helmsman struggled to keep the ship parallel. 'We've got nothing here, only a few fish.'

'We don't want fish, and we're not pirates.'

'What the hell are you then?'

'We're looking for someone. For three people. A man and a girl and a boy'.

There was a silence that filled the sea and the sky. To Bara and Tam it seemed the blood stood still in their hearts. Time was suspended in the few seconds it took Stark to recover himself.

'Never heard of them,' he shouted. 'We're fishermen here, not a bloody boarding house.' The man in the blue tunic looked across the water for a moment.

'All right. If that's the way you want it. We'll have to come and see. Stand by while we grapple you. If you try to get away you'll get hurt, and the boat too. Our irons are heavy.'

Stark spat furiously, then strode over to the companionway. He glared down at Tam, who stood at the door of the cabin.

'What the bloody blazes do I do now?' he whispered. 'I'm not having my boat sunk just for you three.'

'Play for time,' said Tam. 'Tell him to come on, and try to find out why he wants us.'

'Well, I'll do that much for you and nowt else. Nowt else at all. See?'

He walked back to the rail. The ships were already very close and the other crew were hauling long grappling beams across their deck.

'Come on then,' shouted Stark. 'Come on over and see. But if you hurt my boat we'll knife the lot of you.'

The sandy-haired captain gazed over the water at him, obviously puzzled by the invitation, and he motioned with his hand for his men to stop hauling.

'Who were you talking to in the cabin?' he called.

'None of your business.'

'Listen, if you've got them we're going to have them. But listen —' and he spoke very slow and clear – 'I swear to you by all the old gods of Erin that we will not harm one hair of their heads. We will take them to Ireland, and that is where they want to go.'

Stark wiped his mouth and scowled, not knowing what to say or do. His indecision was resolved by Tam, who climbed the companionway and appeared by the rail at his side.

'What do you want with us?' he said, his face black with suspicion.

'Are you the man who has the golden woman and the flaxen boy?'

'What if I am?' Tam's heart was thudding against his ribs.

For a moment the Irish captain stared across the water at him, then his face split slowly into a wide smile. Even to Tam's suspicious eye it was no smile of malice or sarcasm, it was a smile of pure delight.

'Welcome to Ireland!' cried the man. 'And about time it is too. Listen, my friend. We've been sailing these waters for more than two months now, two whole months on this damn little patch of water, just waiting for you three.'

His friendliness was disarming, but Tam remained suspicious.

'How do I know you won't murder us or torture us or rape the girl?' he shouted.

The man looked shocked.

'We are not like that,' he said gently. 'We do not murder and torture and rape.'

'Prove it,' said Tam, still surly. The Irish captain leaned back wearily against the ratlines and folded his arms.

'Indeed you are very difficult,' he said, 'but I suppose you have good reason. Listen now, does this convince you? I know, I *know,* that you have been compelled to come to Ireland. I know you have resisted many times but always you have come on. I know that only the boy has never wavered.'

Tam stared at him, then he turned and called to Bara and Con. They came slowly up from the cabin and stood with Tam by the rail. For a moment of silence the captain of the great ship gazed at them through the gathering mist, then he gravely raised his arm in salute.

'You are welcome to Ireland,' he said. 'The dark man and the golden woman and the flaxen boy.'

Tam grinned sheepishly, fingering the black knots of his beard as he glanced at the ragged clothes and tangled hair of his two companions. Con's face was streaked with smears of tar and his chin was stuck aggressively on the rail as he tried to peer over the side. Bara's blue shift was torn, her strained face reflected the months of danger she had come through.

'Do you really want us?' called Tam. 'Are you sure it's us you want?'

'Quite sure. Will you come over if I send the boat?'

'The horses!' Bara leaned urgently over the rail. 'We can't leave the horses?'

'Horses? What horses?'

'Two horses. In the hold.'

'You'll have to leave them. We can't get horses from your boat to ours.'

'No!' Bara gripped the rail, her knuckles white. 'No, I won't leave them. I won't.' Her voice rose to a scream and Tam looked at her in concern. 'I couldn't,' she said, calming herself as she caught his glance. 'I couldn't. Dark saved our lives I don't know how many times. He's one of us.'

Eventually it was decided that Stark should sail on to Rosslare under escort from the big ship. His reluctance to do so was soon overcome by the sight of Tam's silver, and the solemn promise of the other captain that there was good whisky in Ireland.

All the time the white mist was thickening around them, barely perceptible at first, but now wafting in swathes around the masts and rigging. Both boats bustled with activity as sails were re-set and a course laid for Rosslare ten miles to the west. When all was ready Bara turned towards the great ship, only to find she could barely make it out in the chill, white mist.

'We'll blow our horn,' yelled the Irish captain. 'Follow the sound.'

'Aye,' called Stark, 'but don't go too quick for me.'

'There's no special channel into Rosslare. It's all deep and safe.'

'See you there then.'

'There's a light at the harbour. Have a whisky on me tonight—' His voice died away in the swirling mist.

Stark strode about the deck, looming out of the mist and vanishing again as he swore at the helmsman and the crew. Bara and Tam stood in the bows, staring ahead, but although they could hear the horn they could no longer see the tall Irish ship. Con stood silently, holding Bara's hand and gazing with startled eyes at the clouds of mist that curled about the boat.

'Will we be shipwrecked, Mam?' he asked.

'Oh no Con, we won't be shipwrecked.'

'But wouldn't you like that?' said Tam, smiling down at him.

'Well, not much. You see, I can't swim.'

'We only have to stand off shore till the mist clears,' said Tam. But even as he spoke the mist was thickening into fog, and soon it was coming at them in cold white billows. They could still hear the horn ahead, but Tam was sure it was fainter. Bara shivered, then she and Con went down to the horses and on to the cabin, where she was glad to put on her sheepskin. The place was gloomy but the smell was less pungent and the cold fog had not yet penetrated. She played a few rounds of paper, scissors, stone with Con, then they lay down on the hard bunks and tried to sleep. Above her head Bara could hear the crew pacing about the deck, but they moved slowly and did not shout to each other. Once again Bara recognized an old companion, the silence of fear. This was an unknown sea and an unknown coast, with only the fading horn ahead as a lifeline to the land. Bara looked over at Con who lay on his bunk, taut as a wire, his blue eyes wide with attention.

The boat moved slowly in the light breezes, all sails set, and there was no doubt they were falling behind the Irish ship. When after a couple of hours of fitful dozing Bara came up on deck again she saw that Stark had stationed a man in the bows, whose only duty was to listen for the distant horn. In a few minutes he could hear it no more. Bara put her arm through Tam's.

'Better?' she asked.

'Much. But I don't think I'll ever make a sailor. Captain!' He called to Stark, who rose out of the fog beside him.

'Aye? What is it?'

'What are we going to do? Where are we?'

'Bloody damnfool questions. How for Chrissakes do I know? I wish I'd never taken t'bloody gold. It's you lot brought us into this.'

'Sorry.'

'Sorry be damned. We're taking a northerly course now, then turning for home before we hit the rocks on yon bloody coast.' He spat ferociously.

'You can't.' Bara leaped forward but Tam caught her arm.

'Oh can't I then? That's what we're doing, my young filly, and if you make trouble, eh, I'll tie you up, that I will.' He wiped his mouth hard. 'The breeze's dead east, it'll be a long beat home, but I'm not wrecking my boat for you or anyone.'

He strode off into the white clouds of fog.

'Oh God,' said Tam wearily, leaning on his elbows on the rail. 'It seemed so easy.'

Bara was biting her lip, and fighting against the tears that stung her eyes. After so much and so long it was more cruel than she could bear to turn back now, a mile or two from Ireland.

'Don't cry Mam,' said Con, clutching her legs and looking up at her. 'We're nearly there.'

'But we're not Con. He's making us go back.'

'But we're nearly there. I don't care what he says. I know we're nearly there.'

Tam turned and they both looked down at him.

'What do you mean, Con?' said Bara, kneeling down.

'What-I-keep-saying.' Con jerked his head impatiently between each word. 'We're almost there.' Tam and Bara looked at each other over his head.

'We'll see,' said Tam shrugging. Suddenly he felt himself struck sharply on the leg.

'Listen!' shouted Con, punching again in his anger. 'Listen both of you. We'll soon be there. I know.' Tam put his hand on Con's shoulder.

'All right,' he said gently. 'Whenever you say you know something you're always right. We believe you.'

The clouds of Con's anger dispersed and he smiled.

'I feel jolly,' he said, jumping against the rail.

Tam and Bara looked at each other with eyebrows raised.

For two more hours they moved slowly through the fog on a northward course. Orders were peremptorily given and acknowledged, boiled mutton and vegetables were served in the galley. No-one spoke more than he had to, and no-one smiled. Con's noisy optimism, which he attempted to share with the crew, only acted as another irritant and Bara had to restrain him by her side before any more of the men swore at him.

Slowly the fog melted from white to grey, and they knew the night was closing in. Black scowls were turned on Tam and Bara, and a few angry words muttered in Welsh. Fog and the night and the unknown rocks of the shore filled every man on board with dread. As darkness gathered Tam and Bara took Con down to the cabin. There was no boat aboard, and no kind of lifebelt, but while walking round the deck Tam had noticed some spars lying against the stern. These they would make for at the first sound of rending timber. They lay down as best they could, Bara and Con on the bunks and Tam on the long table, but they knew they would not sleep. All on board but Con were tensed for the first sign of shipwreck.

'We'll soon be there,' said Con happily, curling himself up like a puppy. 'See you in the morning.'

Tam and Bara lay stiffly, holding each other's hands, and unwilling to talk any more of danger and death. Each knew the other was afraid, but each drew courage from the current of trust and love which flowed between them. Danger was diminished, even death was endurable, if they could face them together. For two more hours of darkness the ship moved warily on.

A yell split the thick silence of the night. The soft tendrils of fog scattered as the cry came again, bursting into the cabin.

'Light on the port bow! Light on the port bow!' Bodies were tripping and shoving and scrambling to reach the port rail, but it was a few moments before anyone could make out the tremulous halo. Tam found himself standing beside Stark.

'It must be Rosslare,' he said. 'It's the harbour light.'

'Aye, I could think of that meself,' growled the captain, peering over Tam's head. 'Mebbe 'tis, mebbe 'tisn't. Mebbe it marks rocks.'

'He said the water was deep.'

'Aye, at Rosslare,' he said. 'How do we know we're at Rosslare?'

'I shouldn't think there's many lights along this coast.'

'Well now, and shouldn't you. And what the bloody hell do you know about it?'

He glared at Tam and spat and turned away. They heard him talking to the crew in Welsh, then he began to bark out orders. Slowly the ship slewed towards the light.

'We're going in,' whispered Bara.

'Come over here,' said Tam, taking her hand and leading her and Con to the spars in the stern. He moved about in the light of the stern-lantern and Bara saw that he was collecting and cutting rope.

'If anything happens we tie ourselves to one of these,' he whispered. Con looked up at him angrily.

'Nothing's going to happen,' he shouted. 'Can't you see, we're nearly there.'

The ship crept through the darkness, moving westerly with much of the sail down. The shimmering halo of light grew as they approached. Stark peered at it through slit eyes, gripping the rail of the afterdeck where he stood by the helmsman.

'For Chrissake,' he repeated again and again, 'for Chrissake.'

The light never bobbed or wavered, so it was either on land or on rocks. Four of the crew stared down from the bows, searching for the flakes of foam that would betray a reef below. But for the short distance they could see through the fog and the dark the gentle swell rose and dipped unperturbed. The helmsman stood tense, ready to swing the wheel at the first cry of danger. Seconds were stretched to minutes and minutes seemed hours to all who waited aboard. Still the ship moved on, heading for the light, with only enough sail to give her some way. The circle of light grew larger and brighter, the dark swell remained unbroken. Suddenly they were astounded to hear a shout from the direction of the light.

'Ahoy! Ahoy!'

The cry came faintly through the fog. Stark spoke to the helmsman and they moved on, straight for the light.

'Ahoy!'

The call was clearer now, and Stark grinned, relaxing his long body in relief.

'It must be the harbour!' shouted Tam.

'Aye, it could be. Anyhows it's sommat.' Stark leaped down from the afterdeck and ran to the bows. He cupped his hands and bellowed. 'Ahoy, ahoy! I want to bring my ship in.'

After a long silence a voice floated back across the water.

'Bring her in then. What's the trouble?'

'Bastards,' muttered Stark, spitting as he returned to the helm.

Suddenly they saw the mole, a dark strip faintly lit by the halo-ed light. Stark yelled orders, the crew ran, the helmsman put the wheel hard over. Slowly they drifted at an angle towards the dark mole.

'Hi, you there! Man alive, you're slow tonight.' The voice came crisply over the water but the figure of the shouting man was lost in the circle of light.

'Where are you going, Collum?' shouted another voice. 'You've missed your berth, man. Too much poteen on board?'

Stark glowered over the rail as his boat drifted alongside, half way down the mole and beyond the circle of light. Footsteps came running, mingled with laughter and shouts of abuse. Three men loomed up in the fog, only to stop dead in their tracks. There was a moment's utter silence. Then one of the men stepped forward.

'Who the hell are you?' he said, his hand on the knife in his belt. One of his companions stepped up beside him.

'Where's Collum?' he shouted. 'Where's his ship?' The third man ran off again into the fog.

'They think we're pirates,' said Tam to Stark. 'They've gone to get more men.' Stark passed his hand across his mouth.

'Listen,' he shouted. 'We're not pirates. We're men from Wales over the sea. If Collum has a tall white ship I don't know where the hell he is. He was supposed to guide us to Rosslare.'

'This is Rosslare,' said one of the men. 'You tell us what you've done with Collum.'

Stark sighed wearily.

'I'm telling you, aren't I? We met him out there at sea. He was meant to bring us here. But we lost him in the fog. We couldn't keep up.'

'We'll soon see,' said the man suspiciously.

'Come aboard then,' said Stark.

'Aye, when me friends come.'

'Can I tie up without you sticking that knife in me?'

'If you want. One man only on the shore.'

Stark and the crew busied themselves with the ropes, then suddenly Con laughed.

'I told you didn't I?' he shouted, looking up at Tam. 'We're there. It's Ireland, isn't it? We're there.'

Bara burst out laughing and hugged him.

'I'd completely forgotten,' she said. 'Of course. It's Ireland. We're really there.'

She flung herself into Tam's arms, and they did not notice how their noisy celebrations angered the crew.

'Aw – shut up,' growled Stark at length. 'We may be murdered yet.'

'We won't,' crowed Con, high up in the shrouds. 'We won't, we won't, we won't.'

The sound of running feet interrupted them. A dozen men appeared out of the fog, each one armed with a stave or a long knife.

'Give us a gang-plank,' called the man who had been watching them.

'No,' shouted Stark. 'How do I know you won't murder us all?'

The crowd on the bank looked at each other, nonplussed.

'We wouldn't do that,' one of them called.

'Then drop those things.'

'How do we know you won't kill *us* then?'

Stark spat. 'I'm a fisherman, not a murderer.'

After long, suspicious arguments it was decided that ten men would come aboard and both parties would keep their weapons. But as the Irish leader came aboard he cried, 'May Brigid blind the first man to raise a knife!' Two men were sent to the cabin and four to the hold. Then the leader turned and saw Tam lurking in the stern.

'Who are those with you?' he asked, trying to peer round Tam's body.

Bara and Con came slowly forward, Con with jaunty confidence, Bara more wary.

'Holy Brigid,' whispered the man, staring at them. 'It's them. It's the very ones themselves. Did Collum find you then?'

'Yes,' said Bara. 'We were to follow him here, but we lost him in the fog.'

Quickly the man smiled, and Bara caught a flash of gold in his teeth.

'It's an honour to meet you,' he said. Bara searched for sarcasm, but she could find none. 'You and the boy. It's a long time we've been waiting.'

'Hullo,' said Con cheerfully.

Tam smiled from Con to Bara, where they stood in the dim light in the stern of the boat.

'We're glad to be here,' he said. 'At last.'

As Bara spoke to the man Tam looked gravely at her, seeing clearly for the first time what the anxieties of a mere five months had done to her face. Up till now he had been too busy, or too scared, or too blinded by love to look searchingly for the girl he had known in London. Now for the first time he saw how her cheeks had sunk, how her brow had contracted, how her mouth had set tight, and his heart ached. He longed to take her in his arms, he longed to restore the light that he remembered in her face. But he stood rooted, and the moment passed.

Two hours later they were all seated round a long trestle in a vast wooden hall. Bara and Tam and Con were at one end, Stark sat far away at the other, and between them down each side stretched the Welsh crew and the Irish harbour men. There were torches flaring in sconces on the wall and four great lanterns on the table, all casting a weird criss-cross of shadows on the two lines of faces. They had eventually manoeuvred the unhappy horses off the ship, and Bara had seen to their stabling and feeding. She had stayed with Dark a long time, stroking him while she talked, and at last she was rewarded with his great soft muzzle in her neck. She felt she was forgiven and she had left him with her mind at ease.

To Bara the banquet was a marvel which she would remember in a cloud of light and noise as long as she lived. With the great platefuls of potatoes and fish and eggs and cheese, there was passed a strange colourless liquid in flagons. It was fiery stuff, but after the first sip, Bara decided it was good, and she allowed her horn to be replenished after every gulp. In less than a quarter of an hour the torches and the faces and the flagons were swimming together in the unreality of a dream. She floated off, somewhere into the dark rafters, and looked down on herself and the crowd in a pool of flickering light. There were faces, faces, faces, all turned towards her, smiling and nodding and laughing. In a surge of love for everyone and everything she laughed back. Lovely, lovely people. She laughed and she laughed, throwing back her sheet of hair and allowing the tears to stream down her cheeks. She knew Tam was there, swaying somewhere at the edge of her vision, staring vacantly and shaking his head. She knew Con was there – his shining mane of hair swam back and forth as he moved among the dogs by the fire. But who were all these laughing men? It did not matter, they were beautiful and she loved them all. Suddenly she jumped up and staggered onto the table. She was aloft, high up, far away among colours and lights. She swayed unsteadily and began to sing. What she sang she hardly knew. The words flowed out in music from long, long ago; songs that Kate had taught her when she was a little girl, an age, a century away. She began to prance her way down the table, hands on hips, stamping and tapping with her feet as she went. Hastily dishes and flagons were clattered out of her path and hands began to clap in rhythm to her songs. Anything that came to her she sang; she sang Loch Lomond, An Octopus's Garden, Where e'er you Walk, A-Roving, Lily the Pink, The Foggy Dew, Six Dukes Went A-Fishing, Ring-a-Ring o'Roses. She sang on and on, swaying rhythmically up and down the long table between the lines of laughing faces and clapping hands. Dimly she was aware of Tam, who stood up now and then, only to sit down promptly, his face glazed and his mouth open. He was lovely, they were all lovely, this was a lovely, lovely place.

Suddenly there surged up before her the huge length of Captain Stark. His heels clattered on the table, his arms swung wildly, his face was wreathed in smiles. He seized Bara's hand and whirled her round and round, then they linked elbows and capered in tight circles up and down the long trestle. The torchlight swirled, faces raced towards her, wheeled, and sped away; Con's head shone like a whirling moon. Then the table rushed up to meet her and she knew no more.

She woke next morning in a small whitewashed room. The sun streamed through a high window and from the angle she knew it must be high in the sky. Somewhere outside there were shouts and laughter. She lay with a blanket over her on a straw palliasse, and her head rested on a soft pillow covered in yellow linen. This much she saw before she was forced to close her eyes again. Her temples ached savagely, and when she moved she discovered that her head throbbed through from ear to ear. She groaned, covering her eyes with her hand, and turned very carefully away from the light. Just then the door opened and a woman appeared. She was round and pink, with hair drawn loosely into a bun, and she wore a shapeless garment of blue linen. In her hands she held a crude brown bowl. When she saw Bara's eyes were open she smiled with an amusement which was more than merely sociable.

'Well,' she said, moving over to the palliasse and placing her bowl on the ground. 'Well, it was some evening you had to be sure. Did you never meet the poteen before then?'

Bara shook her head painfully and tried to smile. The woman laughed as she wrung out a handful of wet moss from her bowl and laid it on Bara's forehead.

'What did you say it was?' asked Bara, closing her eyes with pleasure at the touch of the cold moss.

'Poteen. It's our drink in Ireland. And they shouldn't have ladled it into you like that, sure they shouldn't. They're a wicked lot, those boys.'

'Was I very drunk?'

'Ah, you were charming drunk. There's some people take it badly and there's some take it beautiful. You take it a dream. You'd charm the water from a stone when you're drunk.'

Bara pulled a faint smile and sighed with relief as another handful of wet moss was laid on her forehead.

'How's Tam?'

'Your man? He doesn't take the drink so well. He sat like a wet pig in a bog most of the evening.'

Bara laughed as love and delight flooded through her, but she stopped abruptly when hammers pounded in her head. The woman went on.

'His mouth hung open wider and wider until you'd think his jaw would drop off.'

'Where is he?'

'Through there. Asleep like a child. And the little lad's down at the harbour with Finn. It's the time of his life he's having. Would you like some soup now?'

Bara declined and said she would sleep some more.

'I suppose I ought to say I'm sorry,' she added.

'Ah no. Sure you gave the greatest pleasure to us all.'

The woman smiled as she backed out of the door, and Bara smiled ruefully back.

When she woke again the sun had left her little room. Gingerly she turned her head and found to her relief the ache had almost vanished. She propped herself up on an elbow. Where there had been shouts and laughter there was now a deep and unnerving silence. No voices, no footsteps, only a deathly hush. Carefully she climbed off her palliasse and stretched. She noticed for the first time that her clothes had been changed and she was now wearing a long white smock with flowers embroidered round the hem. She looked down at it admiringly, then turned to go out.

She opened the latch on the wooden door, expecting to find herself in a corridor, but instead she found she was out in the sunlight. Yesterday's fog had vanished but there was still a white shimmer over the sea ahead of her. Down a gentle green slope was the harbour, and she saw now where everyone had gone. About fifty people, men and women, stood in a silent circle on the shore. They were bareheaded and some of the men held caps in their hands. As Bara approached she saw that they were looking at a body stretched full length on the ground, and alongside it a few large chunks of wet timber. Tam detached himself from the group and came slowly up the slope to meet her. He put his arm round her shoulders and looked back at the body.

'It's one of Collum's crew,' he whispered. 'A fisherman just brought him in. The ship was wrecked in the fog on the Tuskar Rock. They haven't found anyone alive.'

Bara's face contracted with pain. Collum and his tall white ship. They stood looking at the silent crowd and the body of the young man on the shore.

'It was a lovely ship,' said Tam. 'They must be good at these things. No-one in England could build a ship like that. And we'd have been on it,' he added, 'except for Dark and Moon.'

Con came slowly up the slope towards them, dragging a huge rope of seaweed. He looked solemnly up at Bara, standing close in front of her.

'They went on the big rock,' he said. His brow furrowed and he looked down at the ground. 'I knew – I think I knew there was a rock,' he went on, drawing on the sandy soil with his toe. 'I think there was – well, once, there was a kind of map of the sea.'

'A chart?' said Tam.

'Maybe. I don't know that word. A map of rocks and things. I think I could've – oh I don't know.' He looked up, shrugging and smiling. 'I don't know. My mind's all smoky. Come on!' he shouted suddenly at Tam, racing off with his seaweed trailing behind him.

Angry heads turned on the shore and Tam raced after Con to subdue him, for the child had already forgotten the drowned youth on the shore.

They discovered within the next few hours how powerful was the Irish reverence for the dead, and they were amazed when they remembered the perfunctory attitude to corpses with which they had grown up. Bara thought of Charley's funeral in Hampstead, to which she had ridden in the cart with Kate (so long ago it seemed hardly the same lifetime). And she knew that his funeral had been considered elaborate and grand. But it seemed that for this drowned boy the preparations and the wake and the funeral would take a night and a day, with no other work done and everyone participating.

The boy was carried reverently up to one of the huts along the shore, and there Bara was allowed to watch while the women washed him and shaved him and dressed him in a pall of purple wool. He looked utterly at peace, as if drowning had been no enemy to him at all. She found it hard to think, as she looked at his composure, of the gasping lungs or the struggling limbs or the final exhaustion and cold. Then the men came again and took him to the great storehouse where they had had the banquet. They laid him on a trestle at one end of the hall, and a man stood at each corner with his head bowed and his arms folded, as at the death of kings. Supper was served in silence at the far end of the building. Bara kept Con strictly subdued while she and Tam concentrated on how they were expected to behave. Supper of eggs and fish was eaten standing and they noticed that at no time did anyone sit down in the presence of the dead.

After everyone had finished eating the people lined up on one side of the hall and slowly moved forward to kiss the boy. Bara noticed the other children had left, so she sent Con away to play with them on the shore. When everyone had kissed the cold brow the watchers changed with four other men and the crowd slowly filed out of the hall.

'Come with me,' said the woman who had cooled Bara's face with moss. 'And he with Finn.'

She pointed to Tam and then to a stocky man of twenty-five or so, with a shock of fiery red hair. 'He can help Finn and the men with the hearse and the grave. We'll do the cooking for the morrow.'

'Cooking?' asked Bara.

'Aye, for the wake after the burial. Times ago they had the wake before the poor corpse was cold, but now we think it's more decent this way. I never told you my name. I'm Joan.'

'I'm Bara.'

'Ah, I know that right well.'

Joan led the way to a long wooden hut in which there were stoves and a huge wooden table. A dozen women were already at work, lighting the sconces, stoking the ovens, laying out great earthenware bowls and enormous rolling pins. Joan pointed out the bins of coarse brown flour, the beet sugar, the leather buckets full of fresh well water; she showed with pride a small jug of precious currants, which she said were made from the grapes they grew at Glendalough away in the west. On the walls were ranged pots of herbs and saffron and vegetable dyes, and above them rows of gleaming copper tins and moulds beaten into curves and flutings. Under Joan's direction Bara worked at pastry and cakes and puddings until her arms ached and her feet dragged. The smells from the ovens were delicious and every so often a head cook would come round with some rich uncooked mixture or a pile of broken cake for everyone to share. Many of the women chattered, some worked silently, many more sang quietly. Their songs were thin and sad, pitched very high, in keys that were not familiar to Bara's ear, and they made her feel that the songs she half-remembered singing in her revelry were coarse and vulgar pieces. Her face was hot at the memory, and she blushed constantly too at the scrutiny of the other women. They were deeply interested in her, and their frank stares did not drop when she glanced back. They simply smiled, or waved their spoons, or went on talking about her just out of earshot. She was reminded too much of the Shepherds' Kingdom. Here, as there, she did not relish the interest she aroused, for it stemmed from some knowledge which she did not share. The old unease returned and she ceased to smile back or respond to the chatter of the women around her. Doggedly she mixed and stirred and rolled her dough, wrapping her fears in surliness and silence. Eventually Joan noticed.

'What's wrong?' she said, more pink and smiling than ever. 'Has someone been nasty then?' She wiped her hands on her apron and looked round into Bara's grim face. 'Is there someone's been upsetting you?'

'No.'

'They like you. We all do so. And it's certain you're very important to us.'

Slowly Bara put down her rolling pin and stared at Joan.

'Last time I was important,' she said, 'was because Con and I were going to be sacrificed.'

'Sacrificed?' said Joan in puzzlement.

'Raped and killed.'

'God's mercy,' said Joan, retreating. 'Raped and killed?' Her face was aghast.

'Yes. I thought that might be why we were important again.'

Joan took her arm gently and led her out of the kitchen into the starry night. She put her plump arm round Bara's shoulders but Bara was irritated and wriggled free.

'This is Ireland,' said Joan softly. 'This is no longer a barbaric land. Indeed it is not.'

She looked down towards the sea, shimmering in starlight. Bara felt the night wind on her face and she knew her fear was dying. 'While we have the Old One,' Joan continued, 'while we have the Old One this will be a beautiful land to be living in. There's nothing a girl or her man or her little lad need fear from us.'

The last of Bara's terror drained away and the muscles of her body relaxed. She smiled and put her hand on Joan's arm. They stood for a few moments in silence, listening to the swish of the waves down on the dark shore. Then Bara spoke.

'Who is the Old One?'

'Indeed he is just the Old One. I don't know any other name. He lives half the year in Dublin and half in Cashel and he is clever beyond all men.'

'Is he a good man?'

'He is wise and he is good. But he says that a boy will come who is greater than himself.'

'A boy?'

'Aye. A boy. Your son.'

PART 3

Beginnings

BARA LAY ON HER MATTRESS in her tiny room but she could not rest. Her mind whirled, leaping from image to image, from elation to amazement to fear. She longed for Tam to return, for the words she had just heard were too much for her to comprehend alone. Con – a leader, a man greater than the Old One. How could Tam be so long, preparing a hearse and a grave? Con to be a king, just as she had seen in her visions; Con blue and silver, moving across the flowered fields of Ireland. It was ridiculous, it made no sense at all. And yet something had compelled them to make the journey. The Old One? The Old One who had told the people that a boy greater than he would come? Oh, when would Tam be back?

By standing on her toes on her mattress Bara could raise her chin just to the level of the window. She knew that somewhere behind her in the west the moon had risen, for a pale light washed out the stars above her and the sea shone a ghostly silver. There was no sound but the swish of the waves and the occasional barking of a dog.

When Tam came at last she had fallen asleep. As she felt his hands on her shoulders and his cold face laid on hers she lifted her arms and tried to pull him down on top of her. But he would not come. He leaned on his elbows, hovering above her in the dark. She ran her hands over his face and through his tangle of hair.

'What is it?' she whispered. He groaned and rolled over onto his side.

'I feel sick,' he said.

'Are you ill?'

'No. It's the funeral. Do you know what happens?'

'I know there's a feast afterwards. We've been cooking half the night.'

Tam rolled off the bed and paced up and down in the dark, slapping himself with his arms.

'You know what barrows are?' he said. 'Like Bela's Knap? Those old burial places?'

'Of course I do.'

'Well, these people open them up. That's what we've been doing. Moving huge stone slabs from the entrance and making a space inside.'

'Inside? What for?'

'Oh it's ghastly in there.' Tam shuddered and sank down on the bed. 'It's full of old skeletons and broken pots and rusty knives and God knows what.'

'Old bones aren't so terrible really,' said Bara, puzzled by the disgust in his voice.

'But a lot of them aren't old at all. They're very new. Some of the bodies are hardly decomposed at all. They're all propped up round the walls still in their clothes. Some aren't even very dusty. And the stench – oh my God.' He leaned over the floor and retched heavily.

'Oh Tam.' Bara had her arm tightly round his shoulders and her face in his hair.

'Let's get out of here. Let's wake Con and go.'

'But how? Where can we go?'

'I'm not staying for that funeral. If we're here tomorrow we'll have to go to it. It takes all day then the wake takes all night. I'm not going into that barrow again.'

'Let's go then. We'll say we felt the Old One wanted us.'

When Bara entered Con's cell she found him awake, standing in his shirt on the bed.

'Mam,' he whimpered, 'I can't get to sleep. I was coming for you.' Bara took him in her arms.

'Why?' she said.

'We have to go. We have to get on. It hurts here.' Con pulled his hand across his forehead. 'We can't stay here. We've got to go on.'

'All right, we'll go on. Tam wants to too. We'll get up and get ready.'

'Oh good.' Con's drooping face dissolved into a smile and he jumped down from his mattress. 'It'll be nice to ride again,' he said as he began to pull on his clothes. Tam appeared in the doorway.

'I've written a note to Stark,' he said. 'I thanked him and wished him a safe journey home. I put in my last bit of silver.'

'So now we're absolutely and finally broke,' said Bara.

'We won't need any more money,' said Con scornfully. 'We'll be all right.'

They moved quietly out into the starry night. The air was sharp and each was aware for a moment of the skin of their bodies. The moon rode high above and in the landscape of grey and silver only the waves moved. Away to the left the light of the dying ovens glowed in the windows of the cookhouse. Dark and Moon stood side by side in the stables, quietly pulling at wisps of hay. Bara hugged Dark's neck and he lowered his head to her. Both horses came out eagerly, their ears pricked, apparently pleased with the briskness of the night air.

Once saddled and mounted, with Con tucked between Bara's arms, they urged the horses forward over the springy turf. Bara was sorry as she glanced back at the kitchen embers that they would not be sharing in that sumptuous feast; but she kept her thoughts to herself. They had no idea which way to ride so they made inland and hoped to find their course when the dawn broke. As far as they could judge in the darkness the country was open, with few trees, and the ground beneath the horses' feet was firm and grassy.

They jogged gently on for three or four hours. Slowly the moon set, withdrawing the ghostly light by which they had picked their way. Bara drew her sheepskin tighter around her, for the night was becoming colder and there was a touch of rain in the breeze. Slowly the dawn crept up. There was no blaze of scarlet, no brilliant disc sailing a clear sky, only a steady encroaching of grey light. The shining summer of yesterday had vanished like a bubble. In the early dawn they passed a group of burial mounds, one freshly dug, and Tam turned abruptly away. 'Shut up' was all he would say to Con's complaints of cold and hunger.

They crossed a small brown river, where they had to lead the reluctant horses over the stepping-stones, then moved up the long gentle slope on the other side. Suddenly Bara looked about her.

'I thought there was something funny,' she said. 'Ever since we landed. I've just realized – there's no rubbish. It's all clean and empty.'

'That's right,' said Tam also looking about him. 'Not a single old car. No TVs, no plastic, no anything.'

'No tins, no old iron, no pylons. Even in Wales there was rubbish.'

'They've cleared it all up. They must have. What a job. That's really good.'

'A scoured land. Beginning again.'

As the drizzle began to fall more heavily they came upon a man in a red shirt and leather breeches digging turf by the roadside. He stood up straight when he saw them, leaning with one arm on his spade, and widened his mouth in a gat-toothed smile.

'You're early across the Carock,' he said, 'on a nasty morning too.'

'We've been riding for hours,' said Tam, drawing up. 'Where can we get some food?'

'Nowhere round here. But you're welcome to this.' The man bent down and picked up a reed basket by his feet. He pulled out a loaf and stoppered jar. 'Bread and milk,' he said, holding them out.

'But we can't take that,' said Bara. 'It's your breakfast.'

'And why can't you take it?' said the man. 'Isn't it mine to give?'

Con settled the dispute by slipping off Dark and running to the food.

'Thanks,' he said, smiling up at the man. 'I like your shirt,' he added, as he sank his teeth in the bread.

'That's very good of you,' the man answered, showing his gaps. 'I like it meself.'

Each of them tore off a lump of bread and took a drink of milk while the man gazed at them. Then he could contain his curiosity no longer.

'Are you looking for someone?' he asked.

'Yes,' said Tam, gulping his milk. 'We're looking for the Old One.'

'Sure everyone knows the Old One is at Cashel in the summer. You're off the road.'

'We're strangers. We don't know where Cashel is.'

'Don't know—' The man's eyes opened wide and brown in amazement. 'Where are you from then?'

'From Wales. Across the water. From England.'

'Ahhhhh.' The man folded his arms with a knowing air. 'Now I know who you are for sure. You're the ones from across the water. The dark man and the golden woman and the flaxen boy.'

'You know about us too?' asked Bara, feeling the familiar grip of fear in her stomach.

'All Ireland knows about you. The Old One can't die till you come.'

Tam and Bara looked at each other.

'Why does he want us so much?' asked Tam.

'Holy St Brigid,' burst out the man, 'youse don't know much. It's a truly ignorant lot you are to be sure. Is there nobody riding with you then?' he asked, looking around. 'Why are you alone?'

'We left Rosslare last night,' said Tam. 'Everyone was busy with a funeral.'

'A funeral? A funeral did you say? I never knew there was a funeral at Rosslare. Holy water, where's that horse?' He flung his spade onto the turf and spun round. 'Oh there's the old bag. How'll I get to her and her right away yonder?'

He pointed towards a grassy mound on the other side of the peat and he began to run across the bog, calling over his shoulder as he went.

'Bear north-west for Cashel. I'd show you but I can't stay. I wouldn't miss a funeral for all the gold in Ireland—' His voice trailed off over the bog and his red shirt vanished into the misty drizzle. Tam shrugged.

'It's crazy,' he said. 'Just bloody crazy. Are they barbarians or aren't they? He'd share all his food with us, and yet drops everything to ride miles through the rain to that foul funeral.'

'It's creepy,' said Bara shivering. 'I wish we could be at Cashel and get it over.'

'When we get to Cashel it'll be only just beginning. Whatever "it" may be.'

'Tam, I'm scared. I'm really frightened. For a few hours it all seemed lovely.'

Tam rode alongside and put his hand on her knee.

'It's all right,' he said. 'Look at Con.'

The boy lay back against Tam's body, humming quietly to himself with a half smile on his face. Bara pulled her sheepskin tighter round her wet shoulders.

'Last time it rained like this was the day before Bela's Knap.'

'Don't think about it. Shove it out of your mind. We'll find food and a place to rest.'

The country was still lush and green, but more undulating now, scattered with copses and woods and occasional small patches of barley. Some had been cut and laid in stooks, but some still stood unharvested, silver-grey, waiting for the sickle and a dry day. They rode doggedly on for another hour or more searching without success for a cottage or a farm. The green land was empty and chill. Then Con sat up abruptly and pointed to the slope of a low hill. Below a rocky outcrop was a stone hut with a thatched roof and smoke trailing from the chimney. As they rode closer they could see a narrow door and three small windows tucked under the thatch.

'It's like a doll's house,' said Con.

'It's like a witch's cottage,' retorted Bara, determined not to be cheered.

A few sheep wandered about the hillside and three scraggy hens scratched near the door, but there was no sign of a shepherd or goatherd. Tam dismounted and beat on the door with his fist. Then he pushed open the door and peered in.

'No-one here,' he called. 'There's a fire and clean hay and a bucket of milk.'

Bara and Con tied the horses to a post, then came running over through the rain and dived thankfully into the warm darkness of the hut. Little light came from the windows and very little more from the glow of the peat in the hearth, but there was enough to see the milk and a loaf of bread and a pile of brown eggs on a shelf. The three of them stood in a line, staring longingly at the food.

'We can't pay for it,' said Bara. 'What can we do?'

Tam's conscience could restrain him no longer. 'We'll eat it,' he said. 'We'll pay somehow.'

Bara shook back her wet tangle of hair and laughed. Then she put six eggs carefully into a black pot that stood by the fire. They found water in a jug and Con balanced the pot carefully on the glowing peat. Tam cut off hunks of bread with his knife and Bara scooped up milk with a wooden ladle.

'This is terrible of us,' she said, stuffing her mouth with bread. 'This may be all they've got to eat for a week.'

'Oh we'll pay it back somehow,' said Tam cheerfully as he blew at the fire. 'We'll wash up.'

'Wash up what? One ladle? Do you know, I don't think I've ever stolen anything in my life before.'

Tam looked up at her in amazement.

'What a good girl,' he said. 'My childhood was one long riot of thieving.'

'Kate reformed you when you came to us.'

'Skin-deep maybe.'

They rubbed their cold hands by the fire and helped each other tug off their wet sheepskins. A faint and delicious smell of wet wool began to pervade the room. Con curled up on a bank of hay, leaving instructions that he should be woken when the eggs were done. Tam and Bara fell in each other's arms into another mound in the corner, and when at last they rose to look at the pot the water had boiled away and the eggs were like stones. Con woke as they began to move about in the steamy firelight, turning over their sheepskins and helping themselves to milk in an effort to ease the weight of the eggs that lay in their stomachs. Sheep bleated occasionally out in the drizzle and hens scuffled round the door. There was no boarded roof and from time to time a straw from the thatch drifted down between the rafters. Suddenly Con looked up.

'Horses,' he said, cocking his head.

'Christ.' Tam whirled round and pulled out his knife.

'They won't hurt us,' said Bara impatiently. 'Not in Ireland.'

'Don't be too sure. We ran out on them. And if it's the people who live here we've eaten their food.'

He pushed Bara and Con into a dark corner and stood by the door. The clatter of hooves and the shouts of men grew nearer. Con filled his hands with stones from the floor and Bara picked up an axe.

The door was flung open and a man stepped into the room. He was unarmed and he leaped back as he saw the point of Tam's knife at his throat.

'Holy Brigid,' he exclaimed. 'Would you murder me then?'

He was the redheaded Finn from Rosslare. Tam lowered his knife and sourly motioned him in as the smell of the grave returned to his nostrils. Then to his astonishment Finn dropped on one knee in front of Bara and Con. Tam burst out laughing, for neither of them looked much like the objects of homage. Con stood damp and gaping, with his mouth open. Bara swung the axe stupidly by her side, uncertain what to say or do. Idiotic wisps of thought rushed through her head. Should she say 'Arise Sir Finn'? Should she bend graciously and raise him with her hand? Finn solved her problem by standing up.

'It's you and the Old One will never forgive me,' he said, dropping his head. 'You were right to go, the Old One wants you. And I was wrong to wait for the funeral. He said when you came to Cashel you must have an escort good and proud. And here's me letting you ride off like beggars in the night, all throught the filth and the unknown ways. May the Holy Brigid forgive me.'

He looked so downcast that Bara smiled and lifted up his chin with her hand.

'It's all right Finn,' she said, 'we're used to riding alone.'

'Sure and I should be whipped like a dog. The Old One will say I am not fit to be put in charge of strangers.'

'We won't tell him,' said Con, pulling down Finn's head and whispering in his ear. 'We'll keep it a secret.'

At that moment there was a shriek outside. The hens squawked wildly, men shouted, and into the hut burst an old woman. She wore trailing garments of black and her face was contorted with rage. She raised a black club in Tam's face and screamed at him.

'Get out! Get out of my house! Thief! Murderer! Get out or I'll kill the lot of youse.'

She swung her club wildly and although Tam ducked he was caught on the shoulder and he spun round, exclaiming in pain. Finn had leaped at the old woman as she swung, and now he had her club in his hands. He pointed it at her as she backed away against the wall, her face a mask of rage and terror.

'Don't you be using your shillelagh on these people, old woman. All they took will be paid for. Look.' He put his hand in a pouch and held out a coin. Bara thought she caught the gleam of gold. 'Will that put it right?'

'Aye,' she said, still against the wall but with her eyes fixed on the coin.

'Take it,' said Finn. Bara came forward to the old woman.

'I'm sorry,' she said. 'We were cold and hungry and you weren't here. We wouldn't have gone without paying you somehow.'

The old woman squinted up at her.

'Would you not then?' she sneered.

'Careful, old woman,' said Finn. She humped over to the fire and placed her coin carefully under a stone.

'Careful of what?' she said querulously. 'It's me that's been wronged, young man. It's old Meg has been wronged. There's justice in Ireland you know. You're the ones to be careful.'

'Soon you will be saying more than you would wish.' Finn strode over to her and gently took her arm. 'Listen, old Meg,' he said. 'These are the ones who will come.'

The old woman's mouth dropped open as she stared at him.

'These are? The ones who will come? These?'

'These.'

'In rags?'

'In rags and owning no money.'

Slowly she turned her head to look at them. Then very slowly, very stiffly, she raised her old skirts and curtsied low. Tam flushed, Bara did not know where to look.

'Please,' she said, moving forward and helping the old woman up.

'It's an honour to old Meg, it's an honour to me in my old age,' said the woman. 'To have you in my cottage. And to have offered you hospitality.' Tam clutched his bruised arm and winked at Bara. 'Holy Brigid, but I'll be remembering this to my dying day.'

'Would you let my men come in and dry themselves, Meg?' said Finn.

'Oh, aye, aye, let them all in. Help me build up the fire, young man. It's a great day for me, this is a great day to be sure.'

As Finn's half dozen dripping men came stamping in, she bustled about, her clothes trailing, moving peat from one pile to another. Suddenly she turned to Finn, pulling him down and whispering in his ear.

'Oh aye, aye,' he said, trying to restrain his face. 'Aye, that'll be fine, old Meg.' As she hustled out of the door, with her face cracked in a huge smile, Finn turned to Bara and laughed. His face was very freckled, his eyes and teeth very bright.

'It's off to her neighbour she is,' he said. 'It'll make a grand story. How she offered hospitality to the ones who will come.'

Con was skipping about among Finn's men, swinging their shillelaghs and running his finger down the flat of their long daggers. Some of the weapons had intricate inlays and some had thin yellow wire wound in whorls on the shaft.

'Is it gold?' said Con, pointing to the wire and thinking to be funny.

'Sure but it's gold,' they replied. 'Good Irish gold.'

By noon the steaming clothes and the damp leather boots were almost dry and Finn said the company must go. The rain was a little lighter, more than half mist, and the sky was a paler grey. They took to their saddles, warm and cheerful, and set off west for the afternoon's ride towards Cashel. Finn rode in front with Tam, then came Bara and Con, and then the five other men of the escort. Bara would have liked to ride alongside some company, but Finn was determined that this was the proper arrangement. They crossed the wide rushing Blackwater and immediately they were in hilly country, among long rides of heather and gorse so yellow it seemed the sun was shining.

'Soon we will take the old valley of the Suir,' said Finn, speaking over his shoulder. 'It's a great crazy river that bends round a hill and takes the longest way it can think of to the sea. But it's a good river for the salmon and the trout, and that's all anyone would want of a river anyway.'

They rode on through the lush grass of the valley, between low, heathery hills. The rain had stopped but the sky was lowering and Finn was sure there would be more rain in the evening, for they could not make out the shape of the Comeraghs a few miles to the south-west. After some three hours at a steady jog they found the valley opening into a wide plain, and Finn turned abruptly north away from Carrick-on-Suir towards some hills.

'I thought we went west,' said Tam.

'Nobody passes the High Crosses without a greeting,' said Finn sternly. 'They were made by the Old People and they are beloved by the Holy Brigid.'

Bara frowned in irritation. What a stupid mish-mash of old stones and the Holy Brigid and the Old People – whoever they were. But she kept her contempt to herself and she was astonished a quarter of an hour later at the height and splendour of the three carved crosses. They stood rooted at the entrance to a sharp little valley, their gnarled surfaces more like wood than stone. The western cross was carved with horsemen and animals and interlacings, the north cross was tall and lean, the eastern stood rough-hewn and stark. As Bara gazed at them in the damp twilight they glistened and grew. She felt their ancient authority, their power to absorb fear, to draw into themselves from human shoulders something of the pains and anxieties of living.

'How old are they?' whispered Tam.

As Bara opened her mouth to reply Con whispered hoarsely, 'When those men – the Vikings – about when they came.' He broke off sharply, scowling.

'Made when *who* came?' said Bara, bewildered.

'The Vikings,' said Tam. 'Look at Finn.'

Finn and his men stood in a line in front of the crosses with their arms upraised. They spoke very softly and in a moment the ceremony was over.

'Up and away!' shouted Finn, leaping onto his horse without touching the stirrup.

'But don't we ever eat?' called Bara.

'Eat. Aye. Food. I'd forgotten,' said Finn. 'The Old One wants you quick but I don't suppose he wants you starving. We'll stop on the road.'

'We might have a stop here too,' said Bara, feeling her anger rise against this cocky young man. 'We've been up since three this morning.'

'No,' said Finn, laughing at her surly face. 'No stopping and no sleeping. Sleeping's for Cashel.'

Bara tugged angrily at Dark's reins and turned her back. She knew she was exhausted, her stomach ached with hunger, the thought of Cashel and the Old One weakened her with fear.

An hour later, at a small inn in Ballypat, they were eating great steaks of baked salmon, with raspberries from the garden and cream from the cow. It was still only early evening but as soon as he had finished eating Con fell asleep over the table with his head on his arms.

'Come on,' said Finn, rising and stretching. 'The lad can sleep in the saddle.'

He bent to lift Con off the bench, then leaped backwards as he received a stinging slap in the face. Bara stood in front of him with her eyes glittering.

'Leave him alone,' she shouted, clenching her fists. 'Why can't he sleep? He's been up nearly a day and a night, why can't he sleep?'

Tam leaped over the trestle and put his arm round Bara's shoulders. He was staggered by her attack on Finn and frightened by the rising note of hysteria in her voice.

'Why shouldn't he sleep?' screamed Bara, trying to wriggle free of Tam. 'Stop bullying us. Leave us alone, just leave us alone. I don't want to go to Cashel, we won't go.'

She turned suddenly, rent with sobs, and clung to Tam, burying her face in his shoulder.

'Leave us for a moment, Finn,' said Tam, as he stroked her hair. 'I'm sorry, but she's had a terrible time. She's tired and scared. She'll be all right.'

Finn rubbed his cheek.

'It's only well we wish her,' he said. 'She mustn't be frightened of the Old One. Tell her. Tell her that.'

And he walked thoughtfully out.

Tam and Bara sat on the bench and slowly Bara's sobbing quietened. When at last she turned her tear-stained face and smiled at him, Tam's heart contracted with love and pity.

'Shall we go?' he said.

'Yes, let's go.'

Con scarcely stirred as Tam gathered him in his arms and carried him out to the waiting horses. Dusk was deepening and Finn gloomily foretold a long dark ride to Cashel. When Bara told him she was sorry he accepted politely but with just a touch of mortification. Tam smiled to himself and thought that Finn would go far in the world.

They passed under the steep black side of Slievenamon and bore north-east for Cashel. They rode in silence, for the men's spirits were low in the damp twilight. Tam rubbed his thumb across the edge of his knife. He believed there was nothing to fear in Cashel, instinctively he trusted in the goodness of the Old One; yet old habits die hard, and he could carcely imagine a time or a place where a long sharp knife would not be a comforting companion. Bara rode in a dream. She felt that but for the solidarity of Con's body between her arms she might float off her saddle and away into space. Her senses were alert, her perception sharp, yet somehow together they made no sense. She rode apart from herself, as when she was drunk; she was two people who watched each other, floating disembodied through the deepening dark.

On and on they rode. Tam knew it was only twenty miles or so, but to Bara it seemed an infinite measure of distance. She was outside time, beyond time, she rode towards the stars. When finally the great rock of Cashel loomed above them, crowned with towers and pinnacles, twinkling red in the light of a thousand torches, she thought she had come to the gates of heaven, or the lords of fairyland.

Hours later, after a bath in a wooden tub, and a meal of delicacies such as she had never seen, she was brought along to meet the Old One. It was only for a moment, the woman said, because he had waited so long for her, and after that she could sleep.

He looked like someone out of an old, old picture, a picture she had seen years ago in a dusty book at home, something Kate had shown her when she was a little girl. His white hair flowed onto his shoulders and his beard lay like a cloud over his chest. Was he called Father Christmas? Zeus? Or God the Father? She could not remember. He lay on his back on a hard bed, covered in a soft blue blanket, and as she gazed at him he turned his head and smiled at her. His eyes were very dark, like unlit pools.

'Sit here by me,' he said, indicating the chair by his bed.

As Bara stretched against the curving wooden back of the chair her whole body slackened. Now she was here she did not want to go, and she motioned the woman to leave. In this room with this old man she felt content. After the hardships and dangers of the last months, here at last was a quiet place. The old man lay still, looking at her and half-smiling. She felt his goodness as a positive warmth in the room, reaching out to her heart as the heat of the fire reached out to her body. She laid back her head and she began to talk. She talked as she had never talked before, even to Tam. She talked as the candle spluttered down and the fire burnt low, she talked into the night and the early hours of the morning. She told him of her long journey, travelling back in her mind to her arrival in Ireland, the terrible loss of Collum and his ship, the voyage across the sea, the savage mountain kings of Wales, the terror of the Outlanders. She told him of Con, and of what Con had suffered, and of what she had endured for him; she told him of her home in London, of old Charley and his garden, of Fred's store and Joddy's stables, of Tam and his books, and she spoke long and lovingly, with tears in her voice, of her beloved Grans. At last she had done. The candle had flickered out, the fire was sunk in embers. She was drowning, spinning on the verges of sleep.

Ralf slowly raised his arm and laid it across her shoulders.

'You are my beloved grandchild,' he said.

For five days they rested on the rock of Cashel, whose great bulk rose three hundred feet above the plain of Tipperary. The skyline of towers and turrets and angled rooftops seemed to Bara translated from a book of legends. On the second morning, when a watery sun shone and martins swooped round the towers, Ralf came out to sit on the terrace wall with her and Tam and Con. In the course of the last fifty years, he told them, the ruined cathedral had been roofed and repaired, and its nave and choir had been lined with green marble dragged in carts from Connemara. It was now the main hall for assembly and eating for all those who lived on the rock. The Norman chapel in the angle of the choir and the south transept, known for reasons lost in history as Mac's House, had needed hardly any repair. Its high stone roof, its vaulting and carvings and intricate doorways, had somehow withstood the horror of the old wars and the erosion of time. In there the Council met and the administrative work of government was done. Ralf himself lived in one of the chapel towers, the one with the pyramid roof. In the old castle, which had been built long ago in the ruins of the western nave of the cathedral, were the kitchens and storerooms, with bedrooms and dormitories above. When Ralf described how the walls of the castle were honeycombed with secret passages, Con opened his eyes wide with excitement. A smaller hall, with the mysterious name of Vikarscoral, was used for assemblies and committees. The Round Tower, ninety-two feet high but still proof against war and weather and time, was used as living quarters by two members of the Council.

The long cobbled terrace where they sat was bounded on one side by a low wall which overlooked the town, and on the other by the grey stone of the hall. Blazing against the walls from one end of the terrace to the other was a tumult of summer flowers; dahlias in glowing red and orange, roses of crimson and lilac and cream, violas and pinks and purple fuchsias.

Ralf described the landscape below them, pointing out the brickworks smoking in the distance, the weavers' quarter in the shadow of the rock, the smelting kilns by the distant woods, the blue Galty mountains to the south-west and the Slievefelims towards Limerick in the west. Green woods and meadows, washed in palest gold, spread to the wide horizon like a sea. Neither on that day, nor on the days immediately after, could Bara regain any solid feeling of reality. Perched on the Castle rock above the town, breasting the plains of Tipperary, she felt suspended in time and space. She had been magically translated from the hard-edged world she knew, where sight and sound and touch were predictable, into a realm of romance where cold towers of stone might vanish at a glance, or the rock itself dissolve into bands of coloured light. Yet at the same time she felt hunger, and sleep, and love, and she well knew that the bed she shared with Tam was now a delectable mound of feathers and no longer the cold hard ground.

On the fifth day Tam was walking restlessly up and down the terrace. 'It's the waiting,' he said, folding his arms and scowling. 'It's not knowing what it's all about. What we're here for. I wish to God they'd tell us something.'

'They think we need a rest,' said Bara.

'Well, we've had a rest. And suspense isn't very restful anyway.'

'Lie back and enjoy it while you can. It's not often you find yourself in a fairy-tale.'

'I can't. I don't like fairy-tales. I want to know. I want to be doing something.'

Bara smiled at his glowering face and the thumbs stuck aggressively in his belt. He was almost handsome, she thought, now that she could see him with his face shaven and his hair cut and brushed. The black shaggy tangle that had lain on his shoulders for so long had vanished on their first day, when the barber had trimmed his hair almost up to his ears. Once again he had a neck. He caught her smiling reflectively up at him and he flushed.

'Don't look at me like that,' he said, standing over her. 'I can't concentrate.'

'Well, don't. Forget it and sit down.'

Con came galloping along the terrace, his silver hair flopping at every bound as he smacked his imaginery charger. His hair had also been cut up his neck but it still lay long and thick over his forehead, hiding the red scar.

'Come here Con,' shouted Bara. 'Come and talk to us.'

'I can't,' he yelled over his shoulder. 'I'm a messenger, I've got an important message.'

Bara shrugged and smiled and leaned on Tam's shoulder.

'Why do they want him so much?' she said dreamily.

'Are you frightened?'

'Not any more. Grandfather's – oh I don't know. He's lovely, he's good. I wish they'd stayed together.'

'Him and Kate?'

'Yes. It would have been beautiful.'

'I suppose they didn't think so. Or he wouldn't have gone without her. Or she would have followed him.'

'She had to look after my dad. He wasn't even born till after Grandfather left.'

'I think there was something in Ralf she couldn't manage. Even if she did love him.'

'She could have managed anything,' said Bara feeling the familiar prick of tears. 'Look how she managed after he left. She managed Great-grandfather, and Charley, then my dad, then me, and then Con.'

'And then all of us lot,' said Tam.

'Exactly. Suz and Jank and Christo and you. All of you. So why couldn't she cope with Ralf?'

'They're still two different people in my mind,' said Tam, 'Ralf and the Old One; Ralf the young revolutionary, and this ancient lord of Ireland. It's going to take some time to fit them together into one.'

'They're a lifetime apart to us,' said Bara.

Just then the huge wooden door of the council chamber opened and Ralf emerged. He moved slowly, his tall figure stooped over a plain staff, but his steps were firm and his voice was that of a much younger man. His long blue gown was gathered at the waist by a blue and white enamelled belt. At his side walked a shorter man, equally old, whose cropped hair was mottled white and sand. He leaned on a magnificent golden crozier over six feet high, enamelled and inlaid and chased, the crook encrusted with ornaments and tiny figures. Bara had never seen an object so magnificent, even in the hands of the Priest King at the Shepherds' Kingdom, and it was with reluctance that she turned her gaze to smile at the man who held it. His eyes of wintry blue moved rapidly and without rest from place to place and person to person.

'You must meet Frost, our First Councillor,' said Ralf smiling. 'He came to join me in Ireland many, many years ago, and even before that we were friends in the revolutionary government, and before that we were at school together in London.'

'That is very ancient history indeed,' said Frost, glancing quickly from Tam to Bara and back. 'Centuries before you were born. Or so it seems.'

'Did you have to escape, like Grandfather?' asked Bara.

Ralf answered quickly,

'We won't speak of that unhappy time,' he said. 'We'll talk of the hopeful present and the happy future.'

'Now that we've been introduced I'll leave you,' said Frost, smiling thinly. 'No doubt you have much family history to catch up on.'

Ralf looked surprised, but he smiled at the departing Frost and lowered himself carefully onto the stone bench.

'Frost has a son,' he said. 'A very clever man. He's called Quint and he's on the Second Council. He's got four wolfhounds he loves like children.'

'Are they a nice family?' asked Bara doubtfully.

'The wolfhounds?'

'All of them.'

'Well, I don't care for the hounds myself,' said Ralf. 'They'd eat you if Quint told them. But he and his father are clever men and they work hard. I'm sure their intentions are good. Now,' he said, laying his plain staff on the ground, 'if you're both well rested we've got a lot to talk about. In fact, so much I don't know where to begin.'

'And I don't know where to start asking,' said Tam, leaning forward with his elbows on his knees.

'It's all so mysterious,' said Bara. 'Uncanny.'

'I suppose so,' said Ralf, laughing silently in the manner of the old. 'Well, this is how it is.'

He leaned back with his elbows on the parapet, his long legs stretched and crossed in front of him. A woman waved from a window in the Round Tower and Ralf raised his arm. The sun was thin but warm, and the rain-washed air sparkled into the blue distance.

'I can't begin to tell you the joy it is to have you here at last,' Ralf said. 'Though God knows it's been at a terrible cost – the loss of Collum and all his men – that lovely ship – terrible . . .' His voice trailed away, then he collected himself with a jerk of his head. 'In fact I think the getting of you three here to Ireland was probably the central task of my life,' he continued. 'Anything else I may have done pales beside it.'

'But why?' said Tam. 'Why?'

Ralf smiled slowly, his chin sunk in his cloud of beard.

'Give me time,' he said. 'I am very old and I need time for the telling of a story. You'll know why you're here soon enough. But first, I expect you realize that a few people are born with the ability to reach the minds of others without spoken words?'

'Telepaths?' said Bara.

'More or less. But in Ireland we call them Speakers. All of them can reach into any mind to some extent, but some are much more powerful than others. But then there are other people as well – lots more of them – who are specially good at *receiving*. Have you heard of them?'

'Receiving – ?' said Tam, frowning.

'We call them Listeners. They also vary very much in their skill. The point is this.' He looked at them both hard, to compel their attention. 'It's difficult to believe, but don't waste time refusing to believe, because it's true. Listeners are people who don't merely receive ideas and impressions from their contemporaries, they receive ideas from the *past*.'

'The past?' said Tam, frowning.

'Yes. They have access – some more, some less – to the whole range of the mental activity of man, past and present. They aren't merely telepaths, who can only receive from some living contemporary human being. They are people who receive from no tangible source whatever. They receive in fact from the mental and imaginative activity of the human race, past and present. They pluck ideas from the empty air. I think there has never been anything like us on earth before. We represent the small beginnings of a new consciousness. We meet like great fish in the depths of the sea. We move in a new element that human kind hasn't ever known before. When our minds move over these frontiers we are free of our bodies and free of the printed word and free of the limitations of time.'

'Christ,' breathed Tam, staring at Ralf.

'Your reading,' said Bara to Tam. 'You said ideas came to you like birds.'

'That's right, that's it. But how does it work?' asked Tam.

'Some people, like Frost and myself and all the members of the First Council, are both Speakers and Listeners. As Speakers we can talk in silence to our contemporaries. As Listeners we can receive ideas from them, but we can also receive from the past. Listeners usually have a particular bent. Most of them receive one category of idea but not another – though a few of us seem open to almost anything. Both of you have a touch of Listener – Tam more than Bara – but your talent is very undeveloped. The point about Con – ' Ralf leaned forward, looking hard at Bara ' – the point about Con is that he is brilliantly and unsurpassably both. Speaker and Listener *in exelcis.*

His gift as a Speaker has hardly begun to develop, but already his gift as a Listener is unique. In depth, in range, in power – there's no-one like him. His loss would have been irreparable. And it became my task to bring him to Ireland.'

'Con . . . but why Ireland?' The confusion of Bara's feelings was so intense she could form only the minor, unimportant question.

'I'll come to that. Give me time. The impatience of the young is very exhausting. Sometimes I thought the effort of getting you here would kill me. My darling granddaughter,' he said, putting his hand on Bara's arm, 'you were so damned obstinate you had me at my wit's end. At first it was easy. After Kate's death you were at your best as a Listener – open, raw, without defences. I had only to keep on repeating "Ireland" and no-one could shake your determination to come.'

'That's right,' said Tam. 'We thought she was crazy.'

'But you gave me some terrible times later. There was no-one else here who could get into you at all, so it all fell on me. In defence of Con and yourself you built walls, you threw up palisades, you raised great earthworks in your mind. In my efforts to blast them down and speak to you I exhausted myself for days on end.'

'*You* exhausted yourself,' said Bara indignantly. 'What about me? I understand a lot now – the presence thing. The Cotswold farm and Old Wat's house and the river in Wales. Three different times when I wanted to turn back to London. My God, you scared me. You nearly blew me to bits in Wales. I was all in pieces, falling around in the dark. Another minute and you'd have made me mad for life.'

'That's terrible,' said Ralf, looking at her gravely. 'I didn't realize I was so strong. All I could thing of was the terror when you turned your back yet again. Just when I thought I had you almost here. I suppose I sent you all my panic as well as my command. I'm sorry.'

Bara smiled at him. 'As long as you don't do it again,' she said. 'But Con wouldn't ever have let me go back anyway. I'd have had to drag him by his hair.'

'Oh, Con was so easy. He never had a moment's doubt he had to come. Still, it was through him I suffered most.'

'Why through him?'

'I could feel your terror just dimly. I knew when you were scared and I knew when you were miserable or in pain – but it came to me through a mist. It was quite different with Con. When he got frightened or hurt it hit me like a hurricane. His feelings came through so raw I felt physically sick. One morning last February his terror swamped me so completely I just fainted dead away.'

'Bela's Knap,' said Bara, staring into space. 'The branding at Bela's Knap.'

'Yes. I feel terribly guilty that I didn't try to make Tam go with you from the beginning. For one thing, I'd no idea of the danger. I didn't realize England had got so barbarous. And also I couldn't have had any knowledge of Tam except through your mind, and I don't think he was there much at the beginning . . .?'

'No,' said Tam, 'I wasn't. Except as something to be avoided.'

Bara smiled shamefacedly and groped for his hand. The flowers blazed against the stone walls, martins arched in the blue air. Her mind wandered off to the old house in Hampstead, now so remote in the time-scale of her memory that she might have left it ten years instead of a mere six months ago. She wondered if Suz still wiped and polished the fantastic golden furniture from Kenwood, and she smiled at the thought of Christo and Jank trying to grow fruit and vegetables on their own. But Ralf was still speaking.

'So I was able to find you,' he was saying to Tam. 'In the end your image came to me so sharply through Bara that I knew your face, your name, where you lived, everything. Because of the fears I felt in Bara, and the blasts of panic I got from Con, I knew they were practically always in danger. And this constant beating of emotion was wearing me down. I've had quite a strenuous few months too, you see,' he added, turning his head to Bara. 'In fact in that time I've become a very old man. Anyway, Tam proved an awkward devil too. He was damned obstinate, and he wouldn't listen at all. But I wore him down in the end.'

'No-one can live without sleep,' said Tam, 'however damned obstinate they are.'

'Exactly. That's what I counted on. But it meant I had to stay awake all night myself.'

'It was a near enough thing in the end,' said Bara. 'In another day we would have been dead. Just to improve the lambing.'

'It's hideous,' said Ralf, his face twisted, 'Don't think about it.'

'By the way,' he continued, bending his white head to Bara, 'I hope it's not too painful – but who was Con's father?'

Tam glanced quickly at Bara, but she replied without emotion.

'They tell me he's called White Michael,' she said. 'He's a kind of savage king round Colchester. Grans told me he had some awful kind of power,' she added. 'Something to do with how he looked at you.'

'I've heard the same,' said Tam. 'The rumours always said he could make anybody do anything.'

'Ah,' said Ralf. 'I thought it might be something like that. He must have been a Speaker, and he was probably a very powerful one.'

'He was fiendish,' said Bara. 'He used his power just to get what he wanted.'

'There are stories about him everywhere,' said Tam. 'About how he can make people do what he wants, and how cruel he is.'

'The abuses of this power could be appalling, though the power in itself is neither good nor bad,' said Ralf. 'It's important to remember that. Its direction is decided by the character of the person who possesses it. It's not a gift that necessarily brings wisdom with it. We're still bedevilled by all our old failures. We're no less greedy and no less cruel and no less belligerent than we ever were. Our passions are still dark and obscure. We've made very little progress in our two million years in reconciling the pulls within us. I haven't much hope of such a contrary creature, all at sixes and sevens with himself, but whatever hope I have is centred here, in this new flowering of the mind in Ireland.'

'Ah,' said Tam leaning forward eagerly, 'Now we've come back to the subject of Ireland. Now, why Ireland?'

'Well,' said Ralf, stretching his arms and letting his chin sink slowly into his beard. 'Ireland. Why Ireland? Why indeed? But Ireland it is.'

'What is?'

'What is? Ah, what. Ireland – Well, we'll leave that till later, shall we? It's nice out here.' Ralph looked about him and yawned. After a moment's waiting, Tam looked round into Ralf's face, then he fell back on the bench with his arms behind his head and laughed softly.

'The old man's asleep,' he said. 'Sound asleep in the sun.'

That evening Ralf took his violin from the wall of his little room and played in the Great Hall. All the people of Cashel Rock, and whoever was staying the night, ate together at the long tables; councillors, governors, emissaries, messengers, cooks, chambermaids, stable-boys, even Quint's wolfhounds came to scrounge what they could find. Bara was introduced to Quint, who was a man approaching fifty but much younger in movements and looks. His greying hair was cropped short like his father's, and his eyes were very blue. Bara was aware that he gazed at her often during the evening, and she noticed too that he did not withdraw his eyes when he caught her glance. She thought his regular, even features superbly handsome.

Every Saturday evening, she was told, there was singing and recitation and playing on instruments. Some of the songs she heard were faintly familiar, echoing in Kate's voice from her early childhood; others were as strange as the songs of the women at Rosslare. Ralf played his violin and the company shouted for more and more. A young man stood in front of the huge fireplace with is arms folded and his eyes closed, and for half an hour recited in rushing verse the story of a battle between the North and the South. Then, raising and tilting his head, as if listening to a voice far away, he spoke for a few moments the words of some utterly foreign tongue.

'It's a tale of Troy,' said Ralf softly. 'He hears the Greek in his head.'

At the end of the evening's entertainment Ralf beckoned to Bara and Tam.

'It's time for you to meet the Council,' he said. 'The Council of Six. You've probably seen them all coming and going, but now you must meet them properly.'

He ushered them up to the end of the hall and held open a thick green curtain. They passed through into a small room, in which a few chairs and chests stood round a peat fire. Coarse woven rugs of green and blue hung on the walls and a huge sheepskin lay across the stone flags in front of the fire. The room was lit by the great yellow candles they had seen used at Rosslare. Six people stood about the room, three men and three women. As Tam and Bara entered the tallest of the women walked swiftly over and laid her arm across Bara's shoulders.

'Welcome to the great travellers,' she said. 'Indeed there are few people have been so far or seen so much.'

'This is Maeve,' said Ralf, with a softness in his voice. 'She is the most talented of us all.'

'No,' said Maeve thoughtfully, weighing his words. 'It is only that my talents are the swiftest. And the least useful,' she added.

Bara gazed at her in admiration. Her dark hair, brindled with grey, was gathered loosely at the nape of her neck, framing a wide and gentle face. Her eyes were brown, shining and amused. She wore a shift of green wool with white fur at the neck, and although Bara thought she must be in her early fifties her body was firm and slight.

'She is a mathematician and a musician and a matchless player of chess,' said Ralf, smiling at her. 'Perhaps I overrate her because she has the gifts I would have liked myself.'

'But I thought—' said Bara, 'I thought you were a mathematician and musician.'

'My gifts are poor stuff. I didn't know how poor till I met Maeve.'

Maeve waved her arm deprecatingly and sat down. An older woman moved forward, unsmiling, and stared hard at Tam and Bara in turn. Bara knew that in such circumstances one was supposed not to flinch, so, much as she would have liked to look away, she returned the glare. Suddenly the woman smiled, a wide smile which split her pouchy face in two.

'You're quite formidable,' she laughed. 'I think you won't be overawed by us. I'm Ellen,' she said abruptly, before Ralf could speak. 'And you are Bara and Tam, the ones who will come.'

'The dark man and the golden woman and the flaxen boy,' said Tam smiling. 'We know how it goes.'

'The Irish like their pictures bright,' said Ralf. 'Ellen is our doctor. She has deep and powerful access to the medical knowledge of the past.'

'By which he means some of my cures work.' said Ellen, laughing a little too loudly.

The youngest of the three women stepped forward. She was small, with long yellow hair and startled green eyes. Bara felt in her something of the timidity of a small animal.

'This is Ness,' said Ralf. 'What she doesn't know about our darkest and deepest thoughts must be beyond knowledge.' The young woman smiled shyly, looking up through her hair.

'He means my subject is the mind,' she said. 'I ought to warn you that my hold on my own sanity can be released and sometimes I am mad.'

Bara could not help looking startled.

'Don't worry,' said Ness, beginning to laugh. 'I can always surface again when I want. So far, at least. With Ralf's help.'

'You've met my old friend Frost,' said Ralf, turning. Frost smiled his thin smile as he glanced rapidly back and forth from Tam to Bara. He leaned heavily on his marvellous crozier.

'Your staff is wonderful,' said Bara, looking at the tiny gold figures on the crook.

'Yes,' said Frost, glancing down.

'It's loot,' said Maeve, only half laughing. 'It's the Limerick Crozier. It came from the ruins of the cathedral at Limerick.'

Frost glanced at her sharply.

'You will have your little joke, Maeve,' he said.

Ralf continued quickly.

'Frost is our lawyer. He is an expert in the framing of laws and the administration of justice. He has organized our constabulary and our courts. If the Irish feel that they are treated justly and their grievances are fairly sorted out – and I think they do – then that's due to Frost.'

'Thank you,' said Frost, looking rapidly round the room.

Ralf beckoned to a tall man who stood back in the shadows. As he stepped uncertainly forward Ellen put out an arm to support him and they saw now that he seemed tall only because he was so thin. His white skin clung to the bones of his face, his eyes and his teeth looked unnaturally large. He smiled slowly as Ralf presented him.

'This is Paedric. He has delved deeper and further than anyone into the theories and mysteries of politics and government.' Tam gazed at him intently. 'He has given us our political organization and our methods of administration, and he knows how they are likely to develop.'

Carefully Paedric sank back in his chair. Bara watched the tendons of his hand where the skin sagged over them.

'And last but not least,' said a young man stepping forward, 'is Cormac. The baby of the Council.'

He bowed ironically. His eyes were black, his pointed beard was black, his square-cut hair was black, his clothes were black.

'Cormac has an eye for the dramatic,' said Ralf smiling at him. 'He thinks he is a Spanish nobleman who was wrecked four hundred years ago on the coast of Ireland.'

The Council smiled indulgently and Tam laughed, but Bara was uneasy. There was something frightening about the pitch to which the young man was tuned.

'Cormac is our expert in applied science, our technologist and our inventor. He knows how to do things. He's alarmingly good.'

'It's not alarming at all,' said Frost.

'No,' said Ralf, 'you're right. That wasn't the way to put it. Well, now you have met the First Council. We're all here because each of us has a very particular gift as a Listener.'

'Ralf has all the gifts,' said Ness. 'He can turn his ear to anything.'

'No,' said Ralf, 'your subject is almost dead to me. No sound at all. I do not understand the human heart.' He paused, then continued, 'As we've not got an expert in economics and trade I have to deal with them as best I can. And with the general direction of things. By election I'm the Lord of the Council.'

'Long live the king,' said Cormac cheerfully.

'I am not a king,' said Ralf, without smiling.

Chairs were drawn up for Bara and Tam, and two goblets filled with wine.

'Is it like the poteen?' asked Bara anxiously.

'No,' said Ralf, 'it's not.'

Bara thought she caught a glimpse of smiles quickly subdued. Finn had obviously reported thoroughly.

'We drink very little wine,' said Frost, making an effort to be genial. 'They grow grapes in the south-west, but not enough for much wine. And the women are always wanting them as raisins for their cakes.'

'Well,' said Ralf, kicking the fire into greater life. 'The Council have heard my account of your adventures and my account of who you are. Now I think they'd like to talk to you themselves.'

There was a moment's pause.

'May I speak?' said Paedric from the shadows. His voice was deep and resonant, at odds with his fragility. 'I would like to know first if either of you think you have a gift as Speaker or Listener.' There was silence as Tam and Bara looked at each other.

'We don't know if we're Speakers,' said Bara, 'We've never tried. But Grandfather tells me I'm a poor Listener.'

Cormac said, 'In many ways you're very lucky.'

'I'm not sure if I'm a Listener,' said Tam. 'I seemed to recognize a lot of ideas when I used to read in London. As if I knew what was coming on the next page.'

'That sounds hopeful,' said Paedric.

'What sort of ideas? What were you reading?' asked Maeve.

'Oh, politics, philosophy, theory of government. Bentham, Plato, Hume, Lenin, Russell, Marx, people like that.'

'Ahhhh.' A long deep sigh of satisfaction came from the dark corner where Paedric sat.

'We'll go into this later,' he said. 'It's just as I'd hoped.'

There was a general stir among the company, but the subject was not pursued.

'Sometime we must test your powers as Speakers,' said Ralf, 'because they're the more dangerous and they've got to be very strictly controlled. But we'll leave it for the moment.'

'Could we just try one thing?' said Ness, leaning forward. Her yellow hair lay like a mane over the red of her shift. 'Could we just see if Bara can speak to Con? That would be very interesting.'

'All right,' said Ralf. He put his hands on Bara's shoulders and told her to close her eyes.

'Think of Con,' he said. 'Try to think only of Con. See his face in front of your eyes. Then think, Con, come here. Come here.' He turned to the rest of the company. 'Everyone else had better think of anything but Con. If he comes, we want to be sure Bara did it.'

Bara closed her eyes and tried to do as she was bid. She conjured up Con's face and she shaped the words in her mind. 'Con, come here.' She repeated them several times as she clung to the image of his face.

'All right,' said Ralf. 'That's long enough to start with.'

Bara passed her hand across her forehead and pushed back her hair.

'It wasn't very good,' she said. 'I could feel my chair and I knew you were all here and everything.'

'We'll see,' said Ralf. 'Meanwhile we've got a lot to ask you and a lot to tell you about.'

'We ought to tell them something more about why they're in Ireland,' said Ellen.

'Ah,' said Tam, draining his goblet. 'At last.'

'Well,' said Ralf, settling back in his chair and stretching his legs. Bara glanced round the company, apprehensive at the solemnity of their faces. Just as Ralf opened his mouth to speak there was a scuffling and muttering outside. Then Finn put his head round the thick curtain.

'I'm that sorry to be interrupting,' he said, 'but I can't control the boy at all.'

Con burst from under Finn's arm and fell headlong into the room. Bara rushed to pick him up and he stood rubbing his head and whimpering.

'He wouldn't let me come, Mam. He said I couldn't. But you called me and I wanted to come.'

'I called you?'

'In my head. Loud as anything. You know you did.'

'Yes, you're quite right.' Bara looked at Ralf, wondering what to do or say.

'She just wanted to know if you were all right,' Ralf said to Con.

'Is that all?' said Con indignantly. 'Of course I'm all right. I thought it was something bad.'

'That's all, Con,' said Bara, kissing him. 'You can go now.'

'I wish you wouldn't do that,' Con grumbled as he went out. 'Just for nothing. I was having a game with the boys and now they'll have gone away.'

'He's right,' said Maeve emphatically, 'we shouldn't have done it.'

'It may be useful,' said Frost, glancing rapidly from Ralf to Bara and back, 'it unites the family.'

'Perhaps we shouldn't have done it,' said Ness, 'but at least we know now there's this between them, and that's important. Ralf's told me about Con's father,' she went on, turning to Bara. 'It explains a lot. I've been watching Con and talking to him for three or four days now and I somehow couldn't get the feel of him at all. Now I know about his father I understand more.'

'Understand what?' said Bara, her voice touched with foreboding.

'Well, what he is. Sun and shadow, dark and light. Christ and Judas.'

Bara clutched Tam's hand. The words frightened her, for they seemed to bear down with an intolerable weight on the small scampering boy who had just run off to find his friends. But Tam was not very interested.

'You were going to tell us why we're here,' said Tam, determined not to be diverted yet again.

'Paedric can start,' said Ralf. 'It was he and Maeve who finally showed me what I was.'

There was a long silence before Paedric spoke from the shadows. He had chosen a seat where neither candlelight nor firelight fell on him, so his deep voice sounded out of darkness.

'A long time past,' he said, 'many, many years ago when I was only a boy, I realized there was something strange about me. Like Tam, I knew the contents of a certain kind of book almost before I'd opened it. My father had been a professor at the remnants of Trinity College in Dublin, and somehow his section of the university library had escaped the book burnings and the wars. So he rescued all the books on politics and government and we always had them hidden in our house all through my childhood. I discovered that I had the ability to absorb and understand them at a glance. As I grew up these ideas became my subject, and from about the age of fifteen I eked out a miserable living teaching them to a few ragged students. There wasn't any way of putting any of these ideas into practice in those days. There simply wasn't any government – just here and there a few tribal chieftans – merely thugs who took what was going. Then I began to hear occasional rumours of a girl in the south-west – near Dingle, the stories said. Although she was only fourteen she was rumoured to be a magical harpist. They said she also played chess like a demon and made long patterns in signs and numbers. All this took two or three years to put together, and by that time the rumours were uglier. People were saying she must be a witch, for her powers were so uncanny they must be from the devil. Her patterns of signs and numbers must be spells, they said, and her harping was a skill given by the devil in exchange for her soul. I began to think she must be like me – so attuned to certain skills and ideas that they hardly needed to be learned. I was still wondering about her, off and on, when I woke up one night in a sweat of terror. All round me in the dark was a scream so terrible my limbs shook. But even in my panic I knew it was the girl from Dingle. I leapt up, and stole a horse, and I galloped till it nearly died. I stole another, and then another. It's over a hundred and fifty miles to Dingle and I rode there in a night. There wasn't any problem finding Maeve. She was locked in a stone hut and they were planning to open up an old barrow grave and wall her in alive.'

'We know the custom,' said Tam.

Ralf looked at him sharply but Paedric was speaking again.

'In the end I persuaded them to let me have her. I had to promise to take her away for ever to the other side of Ireland and I had to give them the great gold ring my mother had left me. I had to give them my horse too, but that was hardly my loss as I'd stolen it anyway.' His voice faded. Ellen rose quickly and passed him the last of the wine.

'Thanks,' he whispered. 'Maeve can go on.'

'He saved my life,' said Maeve. 'They were going to wall me up till I starved or suffocated. Paedric came for me in the nick of time, just like a hero for a princess. But oddly enough, and against all the traditions of romance, we didn't fall in love. But we've been friends for forty years, and we always will be.'

'For a little while,' said Paedric softly. 'For a little while.'

Maeve's brow contracted, but she continued. 'I went back to Dublin with Paedric and we worked together there. He's ten years older than me and he looked after me like a brother. I earned money or food teaching maths, though heaven knows I'd got the sense to conceal most of my knowledge and I kept it very simple.'

'Simple for her,' said Ralf.

'I also hired myself out as a singer and harpist. And later we thought of exhibition chess games.'

'She was never beaten,' murmured Paedric. 'She made twice as much in food and goods and money as I ever did.'

'They were a poor exchange for my life,' said Maeve. 'Anyway, we talked. For those first days and weeks, how we talked. We explored each other's gifts and we probed each other's minds for more. We found out the limits of our skills and we experimented in improving them. We called ourselves Listeners, and the name has stuck ever since. Then we turned our minds to the cry of panic, which I'd never uttered aloud but which had carried to Paedric in his sleep a hundred and fifty miles across Ireland. For months we tested and experimented, first on ourselves, and then (unknown to them) on other people. The results were terrifying. We discovered first that we could send urgent feelings to each other as and when we liked. But we couldn't transmit precise ideas or anything of any verbal complexity. That was all right, and not unheard of. What frightened us was the discovery that certain people were so sensitive in receiving us that we could manipulate their very thoughts and actions. We discovered in fact that we were not only Listeners, but very powerful Speakers. There were people to whom we could speak as if we were the voice of their own minds. We drew up a code, to govern the use of our powers. We regarded it as law, and we've never broken it.

'After this we thought we must find out if there was anyone else like us in Ireland. We travelled hundreds of miles, stopping at inns and markets and fairs, listening everywhere to see if we could pick up any rumour of people like ourselves. For a while we found nothing. Cormac wasn't yet born, and he's the only other native Irishman here.'

'I told you I was the baby,' said Cormac.

'You make a creditable baby,' said Frost.

'Ellen's from Scotland and Ness is from Wales,' said Ralf.

'Well,' Maeve continued, 'then an odd thing happened. We both began to feel something, away in the south-west, somewhere in Kerry or beyond. There was something there. We sensed – I don't know what to call it – a density, a vibration, a locus of something akin. We walked and we rode and we questioned and we searched, but we couldn't find what we knew was there. Someone either didn't realize his powers, or he – or she – was deliberately withholding them. In the end we gave up.'

'But for all your journeying you hadn't gone quite far enough,' said Ralf, smiling widely. 'You never ventured out to the Blaskets.'

'What fools we were,' said Maeve. 'We made excuses for ourselves because we were both afraid of the sea. Anyway,' she went on, 'then we decided to combine our powers and try to send out the image of Ireland – the idea of Ireland – into the ether. If there were other people like us in England or western Europe we felt we must try to assemble them. Because we'd come to feel by now that something was happening in the evolution of our species. Some innovation, some mutation, some new source of psychic energy, some new pattern of radiation – we didn't know what it was, but we knew it had happened, and it had happened to us.'

She rose and began to pace about the small room, clenching her hands.

'We began to have glimpses of a new civilization, a new society, a new consciousness. We saw the frontiers of darkness receding before us. So we put out all our strength, night after starry night, throwing the word Ireland into the hollows of space. For months nothing happened and no-one came.'

'But in the end you brought me.' Ralf rose slowly and leaned on the chimney-breast, staring into the fire. 'I knew then that I couldn't resist any longer. I'd had six years of the Blaskets. Life in winter was so hard, I don't know how we endured it. My fingers were raw and my muscles seized up with the cold. Except in the evenings we never rested from the fishing or the kelping or digging in our stony earth. But in the summer—'

Ralf stretched up and stared unseeing through the window.

'The old man is wandering again,' said Cormac, grinning.

'Let him be,' said Ellen.

'In summer the islands floated in silver and blue. We seemed to swim in sunlight all the summer long, out in the uttermost west.' Ralf shook his white head. 'The past is very present to the old,' he said. 'All through those six years my mind was very much occupied. I was discovering things about myself every day and to begin with I was frightened. Very cautiously I began to experiment with my powers, and they flowered and grew with such magical speed I was overwhelmed. When I first heard the call of Paedric and Maeve I withdrew in utter panic. I was determined they shouldn't find me – yet when they left the west I felt abandoned, as if my own kin had gone. Then they began again, calling at night from the darkness of the sky, it seemed from the stars themselves. Well, in short, the noise they made in my head became more than I could resist. I couldn't sleep.'

'Just what you did to me,' said Tam.

'Just what I did to you. So one summer's day in 2009 I sailed my boat to the mainland, I gave a man six lobsters for a scraggy little pony, and I rode off to find Paedric and Maeve.'

Maeve stood in front of him and took his hands in hers. 'Oh Ralf,' she said, laughing through her tears, 'what a prize we brought to Dublin, what a prize.'

The Council met again the next day in the Great Hall. The morning was brown and grey, with light falls of rain shrouding the roofs of the town below and the green expanses beyond. Tam had scarcely slept. For half the night he had paced up and down their little room, scowling and laughing and smacking his hand in his fist. 'It's fantastic,' he kept saying, 'it's so fan-bloody-tastic. It took a million years to get to where our grandparents got – and they were so damn stupid they let the whole thing blow up on them. Now we can do it all over again, inside one lifetime. One lifetime. Don't you see?' He knelt by Bara's bed, emphasizing with his hands the urgency of his words. 'They had to find it all out by experiment and hard work. Painful and slow. My God, how slow. But we'll just know it all, we'll just know. It's the most exciting thing that's ever happened on earth.'

Bara turned over and pulled her blanket round her neck. She felt inadequate and therefore cross. Somehow this electric excitement that ran through Tam had passed her by and she could not respond to him except with irritation. Why didn't he shut up and go to sleep? Somewhere at the back of her mind was a cloud of unease. Sleep (if ever she could get any) would perhaps disperse it, or at least obliterate it for a night. As she tossed about, trying with half a mind to listen to Tam, trying to catch some spark of his excitement, she found herself haunted by the image of Con's face. Con was at the heart of this vast and terrifying mystery, the first of his kind in all the history of the world to be so endowed. She withdrew into a cocoon of maternal fear and love, and ceased altogether to listen to Tam.

So in the morning she and Tam were irritable with each other.

There were concerned glances from some of the Council, as if they knew that the night had gone amiss. But Tam noticed nothing. He could not wait to hear more. He cut into the preliminary murmurs of politeness and his dark eyes blazed. Frost looked at him very intently.

'Could we go on?' said Tam leaning forward in his chair: 'You'd just brought Ralf to Dublin. What happened then?'

'Once we had Ralf we began to learn fast,' said Paedric. His skin was yellow in the hard morning light but his bones seemed less emphatic. Bara noticed how tightly he grasped the arms of his chair, as if he were having to concentrate mind and body in a great effort.

'Ralf's range as a Listener far surpassed Maeve's or mine – though in certain fields he was not so reliable or so detailed. And his powers as a Speaker surpassed ours a hundredfold. We never forgot what had nearly happened to Maeve in the west and we all three kept our skills very secret. We set Ralf up as an inventor, making sure that his inventions were only a step or two beyond what people thought possible. He improved on the pottery kiln, as it then was; he produced a simple system of cogs for raising water from wells; he introduced lime in the smelting of iron; he invented a crankshaft for the woodworkers' lathes – and a thousand other things.'

'It was very frustrating,' said Ralf smiling. 'That's why I feel for Cormac now. There was so much more I could have done – but I didn't want to be burnt or walled up in a grave.'

Tam frowned. 'But those are such simple things. When you came here fifty years ago — '

'Forty-eight years ago to the Blaskets. 2003. Forty-two years ago to Dublin.'

'Forty-eight – forty-two – whatever. Surely there was a basic technology still operating in England?'

'Certainly there was, though it was showing signs of very rapid collapse. All that was in *England*. You're forgetting the history of *Ireland.*'

'I never knew much of it. A little about the wars.'

'Ah. Then you'll have to be told more. In 1993 Ireland embarked on the bloodiest civil war in the history of the world. The south called it the Holy Crusade, the north called it King William's War. In three years a population of nearly three million souls was reduced to a quarter. The carnage was appalling, the destruction of cities and towns and villages was almost total. Entire industries, all the great docks and all the fishing fleets, the ports, the colleges, the libraries – everything vanished in a madness of destruction. Dublin was a sea of blood and bones. The accomplishment of two thousand years was

wiped out in three years of total war. And all in the name of God.'
Bara shuddered. 'I'd no idea it was like that.'

'The name of God is no longer mentioned in Ireland,' said Cormac.

'That's why we've heard so much of the Holy Brigid,' said Bara.

'That's why. She's God now.'

'So at the end of the war there was nothing?' said Tam. 'Total
destruction of industry and technology and science and government
– and all the books and blueprints that went with them?'

'Nothing left at all,' said Ralf. 'Everything was pulverized. That's
why it was reasonably easy to clear up the mess. We did it in ten
years. But by 1996 Ireland was a Stone Age land again. Even the
smelting of copper and tin for bronze had to be re-invented.'

'But surely you've been able to accelerate things since then?' asked
Tam, puzzled. 'People would begin to be glad of simple machines
and technologies.'

Frost shifted himself in his chair and Ralf glanced at him quickly.

'Well, you'll see for yourselves what we've done in fifty years. In a
mere half-century we've done things our ancestors took thousands
upon thousands of years to contrive. We have all the basic
technologies of a highly developed primitive society. By which I
mean we haven't yet faced the colossal implications of the next step,
which is the creation and use of electrical power. There are some who
think we should go faster,' he added, his chin sinking in the cloud of
his beard.

'The boy is held back,' said Frost, nodding at Cormac, with anger
in his voice. 'His head is whirling with ideas that could only benefit
us.'

Cormac folded his arms and glowered at the ground. The long
silence smouldered.

'Well, they'll have to know sometime,' said Ellen at last, rising
heavily to her feet and moving over to the window.

Bara was frightened and her hand sought Tam's, but his mind was
so intent on the conversation he gave it only a perfunctory squeeze.
He stared from face to face, bewildered by the sudden intensity of
feeling in the room.

'What is it?' he said. 'What must we know?'

Ellen stared out of the window, Ness pressed her hands hard
together and gazed at Ralf, Frost twisted the rings on his fingers. At
last Ralf spoke.

'We are a divided company,' he said slowly. 'We have in our hands
a power that terrifies us.'

'It doesn't terrify me,' said Frost shortly. 'I welcome it.'

Ralf continued, ignoring him. 'We are like necromancers, like magicians, like the greatest wizards the world has ever seen. We can conjure marvels from the empty air.'

'We are gods,' said Maeve. 'No less.'

'Western civilization lasted two thousand years and more,' Ralf continued. 'A hundred years ago it began to fall apart. By the early years of this century it was a rotting corpse. In half a century, just half a century, we could create its duplicate in roaring health again.' He rose slowly and leaned against the wall by the fire. 'If we wanted to,' he added.

Cormac jumped to his feet, his black eyes shining, and began to pace up and down in front of the company.

'Something must be decided,' he shouted, 'and by the Holy Brigid it must be soon.'

He stopped in front of Tam, and glared down on him. 'It's myself is the subject of a war,' he said. 'I am a battleground between these people. But I am also a man, and soon I must make a man's choice. But I do not know which way it is I should be turning.'

'I don't understand,' said Tam.

'Oh, it's simple enough, for sure. Frost and his people want me to be tearing on. Ralf and his lot want me to be holding back.'

'Our decisions have been left in abeyance,' said Maeve, 'while we waited for you two and Con. Now you're here we can't put off our quarrel any longer.'

'Roughly we stand like this,' said Ralf. 'Frost and Quint and many others are for pressing on towards an industrial and technological society. With Cormac's help we could do it, but Cormac isn't certain what to do.'

Cormac kicked angrily at the fire.

'I want to let it out,' he said. 'What I am damming up in my poor head will be bursting my skull one day. But I don't know.'

He slumped down on a bench with his head in his hands. Ralf went on speaking.

'Ellen gives Frost modified support, becaue she's anxious for advances in medical and scientific techniques.'

Ellen glanced at Paedric, whose great lids were closed, and her brow tightened in pain.

'Maeve's interests and skills leave her unimpassioned about the form of society we create. But she leans towards the position taken by Ness and myself.'

'Oh yes,' said Maeve, 'I dislike noise and speed and dirt. That may sound trivial,' she added, 'but I think it covers a lot.'

'Ness and I are for slow and sparing use of our powers,' Ralf continued.

'Yes,' said Ness, shaking her yellow hair and struggling to subdue the turmoil of feeling in her voice. 'We must go slowly, we simply must. We can't subject our species again to the strain of a full urban and industrial society. We aren't built for it, we can't take it. Not at this point in our evolution anyway. And now – unlike any other species that's ever existed – we've been given a second chance. We've got a choice, a chance to begin again, and we must not get it wrong.' Ness's voice had risen and she was near to tears. Ellen put an arm round her shoulders.

'I find this hysterical and embarrassing,' said Frost. 'The decaying society I left behind in London forty years ago still had enormous possibilities. Of course there were mistakes, and we don't have to repeat them. But people shouldn't have to live their lives bounded by thoughts of food and shelter. You shouldn't have to live like Ralf on the Blaskets. Technology can supply relief, technology can free us from the life of a primeval peasant – for primeval peasants is what Ness would have us be. No light except from candles, water from polluted wells, no sewage disposal at all. Tubercular milk, ring-wormed pork, blighted potatoes. No time for anything but the struggle for warmth and food. A depressed agrarian society, weighed down in poverty and disease and dirt.'

'It's a travesty,' said Ness tightly. 'A complete travesty of what I want.'

'It may be a travesty of your rosy dreams, but nevertheless it's what we'll get.'

Ness rose to her feet, oblivious of the company about her and stared into the fire. 'Think of this planet to our early ancestors,' she said. 'The clarity, the colours, the sounds they heard. Of course they didn't notice their good fortune – it was just what they were born to. Nevertheless, the planet whose children they were gave them all they needed to grow into their full humanity. We must not destroy – we dare not destroy – for a second time that relationship with the earth.' There was a long silence. Frost shifted angrily in his chair and Tam clenched his hands in embarrassment.

Then Ralf spoke. 'I'd like to read you something,' he said. 'The others have heard it before, but it's very short.' He delved into a pocket of his long blue robe and pulled out a frayed sheet of paper, brown at the edges. 'When I was a schoolboy in London in the eighties of the last century,' he continued, 'I had an old schoolmaster called Greatorex. I was very fond of him and I kept up with him when he retired. I used to go to his second-hand bookshop and read Greek with him. Just before he died he wrote me this letter. This is a paragraph from it:

' "We are so diabolically adaptable there's almost nothing that we won't be able to endure. As long as there's food and shelter we can survive anywhere on earth and in almost any circumstances. But only at a cost, and for me the cost is too high. We can survive in concrete, in dirt, in noise, in twilight, in filthy air, in loneliness, and in crowds. But we can only do so by retreating from our full humanity, only by surrendering again the territory we have unbared from darkness. We can adapt to anything, but only by a betrayal of our kind. Our poor starveling souls are shrinking in the prison we are making of our earth. I want no man's drugs, I am glad to die." '

'I've kept it all this time,' Ralf said, stowing it back in his pocket.

'I think that's right in many ways,' said Paedric at last. 'But I think we all agree we must have a technology of some sort.' His voice was deep and resonant, though his lids were closed. 'We must have bricks and cement and ships and looms and metal. We've got them in a basic form already and we must keep them and perhaps develop them a little further – an intermediate technology.'

'It's not enough,' said Frost, striking his staff on the ground.

'It's too much,' said Ness.

Frost rounded on her, his eyes glittering, and Ness shied as if she had been struck.

'You and thousands like you have a phobia,' he said. 'A psychological condition which needs curing, and damn soon. You're terrified of machines. You feel threatened by the simplest piece of machinery, you resent the cleverness it implies, you can't bear its alien behaviour. You and your kind are holding us all back in a life of primitive squalor. Just because you're frightened of machines.'

'I don't think that's fair,' said Paedric. 'Ness has reasons, not phobias. I'm with her and Ralf against industrial cities. Industry needs cheap labour, so an advanced technology has got to lead to cities. We couldn't stop them. So my feeling is that we leave the dynamo and the radio and all the various engines of power where they are now, in Cormac's head.'

'Where they will soon burst my skull,' said Cormac angrily.

'You'll kill the boy,' said Frost, rising suddenly and striking the ground again. 'At the barest minimum we need to import coal. Even if we have to go to Wales and mine it ourselves.'

'We've seen – at least some of us have seen – what coal and steam and electricity and oil and nuclear power can bring us to,' said Ralf. 'Frost and I have seen it in full growth, and Tam and Bara have seen its ruins. In a period of about two hundred years we almost murdered this planet and ourselves with it. A planet dead and the race of men extinct. We just dare not try to travel the same road again.'

'No,' said Ellen. 'But perhaps a more calculated one. It should be possible. Now we're so aware of the dangers I think we could control them.'

'I think so too,' said Tam, rising suddenly. Every face turned abruptly towards him, and Bara stared in amazement at the excitement shuddering in his hands.

'I think we could control it,' he said.

'We?' said Ness gently.

'I mean – I mean, you could. Oh and me too, if you'd let me help. I think Ellen ought to have proper medical equipment and proper machines for surgery. It's stupid to know you could have them and then choose not to.'

'Of course it's stupid,' said Frost, speaking very fast and darting his eyes round the company. 'Stupid and wrong. To repudiate voluntarily what you know you can do. It's limiting to human fulfilment. A divine curiosity is one of our greatest gifts. We have to, we must find out; explore; press our skills to the limit. If we don't we are abrogating our destiny as men.'

Everyone gazed intently at Frost, and there was a long silence when he had finished speaking. Then Tam continued.

'I don't think, myself, that we dare try to repeat the whole mess again. Only Bara and I know what the wreckage – the rubbish – the muck – of a full-scale industrial society is like. And the human wreckage that goes with it. But surely it's possible to select what you'll invent and discard whatever might lead to harm,' he said.

'Everything can lead to harm,' said Ralf slowly. 'Every important discovery that was ever made, every new invention that was ever conceived. You can't wield that kind of control in the sort of free society I want us to have.'

The rain had cleared and the noon sun streamed through the high windows of the hall. Bara looked with foreboding round the company, and shivered at the disintegration she felt around her. Ralf rose wearily to his feet.

'I think we should break off,' he said. 'If everyone agrees.'

There was a general murmur of assent as they all rose to their feet. Ellen and Cormac helped Paedric from his chair and supported him as he walked. Ralf put his arm round Bara's shoulder and they moved out onto the rain-washed terrace, where the jumble of late flowers glowed against the grey stone of the Great Hall. They walked over to the parapet and looked down onto the roofs of the town. Bara did not notice that Tam stared angrily after them, then turned on his heel and walked away with Cormac. Nor did Ralf know of Maeve's eyes following him from the hall.

'I'm tired,' said the old man, leaning on his staff. 'And full of fears. I'm supposed to be the all-wise, the all-confident, the all-powerful. The Old One, who has the keeping of Ireland in his hand. But I'm not any of these.'

'You didn't like what Tam said.' Bara was warmed by the weight of his arm on her shoulders.

'I was surprised. But he's very excited. It's all so new to him.'

'Were you thinking of him to take – I mean Paedric—' She stumbled, wishing she had not begun.

'Yes. Paedric has very little time left. I expect you realize he has cancer. It's chiefly his disease that leans Ellen towards Frost. Tam's talent seems very like Paedric's. If he proves himself we'll need him to take Paedric's place. And I think he'll prove himself very soon.'

'What about your other fears—?' Bara spoke hesitantly, flattered by his confidence but uncertain what was expected of her.

'My fears. Yes. Chiefly I fear the curiosity of man. Sex, hunger, warmth – these we can satisfy. But curiosity – I don't know. Man's curiosity is so intense you could think of it as one of his basic properties. It's so restless, and so uncontrollable. I think it's the greatest danger to our second future. And now it's so much easier to satisfy than ever before. Since we discovered our access to the past and present mental world, our curiosity has been stimulated even further. If that's possible.'

'A lot seems to turn on Cormac,' said Bara after a pause.

'He isn't the only inventor, he is simply the best. If he were the only one, then everything might turn on his final decision. Even as it is, what he decides will have a great influence on his companions. If he decides he wants to proceed to electrical power I don't know what will happen. Peat and coal and steam are limited – I think manageable. But electricity. And after that? What's to stop the next Cormac moving on to nuclear power? Something like this had to be decided once before, you know.'

Ralf looked down at the cobbles at his feet, talking more to himself than to Bara. But she listened absorbedly, her eyes on his face. 'A hundred years ago there were scientists – Szilard, Fermi, Einstein – who believed they should deliberately turn their backs and refuse to use the things they had made. But they were outvoted – overruled – and Hiroshima had her bomb. I've never seen real nuclear wreckage, because no-one ever dropped a bomb on Europe, but I've seen enough reactor accidents to know what happens. I've seen nuclear burns and radiation sickness and deformed babies. I've seen a huge tract

of dead ocean where plutonium waste escaped. Frost's seen it all too.
So why can't he understand? Why can't he?'

'He thinks the advantages are worth the suffering,' said Bara.

'Yes, you're right. He does. It's a total deadlock. Poor Cormac –
he's only a boy. Ness worries about him. She feels – she feels he's
already strung far above pitch. Another turn or two – the strings
could break.' His voice trailed away. 'It's hard for him to face such a
temptation to power.'

'How will he decide? Do you know?'

'No, I don't know. I hope it'll be in our favour. I think he'll
eventually opt for restraint. Frost and Quint will be very angry. The
Council may even break apart.'

Bara laid her head against Ralf's shoulder.

'Oh Con,' she said. 'Con, Con.'

'Con?'

'What will it be like for him?'

'Like it is for me,' said Ralf. 'But harder still.'

The next morning Tam and Bara were to begin a long ride round the
south and west. They were to be away a month or more, visiting the
towns and the farms and the villages and the small industries. The
east and north they would visit later from Dublin. Quint and Fergus
were to be the guides, and they were told that Cormac would come
too, when he had finished his drawing of a new four-heddle loom.

Bara, to her misery, could come nowhere near Tam. Although she was
in his company most of the day and all the night, she felt he had
vanished from the body she knew. There was a wild look in his eyes, he
never sat still, he hardly slept. Sometimes he stood trembling and staring
into space, his face flushed and twitching. The man she loved was
absent, his body inhabited by some creature she did not know; he was
bewitched, a changeling, an alien being. She was frightened and she
retreated more and more often to the company of Dark, whom she rode
hard and far across the country until he was in a lather and she herself
was too exhausted to care about Tam. She knew all the time that she
wanted him, that she needed his reassurance, but however she tried she
could not share his excitement, and she knew this made him angry.
Their muddled feelings stood between them like a thick cloud.

On the night before they were to leave for the west, Maeve beckoned to Bara and asked her to come to her room in the tower for a mug
of tea. Bara had quickly acquired a taste for the acrid drink that was
known as tea and always drunk after supper, so she went eagerly to
Maeve's room, not only for the tea but because her first ad-

miration of Maeve's autumnal beauty had not diminished. Besides, she was lonely and miserable. Tam had strode off to talk to Cormac, Ralf was surrounded as usual by people with requests, Con was away with his friends and the dogs. Maeve lived in one of the towers high above the terrace overlooking the town. The room was small and round, with six narrow windows and a large fireplace. A low bed followed the curve of the wall; three chairs, a table, and a huge carved chest were spread about the room. Both floor and walls were covered with thick rugs in shades of blue and green and yellow. Bara's strained face lit up with pleasure and Maeve smiled at her.

'Do you like my room?' she asked, with the amused edge to her voice that Bara found both attractive and disquieting.

'It's lovely, it's really lovely,' said Bara, over-emphatically. She was afraid of being thought merely polite. 'All these marvellous colours—'

'Ah well, you see I'm in charge of the dye works in the town.'

'You? But I thought music and mathematics—'

'Oh yes, those are my real subjects. But I have to do something useful too, you know. My time's half spent in calculations for builders and shipwrights and metalworkers and people like that – and half down at the dye works.'

'I see. They really are lovely colours. Not exactly this or that. I wouldn't know names for half of them.'

'We're getting more skilful. The dyes are all from common plants – the blues come from centurea, and reds from tormentil, yellows from vetch and betony and mignonette – things like that.'

Bara stood by the plain wooden table and gazed down at a magnificent chess set. The pieces were of natural polished wood, the Black of oak, the White of sycamore, and each stood nine inches tall. The board was an inlay of pale and dark veneers, beaded round the edge.

'It's beautiful,' said Bara. 'Really beautiful. Is it very old?' There was the flicker of a pause before Maeve answered.

'Well now – about thirty-five years I suppose. Actually, your grandfather made it for me.'

In her surprise Bara turned round quickly, but Maeve was quicker still. She was closely examining a poker and already speaking a little breathlessly.

'This is another historic object,' she said. 'This was the first piece of faultless iron smelted and forged in Ireland since the Wars. And it's thanks to Ralf.'

'Grandfather again?'

'Almost everything is thanks to him. He showed us how to add lime in the smelting.'

The kettle on the fire began to splutter and hiss.

'I've got three kinds of tea here,' said Maeve, resting her hand on a shelf by a row of brown pots. 'There's agrimony and calamint and marjoram.'

'Agrimony please. I love it.'

As Bara settled herself in a chair Maeve glanced round at her and smiled. Bara's face had relaxed, her brow was unfurrowed, her hands lay slack in her lap. Maeve poured the tea and they sat for a while crouched over the fire in companionable silence. Then Maeve said, 'I'm sorry Tam's being so difficult.'

Bara was startled. 'How do you know?'

Maeve smiled. 'For sure I know. It'll take you some little while to get used to all the things we can know.'

Bara looked at her broad, calm face, then she turned and gazed into the dusk.

'I don't know what's the matter with him,' she said desperately, a sob seeming to solidify in her throat. 'He's completely changed. He doesn't notice me and when he does he's just angry.'

Maeve did not speak for a long time, then she said softly, 'I think someone is on to him.'

'On to him? Trying to get him from me?'

'Oh not that. But someone's not obeying the code. Someone's trying to manipulate him for their own ends.'

Bara stood up slowly, anger flooding in over her misery.

'Of course,' she said. 'Of course that's it.'

'I don't know that it's "of course",' said Maeve mildly. 'It's only an idea. And I don't know who it would be.'

'It's Frost,' said Bara vehemently. 'He wants Tam to support him.'

'There are others,' said Maeve. 'Don't be too quick to jump to conclusions.'

'But who else could it possibly be?'

'Sure now I can't discuss the members of the Council with you,' said Maeve a little sharply. 'Or the Second Council either.' Her voice softened again. 'I shouldn't have said as much as I have, but I could see you were very unhappy. What's happening to Tam is temporary and artificial. You can be sure of that. I'll sort it out myself and everything will be all right. Ralf should have told you this really, but he wouldn't have noticed anything was wrong, and anyway he'd never believe anyone would do such a thing.'

'I remember he said he was deaf to Ness's subject. To – human feelings and things.'

'You remember that? He's got only two weaknesses where the rest of us have a hundred. But both of them are exactly covered by this.'

'I'm afraid I don't understand.'

'Well now, he finds it very hard to believe wrong of anyone. He assumes until it is too late that everyone is as honest as he is himself. He could hardly believe that anyone would try to manipulate Tam.'

'Oh. What's his other weakness?'

'Ah. Yes. Well, he does not notice the state of people's feelings.' There was a note in Maeve's voice that Bara found embarrassing, so she said no more. But Maeve continued, speaking so softly she seemed to have forgotten Bara altogether. 'Why he doesn't notice I don't know,' she said. 'It's a deep and unhealable wound. Ness says something to do with his childhood.' Bara could scarcely hear her words. 'Whatever the reason the wound is incurable. I know. I know better than anyone. He can neither give nor receive love.'

The words rang in Bara's head that night until they became an agony. He could neither give nor receive, receive nor give, give nor receive love. So that was why Kate had let him go. That was why she had chosen to live half a century alone. Kate had known, as Maeve knew. Bara lay sleeplessly on her back, her heart aching with pity and her eyes sore with the tears that would not come. Now she knew the seed of the mystery which had nagged at her so long. Two such women, Kate and Maeve, and he could not love them. Compassion overwhelmed her, for Kate, for Maeve, for Ralf, for all the miseries of men and women. She clutched her pillow tight, and at last the relieving tears flowed.

Next day the air was sharp, the skies were white and blue. The prospect of riding through the country in this summer weather was welcome to all who were to go on the journey. Bara ran leaping towards the stables to saddle Dark and for the first time in many days Tam watched her and smiled. In the cheerful bustle only Maeve seemed out of place, leaning wearily against the stable wall. Ralf intended to ride with the party as far as he felt able, and by then perhaps his place would be taken by Cormac, who was to follow after.

A door in the tower burst open and Ellen came running clumsily. Her pale hair flew in wisps about her face as she waved a piece of paper in her hand. Maeve stood up straight and stared at her intently.

'Quint!' called Ellen. 'Hey, take this!'

Quint groaned and smiled down at her.

'Not more plants?' he said.

'Of course.' Ellen laughed loudly and slapped the flank of his horse. 'Watch out for all of them and fix exactly where you find anything.'

As Ellen turned away she saw Ralf watching her. She shrugged and her face flushed. 'I'm tired of all this primitive witch-doctoring,' she said. 'Herbs and simples and all that stuff. I want some proper drugs.'

'I know. I know how you feel,' said Ralf. Ellen clicked her tongue in exasperation and turned away, then paused and stiffened when she saw Maeve. The two women looked at each other in silence. Bara watched them from behind Dark, sensing the tension.

'I'm sorry,' said Ellen quietly, lowering her eyes. 'I shouldn't have done it.' Then she moved heavily back to the Hall.

The cavalcade was ready to go. Although they would stay at inns where they could, they had three pack horses carrying bedding in case it should be required. Quint was the leader of the expedition, and Tam rode beside him. Bara had Con between her arms on Dark's back, with Ralf flanking her on one side and Fergus on the other. Finn had two companions to help him with the horses and the baggage in the rear. Just as they were leaving Finn reported with a puzzled frown that Cormac was locked in his room.

'Never mind,' said Ralf. 'He gets taken up with things. He'll come when he's ready. Maybe not for a day or two.'

They clattered along the terrace and down the steep ramp into the town. Quint's four wolfhounds were leashed to his saddle, and trotted alongside, as they had been trained, without entangling themselves or the horse. No-one went near them except Quint. Even Con had learned to be wary. Men in sheepskins, women in coloured shawls, barefoot children in leather tunics – all gathered in knots in the streets to see the procession go by. They waved and shouted and laughed, and there were also murmurs in which Bara caught the word 'Con' time and again. The boy bounced and laughed in the saddle, his silver hair flopping from side to side. Then Fergus began to sing. The song was obviously well-known, though Bara could understand no word of it, for the people in the street joined in. Ralf turned his white head to her.

'It tells of the Irish hero Cuchulain,' he said. 'It describes his setting off on a great journey. I hope your own journey won't be quite so adventurous,' he added.

'Fergus is on the Second Council, isn't he?' asked Tam turning in the saddle.

'He is,' said Ralf. 'His head is not only full of poetry and music, it is full of ideas too.'

'Curious ones,' said Quint, squinting round.

'Not altogether,' said Ralf. 'He wants us to build a life here based on the old heroic society. And the structure of the heroic society has a lot to be said for it. In the right circumstances it's very stable, and I like its virtues of affection and loyalty and courage. Dignity and order have a high place in it too.'

'But it's a society for hard times rather than good ones,' said Tam, turning again.

'I think you're right,' said Ralf, looking at him with approval. 'It's for a people beleaguered by enemies or an unfertile land. A heroic society needs heroics to sustain it. The kind of society I want hasn't a place for heroics.'

'That's right,' agreed Tam. 'Without feats of arms and physical courage the glory would all drain out of it.'

'As I said,' said Quint, 'curious ideas Fergus has.'

Sometime in the early afternoon Ralf turned back for Cashel, and Bara felt a loss of warmth when he went. The country was flat and rich, chequered with small fields of grain, some still standing, some already cut and stooked. Squares of dark brown wheat alternated with barley of silver-green, and here and there between were the patches of brown earth where wild flowers had been harvested for teas and drugs and dyes. All over Ireland Ellen had organized orderly fields of digitalis and poppies, henbane and marjoram and centuary. She was constantly experimenting with new drugs from plants, and as they rode Quint would point with mock disparagement to patches of her new hopefuls, all neatly fenced and labelled. But not all the fields were Ellen's. This flat lush land towards Limerick was chequered with coltsfoot and betony for tobacco; soapwort for washing and cleaning; bluebells and arum for starch and glue; rosebay and parsnips for alcohol. Only soapwort and rosebay were still in bloom, but every patch was clearly marked with a wooden board. Flax grew by all the streams and small rivers, on the higher ground was heather for fuel and thatch, and everywhere in between, high up or low down, were patches of potatoes.

In the late afternoon they joined the valley of the Mulkeir and passed through the Limerick dye-fields. Finn rattled off the varieties of sorrel and bedstraw and tormentil and centurea and betony and mignonette – but added there were plenty he didn't know, and anyway they couldn't all be grown in this particular soil. Bara's head reeled with all she had seen.

'You'll have to write it down for me, Finn,' she said. 'I can't remember it all.'

'Well,' he said, 'you make your paper from nettles and your ink from irises, then I'll write it down for you.'

Bara rubbed her cheek on the soft down pillow in her bed in Limerick. She looked over at Con, sleeping in a bundle, and wondered when Tam would come. He and Quint had stayed on after supper drinking wine with the young governor of Limerick, but he had said he would not be long. In the course of the day's riding he had begun to return to her at last, as Maeve had promised, but as yet her hope was only flickering. Then, suddenly, Tam was there, with his arms fiercely around her. His love had rushed back at him in a torrent so compelling that Bara was swept away in the dark flood. He was past laughter, past gentleness, longing only to give his heart for the mean weeks in which he had rebuffed her. She rose to him, at the height of her spirit, and her misery withered like a winter leaf. There was no longer any need of explanation or forgiveness.

The next morning they rode through Limerick. The governor, Rory, was a fair, talkative young man, immensely proud of his tumbledown city and eager with plans for development. He and his council had recently decided there was to be no more plundering of the old walls for building; nevertheless, he was anxious to point out, he was no mere conservationist. Limerick looked to the future.

First they were shown round a huge pottery, which made vessels for the whole of Ireland. The old man in charge had curling grey hair to his shoulders, and he was proud of the quality of his pots.

'It's the few wasters we have now,' he said, in an accent so broad Bara could scarcely understand. 'In this workshop we have the old up-draught kiln, but we're replacing them all by the down-draught. The heating is more even there. But it's little enough we have go wrong since the Old One came.'

'Came here?' said Tam.

'Aye. He was spending a month or so some years back and by Brigid he put us right on a mountain of troubles. It's him as invented the slip-casting. Here's a wee dog now. He's a slip-cast. We'll give him to the little lad.'

Con smiled broadly and held out his hands for the china dog. It was a wolfish looking animal, painted brown and white, with a deliberately cracked glaze.

'Thank you,' said Bara. 'It's a lovely animal.'

'Ah, it's just for the sport,' said the old man. 'Out of working hours and all.'

Con had been looking worried ever since they came to the kilns, and the gift of the dog dispersed his gloom for only a few minutes. Once again his brow furrowed and he wandered back by himself to the ovens. He stood staring at them so long Bara went over to fetch him.

'They're so small,' he said, looking up at her with a puzzled frown.

She recognized the signs of something echoing in his mind. 'How do you know they're small?' she said. 'You've never seen kilns.'

'I have. I must have. Somewhere. I *know* these ones are small. And why don't they do this instead?' He picked up a lump of dry clay and began to draw on the side of a cold kiln. He drew the usual dome, in section, raised off the floor, with a fire to one side, then he drew another dome over the top, with an outlet in the roof.

'This way the heat gets all round,' he said. 'And there's no fire or smoke in with the pots.' The old man had walked back to them and he stood looking at the drawing over Con's shoulder.

'Were you thinking of that yourself now?' he asked.

Con shrugged.

'I think he did,' said Bara.

'That's a muffle-kiln. We have some in the new shop across the road.'

Con gazed at him, then threw down the clay and stamped on it angrily.

'But it was marvellous clever of you to think of it,' said the potter, trying to mollify him. 'And you so young and all.' The old man gazed after him as the boy tramped away. 'He has the new world in him to be sure,' he said.

There followed a week of shining summer weather. Soon after Limerick they left the lush country of grain and cattle and found themselves in stoney moorlands, rising to mountains or dropping sharply to the sea, where crofting was the only farming possible. Bara was delighted with the corbelled stone cottages, built like tents, and with the long stone houses weighted with boulders against the Atlantic storms. They rode through heather and gorse, by sundew and asphodel, by foxglove and bilberry, they saw red deer on the hills and foxes in the valleys. Merlins and peregrines hung and swooped above them, swallows cut long arcs across the sky, Quint's hounds bounded like wolves across the hills. Sometimes Fergus would sing, or recite long legends of Ireland, while Con gazed and gazed and asked for more.

Tam was full of love again and his high spirits led them into danger more than once, as they galloped their horses across treacherous stony ground and urged them over the sudden brown streams that appeared without any warning in their path. Con shouted and laughed with Finn, shot with his new bow, learned to wrestle and box, and once again tickled for trout in the clattering streams. Once Bara found Finn sitting apart on a rock in the heather, his chin in his hands, staring at Con. When she asked him what was wrong he simply shook his fiery head, unsmiling, and said it wasn't that easy to live with a magic boy. Con had made half a dozen improvements to the mechanics of Finn's crossbow, and he had demonstrated to Finn, the great wrestler, three entirely new throws.

Quint was good-humoured and attentive, his bland blue eyes constantly flickering from Bara to Tam and back, anticipating their moods and wishes. But behind that camouflage of open blue Bara knew he was searching, studying, debating; and often when he looked at her she knew he was staring straight through her clothes. Sometimes when she found him closer than she expected, she was shocked by the surge of feeling that rose through her. He would smile slowly, as if he knew, and turn away. More and more often she found herself seeking him out and riding in silence beside him. One day, when his knee touched hers, she pulled away in panic, sharply reminding herself he was old enough to be her father. As she formed the casual words in her mind her throat suddenly constricted and her eyes stung. The buried memory of her lost father came rushing up at her, to be immediately swamped in the image of Kate. She gazed towards the roaring Atlantic, slapping on the cliffs of Brandon Head, but the sea was misted in tears. Lenny, her father, lost so long ago; poor crazy Charley; her enfolding, loving Grans; the tug of the past overwhelmed her and she no longer knew where she rode. When Tam found her, hours later, sitting in the dusk on the edge of the cliff, she was cold and far away, invaded by memory, stunned by the crashing of the sea.

The next week was bright but there was little warmth in the sun. They remembered autumn, and pulled their cloaks of wool and leather close to their shoulders. The cliffs, the mountains, the crests of the sea were all sharply defined in the crisp air. Since leaving Limerick they had come across the Feale and through the hills to Tralee, then out along the Brandon peninsula to Slea Head, in sight of the Blaskets. Many of the seabirds had left for the ocean, but there were still gulls and shags and fulmers and kittiwakes, whose cries rode above the booming of the sea. Sometimes they saw seals, basking on rocks or raising inquisitive, whiskered heads from the waves. They had travelled south by the lakes of Killarney, through lonely mountains to Bantry Bay, and now they were to turn their backs on the Atlantic and make their way home to Cashel. Bara was enraptured with what she had seen. The cliffs and the mountains and the boundless sea filled her eyes and her ears and her dreams at night. She rode on the wind, she was swept up in the freedom of the great birds. Exhilaration blew around her, like hair blowing in a gale. Quint gazed and gazed and smiled his slow smile. One day, when the afternoon sun was warm, he headed Bara off from the main party and rode with her down Glengariff. He had something particular to show her, he said. Every kind of shrub and tree and plant grew in that lush silent glen. Near the sea they dismounted and Quint walked ahead. The air was very still.

'Look,' he said at last, pointing to a group of small trees. 'Arbutus. The strawberry tree.' Bara stepped ahead of him into the grove, her heart pounding. She felt Quint's hand on her arm and his lips on her hair. Between two heartbeats time stood still. His grip tightened and he began to turn her round. Suddenly her muscles moved again, she tore for Dark's back and in a desperate confusion of feeling leaped into the saddle and galloped up the glen. Tam said nothing, but that evening he was thoughtful and she wondered what was coming. She had done nothing wrong, and if he was angry with her she would be angry back. But he did not seem to be angry, merely silent. Presently he began to talk about all they had seen. In the six weeks they had been away they had visited the potteries and the dye-works at Limerick and the open-cast coal-mines south of the Shannon. They had seen the cement works at Tralee, the iron foundries and steel-works at Killarney. They had watched men panning for river gold, they had visited many small boatyards on the coast, and the shipyard in Bantry Bay. All along the shores they had seen the cultivation and gathering of seaweed. They had heard in detail about the silver mines north of Limerick and the slate quarries south at Clonakilty. And everywhere they had come upon the small turf stations, where machines like cider-presses crushed the loose fibres of peat into solid blocks. Every evening in the crofts and inns where they stayed they had eaten crayfish or lobster or crab or prawns fresh from the prolific sea.

This evening, the last in Bantry, Tam rose early from his meal and took Bara's arm. She was startled, for the company usually sat talking and drinking after supper, and she glanced at Quint who was staring at Tam. But she followed where she was led, down the path to the dusky shore. If Tam was going to be angry, he would get as good as he gave. Across the estuary the Sugarloaf Mountain blackened against the pink sky. And still Tam did not speak. Bara's irritation rose, sharpened by guilt.

'Oh for goodness' sake,' she said, stopping in her tracks on the shingle and pulling away her hand.

'Sorry,' he said, astonishing her. 'Sorry. But I'm worried. In fact I'm scared.'

'Scared?' Bara wrinkled her forehead, bewildered.

'Haven't you noticed anything?'

'What sort of thing? I've noticed thousands of things – mountains, crofts, birds, badgers. What do you mean?' Tam stood with his arms folded, staring at the twilit sea.

'Everywhere,' he said, 'everywhere we've gone, there's been some mystery. Something we weren't allowed to see.'

'We saw everything.'

'No, we didn't. We were supposed to think we did. Look, even in this estuary we've seen only one big shipyard.'

'But there is only one.'

'No, there isn't. There's a far bigger one, over there, hidden beyond Bear Island. A boy just happened to ask me if we'd seen it.'

'Well, we don't have to see everything I suppose.'

'I don't believe Ralf knows about it. I don't believe he knows about the high-carbon steel they're making at Killarney. I don't believe he knows they're using blast furnaces. I don't believe he knows they're making cargo ships twice the size that's authorized.' Bara stared at him as he seized her arm. 'And I don't know what the mysterious hum can be. I heard it in Limerick and I heard it in Tralee and I heard it in Killarney. It's some kind of power. A generator. Based on peat, or water I suppose – something, anyway.' He began pacing up and down the muddy shore. 'You remember at Tralee Con said "What's that funny noise?" and Quint pretended he couldn't hear it and hurried us on? Don't you remember how abruptly we finished our tour of the iron-works, when we seemed to be only halfway through? And now the boats. Quint said this was the greatest boatyard in the South – then this boy cutting turf asked me if I'd seen the *really* big one over there.'

'So they're settling the matter on their own,' said Bara softly. 'Frost and Quint and Cormac and the rest.'

'I think they are.'

'Who are these people anyway?' said Bara. 'Who is it doing what Frost wants?'

'They must be mostly young, like Cormac. Too young to remember Ireland in the wars. They probably think of the old industrial societies of Europe as the most magnificent pinnacle of man's achievement. God, it's frightening.'

'They must think it's all so wildly exciting and new.'

'Yes. Building a shiny, affluent, modern world. Technology equals progress.'

'I'm surprised people who think like Ness don't come and break up these new machines.'

'I think they will. I'm sure they will. The new Luddites. Frost's right about that – there *is* a real terror of machines, specially among older people who saw what scientific weapons of war can do. We've got to strike a path between these extremes. Ralf's path. We've got to find it and make it appeal and make it work. And by God we must do it soon, before Frost and Quint and Rory and the rest of them have Ireland humming with secret machines from end to end.

Poor Ralf. He thought he was conducting an honest debate. And he thought his ideas were winning. It's treachery,' said Tam, suddenly fierce. 'Pure, black treachery.'

Bara looked at him.

'I did think at one time you wanted it that way. Technology – progress – and all that.'

'To start with, yes. Then when I began wavering someone took me over and made me go on thinking it. Someone wanted me to want it.'

'Frost. Or Quint.'

'No, not them. Someone very – very passionate and upset. Anyway, we've got to go back. And for God's sake don't let Quint know that we know. Otherwise we'll probably *never* get back.'

Bara was shocked and angry.

'You can't really think they'd do anything – anything like—?'

'An unfortunate accident. We fell off a crag or into a river. The horses bolted. Anything.'

'Don't be crazy. He wouldn't dare. He's not like that.'

'Isn't he,' said Tam grimly. 'Your trouble is you've got a weakness for men with faces like cardboard heroes.' Bara turned on him angrily, but he went on. 'And by the way, you might avoid arbutus groves in future.' Then he strode off alone up the path into the darkness.

They reached Cashel three days later, at the end of August, on a pale rain-washed afternoon. The fields near the town had been unusually empty, and there was silence in the streets. Many of the windows were shuttered. Quint frowned and kicked his horse into a trot. Finn called to a face at a window, but the shutter was promptly slammed. Bara shuddered and remembered Monmouth, the plague town.

'What's wrong, Mam?' asked Con, staring about him, his voice sounding unnaturally loud.

'We'll see. We don't know yet,' whispered Bara. As they approached the ramp up to the castle they came upon small groups of people, many of whom turned their backs in silence. Quint reined in by a group who did not turn away.

'What's the trouble? What's happened?' he said. A youth stepped forward to speak but an old woman put a bony hand on his shoulder.

'Shut your mouth, Liam,' she hissed. 'Let the Old One be telling them.'

Quint muttered in anger and urged his horse up the road to the castle. There were crowds gathered on the incline, but he did not stop to speak to them. Ellen was out on the terrace, talking to a group of townspeople, and she moved forward as she saw them riding up the hill.

'Come in,' she said, with no word of greeting. Her faced looked swollen and red.

They all dismounted and men moved forward to take the horses. Quint strode rapidly after Ellen, followed by Fergus, but Tam and Bara hesitated, unsure if they were wanted. Then they followed also, leaving Con with Finn, and entered the gloom of the Great Hall. At the head of the long table Ralf sat with his head laid on his arms, the whiteness of his hair and beard shining against the black wood. Ellen laid a hand on his shoulder.

'Quint is back,' she said. 'And all of them.'

Ralf raised his head slowly and looked at them.

'Cormac is dead,' he said. 'He cut his throat this morning.'

In the evening in the small room behind the Hall, they heard the story of Cormac's death. All the Council were there, with Quint and Fergus from the Second Council as well. Paedric's eyes were huge in his hollow face, even larger, Bara thought, that they had been six weeks ago. Ness was white and drawn, endlessly twisting her fingers in her lap. Frost's mouth was set in a grim line, more of anger than grief, and Maeve would meet no-one's eyes. One by one the Council took up the story. As the travellers knew, Cormac had never followed them, although they had expected him. Apparently he had stayed in his room for days, opening his door to no-one except the man who brought him food. He would see nobody – not Ralf, not Ness, not anyone else. Sometimes they heard him shouting, sometimes he wept. And not one of them could reach his mind. Although he was so sensitive a Listener nobody could get through to him, for he erected barriers against them that even Ralf could not penetrate. Nor would he use his powers as a Speaker. He would not communicate at all. Once when they began to break down the door he screamed that he had a knife at his throat and would kill himself if any one tried to enter. They put sedatives in his food, but he either smelled or tasted them and he threw his dish at the floor, shouting that he would not be poisoned.

Then for the whole of August he was quiet. He ate his food and they could hear him moving about his room. They thought he was working, they assumed the crisis was over and that one day soon he would open his mind to them and appear again in person.

Then, at dawn that morning, the people who slept in the east side of the castle were woken by a wild scream, followed by a clanging and shattering throughout the building and the courtyard. Cormac was out, his black eyes blazing, and in his hands an enormous axe. He tore through the yard, swinging to right and left at milk-churns, horse-troughs, handcarts, windows, rending and smashing as he went. Then he wheeled into the Hall, swinging at the benches and the sconces and the platters by the wall. A child who peeped in had had his arm broken. Then Cormac had rushed out onto the terrace, whirling his axe above his head and shouting wild words over the roofs of the town.

'The demons have me!' he had cried. 'The demons have me in their power and sure as the lights of hell they will destroy me. But I will be taking youse all with me, I will not be going down alone, I will go in the company that made and broke me, so help me holy Brigid.'

Then he had leaned on the parapet and sobbed. A crowd of men gathered near him and a few had begun to approach cautiously. But as soon as Cormac heard them he had wheeled around, grasping his axe and crouching to spring. The men withdrew and suddenly Cormac leaped away and made for his room. Ness had let out a terrible cry and begun to run wildly after him.

'I heard him, I heard him!' she had cried as she ran. 'I heard his mind. Catch him, oh for Christ's sake catch him!' But Cormac had barred his door in their faces and they had had to break their way in. He lay in the middle of his room with a knife in his hand and his head in a pool of blood. Ellen had rushed forward, but there was no repair possible to that gaping wound.

Later they found what he had been doing all the weeks he was closeted in his room. His meticulous plans and drawings, all his calculations and inventions, years of work, had been methodically sliced into tiny shreds of paper. Paper lay in mounds all over the floor. Each plan, each drawing, each chart had been carefully cut down and across, in straight lines, a thousand times, and left in scraps so small they were wholly inintelligible. Chalked on the stone above the chimney piece there were two columns, one labelled NOW and one FUTURE. Under the first was a list of words which meant little to most of the company: *blast furnace, sheet metal, welding, high carbon steel, dynamo.* Under the second were words which meant even less: *hydroelectric, radio, piston engine, aircraft, uranium.* Maeve told Bara later that Frost had thrown himself against the wall, striking it with his fists, in a frenzy of rage and weeping. She had never seen him lose control before. It was a horrible exhibition, she said, for they all knew it was not grief for Cormac that stirred him, but the loss of Cormac's skill.

At the end of the story Ness swung back her yellow hair and darted towards the door. Maeve attempted to go with her, but Ness pushed her gently back.

'Don't come,' she said. 'I'm all right.'

When she had left Ralf spoke.

'She thinks it's her fault,' he said. 'She thinks she failed Cormac and failed us all. She knew he was near to madness, but she thought our decision on the future would be soon, and once it was made he would steady again.'

'We all share the blame,' said Paedric, clutching his chair. 'We shouldn't have left him in doubt so long. We should have come to our decision long ago.'

'Of course we should,' said Frost angrily, his eyes darting round the company. 'To deny a boy like that – I knew it was wicked, and now we know it was murder. We've killed that lad between us. The all-wise, all-powerful Council. We who pride ourselves on our humanity. You can't deny a gift like that and get away with it. There's never been on this earth a creature gifted like Cormac. There's nothing he couldn't have made. And what do we do? We murder him. And we'll probably do the same to the next one.'

'The next one?' said Tam quickly.

'The boy – Con.'

Bara leaped up, trembling.

'No!' she shouted, clenching her fists. 'I'll take him away. I'll take him away where you'll never find us. I'll kill myself before I let you do that to him!'

Tam seized her hands, and Ralf's arm was round her shoulders. Suddenly she subsided, weeping.

'What a thing to say,' said Ellen, glaring at Frost.

'It needed to be said,' muttered Quint. 'We'll meet the problem again – and worse – in Con.' But Tam had taken Bara away.

In the course of the next few days Bara realized that Ralf was now an old man. Old he had been before, but he had borne his age with such energy that he was not dominated. Suddenly age was pressing down on him and he was sinking beneath the weight. Two nights after Cormac's death Bara went to find him in his room, thinking of him not as the Old One or the leader of Ireland but as her grandfather who was weary and alone. His violin hung on the whitewashed wall and a small fire flickered in the grate. He smiled and put his arm round her, and she hoped that the warmth of her body would comfort him, but he was sunk in lethargy. They sat in silence, staring at the little fire. After a while Ralf spoke, and his thoughts were so far from Bara's that she took a moment to understand him.

'How was the old house?' he said.

'The old—?'

'In London. Did you still live in my father's house?'

'Oh that. Yes. I told you, I was brought up there.'

'Did you tell me?'

'When I first came here. The first night. I told you everything. I told you about my father—'

'Ah, Lenny. I remember. The son I never knew.'

'I hardly knew him either. He died of cholera when I was five.'

'I remember. You told me. Let's talk about Kate. All night, if you like, we'll talk about Kate. And you shan't cry, for I shall have my arm round you. And I hope I shan't cry either.'

For hours they talked, deep into the night, just as on the day of Bara's coming to Cashel. Once again Ralf wanted to know all she could remember of Charley, of the old house, of Kate, of her friends, of Tam as a boy. He in his turn told her of his father Philip, of his school, of Frost, of Greatorex, of the Revolution and Bradwardine, of the days when London had been a prosperous, shining city. But he veered back to Kate again and again; his memories swept over a lifetime, but always they returned to her.

'I ran away from her,' he murmured. 'I know it now. I've always told myself that she wouldn't come with me, and I've felt very bitter. But it wasn't that at all. I had to run away from Bradwardine and the police, but I ran from Kate too. I couldn't return what she gave me. I just couldn't do it.' He buried his face in his hands and Bara did not know what to say. In a moment he went on. 'Later it was the same with Maeve. I simply couldn't give her what I wanted to give her – I couldn't give her what she gave to me. Oh, two such women.' He groaned and rolled his head against the wall. 'I had no trouble with my body. That was easy. They had all they wanted of me, and more. But I couldn't love them, I just could not love them. My mother bitched it up for me long, long ago.'

Bara stared at her hands, feeling uncomfortable and inadequate. She did not understand, and she felt too full of pain for Kate to care much about his misery.

The room was cold and dark when Ralf finished speaking. As Bara sat waiting for him to go on, he fell suddenly asleep and his head sank onto her shoulder. She shifted slightly to take the weight of his head more squarely, and determined to stay there till he woke. Overlaid by the down of his beard, her hair glittered red in the last of the firelight. When Tam found her in the early hours of the morning she was cold and stiff, but still supporting Ralf. Together they managed to lay him on his bed without waking him, then they covered him with the great patchwork quilt Maeve had made him when they both were young.

In the middle of September the move back to winter quarters in Dublin began. Small bands of horsemen and loaded carts left every day for the winter capital. Most were glad to be going, even the local men, for Cormac's death had turned the air of Cashel bitter. He had been buried under a great tumulus, a mile from the town, and it seemed all the able-bodied men in the south had come to dig the earth. The inner chamber where his embalmed body lay was lined with slabs of Connemara marble, left from the repairing of the Great Hall forty years before. There had never been any deaths among the First Council, so there was uncertainty as to what should be done. Ralf had not pressed his desire for a simple funeral. He had retreated, with the rest of the Council, before the clamour of the thousands who wanted the full traditional Irish obsequies. A committee of townspeople had taken the matter in hand, and Quint and his father had announced that they would be delighted to serve in any capacity. Frost appeared constantly in public, subtly encouraging the transformation of the dark and splendid Cormac from man to god. Quint was busy everywhere, cheering on the diggers, devising a ritual, and himself speaking the elaborate funeral oration from the crest of the tumulus.

'It's strange the way you people talk in public,' said Tam to Maeve, as he listened. 'So stately and formal and – resounding.'

'It's expected,' said Maeve. 'We all love words in Ireland, and that kind of oratory is loved best of all. You'll be learning it yourself,' she added, smiling at him. After the interment, the wake had lasted for three days. Much poteen was drunk, fiddling and dancing filled the day and the night. But to Bara it sounded with a frenzied ring; she sensed fear behind the jollity, and she was relieved when the celebrations slowly faded away and the tired crowds set off on their journeys home. Tam felt none of Bara's curiosity. Like Ralf, he was disgusted with the long rituals of death. Now he stood with Bara on the parapet, watching the people go home through the town below.

'Where is everyone?' he said, frowning in consternation.

'Who?'

'The Council. They've vanished for days. Where are they?'

'Oh they're around,' said Bara. 'In the background somewhere.'

'I don't like it.'

'But why? Most of them don't care for Irish funerals.'

'Well, they shouldn't let themselves get so much in the background. Quint and Frost aren't in the background at all. They're right in the foreground, slap in the middle of the people's eye. They'll be taken for the bosses soon, and that's just what they want.'

Bara looked at him with concern.

'You must tell Ralf,' she said. 'About that, and all the other things too.'

That evening Tam demanded to see the Old One. Since Cormac's death Ralf had done very little work, either waving it aside as unimportant or pushing it away until after the funeral. Tam's attempts to speak to him in private had been frustrated several times, and if by chance he had happened to find himself alone with Ralf, his opening comments had been adroitly resolved into pleasantries. Ralf did not want to hear. Tam became more and more exasperated, but Bara was filled with pity, for she knew that for a time at least Ralf had retreated into his own meditations and memories, into the private world within his skull. The piercing darkness of his regard had not faded, but his mind now moved apart, no longer following the focus of his eyes. Maeve was constantly at his side and the anxiety in her sidelong glances was not lost on Bara. The Old One was giving up, and still he did not know the worst.

Then Tam received a message that he could see Ralf that evening. Dusk closed early and the wind rose. At first it played in sudden gusts, driving the autumn flowers against the grey walls of the Hall, then dying away to let them rise again. Gradually the gusts increased in ferocity and the respite between them was shorter, until there was no slackening at all in the solid torrent of wind. Glowing in the gloom, the flowers bent and thrashed and finally broke. The light mist blown in by the first gusts thickened into drizzle, and by nightfall a black, thudding rain tore slanting down from the back of the wind. The forces of the night split and shrieked round the unyielding towers of Cashel. Wind screamed round the corners, rain drummed like pebbles on the roofs, windows rattled, doors moaned on their hinges. Over a constant substratum of sound each new burst of fury screamed and died away, to be immediately succeeded by another rising shriek and then another, in an ever increasing crescendo of tumult. Water edged round the joints of windows and slithered along the sills. The gutters were swamped, the drains spluttered and belched as they overflowed onto the yards and courts. The inhabitants of the Rock drew their jackets round their shoulders and crouched fearfully over their fires. Buckets and rain-butts swirled up to the brim, then splashed in cataracts onto the cobbles below. When Bara and Tam emerged, enveloped in cloaks, in order to cross the courtyard to visit Ralf, their ears were assailed and filled, to the exclusion of all other sound, with the roaring of the storm. Leaning against each other, pushing head-down into the weather, they reached Ralf's door. When Bara entered the bare room she was struck full in the face by the heat from a blazing fire, and she was startled, even on such a night, to find Ralf crouched so close over so fierce a blaze. But he rose to greet them cheerfully, helped them off with their wet cloaks, and passed them each a cup of the precious wine from the west.

'All right,' he said, smiling. 'If you're dry and warm again, tell me the worst.'

Tam was stopped in his tracks.

'You know – ?'

'You are forgetful,' said Ralf wearily. 'Of course I know you're troubled. If I bend my mind towards you for one moment, I know you're troubled. If I cared to set myself to it I'd soon know exactly why.'

'Of course,' said Tam, contrite. 'I keep forgetting how it is round here.'

'Well, tell me the worst.'

Ralf settled himself close to the fire again, and Tam and Bara sat on the bench by the far wall. The firelight shone on the polished surface of the violin. Wind moaned, rain beat on the window. Tam then told him all they had noticed and suspected on their journey. He spoke of the strange hum at Limerick and Tralee and Killarney, of the abrupt ending to their tour of the iron works, of the unseen boatyard behind Bear Island, and a dozen small unexplained details which had bothered him. He finished his recital, but Ralf said nothing, and they wondered if he had fallen asleep. But at last he rose and moved slowly over to the window. He leaned on the sill and stared out into the dark. The wind roared and screamed, assaulting the tower that rose into the night above their heads.

'I knew,' he said. 'I knew all the time. But I didn't want to know. The implications – the necessary action – I didn't want to face them. I'm too old, and too tired. I thought if I kept the problem from my mind – if I avoided confrontation – it might solve itself. But I was wrong. And now perhaps I've betrayed the country that was mine to make.'

He dropped his head in his hands and said no more. After a moment Tam and Bara crept softly away. They stood on a stairway whose window looked over the dark town, and listened to the howl of the wind and the clatter of the rain. Tam put his arm round Bara's waist and she saw to her astonishment his eyes were full of tears.

'The power is gone from him,' he said. 'The power is gone, and now he's only a sad old man waiting to die. The power is looking for somewhere else to settle.'

'One day it will be Con's,' said Bara, moving tight against him.

'But not yet. Someone must hold it for him. And it must not be Quint. If we want our species and our planet to survive their second chance, the power must be kept from Quint.'

Bara looked up at him as he stared into the blackness of the storm. She was dismayed by the hard edge to his voice, but she saw from the set of his jaw that battle with Quint was already joined.

The Great Council, comprising the First and Second Councils, met in formal session the next morning. The Great Hall was dark and cold, its drabness intensified by the huge black vault of the roof, but the wind had subsided in the night and the fury of the rain had passed. The Rock of Cashel glistened like a cliff wet from the sea. Ralf held himself erect, refusing Maeve's arm, and only a few recognized that he was merely the shell of his old authority. Supported by Ellen and Quint, Paedric moved slowly to the nearest chair, where he folded himself in exhaustion and closed his heavy lids. Bara could not bear to look at the grey tautness of his skin. She turned to smile at Fergus, who was trying to subdue his spirits to the solemnity of the occasion, and she busily avoided the steady gaze of Quint. Ellen was feeling cool, for once, so the natural flush of her face was soothed, and at this early hour of the day her hair was less straggling than usual. Bara noticed with surprise how carefully she avoided the eyes of Maeve. She remembered the silent confrontation in the stableyard, when Maeve and Ellen had stared at one another, and she was certain something had happened between them. Ness came in late, wild of eye and twisting her fingers into knots, but when Fergus shouldered his way to her side she smiled and her hands were stilled. Frost sat quietly next to Ralf, turning the rings on his fingers and glancing sharply from face to face. Quint moved everywhere, arranging chairs, joking, laughing, helping the women to their seats. Tam glowered, in his surliest mood, and Bara eased him as far from Quint as she could. As a person Quint was odious; as a body and a pair of searching eyes he was compelling. She sat trembling in his magnetism, only to find herself held in the puzzled gaze of Tam. She smiled quickly and switched her attention, but Tam's eyes sought out Quint and stayed upon him.

The First Council sat in a row along the top board, and the Second at two long trestles at right-angles. Bara and Tam were at the corner of the top table, where it abutted onto one of the trestles. Frost struck the ground with his crozier and Ralf rose slowly. He leaned forward, his knuckles on the table before him, and he did not raise his head as once he would have done. The long billows of his beard fell almost to his hands. There was an unnatural hush in the Hall, expectancy lay heavy on the air, and every eye was on Ralf. Many had theories and suspicions, but no-one knew positively why he had convened this rare gathering of the Great Council. There had not been a Great Council called for fifteen years, not in fact since the astonishing powers of a small boy called Cormac had first made themselves known. Ralf spoke.

'I've called this Council,' he said, 'for one simple reason. I say simple – the reason itself is simple, but the solution to the problem it poses may be very difficult. The plain fact is that Ralf the Old One is becoming rapidly much too old. I would like to quit before I am too senile to see the necessity.' There were shouts and low protests from all over the Hall. Ralf raised his head and smiled, forcing back his shoulders until he was looking up into the dark recesses of the roof. 'You are very kind,' he said, 'and very polite. But I think many of you will have realized that since Cormac's death I have been rapidly losing the battle with old age. I find that my mind is taking on a will of its own. It begins to lead me on long journeys which I did not inaugurate or expect, and I find that instead of concentrating on problems of government I am merely dreaming of my youth. This is the mark of a lost battle, and I cannot any longer pretend to be the leader I am not. Someone must have my place.'

There were loud shouts of protest from all over the Hall, and Bara heard an undertone of murmurs which seemed to say 'Con'. Quint smiled blandly at the roof and Frost darted his eyes round the table. The rest of the First Council stared miserably before them and Ness dropped her head in her hands. Only Tam on the upper table kept his eyes up, staring intently at the faces below and around him.

'Those who cry "no",' continued Ralf, 'have all my thanks. But they mistake the appearance for the reality. I believe I look much as I have looked for several years, but the man within is very different. I assure you all that I am no longer fitted to be chief of all Ireland, let alone the director of the strange and unexpected destiny that has been offered to our kind. I have done what I can for this marvellous planet, and for the dominant species which tenants it. Since I was a small boy, in another world, over eighty years ago, when our planet almost died, I have cared deeply about its fate. I've regarded our species as temporary tenants, whose duty was to hand our home undamaged to our heirs. The astonishing new powers which have developed among us in the course of the last century have hedged us about with temptations and choices even more difficult than those which faced our forefathers. I am no longer fitted to face them. I have been a greatly privileged man and I have done what I could. But I have had my day.'

He sat down slowly and folded his arms. There was a moment's utter silence, then in the broken light of the tears which welled into her eyes, Bara watched the desolation that spread through the company. Many sat with their heads in their hands; some stood; some moved aimlessly; one brown old man beat his fists on the table. At one time or another all had paused to realize that the Old One could not be there forever, but most of them had shied from the thought and forgotten it. Only Frost had not forgotten, nor Quint, nor Tam. Bara saw them glance sharply at each other and as swiftly look away. Ralf had been revered beyond the lot of most men, but it was not only a sense of loss which filledthe Hall. Every man and woman there saw a time of struggle and disintegration ahead. Once Ralf was gone, the tranquility of the last half-century could no longer hold. In time Con would come – all were agreed on that – but in the long interregnum ahead there could be chaos and even war. Every member of the Great Council, every man and woman in the town, and in the end all the people of Ireland, would be compelled to take sides, for now the great decisions about the future could be postponed no longer. Frost and Quint and their supporters had lurked in the shadows long enough. Now they would emerge in a determined attempt to see that Ireland developed again the technology that she had once shared with the Western world. Even those who felt that Frost was right were filled with foreboding at the inevitable struggle ahead, and those who felt he was wrong saw Ralf's vision of Ireland blasted in a summer's span.

That night when Bara was putting Con to bed in his little white room he looked up at her enquiringly.

'Is the Old One dead?' he said.

'Ralf? No, of course not. Why?'

'Oh, I just thought. I sort of felt something. But I wasn't sure. And Finn's been kind of funny today.'

'How, funny?'

'Well, he hasn't been quite there. I mean, he didn't hear when I talked to him. He didn't take much notice of me.'

Bara laughed and hugged him and he buried his face in the swathes of her hair.

'Too many people take too much notice of you,' she said.

'Oh I know. People are always noticing me. Am I very beautiful or something?'

'No you're not. You're an ugly squint-eyed, snub-nosed dwarf.'

Con laughed and rolled his head on his pillow. When his hair fell back the scar showed white and lumpy down his forehead.

'I didn't do any lessons today,' he said. 'Finn said I needn't.'

'What did you do then?'

'I played chess with Maeve. She's quite good, I can beat everyone else.'

'Oh yes?'

'Then I wrote a story in Gaelic about a big fight. Two warriors on horses in a river.'

'You wrote it in *Gaelic*?' Bara stared at him, retreating a little.

'Yes. What's wrong? Gaelic. You've heard of *Gaelic*, haven't you?'

'I didn't know you knew it, that's all.'

'Well, I do now. Paedric gave me some lessons.'

'I see. Well you'd better turn that brain off now and go to sleep.' She blew out his rushlight with shaking breath and Con sighed contentedly.

'I'm glad the Old One's not dead,' he said. 'I think he must be God.'

The following week was filled with meeting after meeting. Knots of people clustered in doorways, at corners, in private rooms. There was whispering, shouting, gesticulating, the running of urgent messages, an air of uncertainty that elated some and depressed others. Everyone knew that this was not mere politicking for a new leader. This was a time out of which must emerge a decision on the future of Ireland, perhaps of the western world, perhaps of humanity itself. The new leader, whether of Ralf's persuasion or Frost's, would merely represent and execute the decision of the majority. Frost and Quint moved quietly about, injecting a word here and a thought there, mysteriously calm in the midst of the commotion. Bara found Quint's admiring glances fewer, for he seemed abstracted and often did not notice she was near him. She felt cold when he would not notice her, then she was ashamed and clung tightly to Tam. In the course of that week she watched Tam emerge as a leader. More and more often people sought him out, more and more often his opinion was required. He was co-opted onto the Second Council, to give him a clearer status, and soon he began to convene meetings himself. His quiet, smouldering presence gave reassurance to waverers, so that those who were afraid of Frost and Quint allied themselves with him and persuaded others to join them. Still Frost and Quint remained unperturbed.

There was little comfort left at Cashel. All but the bare minimum of furniture and equipment was clattering north along the road to Dublin, taking half the people of the Rock with it. The walls of the Hall were stripped of rugs and platters, the offices were emptied of their piles of paper and books, the library was depleted, there were not enough blankets to meet the encroaching cold. Meals were usually tepid and often inadequate. The land was changing leaders, the people were moving house, there was a bitter scouring of the old comfortable world they knew.

One evening Bara wandered up to Maeve's room in the tower. Tam was busy, talking as usual, and Con was asleep, but Maeve would surely be welcoming. The turret stair was cold, and moisture ran down the stone wall. Bara's knock was not answered, so she tried again.

'What is it?' called Maeve, more sharply than usual.

'It's me. Bara. Can I come in?'

'Oh. Wait a minute.' There were murmurings within the room and Bara was about to turn away, feeling an intruder, when the thick door was opened.

'Come in,' said Maeve, smiling. 'I'm sorry, we were talking.'

As Bara entered she saw Ellen huddled over the fire. Her face was puffed, as if she had been crying, but she smiled at Bara and began to pin up the errant wisps of her hair.

'Sorry,' said Bara awkwardly, feeling her welcome had been more polite than warm. 'I didn't come for anything special. I'll go away.'

'Oh no.' Maeve took her arm and turned her towards the cushioned bench by the wall. 'I'm thinking we've had enough of our conversation anyway. A little interruption is very welcome.'

Maeve wore a long dress of dark blue wool and Ellen was in black. The carved wooden chest had gone to Dublin, the rugs were stripped from the walls, only the firelight seemed alive in the gloomy room.

'Have you any news for us?' asked Maeve, thrusting at the peat with Ralf's poker.

'News? No, I never seem to know anything,' said Bara. 'Tam's so tired at night he just sleeps.'

'Doesn't he say anything at all?' asked Ellen, rubbing her eyes.

'Only that he's worried stiff. One day everyone seems to want Ralf's ideas to succeed, then the next day they all think differently.'

'The idiots.' Ellen rose angrily, pulling up her bulk by the stone mantleshelf. 'It's obvious, isn't it?'

'So it is,' said Maeve, staring at the fire. She sighed and leaned back. 'Sometimes I think we'll never win through, Ellen. Our gifts are too big for us. Too tempting. There'll always be unscrupulous people who'll misuse them.'

'Nonsense,' said Ellen briskly. 'We're going to win. We've got to. We'll just have to fight back, that's all.'

'Oh Ellen, you wouldn't do it again, now would you?'

'No, of course not. You know that very well. It was despair for Paedric that drove me to try it on Tam.'

'Tam?' Bara was so bewildered by their conversation her thoughts had wandered away, but Tam's name brought them sharply back. 'What did you try on Tam?'

Ellen moved over to the window and folded her arms.

'About the time you arrived,' she said, 'I realized that I'd never cure Paedric. I've had such success in my life as a doctor I was confident I could cure anything. But his cancer utterly defeated me. I knew I could do nothing to help him without the old medical techniques. I knew from my powers as a Listener just what I should need, and I also knew that in Ralf's chosen state of society I'd never get it. I'd always remained rather apart from the great debate on the future, but I'd always longed for proper tools of medicine and surgery. With Paedric getting worse and worse my longing for them became a passion. I began to support Frost in public and he still counts me one of his allies. When Tam came I recognized a power in him I wanted for our cause. I wanted it so much I broke the first and holiest rule of our society. I set myself to influence his thought in our direction. I worked on him night and day for two or three weeks, and I knew I was succeeding.'

'Of course,' said Bara. 'Those awful weeks when he sort of left me, when I told Maeve.'

Ellen went on, ignoring her. 'Then suddenly there was a kind of blockage. It's difficult to explain; but I couldn't get through to him, and it wasn't because of any resistance on his part. Someone was deliberately in the way – and that's how I knew I was found out. The morning you all set off for the West I saw Maeve looking at me in the courtyard, and I knew who it was had blocked me. I was utterly ashamed and I stopped at once. That's the whole story.'

'Ellen is susceptible to shame,' said Maeve, 'but that isn't true of everyone. I think we know the reason for Tam's present problem. Why people keep changing their minds when he thinks he's persuaded them. Every day his arguments get people round to Ralf's way of thinking, and every night Frost and Quint and their friends undo his work.'

'They're both very powerful Speakers,' said Ellen, turning from the window. 'And there are plenty of others to help them. They're simply manipulating minds to their own advantage.'

'But why can't you all do just the opposite?' asked Bara – but before she had finished speaking she knew she had been stupid. Maeve and Ellen were gazing at her.

'Don't you understand a thing about the story I've just told you?' said Ellen.

'Yes – I know – sorry.' In her confusion Bara turned her face sideways, into the hair which fell across it. 'I do know it's the first rule. You mustn't ever use your power as a Speaker to manipulate. But at a time like this – can't the rule ever be broken?'

'No, it can't.' She had never heard this icy edge to Maeve's voice before. She shrank back against the wall, feeling Maeve's warmth wither like a dryness in the air.

'It's so important,' she murmured. But she could defend herself no longer.

'You'll learn which is the more important,' said Ellen.

'And you must learn soon,' said Maeve, still remote. 'Con's mother of all people must have her priorities right.'

Bara leaped to her feet, her fists clenched, unable to take the lecturing of these old ladies a moment longer.

'Godalmighty hell!' she shouted through her tears. 'I didn't ask to be mother to a sort of – a sort of magic king. I want him for myself,

I want an ordinary boy and an ordinary life. I hate this place and I hate all this fuss about Speakers and Listeners and what's to happen next. I never asked for it to be like this.'

Her voice was choked in sobs as she doubled up in a fury of weeping. Immediately Maeve had her arms round Bara's shoulders and her cheek on the girl's hair.

'There,' she said softly, relapsing into her native turn of speech, as she always did when she was moved. 'There now, I'm sorry. It's rough and hard I've been. It's a terrible destiny has been thrown on you, and you so young. It's a terrible thing to have to carry. But you're good, and you're strong, and you'll carry it, and one day it's the proud girl you'll be.'

Ellen took Bara's hands and smiled down on her tear-ravaged face. 'You are the best and bravest girl I ever knew,' she said.

Bara scarely heard her. 'Grans, Grans,' she sobbed inside herself. 'Grans, were are you? I want you here, I want you.'

They laid her on Maeve's bed and covered her with soft rugs. Ellen gave her something hot and sweet to drink, and almost instantly she slept.

At dusk two days later Bara returned from a ride on Dark. Con, who had been with her, rushed off to find the groom, for he had some new idea about stirrups which Bara had not listened to, and he wanted a more sympathetic audience. Bara felt dreamy and abstracted. It was a melancholy evening, with no birds singing and the autumn leaves hanging dankly in the mist. She gave Dark an armful of hay, rubbed her cheek on his neck, and wandered off to the tack-room. It was a dim, friendly place, smelling of leather and wax and soap. She propped her elbows on the shelf of the small window and cupped her chin in her hands. She swore afterwards she was thinking of nothing, or of nothing more than dimness and warmth, but when she heard a soft footfall behind her she knew it was Quint. She stood absolutely still, her muscles too weak to move. When his arms closed round her and his hands moved over her breasts she sank back against him, forgetting everything and everyone. He kissed her neck, then slowly turned her round. He watched her for a moment, half smiling, then he looked down at her breasts rising and falling fast, and he smiled again. Slowly his arms tightened and his mouth came down on hers. Then, as she melted against him, the door banged open. Quint stepped back quickly, and even now he did not lose his suavity.

'I see you have a talent for dramatic entrance—' But before he could finish Tam's fist struck his jaw.

Afterwards they always maintained the fiction that Quint had attacked her and Bara had struggled to get free. Bara never knew if Tam believed the story, but when he had seemed to assume that those were the facts, she had agreed with profound relief. She was sick with herself, for she knew that, far from resisting, in another moment she would have lain down in Quint's arms. But the figment seemed necessary to them both and they always maintained it.

The enmity between Tam and Quint was now open for all to see. Neither any longer made any attempt at polite concealment. They did not speak to each other, they would not ride in the same party, they would not eat at the same table. People whose appetites flourished on scandal gazed avidly and reported every move. Those of a more sombre nature saw in this open hatred yet another threat to the peace of Ireland.

Ness's long struggle with madness, which had loomed since Cormac's death, was drawing to a close. Her fingers, once ceaselessly twisting, now lay still in her lap, her green eyes no longer roved abstractedly from face to face. Once again she listened and smiled and understood. She had spent many hours of many days with Ralf, searching for delivery from the maze of fantasy which threatened her. She learned to acknowledge that her control was not as sure as she had supposed, that her descents into her own unconscious were red with danger, and she also came to believe that she was not after all responsible for Cormac's death. The mind, totally overturned in lunacy, was inaccessible to her. Nevertheless she had learned from her experiences on the fringes of sanity more than she could easily assimilate. Bara stood in awe of her. She knew that everyone senses to some degree the feelings of others, but Ness's power was a thousandfold that of other people's, and her perceptions extended the length and breadth of Ireland. She had not entirely conquered space, but here in Ireland she was as delicately tuned as a harp to the currents of feeling that swept through the people of the country. She heard, and she reported to Ralf, the increasingly bitter emotions which stirred the minds of thousands over the future of Ireland.

Ralf could now work only in the morning and late evening. His long hours with Ness exhausted him to such a pitch that he had to sleep the afternoon through. But after the evening meal some pulse of energy returned and stayed with him to the early hours of the morning. He knew he was driving himself hard, when he should have been living the life of an old horse put out to grass, but he could not ease up yet. Too much was at stake, and there was a specific task for him to do.

The Council no longer met as a Council, for Paedric was now too ill to move from his bed; and Frost and Quint would not come. So Ralf, Maeve, Ellen and Ness met one evening in late October, not in the Council Chamber but in Ralf's room. Tam and Bara were invited, and wine passed in goblets of thin, pellucid glass.

'They're lovely,' said Bara, running a finger down the long stem. 'They really glitter.'

'That's oxide of lead,' Ralf said. 'It makes the glass dense and shining. I showed them that a long time back. But the gold vine-leaves – that's Cormac. Just before he went mad he scribbled down an idea for using gold leaf in glass. It seems to have worked.'

'Indeed it has. Cormac couldn't have a more beautiful epitaph,' said Ness, revolving the glass in her fingers. The others looked at her and smiled, relieved past words to see her well again.

'We have a job to do,' said Ralf, stirring himself. 'We know what Frost and Quint and their friends are doing every night and we have to do something about it. They're pouring all their energy as Speakers into the minds of the people, and they're directing the energies of their supporters to the same end. In order to get what they want they're breaking the code they swore to uphold. Thousands of people are having their cherished beliefs overturned in a single night.'

'Frost has played his blackest queen,' said Maeve.

Ralf kicked at a log on the fire and a shower of sparks fell.

'I don't know if I'm more angry with them or myself,' he said. 'To think I've trusted Frost for over half a century.'

'You trust everyone, and you shouldn't,' said Maeve quietly. 'I told you a long, long time ago.'

'Oh I know. That's why I'm so angry with myself.'

'We'd better begin,' said Tam, always restive for action and an end to talk. 'We know what we have to do.'

Ralf leaned back wearily and Maeve spoke for him. 'We must be absolutely clear that we *do* know. We must not, in any circumstances, for any end, break the code we've sworn to.' Bara had never seen her so intense. Her calm face was strained and her hands were tightly clasped. 'All that's open to us is to block the efforts of Frost and Quint. We are absolutely not permitted to substitute our own beliefs. Blocking is all that's allowed. Is that clear?'

'Maeve is our conscience,' said Ralf, smiling at her.

She took no notice but gazed at each person in turn and waited for each to nod. Bara felt that Maeve's look lingered longest on her and she trembled as she lowered her head.

'Wait,' said Ness. 'Ellen is divided.'

'All right, all right,' said Ellen, shifting in her chair. 'I was about to say so. I'm not such an ass as to try and keep my feelings secret in *this* company.' She smiled tightly, staring at the fire. 'You all know my thoughts. I'm no longer prepared to support Frost and his faction because I feel they're going to blunder on without a stop. In a hundred years he and his successors will have us all at the point our ancestors had reached a hundred years back. And very likely this time they'll succeed in killing themselves or the planet or both. But my own subject makes me feel we've got to move a little further along the path to an intermediate but skilled technology. Health is important, and at the moment I just can't do what I should. I'm like a combination of a witch-doctor and a village quack.'

'You do marvels, Ellen,' said Maeve.

'Not marvels enough,' snapped Ellen, ungrateful for the compliment. 'I'm frustrated at every turn. As a good Listener I know what I need and I know what I could do. But I must have a higher degree of technology to get on with it.'

There was a long silence before anyone spoke. Then Ralf turned his head to her.

'It's a real problem. When this crisis is over we'll turn all we've got to solving it. But just for the moment, will you postpone it and help us block Frost?'

'Oh, of course,' said Ellen. 'I always meant to.'

'Then let's begin.' Ralf settled back against his chair and closed his eyes.

For four hours they bent their peculiar powers to the obstruction of Frost and Quint. Tam and Bara had to break off frequently for rests, to relax their concentration and stretch their legs, but the other four never moved. Frost, Quint and their assistants were gathered in Frost's room on the far side of the Great Hall and the four experienced Listeners found no problem in locating them. What exactly it was they did they could not explain, even to each other, but by focusing with steady negative responses on the image of their opponents they knew they were blocking the force of Frost's message to the unwitting people of Ireland. The endlessly repeated pattern – *Frost is right, Frost is right, Frost is right* – was held back at its source.

Exhausted as if they had not slept for a week, the six people in Ralf's room fell into their beds at five in the morning. Frost had given up shortly before, when the patterns of his anger registered by Ness were beginning to break her apart. The next night was the same, and the next, and the next, though on each occasion the battle was joined with greater subtlety and in larger numbers. Frost increased his forces and spread them throughout the town, making the task of locating and blocking them that much more tiresome. But Ralf had also greatly increased his numbers, and after a few nights' work he felt his supporters had mastered Frost's. On the last night of the battle, when Frost gave up this particular tactic, Fergus was particularly delighted with what he had done. He had soon discovered that the small group of enemy Speakers for which he had been made responsible were weak in their powers, so instead of merely blocking them with a wall of negative response he had filled their heads with a jumble of epics in ancient languages, from Assyrian to Icelandic. Ralf laughed, but he forbade Fergus to do it again, for he did not care to think about the probable mental state of the Speakers to whom Fergus had given his attention. Bara noticed that Maeve did not laugh.

'Fergus,' she said, with no glimmer of amusement, 'you must not play around. We don't know what we can do with these powers, and until we know we've got to believe they're very dangerous indeed.'

Fergus hung his head politely but Bara saw him wink at Ness. Maeve was heavy-fisted when it came to the powers of the mind, she thought. No other subject ever translated that serene, half-smiling face to lines so old and hard.

Meanwhile, nothing was decided, for nothing could be agreed. Ralf wished to have the succession settled quickly, before they left Cashel for Dublin at the end of the month, but Frost would not agree. Cormac was dead, and Paedric could no longer attend, therefore the Council was without authority. If Ralf insisted otherwise, he would resign. Ralf replied that if he resigned the remaining members of the Council would decide without him. In that case, Frost replied, his eyes glittering with threat, it would be the worse for Ireland.

One warm October afternoon Bara sat by the parapet in the sun, her eyes half closed, her mind drowsy and peaceful. Fifty yards away, along the terrace between the parapet and the wall of the Great Hall, Con and a small girl called Biddy were trying to catch a late butterfly which flitted round the blue clumps of Michaelmas daisies. They had a large shrimping net, and the capture should have been easy, but they were so clumsy and excited they lurched and missed the creature time after time. Finally there was a shriek from Con.

'I've got it Mam! It's in the net,' he called.

Bara rose lazily and sauntered towards him.

'What kind is it?' she said.

'It's a Brimstone.'

'How do you know?'

'Oh don't be stupid. Of course I know.'

'Well, let it go when you've looked at it.'

'In a minute. Look, it's really nice.'

The brilliant, velvety creature closed its wings and abandoned the useless attempt to escape. The three heads bent over it and the little girl poked it with her finger to make it open its wings. Suddenly Con put his hand inside the net and grabbed the folded wings between his finger and thumb.

'Con!' cried Bara. 'Don't do that. You'll hurt it.'

She took a step back to give him room to free the creature, but instead he withdrew his hand, still clutching the butterfly, and ran rapidly along the terrace.

'Con! Come back! What on earth are you doing?'

Then she saw his face. He had stopped twenty yards away, still holding the butterfly and staring back at her. She hardly recognized him. His face was contorted, set in an expression of ferocity she had never seen before. Then slowly, still watching her, he tore both wings off the butterfly's body. Biddy shrieked and burst into tears, Bara shouted in fury. But as she ran at him, to strike him with all her strength, his face crumpled, he dropped his head in his hands and sank to the ground in a frenzy of weeping.

Over the wall someone laughed, and Bara stopped in her tracks. Before she fully realized why she had halted her mouth was dry and her thighs were trembling. The laugh came again, a cold, glittering sound. Only one man in the world had a laugh like that. Her heart thudded, her blood ran in crystals of ice. She wanted to move, to run and peer over the wall, but her legs would not obey her. Then through a postern in the stones she caught a glimpse of a running man, with a head of quaking, silver hair, the colour of the moon. Light drained from her eyes, her knees folded, and she fell fainting onto the cobbles.

When she came round she found herself in Ralf's little room, with Ralf and Tam gazing down at her. Con sat shuddering by her side.

'Mam!' he cried, when he saw her open her eyes. 'I didn't do it. I didn't. Something made me. I had to. I couldn't help it.'

She took his hands and squeezed them.

'I know, Con.' Then she turned to Tam. 'White Michael's here,' she said.

At last she had persuaded them that she was not deluded. Tam was scowling blackly, but Ralf's face was drawn and grey, older than Bara had ever seen it,

'It's terrible,' he muttered, clenching his fists. 'Terrible. That power he had. A Speaker like that with no code to restrain him. Only this great naked power bent to his own ends.' He rose to his feet and stood staring unseeing at Con's flaxen head. 'He adds an appalling complication to our lives,' he continued. 'We don't any longer have one clear-cut issue. We now have a third alternative – anarchy, dictatorial power, barbarism once again. Oh God.' The old man dropped his head in his hands and Bara's heart was torn for him.

'There's another thing,' said Tam. 'We don't know what he can do as a Listener.'

'No,' said Ralf. 'We don't. He hasn't shown us that yet. I only hope to God his power as a Listener is less than his power as a Speaker.'

'He made Con tear the butterfly, didn't he?' said Bara.

'Of course,' said Ralf. 'And he can make him do it again. And again. So what do we do?'

'Kill him,' said Tam.

Ralf gazed at him aghast.

'*Kill* him? For what?'

'Because he's evil. Because he'll destroy us.'

Ralf turned wearily and stood looking out of his window over the town and the autumn country beyond.

'You can't,' he said. 'Don't do it, Tam. Even when I'm dead, don't do it. I've worked half a lifetime to create justice in this country. Don't turn the corner back to barbarity. It's a road that's always open and inviting and easy. Even so, don't do it.'

But Tam only shrugged and strode from the room.

Suddenly the days were cold, shrouded in a harsh mist which persisted from dawn to dusk. The leaves of the oaks and beeches hung damply and without life. The fires of autumn were subdued and no sun burst through to warm the chill of the air.

There was one last ritual to be completed before the departure for Dublin. Every autumn at the end of October was held a magnificent stag hunt. Ralf hated it, and had tried to stop it long ago, but he had not in the end felt able to press his objection against the enthusiasm of the people of the south. Indeed the hunt had grown rather than diminished in importance, for Quint had wanted his hounds to lead the pack and he had worked since he was a boy to raise the hunt into the second festival of the year, lesser only than the great spring festival in March. People came to join the hunt from a hundred miles around, bringing their horses and their wolfhounds and deerhounds, carrying their food and often tents as well. The town was always thronged with visitors, every spare room occupied, and both floors of the two inns packed out. Now the Chief Ranger and his men had been out for a week, locating likely stags; the grooms had been rubbing and waxing and polishing till the harnesses shone; the few remaining cooks and kitchenmaids had enlisted help from the town and worked half the night on the banquet to come. By old tradition the banquet was carried by horse and cart to the site of the kill, and there warmed and eaten as a kind of gigantic picnic. Therefore the Rangers had to find a stag not too distant, and they had to try and direct the killing towards rather than away from Cashel. They had a difficult task, and they allowed their resentment to needle the kitchen-staff all the year round. Bara came upon Con one morning, trotting across the courtyard behind the Chief Ranger, tugging at his tunic. Shawn was a huge taciturn man with a bushy red beard. He had no time for Con, and Bara watched Con's outrage with amusement. Suddenly he seized Shawn's tunic with both hands and swung on it.

'Let bloody go, ye small devil,' growled Shawn, halted in his stride.

He struck at Con's hands and Con yelled as he dropped to the ground.

'You're a beastly, cross old man,' he shouted, shaking back his shock of white hair. 'If you won't listen to me I won't – I won't – well, I won't ever talk to you again.'

Shawn glared down at him, then suddenly he folded his arms and laughed.

'Holy Brigid,' he said, 'it's the little fighting cock ye are to be sure.'

Con's upturned face shone.

'Then you'll take me hunting?' he asked eagerly.

'No,' said Shawn, stern again. 'That I won't. Hunting's for men.'

He strode off leaving Con stranded in the middle of the yard. The boy wandered dejectedly towards the stables, trailing his feet, but before Bara could follow him she heard a bellow from Shawn.

'I'll whack you with your own greasy ladle, woman,' he roared, 'and I'll be sticking yer kitchen trollops on the spits for the feast, so I will.'

Bara rushed delightedly round a corner and through an arch, where she could see Shawn's broad back at the door of the kitchen. Screams came from within, some of mirth, some of fury.

'Get away with ye, ye red slob of a foul-mouthed caveman,' screeched Patsy, the head cook. 'Get away from my kitchen, or it's no food at all you'll be having on the hunting day.'

'Fat guzzling sows,' roared Shawn. 'You'll bring the bloody food to where my stag is, or I'll wind its wet guts round yese all.'

He ducked and leaped away as the lid of a huge pan came skimming through the air. Bara expected him to laugh, but he did not. Perhaps it was true what they said, that Shawn hated the human race. He loved only the animals he hunted and the forests he tended, and it was only when someone spoke of these that he would pause in his long stride and listen. In his cups he never laughed or sang with the rest of the company. Instead he would lean forward on his elbows, talking quietly and steadily, whether anyone was listening or not, of the habits of voles and foxes and owls and stags, or the seasonal comings and goings of butterflies, or the slow mysterious growth of trees. The only day of the year on which he was forced into public prominence was the day of the hunt, and that day he hated.

A pale sun shone fitfully on the morning of the hunt. Scuds of thin cloud moved across the sky in a sharp wind. Before dawn the horses were out in the stableyard, stamping and blowing in the full splendour of their ceremonial harness. Their manes and tails were plaited with coloured straw, their tack gleamed, their flanks glowed with embroidered saddle-cloths. Bara leaned against Dark, watching his breath turning to clouds of mist. The concourse was like a horse fair. By seven o'clock the yard was thronged with riders, all wearing soft leather breeches and their finest ceremonial sheepskins. Con was furious at being kept at Cashel. Bara had had to leave him sulking in bed, there to wait for the party from the kitchens, who would bring him to the feast. Ralf had excused himself from the hunt, as he always did, but he would ride later with Con and the kitchen staff to meet the others for the banquet. Meanwhile he had come to see them off. Bara gazed at him in awe. He looked marvellous in his best sheepskin, thickly embroidered in green and gold, his cloud of hair and beard lying softly on his shoulders. If you did not know him for a man, she thought, you would follow Con and take him for God – the portrait he presented seemed exactly what the human mind required.

Ellen was mounted on her roan, Aescalapius, a horse oddly unlike herself, being long and spindly and delicate of movement. Ness rode a bay and Maeve was astride a huge piebald she called Checkmate. Frost was on his Arab and to Bara's surprise he seemed in high and friendly good humour. His eyes were as restless as usual, but he spoke cheerfully to everyone near him and seemed to avoid no-one. Tam in his gold and red sheepskin stood quietly by Moon's side and gazed at Frost.

'He's strange today, isn't he?' said Bara.

'Very. And he's blocked off. I can't get near him.'

'That's a bit sinister, isn't it? Why should he bother to block off?'

'I don't know. We'd better look out, that's all.'

'Hey, who's that?' Tam was pointing at the back view of a hooded man on a white horse.

'I don't know. There's hundreds of people here.' But as she looked at the hooded back Bara felt a chill in her blood.

Everyone began to move out of the stableyard into the Great Court. Quint was already there, with his own four wolfhounds and the pack of castle deerhounds as well. Although Shawn, who rode a huge Arab, was the acknowledged leader of the hunt, Quint was the official Master of the Hounds. Bara could not choke down a catch of admiration as she watched him sitting still and straight on his white horse, the red and gold threads on his sheepskin shining in the morning light. He turned to her and smiled square in her eyes, but she was resolute enough to turn sharply away. Against the grey cobbles and the stone walls of the Hall the throng of people and horses glowed like a field of flowers. Brown and gold, silver and green danced together as in a tapestry freshly finished the night before. The sounds were of clatter and clop and shout and jingle and bark, the smells were of horse and dog and leather. Here at last was something of Bara's brilliant vision of Ireland, the vision she had shared with Suz and all the thousands of others far away in London, who had felt the spell of the new legends blowing from the west. Tam touched her arm and smiled. 'Come on,' he said, 'we're off.'

The morning's ride was long and hard. The two stags Shawn had marked for quarry had moved in the night, so two hours of sun and rain had passed before the halloo was raised. Bara did not try to keep up with the leaders, though Dark strained hard on the bit, for she disliked the howling of the dogs and she had no desire to see the stag driven to panic and torn to death. By midday the hunt was spread wide across the woods and meadows ten miles south of Cashel, and some tired riders were thinking of returning home. Bara had become separated from everyone she knew and she rode now with some villagers from the south. There were four red-faced men and a black-eyed woman, all well into middle-age and not greatly at home on their ponies. They made it plain with many winks and relapses into Gaelic that they had come only for the free food and liquor.

'And also the hell of it, to be sure,' added the woman, winking heavily.

'Now we won't be hurrying ourselves,' said a man with a carbuncle on his cheek. 'We'll wait till we hear the horns – then by Brigid we'll make haste.'

They all laughed, ambling behind Bara over a wide expanse of wet heather. A misty drizzle began to fall. Bara's quiet content drained away, leaving her wet and lost. Hunting was a greatly overrated sport, she thought, as she stared gloomily at the faces of her companions who seemed even more cheerfully noisy since the rain began. Suddenly they heard the horns, sailing clear and high above the baying of the hounds. With yells of delight Bara's friends turned their ponies and headed over the heather towards the sound. Dark wanted to move at twice the speed of the old hacks beside him, but Bara held him in, afraid of appearing unfriendly and greedy if she rushed ahead.

They took over an hour to find the hunt, by which time they were hungry and cold. The dead stag lay on open ground at the foot of a rocky hill. Shawn was working at it with a long bloody knife, while a large group of men, including Quint, stood around to watch. The hounds, still wildly excited, were held with difficulty in a tumultuous pack. Nearby were six enormous fires, round which circled cooks and serving men. The smell of crackling roast meat filled the air between the hill and the woods nearby, but those with their noses already down a mug of poteen had them filled with a smell even sweeter. Bara looked about in the huge throng for someone she knew, and at last she found Maeve, stirring a cauldron of soup by the side of a fire. Her face was red and glistening with sweat.

'Come and help me serve,' she called to Bara as she picked a ladle off the grass. 'It's ready now.'

Everything except the meat had been cooked in the castle kitchens the night before, so now it had only to be heated. As she ladled the steaming soup Bara caught sight of Ralf, carving up a suckling pig with an enormous hunting knife, and a few minutes later Tam swung past, laughing like a man already tipsy and clutching to his chest a huge earthern vessel of poteen. Bara waved her ladle at him, smiling at his exuberance. His darkness seemed lit from within, his face was all shining eyes and laughing mouth. Her heart turned over, she adored him. She returned to her ladle and the impatient queue, and began again to scoop the thick broth into bowls. But suddenly Tam was at her side, and before she knew what he was doing he had tipped half his huge jug of poteen into the soup.

'Tam!' she screamed, pulling at the jar. He put it down obediently, then suddenly grabbed her round the waist and kissed her hard. Her fury and embarrassment melted in the cheers and hoots of the surrounding crowd. Round the edge of Tam's face she could just see Maeve, with her head thrown back and her face split with laughter. She fell out of Tam's arms, delighted with everything and everyone. It was going to be a marvellous day after all.

By late afternoon the mist had cleared and a pale golden sunlight shone on the heather. Frost, still as genial as he had been in the early morning, gathered the members of the two Councils on the rock at the foot of the hill, and produced from his saddlebags four bottles of the precious Bantry wine. Many of the Council were already too full of poteen, and all were warm and content. They sprawled comfortably on the heather, or propped themselves against the boulders, in varying degrees of drowsiness, but however replete no-one was churlish enough to refuse Frost's wine.

'Why not take your coats off?' said Frost to those who still wore their sheepskins. 'It's really warm. You'll see.' Quint leaped up, cheerfully collecting the discarded coats, while his father moved round with the wine. Bara noticed vaguely that Quint carefully separated his own coat, his father's, Tam's, and Ralf's, then threw the rest down in a jumble on one side. It seemed curious – but her mind slid drowsily away from the oddity of his action and came to rest on the glittering embroidery of the coats. Silver and blue for Frost, green and gold for Ralf, red and gold for Tam, gold and red for Quint. Red and gold, gold and red – she rolled over on Tam's arm and fell into a shallow doze. When she half-opened her eyes a few minutes later she saw that Quint and his four deerhounds were sitting by the four selected coats, and the dogs were smelling them avidly. Dogs have peculiar pleasures, she thought, dreamily reaching for the remains of her wine. Quint smiled at her and drooped his head, as if to say he was half asleep. Beside him, with his back to Bara, sat the hooded man. Could it be—? No, she would not think about it. She forced her attention away and allowed it to slide off into drowsy contemplation of the company. Tam lay snoring with his mouth open, Ralf was dozing against a rock with Maeve's hand in his, Ellen was drinking intently, with the concentration of one who has already had too much, Ness sat gazing dreamily at Fergus, who stood twenty yards away in the clearing in front of the woods. He and his friends were fiddling like madmen, tapping and twirling and hallooing while the dancers flew in reels so wild that half of them fell over and rolled in hysterical laughter until they were retrieved by their friends. No-one had yet given a thought to clearing up the spread of crocks and pots and embers and bones and jars and mugs that littered the stony ground in all directions. Bara's eyes began to ache. The dogs were still sniffing excitedly round the sheepskins. She knew she should be thinking about something, she should be focusing on some problem which eluded her. It rolled uncomfortably at the back of her mind, like a piece of gristle that would not be swallowed. But the sun was warm, the heather was soft, she was full of food and drink. She closed her eyes again.

Sometime later she was roused by the sound of Frost's voice. He was standing up, stretching himself, and smiling down on the somnolent company. Quint and the dogs had vanished. The sun shone on Frost's silver head, and the expression on his face was almost mellow.

'Come on,' he said. 'I think we need a walk. A little exercise.' Faces turned blankly up at him. 'Let's go up the hill.'

'Why?' said Ellen. 'I won't.'

'It's a good idea,' said Tam, climbing to his feet and dusting himself down.

'Good.' Frost glanced sharply at him, then passed him over a

folded sheepskin, gold and red. Gold and red? Was that right? Bara
rubbed her eyes, and stood up, quenching the tiresome prick of
anxiety. She shook out her hair, and held her hand down to Ralf.
'Good idea' he said, smiling up at her. 'I'll take a walk. Pull me up.'
Slowly he thrust his arms into the sheepskin that Frost held out for him.
'It'll be cold up there,' said Frost. 'We might see the mountains
from the top.'
'Let's try,' said Ralf. He looked down and smiled at Maeve, who
squinted up at him from where she lay propped against a rock.
'Coming?' he said, holding out his hand.
'Too lazy,' she said, smiling and closing her eyes. 'I'll see you later.'
Bara looked at them with love and envy. They had been lovers and
companions for forty years, and during that long and often difficult
time they had learned that Maeve's love was enough for both of
them. Now they had reached their gentle Indian summer, and there
was no more pain but only peace between them.
Ralf and Frost set off slowly, on an upward path, picking their way
between rocks and heather. Tam caught up with them but Bara
trailed a little behind. There was something odd about Tam's back.
The sheepskin – why did it look too big for him? She shrugged,
caught him up, and they moved on, ahead of Ralf and Frost.
'Hi!' called a voice from below. 'Wait for me.'
Quint emerged from round the side of the hill, moving rapidly. As
he ran he seized the remaining red and gold sheepskin off the ground
and struggled into it. He slowed when he was just behind Ralf and
his father, and made no attempt to catch up with Bara and Tam.
Fifteen minutes' climb brought them to the crest of the hill. They
stood in a group, enjoying the sharp breeze in their faces, and gazing
across at the distant mountains of the south and west.
'Let's go and sit there,' said Frost, pointing to a grassy hollow a few
yards down the far side of the hill.
Bara saw that Ralf was both surprised and delighted at the
friendliness of Frost. He was anxious to reciprocate, so he fell in
readily with all Frost's proposals. But she also noticed that Tam was
scowling. As he had slowly wakened from the effects of the poteen, he
found himself filled with fears he could not formulate. He took
Bara's hand and moved down the slope behind Ralf and Frost, but
he glanced back at Quint still standing on the crest. As the four of
them arrived at the hollow Quint turned his back and whistled
shrilly down the slope they had just ascended. Bara felt Tam's grip
tighten, then suddenly he crushed her hand so fiercely she cried out.
'Christ,' he whispered. He was as white as a sheet and staring up at

Quint. Suddenly he leaped for Ralf, pulling Bara after him.

'Run!' he yelled, 'for God's sake run! There – those rocks – over there!' He pushed at Ralf who staggered and almost fell.

'Tam, are you mad?' screamed Bara, tugging at his arm.

But Tam was heaving and pulling at Ralf, shouting wildly in his face as he tried to drag him along. Ralf fell heavily, tripping over a boulder, and at that moment the first of Quint's wolfhounds leaped over the crest of the hill.

Bara doubled up behind a rock shaking with fear. Tam let Ralf lie where he had fallen and fumbled round the old man's waist. But there was no knife and he had left his own in his saddlebag, on the far side of the hill. A second hound appeared behind the first, and there was no mistaking the murderous excitement in their eyes. Tam seized a sharp stone and crouched over Ralf's struggling body. The first leaping hound received the point of the stone in its mouth, and fell, pouring blood over Ralf's legs. But the weight of the second hurling body knocked Tam off his feet and he rolled helplessly down the slope. Somehow Bara found the strength to stand. She rushed from the shelter of the rock, flinging stones at the animal's body, but they were not heeded. She threw herself on the dog's hindquarters and pulled with all her strength, but the creature did not even turn to bite her. It tore and shook at Ralf's weakly flailing arms until it had found the way to his neck. As Tam hurled himself at the dog's head, Ralf screamed and lay still. The dog sank onto his body, with its teeth in his throat.

Quint and Frost stood looking down at them. Tam crouched like an animal over Ralf's body, yelling wordless horror at them, but Bara made no sound at all. For as she watched, their faces changed imperceptibly from Quint and Frost to Cantor and Grett. She moved slowly backwards, every faculty suspended in terror. Suddenly there was another dog. She closed her eyes, uncertain whether it was a vision of her mind, but as she opened them a fourth animal leaped over the hill. Their mouths were white with froth and their haunches quivered as they collected themselves for the spring.

'Tam!' screamed Bara, 'Tam, Tam, Tam!' The dogs leaped down the slope towards him. The light left Bara's eyes and the sky reeled as she stumbled half to her knees. Somehow she forced her head down and her legs held. She heard a roar of pain and as the sight swam back into her eyes she twisted her head to where Tam's dead body would be lying beneath the dogs. Then she squeezed her eyes again, still uncertain if she could trust them. For Tam was standing upright, besides Ralf's body, and the cry had not been his.

'Look,' he said, scarcely able to whisper. Above them on the slope lay the bloody body of Quint, his throat torn apart, his face savaged, his sheepskin in shreds. Blood still pumped from his carotids, circling his head in an ever deepening pool of red. Further up the slope stood Frost, his face dead white, his eyes staring. They turned away from him in loathing and fell into the circle of each other's arms. Neither could speak, and neither could weep. They were sick and shaking, unable to think of what they must do.

'Tam!' whispered Bara at last.

'Don't talk. I can't.'

'Tam, it's the coats.'

'Coats? What coats? Why aren't I dead? Why? They came at me. They leaped at me.' He shuddered violently, rubbing his cheek on Bara's hair, then very quietly began to weep.

'Oh Tam. Tam, listen. The coats. Frost gave you Quint's coat and Quint took yours. By accident. Dear God, thank heaven.'

. It took him a long time to understand, for a storm of tears shook them both and they stood helpless in each other's arms. Then, still half-blinded, Bara laid her sheepskin over Ralf's bloody head. She closed his terrified eyes and she covered his throat with swathes of his hair and beard, now felted and dark with blood. They left Quint's body where it lay and they took no notice of Frost, who had stumbled off in panic down the hillside. Shivering and clinging to each other, they returned over the crest of the hill and climbed to where they had left their friends.

Half an hour later Finn and Fergus and some other men returned with Ralf's body and laid it tenderly on the stony ground. At a signal from Ellen, Fergus turned back the cloth that lay over Ralf's face. The scream that was torn from the depths of Maeve's body haunted Bara's nights and days for the rest of her life. The afternoon passed into the borders of nightmare. People came and went, Con was hustled in bewilderment back to Cashel, Quint's body was carried down the hill, a group set off to look for Frost, the huge disorder of the banquet was cleared away in silence. For an hour there was no source of authority. Ralf and Quint were dead, Frost had disappeared, and Maeve had vanished alone into the woods. Fergus directed a small group who washed Ralf and Quint and raised them, wrapped in linen, onto two low carts. Finally it was Ellen who roused herself. She felt unsteady on her feet, but she knew the full force of shock had not yet hit her and she must act while she could. She had half-expected Tam to take charge, but for an hour he had not moved from the rock where he sat with his head in his hands. Bara was at his feet, so mercifully numb she could think of nothing at all. At last Tam began to mutter.

'I've got to get moving,' he said, as if to himself. 'The facts – I've got to make sure people know the real facts. Before Frost gets back. Before his story. I must tell people what happened.'

'There's time enough,' said Bara dully.

'No there's not. No time. Frost might be talking already. People must be inventing explanations. I've got to tell them the truth.'

He forced himself to his feet and Bara was appalled by the whiteness of his face and the unsteadiness of his legs. In all the dangers they had been through together she had never seen him so broken. She stood up and took his arm. He smiled down at her and although he said nothing she knew he was grateful. They moved slowly through the silent crowds until they reached a boulder in the middle of the open ground. Fergus came shouldering his way towards them, his face tight. Tam handed him a cooking pot and told him to beat it with a ladle. As Fergus struck resounding blows on the pan Tam climbed heavily onto the boulder. He stood with his head down while every member of the huge company laid down whatever he or she was doing and moved slowly towards the rock. In a few minutes there were three hundred people gathered round Tam. Suddenly Bara noticed the hooded man on the edge of the crowd, and she saw when he turned his head a glimmer of silver beneath the hood. So it was him. Sick and despairing she turned back to Tam. At last he raised his head.

'You all know the Old One is dead,' he said, his voice unsteady. 'And he did not die peacefully in his bed. And he did not die simply because a dog went mad and killed him. He died because he was murdered.' A gasp rose from the crowd and moved like a wind across the meadow.

Tam held out his sheepskin for the crowd to see. 'This coat saved my life because it smells of Quint. For Quint's hounds had been ordered to attack and kill both Ralf and me. They had been taught the smell of our sheepskins. But by an accident, frightful for Quint and heaven-sent for me, I took Quint's coat up the hill and he took mine. So the bodies who lie there are not those of Ralf and myself, as they were meant to be, but of Ralf and Quint. This was a murder most carefully arranged. Frost and his friends will try to tell you it was a hideous mistake. They will tell you the hounds went mad and have been killed. They will point to the body of Quint and ask why Frost should want to kill his own son? The answer is as you know. Frost did *not* want to. His object was the same as Quint's – to have the hounds destroy Ralf and me. It was he who persuaded a few of us to walk over that hill to our deaths. But he didn't know – no-one knew except the hounds – that I was wearing Quint's coat and he was wearing mine.

'When those dogs leaped at me—' Tam paused and closed his eyes.

Bara saw his hands clench as he tried to steady his voice. 'When those dogs leaped at me I gave myself up for dead. I waited to be knocked over and torn to pieces. But suddenly they stopped in their tracks. They were mad with excitement, but still they stopped. They sniffed me for a moment, then one of them suddenly turned his head up the hill towards Quint. They both growled, then faster than wind they both leaped onto their master and tore him apart.' Tam covered his face with his hands.

'It doesn't matter about me,' he said, as he raised his head again, 'they wanted me out of the way because I am the protector of Con, and they wanted Con to bring him up in their own way. The murder of Ralf is what I shall leave you to think about. Everyone of us knows what the Old One has done for Ireland and for the species of which he was a member. Everyone of us knew his justice and his wisdom, everyone of us had felt his goodness and his love. The only fitting memorial we can give him is the Ireland that he wished for.'

Fergus murmured some words nonsensical to those about him: 'Mark Anthony speaks over the body of Caesar,' he said.

Many in the crowd were openly weeping and there was a crush round Ralf's bier that the carters could hardly control. Tam climbed down from the boulder, but Bara would not look at him. She knew his grief was real enough, but the end of his speech sickened her. He should not have taken advantage of such a moment to bend the crowd towards Ralf's hopes for Ireland. People made way for her as she moved alone toward's Ralf's body, but she did not allow herself to think of Ralf. That terrible time would have to come, but it must be later, in the silence of her room at Cashel. She kept her mind on Tam, trying to accept that he was by nature a leader and a politician, and that even in genuine grief or rapture he would always be aware of the advantageous course.

She stood by the cart which carried Ralf's body and she covered her face with her hands, for she knew that was expected. But once again a dullness of mind and muscle had settled over her and she stood thinking of nothing. The hooded man had vanished again and she was determined to banish him from her mind. She was aroused by a sudden shouting some yards away, near Quint's body. She pressed her hands on a woman's shoulder and pushed herself up onto a rock. From there she could see a turmoil round the body of Quint. A stone flew throught the air, then another. The shouting rose and the turbulence in the crowd spread like waves. Now there was a fight raging by the cart on which Quint's body lay. A tangled knot of men and women, many of them half-drunk, were hurling stones, while another small group tried to defend both the corpse and themselves. The attackers were gaining ground, able to beat back any who attempted to join the defenders. They were yelling abuse, cursing Quint and his father, screaming threats to the body and those who tried to guard it.

'Give him to the dogs!' they yelled. 'Give the bastard to his own dogs! They'll tear him up, they'll pull him apart.' All the men protecting the cart were hurt, and some were bleeding badly.

'Tam!' screamed Bara uselessly, her voice swept away in the rising tumult.

'Tam! Fergus! Finn!' As she screamed she saw them, trying to pull away the outer fringes of the attackers, but their efforts were of little use, for the crowd was swelling every moment. A woman ducked under the guard of the defenders and began to tear savagely at the covering over the body, and before the men could throw her back she sank her teeth in the leg of the corpse. The defenders were overwhelmed and Quint's body was engulfed in clawing hands.

As Bara leaped from the rock, sick with the sight before her, she caught a glimpse of the hooded man on the edge of the fighting crowd. His face was rapt, his eyes half-closed, his hands clenched in concentration. Immediately she knew he was compelling those people to fight, he was compelling the old woman to bite at Quint's leg like a dog. Flames of anger rushed through her body, but before she had moved a dozen steps towards him she was stopped rigid in her tracks. The blast of a horn rang out with a ferocity so brilliant the clouds seemed to shake. Again and again it blew, and it did not cease until every member of the crowd was silent and still. Shawn sat astride his great hunter, his horn still to his lips, and beside him on her roan was Ellen. She looked like thunder as she rode slowly, with Shawn beside her, through the parting crowds. When she reached Quint's body, now hanging bloodily half off the cart, she drew in her reins and spoke.

'What this man did was shameful,' she cried, 'but in doing this to his body you only add shame to shame.' She turned to the bleeding men who had defended the corpse. 'Those of you who defended your charge did well. Wrap him up, see to your wounds, and take him home to Cashel.'

Bara stared. This was the dumpy, red-faced woman whose hair was always falling down. She looked no different, perhaps even redder and wilder than ever, but somehow she had assumed an authority that not one of all these drunken, fighting men and women would question. Shamefacedly the crowd broke up and as they separated Bara could see Tam and Fergus standing sheepishly in front of Ellen.

She ran towards them and heard Fergus speak.

'You did what we could not,' he said, looking up.

'We were fools,' said Tam. 'We never thought of Shawn and we never thought of horses.'

'It worked,' said Ellen, grinning. The light of authority had vanished from her face as if it had never been. She turned to the man by her side. 'Thank you Shawn, I never knew it could sound like that. I only hope my hearing won't be impaired'.

But Shawn did not smile, he merely inclined his head and turned his horse away.

'He's only confirmed in his contempt for the human race,' said Fergus.

Then the long, dreary pull back to Cashel began. Frost was brought in that evening, having been found wet and exhausted wandering in the heather, miles from the scene of the hunt. He had lost his sheepskin and ripped one of his shoes, but he clung tenaciously to his magnificent crozier, permitting no-one to carry it even when he was in the saddle riding home. He had refused to accept any covering, so his white head glistened with the evening rain and his shirt clung damply to his body. His eyes darted more rapidly than ever, but since his capture he had not spoken a single word. The men who brought him home were relieved to be rid of their charge, for his silence had unnerved them. He had apparently made no protest when he was found, nor shown any resistance, except when the men offered to take his staff. But he had spoken no word in the four long hours he was in their company,

Ellen and Ness were the only remaining members of the First Council. Maeve had vanished into the woods, where Tam's search party had been unable to find her, and Paedric lay dying in his room. When Ness and Ellen met in the Council chamber that evening they decided they would invite Tam and Bara and Fergus to share their decisions. All of them were exhausted in nerve and bone, but Ellen was determined that decisions must be made at once. As they were settling themselves a messenger arrived to say that Frost was back in Cashel. Ellen suggested they invite him to the Council, but before she had finished Tam leaped up.

'But why?' he shouted. 'Frost's a murderer. We can't have him here.'

'Oh Tam,' said Ellen wearily, passing her hand across her forehead. 'We do have justice in Ireland you know. We have fair trial.'

'Then arrest him.'

'In due course. But first we must see him. He is still a member of this Council.'

Tam folded his arms and scowled. When Frost appeared at the door he was wearing a dry tunic, but he was still clutching his staff. As his eyes darted crazily from one face to another Ness retreated and covered her face with her hands.

'Frost,' said Ellen, standing up. 'We are about to vote you off the Council. Then you will be arrested.'

Frost stood absolutely still, moving only his eyes. Then, very slowly he smiled. They waited a moment, and another, and another, but still he did not speak. Ness stepped quickly forward.

'Would you like to go to your room, Frost?' she said. 'You may if you like.'

Without protest, without ceasing to smile, Frost turned quietly and went away with the messenger.

'He's mad,' said Ness, turning to Ellen. 'He's far, far gone. He thinks he's the power that's going to rule the world. He thinks he has only to be patient. He thinks his cunning and guile are invincible. He's absolutely sure he'll prevail.' She shuddered. 'It hit me hard as soon as he came in. The stench – ugh.'

Fergus slumped heavily into his chair. 'I'm that tired,' he said. 'But I don't believe I could be sleeping at all.'

'We're all grey with exhaustion,' said Ellen, looking round, 'but we can't sleep yet. When we're finished I'll make sure that we all do. Sleeping drugs are the least of our problems.'

'I can't take it in,' said Bara wearily, leaning her head back against the wall. 'Ralf dead, Quint dead, Frost mad – they're just words. They don't mean anything at all.'

'They will,' said Ellen, 'all too soon. Now, I think that tomorrow we must be able to announce the successor we propose, so the people can approve or disapprove. And we must be able to announce the time and the nature of Ralf's burial. First, the leadership.'

There was a long silence before Ness spoke.

'You and Tam are the only possible candidates,' she said to Ellen. 'it's not for me and I know Maeve wouldn't have it at any price.'

Tam leaned forward with his hands on his knees and Bara could feel the excitement rising through him like a wind. But he spoke evenly.

'We must have it clear,' he said. 'Are we agreed that this leadership is an interregnum – a sort of protectorship till Con is old enough to take over?'

'That's what I had in mind,' said Ellen.

'And myself,' said Fergus.

'It was what Ralf wanted,' said Bara.

'Then we're agreed,' said Ness. 'Ellen, you're the senior member. I'm sure you would be accepted.'

Ellen rubbed her chin.

'But I don't want it,' she said slowly. 'Medicine is my work and my art and my life. I don't want to be distracted from it by administrative cares and all the problems of justice and education and trade and welfare and whatnot. I just don't want it at all. But I'm hesitating for one reason, and one reason only.'

'I know it,' said Ness.

'But I don't,' said Bara. 'What is it?'

'I should have liked a woman to have the task,' said Ellen. 'I would have liked my sex to have a chance to show what it could do. And I wouldn't like the people to think that Tam was chosen leader simply because he was a man.'

'But that's an easy one to explain,' said Fergus.

'Easy,' agreed Tam. 'If I'm to be the man I'll tell the people why. I'll tell them you resigned to me because you didn't want to abandon your medicine.'

'Tam,' said Ellen, looking straight at him, 'you're a marvellous boy, but you've got a lot to learn.' Tam flushed and turned away. 'You don't present people with a quasi-alternative like that. You don't offer them a focus of disaffection on a plate. And God knows there are plenty of disaffected already. Rory of Limerick will take Quint's place, and White Michael might even be his ally. No. You say – here am I. Will you have me?'

'She's right,' said Ness. 'If they refuse Tam – which they won't – then is the time to talk of Ellen.'

'Yes,' said Tam humbly. 'I see that.'

'He's a good boy,' said Fergus. 'See how fast he learns?'

'Good,' said Ellen. 'And now the funeral. What about that?'

'Does anyone know what Ralf wanted?' asked Tam.

No-one answered, then Ness said dreamily, 'The disposal of the human body has been a perpetual problem for our species.'

'Maybe,' said Ellen sharply, 'but we can't muse about that now. The point is, what do we do for Ralf?'

'I'll look in his room' said Bara. 'Perhaps he left something that'll help.'

'Yes, do that. And let us know first thing in the morning.' Ellen rose and rubbed her face. 'And now some sleep,' she said.

'Sleep,' said Fergus, 'that knits up the ravelled sleeve of care.'

'What's that mean?' asked Bara.

'Oh I don't know,' said Fergus irritably. 'It came into my head.'

'We will none of us be able to sleep tonight without help,' said Ellen. 'We'll go to the kitchen for some warm milk and I'll put a strong dose in it. Holy Brigid help us all.'

A metallic laugh suddenly filled the room and a head the colour of the moon flashed past the window.

The next morning, the first of November, dawned cold and grey. The wind had risen in the night and the people in the great crowd which had assembled below the parapet of the Rock stamped their feet and blew on their hands. Shawn appeared on the parapet and every face looked up at him. He raised his horn and blew. At the end of his call Con was lifted on to the parapet beside him, and a murmur like the sound of distant waves rose from the crowd. Con stood wide-eyed and scared, looking down on the multitude. He was dressed in a short white tunic of wool, held in at the waist by a belt encrusted in emeralds. Even in the dull light his hair shone silver. He clenched and unclenched his fists, longing to get down and away from the gaze of the people, but he could not escape, for Tam stepped up beside him and took his hand. Tam was in black and silver, in dramatic contrast to the whiteness of Con, and in his left hand he carried a plain staff of black bog oak. There was a long moment's silence, then Tam began to speak.

'I ask you to accept Con,' he cried, 'as your future leader in Ireland. In ten years' time, when he is sixteen, I ask you to accept him as your chief, for he is the great-grandson of the Old One and he will be well fitted for his task.'

The was a moment's hush, while Bara's heart stood still, then there erupted from the crowd a roar that seemed to shake the rocks and towers of Cashel.

'Con, Con, Con!' His name was repeated again and again above the tumult.

'Raise your arm,' whispered Tam.

Con lifted both arms wide, his eyes roving unhappily over the crowds, and the roaring redoubled. Coloured caps and bonnets and hats flew like fireworks through the air. Suddenly Con smiled, for it was really quite funny. Like a party. Then, just as he was beginning to enjoy himself, Tam turned him about and he jumped down into Bara's arms.

'They like me,' he said happily. Bara kissed his hair but she could not speak. Here again were the images of her dreams, but now they were warm and solid. Con in white and green, king of the hills and fields of Ireland. She wrapped him in her cloak, for he was shivering, and turned to watch Tam. He held up his hand for silence.

'As you know,' he said, 'Con is the boy the Old One promised you, and what the Old One promised he fulfilled. You have been hearing for some time now about those who will come – the flaxen boy, the golden woman and the dark man. You knew us as a kind of story, a legend from a children's book, but now you know us in fact, as people who live among you. The Council has now proposed me as leader, and I ask you to confirm me as Protector for the time of Con's childhood. If you will have me I will swear to do my utmost to establish the Ireland that the Old One always hoped for. We will use our most gifted Listeners until we can achieve and maintain a life in which no man is hungry and no man is cold and no man is unwillingly idle. We will have competence and we will have health and we will have beauty and we will have content; but there we will stop. We will not blacken our green country with smoke, enmesh it in cables and wire, smother our fields in concrete and factories, or poison our prolific sea with rubbish. And when we have achieved our balance – found our point of equilibrium – then we will turn our eyes outwards, to Wales and England and Scotland, to see what they are making of their countries, and then to Europe and the world. I ask you to accept me, Tam the dark man, to hold Ireland for Con.'

There was silence, then a murmur of assent, then a swelling volume of approval. Finally, 'Aye, aye, Tam, Tam!' thundered from the crowd, and only a few were silent. They stood together, some fifty of them, a little apart, and among them stood a tall, hooded man. They did not assent. Tam saw them, but he did not look directly. Instead he raised his arms and smiled at the main body of the crowd.

'I thank you all,' he cried. 'Your trust means much and I shall not abuse it. No man but Con will ever be able to follow in the footsteps of Ralf, whom all of us loved. But I swear I will do all in my power to be worthy.'

He lowered his arms and folded them across his chest. Bara was amazed at the ease with which the grand oratorical sentences flowed from him. Until yesterday she had never heard him speak more than two or three sentences together, yet he now stood on the parapet, apparently perfectly at ease, the focus of a thousand eyes, and speaking what had to be spoken.

'You will want to know,' he continued, 'what we should do for the funeral of the Old One. Perhaps you have had it in your minds, as I had, that we should dig a magnificent barrow for him, the greatest that has ever been seen in Ireland.'

There were cries of 'Aye, a barrow, a cairn.'

Tam continued. 'Last night we searched for his last wishes in his room. We hoped he might have written something down. And sure enough, we found this.' He reached into the pouch on his belt and withdrew a scrap of paper. 'I'll read it to you. It's very short and very surprising. It reads "I would like a ship burial, into the west." And that's all.'

Murmurs of surprise rustled through the crowd. There were mutterings and shruggings as people turned to each other in bewilderment.

Tam continued. 'Fergus knows about the ancient world long before our time. Stories and poems of ship burials, many of them in strange tongues, come to his mind when he opens it. He has told me what must have happened.' Tam spoke for another few minutes, then he raised his arms again. 'I call on you all,' he cried, 'every man and woman and child in Ireland who wishes it, to gather in the morning, one week today, at Slea Head past Dingle.'

There was a roar of assent from the crowd, for the prospect of a holiday and a funeral were great over-layers of grief. Tam waved and jumped back off the wall. Out of sight of the crowd he slumped onto the bench under the parapet. Ness and Ellen, Bara and Con, Fergus and Finn, Shawn, and most of the remaining inhabitants of the Castle, stood grouped round him, smiling and relieved.

'It went well,' said Fergus. 'You did it fine.'

'All we wanted,' said Ellen.

'Except for the small crowd,' said Ness, 'by themselves, over on the right.'

'Yes, I saw them,' said Tam. 'White Michael too. Damn, this silver stuff prickles.' He tore off his cloak and tossed it on the ground. Bara threw back her head and laughed wildly.

'There, there,' said Ellen, putting an arm round her shoulders. 'He may be funny but he's not that funny.'

Con grabbed Tam's cloak and wrapped it round his own small body. Yelling with excitement he skipped and pranced in whirling circles until he fell with giddiness. Tears ran down Bara's cheeks and before she could stop herself she was crying. Tam stepped forward and took her in his arms. She leaned against him, racked with sobs.

'Come on,' he said softly, 'We'll go to our room.'

Bara felt her skull would crack, there seemed to be so much whirling inside it. Misery, excitement, foreboding, love and hate, all at sixes and sevens, all escaped at the same moment from their appointed places in her mind. Shapes and colours beat about in the bony cage that was her head; the remote and tiny object that was herself could not control them. Tam darkened their room and she lay for a long time quietly in his arms, until at last some kind of order settled through the drifts, like a net falling through water.

There followed a black week. The cruelty of Ralf's death, and the hollowness of Cashel without him, were miseries not yet blunted by time. For many the future stretched infinitely, remote and grey.

Tam was everywhere, with Finn at his right hand, investigating the tides and currents, finding and paying for a decent ship, arranging crowd patrols and latrines and ceremonial. He worked all day and half the night, sometimes in Cashel, sometimes away at Dingle, and Bara rarely saw him. Almost everywhere his authority was cheerfully accepted, but there were constant rumours about the dissidents.

Some said they had called themselves the Hundred Men and sworn to uphold the ideals of Frost and Quint; others said they had retreated to Limerick, where they had been welcomed by Rory, the young governor who had shown Bara and Tam his town. The Council knew White Michael must be with them. He was keeping himself very secret, shrouding his silver hair in the hood of his cloak, and as far as the Council could tell his power as a Speaker was lying fallow. No doubt he was listening, and watching and waiting. For the moment the Council hoped he and the other dissidents could be ignored, but after the funeral, when the government was settled in Dublin for the winter, they would have to be met, and perhaps offered representation on the Council.

Four days after Ralf's death Maeve returned from the woods. She walked in early one morning, shrouded in a grey shepherd's cloak, and it was noon before Bara knew she was back. When she came to eat in the Great Hall at lunch-time she seemed entirely composed. She said she had been staying alone in a charcoal burner's hut, which was what she had wanted to do. She apologized for not having been around to help, but she had needed a few days by herself; now she was all right and prepared to do whatever was required of her. She was pale, and her brindled hair had lost its shine, but her serenity seemed absolute. Bara wondered how she had subdued in so short a time the desolation which had betrayed itself in her scream over Ralf's body. It was only when she caught Ness's glance of concern that she began to wonder if all were as well as it appeared. She began to realize something had gone from Maeve, something had withdrawn, something barely perceptible had shrivelled. A deep sadness crept through her, embracing more than she could define. When she left the table she went straight to Dark, and laid her head for a long time against his neck.

Early in the week the crowds began moving west. Soon every road and track was filled with horses and ponies, donkey traps and dog traps, small covered wagons and every shape of farm cart. Women in bright shawls bustled from one group to another, children skipped among the boulders and the heather, men shouted abuse at each other's horses and drank from flasks of poteen. Fiddlers played by the roadside, extracting money or food or a drink where they could, and the cannier families set up stalls for the sale of apples and gingerbread, eggs and ale, milk and bread. The crowd was rowdy and cheerful, thousands strong, exhilarated by the journey west.

Sitting on Dark, on a hill-side west of Cashel, Bara felt sickened by them, for the loss of Ralf seemed to have no meaning for them any more. But Ness and Fergus, who were with her, told her she had much to learn about the Irish and their feeling for a funeral. The shock was there all right, they said; you could feel it in the people's restlessness, and you could hear it naked when you talked to anyone alone. But this was one way of dealing with grief, and the Irish had perfected it.

Bara found she could not put her mind to anything. Each fresh bout of misery was succeeded by a stretch of calm, but it was a calm of withdrawal which brought no lasting peace. She slept profoundly, but her sleep was a kind of drowning and she woke unrefreshed. It was impossible to believe Ralf was no longer there, in the Hall, in the council chamber, in his small room. All the time she wanted to talk to him, to tell him something about Con, even to ask him about his funeral. Often in her restless wandering she went down to the whitewashed cellar where he lay. Ellen had preserved his body and Maeve had covered him with a cloth of brown and saffron and gold. Once Bara lifted the coverlet and stroked his thick, white hair. She thought of Kate, in another world and another time, and she thought of the remote, alien city where she and Ralf and Kate had been born.

All the time she wanted to talk to Maeve, but she did not dare. Maeve had smiled at her, but had not spoken, and Bara could not tell if her composure was fragile or strong. Whichever it was, she knew it was hard-won, and she did not dare intrude without invitation.

One morning Finn came up to her in the courtyard. 'I've been thinking,' he said. 'I've been thinking Con is the most precious thing in all Ireland now. The people count on him for the future time.' His broad face was troubled.

'I know,' said Bara.

'Well, it's frightened I am. If anything happens to that boy they'll have me limb from limb. Tam will be too busy now to mind him and it's me will have the whole burden of him.'

'You're right,' said Bara. 'You must have help with him. And Con will need some regular lessons soon, and teachers and books and things.' Finn stared at her.

'Teachers? Books?' he said incredulously. 'And who'll be able to teach that boy? I'm wondering if you know your own son.'

'There must be something he can be taught,' said Bara helplessly. 'At least he can be shown what to put his mind to.'

'Well, he knows all I can teach him,' said Finn. 'He just *knows*, I'm telling you. He *knows* about boat-building and archery and wrestling and riding and hunting and sailing and growing potatoes and all. He *knows*. It's just that he's not big enough yet.'

'I hope you'll stay with him, Finn,' said Bara, suddenly worried that Finn might want to return to Rosslare. 'He loves you and you've been wonderful.'

Finn stuck his thumbs in his belt and tried not to show his pleasure.

'Well,' he said, 'now they've put me on the Second Council—'

'Have they, Finn?' said Bara.

This time he could not conceal his delight.

'Aye. Because of how I've been with Con, they say.'

'I'm glad. That's wonderful.'

'Aye. And being on the Council now, I'll have to be leaving Rosslare to live around Cashel and Dublin.'

'Yes, you will.'

'So I'm thinking I might as well make Con my business too.'

'I'm very, very glad. And we'll get you help.'

'Aye, we'll do so. And we'll talk about it on the Council.' He grinned and winked and strode away.

The main encampment was centred on Ventry Bay a few miles east of Slea Head, but the flat land quickly became so crowded that the camp spread east around Dingle and up the valley north of Milton. The day before the funeral Bara rode with Maeve up the hill of Ballsittra and looked down on the crowded plain. The weather was clear and cold; the scene below them, and the hills beyond, stood sharply defined.

'It's like an enormous army,' said Bara. 'Thousands and thousands of people. With all the little tents and wagons and shacks and fires.'

'They seem like toys,' said Maeve, 'and we are gods.'

Beyond the camps the icy sparkle of the sea spread into the west. Bara wondered what she could say. It was the first time she had been alone with Maeve since Ralf's death, and she wanted desperately to open the locks that stood between them. But as she sat in uncertainty Maeve smiled at her and spoke.

'You've been avoiding me,' she said, with the old amusement in her voice again.

'Oh no – I mean—' Bara was utterly confused.

'It was nice of you, but you needn't. I can talk about Ralf. Anything.'

'I don't know how you can,' said Bara. 'So soon. I hardly can.'

'I don't know either. You see, it's not just the loss of Ralf. He and Ellen and Paedric and Frost and I – we worked together and cared for each other half a lifetime. Then later there was Cormac and Ness, and we loved them too. Suddenly it's all gone. The fellowship's ended. The Round Table's dissolved.'

'It's terrible. I don't know how you can bear it.'

'One finds unexpected resources. I don't know what they are, but they're there.'

'You mean you can talk about Ralf to anyone, any time?'

'In daylight, yes. You may have noticed I tend to vanish at night. Darkness is an undermining thing – it always has been. Our symbols of hope and happiness have always been bright. Our symbols of terror and despair are dark. We are absolutely creatures of the sun.'

Suddenly Bara felt intensely irritated. Her own throat was tight with the effort of keeping back her tears, yet here was this woman sitting serenely on her horse and lecturing her about symbols. Her voice rose in bitterness.

'You're a cold fish,' she said. 'I don't think you feel anything at all. You're so clever and so beautiful and so – so everything. But you're just a shell. I don't believe you loved Ralf. I don't believe you can love anything.'

She turned Dark roughly, digging in her heels, and drove him into a canter down the plunging path. But the bleakness of Maeve's face remained with her, and she hated herself that night.

The boat lay at anchor two hundred yards from shore. To Bara and a thousand others high on Slea Head, it was a toy far below them, carefully fitted with miniature masts and sails and rigging; to the crowd below on the narrow shore it was a hulk against the sun, all bulwark and hull. Around and beyond it, scattered on the swell, were six great rowing boats manned by crews whose task was to tow the vessel into the full outward pull of the tide. It was an hour before sunset, with the sea broken in long splinters of silver. The burial ship rode quietly, her sails furled, bearing on a plinth amidships the body of Ralf. He was covered in a pall of green, embroidered with silver, and green flags lazed in the breeze above him. The pall and the decks were littered with late flowers, roses and dahlias, Michaelmas and chrysanthemums, gathered from fields and gardens all over the south. Ralf's bier had been buried in flowers and leaves and branches as it was pulled from Cashel to Dingle, and the towing boats had been filled knee-deep as they lay drawn up along the shore. Now there was a lull, for everything was prepared.

The sky was a wash of silver-grey, the round autumn sun hung in mists of orange over the sea. Ten men under Fergus were stationed on the ship, ready to weigh anchor and run up the sails when Fergus lit the pyre. Two jolly-boats stood by to take them off, the four others stood out with towlines to help the ship on its way. Tam had hoped to have the pyre lit immediately the sun vanished, but unless there was a strong offshore wind the turning tide would not be running hard enough to carry the ship westwards. Even so, contrary currents might still wreck her on the Blaskets. They had to be content to wait until half an hour after sunset, when the tide would be pulling hard, and with luck an offshore breeze would overhaul the task of the men sweating in the row-boats.

Bara knew that Tam and Fergus had found the organization of the ship-burial almost beyond them. The problem of integrating tide and wind and sundown with some form of ceremonial seemed impossible. Nevertheless, Fergus had loved the task. He had devised form after form of ritual, each more complex than the last; produced oration and lyric from every age of the world; contrived and arranged and reorganized until Tam's hair stood on end. Finally Tam's temper had flared. Fergus had retired in an angry sulk, and in an hour Maeve had produced a form of ceremony more or less agreeable to everyone. Tactfully she had included many of Fergus's ideas; she agreed to speak briefly herself, and she insisted Fergus be given the honour of lighting the pyre on the ship. So it was that Maeve stood alone on a rock at the edge of the cliff, and Fergus stood far below her on the ship's deck with a smouldering torch in his hand. To Maeve on the cliff top he was a fleck on the sea; to Fergus, she was a small cairn silhouetted on the sky.

The crowds were spread all over the headland, and down below along the strip of pebbled shore. Tam had woken in a sweat more than once that week, dreaming of figures tumbling between the cliff top and the sea. Around the tip of the headland, where Maeve and the other members of the Councils stood, a rough wooden fence had been thrown up, but there was half a mile on either side where anyone might fall. Finn had tried to organize a line of strong men linking hands, but every time he turned away the links dissolved and wandered off, intent on a bite of supper or a mouthful of poteen.

Tam stood with folded arms glowering at the sea. He felt this was an idiotic place to have chosen, but once announced it could not be changed. He should never have allowed Fergus's overblown sense of drama to rush him along like this. He felt resentful with Ralf too. If the old man had stopped to think for one moment he would never have made such a ludicrous request. He caught Bara's eye and she smiled at him across a patch of gorse. He melted enough to smile in return, but his irritation still prickled. He hoped no idiot would fall over the edge of the cliff. He hoped Maeve's words would not sound stupid. He hoped the bloody ship would move, and not just fall flat on its side on one of the Blaskets.

'Bloody flaming hell,' said a voice in his ear. He turned sharply to find Ellen smiling at him.

'That what you were thinking?' she said.

'How did you guess?'

'There's a black cloud all round you. You don't have to be psychic to see it. I can almost smell it. Do you know something?'

'What?'

'You're the only person here in a temper. Among all these thousands and thousands.'

'How do you know?'

'Well, just look. Everyone is expectant and exalted and thrilled.' Tam turned and looked about him. It seemed to be true. In some parts of the crowd there was bustle and noise; other groups were quieter, staring at the sinking sun or at the ship; but everyone looked absorbed and content. Tam smiled ruefully and held Ellen's motherly arm in his own.

Bara moved into the group that stood around the rock at the tip of the headland. Maeve stood quietly, wrapped in a long cloak of black and gold, whose edges moved in the breeze, and her head was down. Bara took a step nearer and stared. The sinking sun threw a glow on Maeve's half-hidden face, and in its light Bara saw the shining tears. Maeve was crying. The cyst of pain had burst and Maeve was crying. Bara began to fight her way through the crowd, shouting Maeve's name. She must at all costs get to Maeve's side, she must tell her how ashamed she was of her cruel words. But rough hands caught at her, Tam was hissing angrily in her ear, the crowd was muttering uneasily. She allowed herself to be led aside, but she was dumb with misery, for Maeve had never even turned her head.

The western sky melted in coral and palest rose. Unhurried, uncaring, the sun swam slowly down towards the horizon. A swathe of pink and silver glittered on the sea. As the edge of the sun flattened on the edge of the ocean, the bustling noises of the crowd began to fade. Slowly all sound subsided, until only the screaming of the birds and the slapping of waves on the rocks disturbed the silence. Bara gazed back at the huge crowd. She felt herself no longer separate, no longer a person apart; the hush was drawing her in and she was afraid. The last edge of the sun sank, and a gasp like the end of a long-held breath drifted up from the crowd. An unearthly glow persisted on cliffs and sea and sky, but imperceptibly the dusk closed in and cold crept up from the dark corners of the east.

The towing boats were manoeuvred into their final positions, the dim figures of the sailors stood motionless by the yards. People began to pull their coats closer round them and many of the women raised their shawls over their heads. Colour was draining from the sky, grey encroaching on coral, black creeping in on rose, brilliance fading to monochrome. No fires were stoked, no torches lit. The people murmured, moving in the dusk, taking up their final places, waiting for the signal from Fergus's torch on the ship below. They must wait, they knew, for the tide to run out towards the west. Suddenly there was a gasp. A call floated across the darkening water from the furthest boat, and Fergus's torch flared up in the gloom. Then Maeve's voice rose above the sounds of a bird and sea, riding strongly on the wind.

'I am not going to give an oration,' she said. 'I am only going to say some words of my own, then some lines that Fergus has given me. You all know that we are here to honour the last wishes of the Old One, who wanted to be given a burial by burning ship, as they used to do in the old days. He wished to be sent into the unknown western ocean, beyond the Blaskets, over the curve of the world. Many of us loved him, for many years, in our several ways. When he first came here, almost fifty years ago, he found Ireland a barbarous country, unrecovered from the wars, at odds with itself. He left us as we are today, a happy and united land, where there is warmth and food and justice for everyone. Now he is only a corpse, but we will honour his dead body because that has always been the way of our country and our kind. We will send him burning, as he wished, into the furthest west.' She paused and there was a faint stir in the crowd. Some wiped their eyes, and others roughly cleared their throats. Then Maeve spoke again.

'These are the words that Fergus heard, from a far country, in a distant time:
Then they set high over his head a golden standard,
They let the sea bear him, they gave him to the ocean.
The spirits of men mourned for him, their hearts were sad;
They could not tell, neither councillors in the hall, nor heroes
    under heaven,
Who received that load.'

Fergus waited for her words to die across the sea, then he gave his order. The sails broke out, white in the gloom; the rowers began to pull, and Fergus held his flaming torch above his head. For a long moment the ship lay still. Then almost imperceptibly she cut the water and a small bow wave swelled towards the cliff. She was under way. The sails flapped and belled and flapped again as the rowers strained on the tow lines. Then the sails sank and the impetus was lost. Tam shifted uneasily. Would the bloody tub never go? In answer a gusty breeze suddenly filled the sails, and in a few moments wind and tide between them left the tow-ropes slack and the ship was making on its own for the open sea. At last Fergus dipped his torch to the pyre. Slowly he walked round the bier, setting it smouldering in a dozen places, then as the shouts from the jolly-boats alongside became more urgent he and his sailors leaped over the rail and left the ship to sail alone. Wind clapped in the sails, the tide tugged, flickers of flame crept up the sides of the pyre. The watchers from the top of the cliff could see the ship move diagonally across the last shimmer of the sun. Then it passed into dark water where the only light was of its own creeping flames.

Bara looked round her in the thickening dusk. Everywhere pale faces stared intently out to sea. Only Maeve did not look. She sat apart with her face in her hands and her cloak pulled tight about her. Bara gazed at her, longing to touch her bent shoulders, but after a moment she turned away, feeling bleak and useless. The fire burned high, fanned by the offshore breeze, and in a moment the first of the sails caught alight. Orange and yellow, red and black, the ship of fire burned on the water. The swell swung in and out of the lurid light, each crest livid with flame, each trough black in shadow. One sail caught the next, small flames flickered up the yards. As the ship caught from stem to stern, from hold to topmast, it swelled in size and seemed to be approaching instead of receding. There were murmurs in the crowd, and muttered explanations, but in a few minutes, when the entire ship was blazing, it began to diminish again, for now the wind had seized the remnants of the topsails and the fierce currents out from shore began to drag it rapidly west. For another half hour the crowd stood silent, watching the peaks of fire diminish into the dark. At last a few people began to stir. Bara was amazed in the dryness of her own feelings to see them smile at one another, to hear cheerful words and even laughter. Somewhere a kind of joy was seeping through. Ness turned to Tam.

'He was a god to them,' she said, 'and now they have none. But it was a marvellous spectacle,' she added, smiling.

'It was a way of disposing of the body,' said Ellen.

'Of all possible ways it was the most magnificent,' said Ness.

'Expensive on ships,' said Tam.

Bara laughed at him and took his hand. He smiled down at her, his teeth very white in the gloom, and they looked round for Con. He came scrambling down from the shoulders of Finn and leaped towards them, his hair glittering. He took their hands and swung between them as they moved off towards their lodging a mile away. He and Tam were talking cheerfully about their coming supper when something made Bara lift her head and look about her. The people were parting for them; not merely separating as people do for others, but creating a deliberate path. They were backing away, staring, calling to those ahead to clear a track. Suddenly the staring was like the Shepherds' Kingdom all over again; fear clutched at Bara and she crushed Con's hand so that he cried out in protest.

'What's happening?' she whispered to Tam.

Tam looked round him and smiled at the crowd.

'It's all right,' he said. 'You'll get used to it. We're important people now.'

Bara smiled tentatively at the people nearest her and was relieved when they grinned cheerfully back. Con was enchanted.

'We're like a procession,' he said. 'Shouldn't we wave?'

'No,' said Tam firmly. 'And I think we'd better wait for the others.'

They stopped to wait for Maeve and Ellen, who were some way behind them, but even when they stood still the crowd kept its distance. Suddenly into a moment's silence there fell a few soft words, and Bara's muscles froze.

'Look,' came the words. 'Look, 'tis the holy family.' And immediately there came an echo in another voice. 'By Brigid, 'tis so indeed. 'Tis the holy family.' Suddenly the low words were everywhere about them, sounding through the excited murmurs that rose on all sides. 'The holy family, the holy family, 'tis the holy family themselves.' Bara turned aghast to Tam and found him already staring at her. His eyes were wide with perplexity and there was no help from him. Then Maeve was beside them, smiling at the bewilderment on their faces.

'You became a legend in Ireland,' she said lightly, 'even before you arrived. Now it seems you're going to become a myth. Ralf's death has opened a gap in their hearts. For good or bad, the Irish are makers of myth, and they seem to feel you'll do very well for a subject. Walk on anyway, and try not to look so appalled.' She laughed at them and pushed aside her wind-blown hair. 'We have so many problems one more will make no difference,' she added.

The crowd continued to part before them and Bara managed to smile wanly as she walked. But she was dazed, deafened by the whispered words which circled in her head. *The holy family, the holy family, by Brigid, the holy family.* She did not know why they suddenly stopped walking. She saw the crowd had thinned into scattered groups, and she saw Fergus pointing up the hillside to where a few fires burned. In the quavering light stood some two hundred men, looking down on the road. They made no sound and they did not move. A little below them, smiling the marvellous smile that had first enslaved her, White Michael stood looking at Bara, with his arms folded and the firelight gleaming on his hair. Did she imagine it, or could she even at such a distance hear the ring of his mocking laughter?

'It's Rory of Limerick,' said Fergus, 'and the hundred men.'

'More,' said Tam, 'many more.'

'That's right,' said Fergus, 'many more. Frost has sown his dragons' teeth.'

Quietly they moved on. Con was wildly excited. He tugged at Bara, trying to make her run, he dragged at her arm to make her swing him round. Bara looked down at his shining face and suddenly his exuberance rushed through her like a gale. She felt the night breeze on her face, she saw the lighted doorway of their lodging ahead, she saw the first stars pricking out. She seized Con's hand and tore with him along the track, the wind in her face, her hair streaming across her eyes. She ran and ran, with Con galloping like a puppy at her heels; so fast and fast and fast one ran at night! But Tam walked slowly, his eyes on the ground, for danger threatened, and there was much to do.